Cross Stroke

ON THE EDGE
BOOK ONE

ELIZABETH HARTEY

LIMITLESS PUBLISHING, LLC

Cross Stroke

First Print Edition: Date 2018

Limitless Publishing, LLC

Kailua, HI 96734

www.limitlesspublishing.com

Formatting: Limitless Publishing

ISBN-13: 978-1-64034-290-3

Dedication

I want to dedicate this book to Maureen N. for raising the person who provided the inspirational antics for Dakota.

Chapter One

TRACEY

It doesn't seem possible. One brief interaction, one night, can change a person's whole life. One mistake...well, um...I suppose it was a series of mistakes, brought me to this place and this conclusion. I don't do well with the whole love thing. Love's too risky, too destructive, too...fatal. That's why my new motto is *there shall be no more falling in love*. The mantra repeats in a silent thrum inside my head, matching the thump of my blood, until it's tattooed on my heart.

Taking a long breath for much needed courage, I tug open one of the glass double doors of the Bernard University Arena for the first time. As I do, my phone rings. Letting go of the door, I step back. Students push past me, coming and going from the rink, like I'm invisible. Since I'm not, I pull my wheeled skate bag behind me to step out of the way of the entrance and slide my backpack off my shoulder to hunt for the ringing phone.

"Come on. Where are you? I don't have time for this." My phone answers me with another ring. I'm already late and should ignore the call, but I'm sure it's my mom and I don't want her to freak out if I don't answer. When I manage to retrieve the annoying implement of technology from the tangled mess of clothes I stuffed in there earlier, the screen lights up with my mom's gorgeous face.

"Hi, Mom. What's up?" Although, I don't know how there can possibly be anything new to tell me since her last call a few hours ago.

"Hi, honey. Just wanted to see how you're doing."

"Great, Mom. I'm doing great." *Just like I was this morning.*

"How are your classes going?"

"No classes yet, Mom. Told you, they don't start 'til next week." I'm so late for practice, but I'm doing my best not to be curt. I know she calls me twice a day *every* day since I've been here, out of love and concern. She didn't used to be like this; an anxious, overbearing mom. I did that to her. But she needs to understand I'm doing better now. I love how much she loves me, but she doesn't need to worry anymore.

"Oh, right. I forgot. So, have you met any new friends?" The same question she asks every time she calls. What she really means is, "Have you met any new *boy*friends?"

"Nope, not yet." *Not since this morning, when you asked.* "I don't have time for socializing, with classes starting, my research, and skating. In fact, I'm headed in for a practice session right now and I'm super late."

"Oh. Okay. I'll let you go then." The thick concern in her voice reaches through the phone and tugs at my heart.

"Mom, I'm good. You don't need to worry about me. It's beautiful here. The school is outstanding. The little house you found for me is awesome. Everything's really good. And I'll see you in November. Please stop stressing."

"I know you're fine, honey. I just like to hear your voice. And remind you, you are a strong and powerful woman, in control of your own destiny," we recite simultaneously.

I remember, Mom. Everything's okay. I promise. I'll call you in a few days?"

"Okay, honey. Love you up to the sky."

"Me too. Talk to you soon."

Although I sense her reluctance to hang up as I disconnect, I can no longer assure her with words alone. I'm going to have to let my actions while here at Bernard speak for my determination to fix my life. I totally get the whole strong and powerful woman thing and controlling my own destiny, the reason I'm giving up relationships. Although, I'm sure it's not exactly what my mom means about taking control. Truth is, she *wants* me to find so-called 'true' love one of these days. She says I'll 'know when the right guy comes along'.

Not. Interested. Finding Mr. Right involves the painful possibility of connecting with too many Mr. Wrongs along the way. It's time to focus on my future sans sticky relationships, which do nothing but screw me over, and not in a good way.

I stop at the front desk and sign in before walking

into the rink area. A shiver runs down my spine. Holy shit it's cold!

Where are the White Walkers? Winter is definitely here.

I snicker to myself, as my thoughts drift to my favorite television show in an attempt to ease my nerves.

Dropping my backpack on one of the benches that line one wall, I sit to put my skates and guards on. I jump up and down to warm up, get blood flowing to my limbs instead of pounding inside my head with nervous energy. Could it *be* any colder in here? Patting my arms to alleviate the feeling of ice water running through my veins, I look around the rink.

Championship hockey and figure skating banners, in neon gold, red and blue, decorate the perimeter walls. They stand out in the glaring overhead lights, like radiating warning signs to remind me how good these teams are. I take a deep breath. The freezing air turns my heated lungs into popsicles, much like the rest of my body. My eyes drift to the ghost mist when I blow it back out.

"Surprised it doesn't freeze into a plate of ice at these temperatures," I mumble.

This rink is much colder than UDel's. Or maybe it's my newfound, uncharacteristic anxiety making it seem like it is. The size of this place is overwhelming. It's gigantic, with hundreds of individual black and gold seats instead of bleachers. I almost expect the Penguins to take to the ice any second. Between the cold and the overwhelming size of the arena, I can't keep my teeth from clattering.

There are only a couple of people on the ice and

they're hockey players, not figure skaters. One of the six foot walls of humanity pushes past me as he comes off the ice. "Excuse me, sweetheart," he says. I don't look at him or acknowledge his comment. Nope. Just step out of his way.

Hmmph. Sweetheart my ass.

Boys are assholes.

Bob, the rink manager, comes up behind me and asks, "Did you sign in for this session, Tracey?" He holds out the clipboard with the required sign in sheet.

"Yes, thanks. Took care of it at the front desk when I came in."

"Okay, good. We like to keep a count of skaters for each freestyle session." He glances up at the digital clock on the gigantic Jumbotron hanging from the middle of the mile-high ceiling. Seriously, they could hold the Stanley Cup in this place. "Cutting it kinda close, aren't you? The session's almost over," Bob continues with a friendly smile, reminding me of my late arrival. Not that he needs to. I'm more than aware of my *tardiness,* as my mom loves to call it.

"No need to be nervous," he offers, as if he can read my mind. "You'll feel better as soon as you take the first stroke on our flawless ice." He smiles again and walks away.

Pinching my eyes closed, I instruct myself to calm the hell down. I can make this work. I will take the lessons I've learned, make changes, and move on with my life. Wait. What lessons? Oh right. Love sucks.

I thought I knew all about the so-called fuzzy, warm things called love. I *so* didn't. Not if what happened with

5

Sean is any indication. I thought I knew what I wanted. I was ready to reach for the stars with two hands, both professionally and personally. Then came Hurricane Sean and everything I knew or wanted was annihilated. Now the only thing I know for sure is I wish I had never laid eyes on him.

Closing my eyes again, I try to will all thoughts of Sean out of my head. When I open them and stare across the shimmering expanse, the lone hockey player on the ice flies past me and glances over. Another shiver flashes down my spine. I don't even know why I feel this trembling rush of nerves. It's only a team practice.

Funny. Skating rinks *used* to be my safe haven. The place where all stresses slid away with the first glide of my blade on the ice. Standing in an arena, waiting to perform, I owned it. The music washed over me, invading my senses, the ice and I became one. It was just my music, the cold, glistening surface, and me.

All that was BS. Before Sean. Yup. There always seems to be either one really stupid or one totally awesome thing which changes your life forever. Sean was my one *really* stupid thing. Things I believed BS evaporated like water on a Phoenix summer sidewalk.

Standing here about to glide onto the ice for my first freestyle session, I'm a complete mess. My heart beats with an enthusiastic attempt to explode against my chest, my stomach is determined to work its contents back out into the world, and the weird Santa jelly-belly shaking of my legs has increased to seismic proportions.

The hockey player zips past me again. The wind of his speed sweeps across my face. As Bob said, this session is almost over, but I only wanted a few minutes to get the feel of the ice anyway. However, when I take the first stroke on the ice, this is not what I had in mind. The feel I was interested in wasn't the one where my ass hits the frigid, unforgiving surface right in front of a pair of black hockey skates.

The skater slides to an abrupt halt to avoid running over me, his sharp blades spraying me with cold shavings. In my frantic state of synaptic overdrive, I forgot to remove my glittery purple skate guards.

"Yeah, those don't work too well on the ice. You might want to remove them before trying to stroke." I look *up up up* until I reach the face of the taunting skater.

Yowsa. His ice blue eyes shimmer like lasers right through the Plexiglas visor of his hockey helmet. Strands of sun-kissed streaked hair peek out from his helmet and frame cheekbones, which would be the envy of every Express model. Absurd. No one looks that good in a helmet.

Did he say something about stroking?

My naughty, sex starved mind drifts for a second to stroking other types of hard surfaces, the kind that could melt cold ice and my bones. Seems the blood has no problem reaching lower regions of my body now.

Stop it.

Right. Sworn off sex. Forever. Well, at least until I can let someone get that close again, *if* I ever can.

But when Hottie McHot wiggles his fingers and stretches his hand out a little further toward me, it's like he has a front row seat to the opening night of my porno imagination. Although my ass has lost all sensation from its imminent fusion to the icy surface, I *can* feel the warm blush creeping up my neck and face.

For an experienced skater, taking off skate guards before stepping on the ice should be as natural as removing shoes before jumping in a pool. It's a pretty lame, rookie mistake.

"No thanks. I'm good." I ignore his chivalrous gesture.

"Whatever. Take it easy, Bambi," he says, slips on his glove, and skates away before I'm able to push myself up.

"Hey, my name's not..." He pays no attention to my objection and his lack of interest is fine by me.

Oh yes. Now I remember the second most important lesson learned since Sean. Never fall for a gay guy, unless, of course, you're another gay guy. Been there, done that, and it was soul crushing. Although I suppose *in technical* terms, Sean is bisexual. It's irrelevant. Because what he truly is, is a cheating, douchebag liar. Okay, maybe I'm still a little angry—and broken. He's the primary reason I transferred from UDel and one of the reasons I don't accept help from the sort-of-magnanimous hottie.

How do I know McHottie's gay? Oh, it has nothing to do with judgie outward appearance observations or judgie anything, for that matter. Nope. I love men who prefer to get it on with their fellow man. And therein lies the problemo. I, Tracey Hayward, have a definite defect in my uterine radar. A fancy way of saying I'm totally fucked when it comes to picking boyfriends. Whenever I fall for a guy, no pun intended, I'm sure to find out his only interest in me is as his new BFF. I'm like a moth to a flame when it comes to gay men. I don't mean in a conscious "I know what I'm doing" kind of way. No idea why. Could be some kind of Karmic thing, God's little joke or something. If I'm hormonally attracted to a guy, after hanging out with him for a while, I'm trying to jump all over him while he's explaining to me I'm a great 'friend' but...No joke. It's happened several times.

The last time was with Sean. I thought for sure a super jock, sex on a stick, quarterback would be a safe bet. I was almost right. Our relationship went way beyond friendship. Except, thinking about it now, we may've skipped the friendship stage. A "friend" would never have treated me the way Sean did. My association with that dirt bag was devastating to the point where I almost didn't survive the deep abyss of heartbreak.

I did some tremendously stupid things as a result, and can never make up for the worry and distress I caused my family. They had my back through the crazy, self-destructive behavior and hours of self-pity, the reason my mother has become the definition of a helicopter mom. But I'm determined to regain my self-confidence. No guy, especially a snake like Sean, is worth giving up what I almost gave up.

Which is why I intend on steering clear of any overzealous attraction to the opposite sex, no matter how much my already used V-card begs me to try to get back into the game. I'm focusing on marine studies and research, with a few figure skating competitions and shows in my free time. No partying, no temptations, no super-hot athletes—including hockey players.

Getting myself to an upright position, nervous jitters flutter my insides again like hundreds of inebriated butterflies. Whoever said nerves and adrenaline were great tools to enhance one's performance was either someone who never performed in front of others or an alien from another planet, ignorant of human physiology. Hanging onto the boards, balancing on one leg at a time to slip off my guards, I realize I'm a normal, nerve wracked human. After placing my guards on the edge of the boards, I push off on freshly sharpened blades, gliding in the *opposite* direction of McHottie.

Yup. Just one look at him and I'm feeling yummy warm sensations right down to my toes, which set off bells and whistles in more ways than one. It tells me one thing. If *I* want him, he *must* be gay.

Never again, and I mean *never* again. I know how it works. It's how it always starts: a chance encounter, a heart-racing glance at a panty melting face and body. The first encounter with my next big mistake. Not this time. My middle name is going to be Snow White while I'm getting my graduate degree. I'm focusing on the new, celibate, Tracey Snow White Hayward and what I need to do right now.

Forget your current state of humiliation. Shake If Off —the apropos advice of Ms. T. Swift's song blaring over the PA system in the rink.

There are only a few people left in the arena since it's the last freestyle practice session of the day. Maybe no one noticed, except for the hottest guy on the planet, that is. Which doesn't matter because, nope, no, nada, nyet, will I get involved with another gay guy—or any guy at the moment—only to get my heart pulverized.

After two weeks off the ice, I only need a few minutes

to get the old skating legs back. My dad was a pro hockey player, so I learned to skate almost before I could walk. The ice is like home to me when I'm not experiencing this unusual nervousness about new surroundings. The Zamboni gears up to make its entrance onto the ice. I glance at the clock. There's about fifteen minutes left in the session; enough time to do some stroking to warm-up, a little footwork and then I'll try a double or two.

An abrupt switch to The Black Eyed Peas "Pump It" interrupts T. Swift's song and I do as the Peas suggest, taking off at a fast and furious speed, back in the zone. The frigid wind turns my cheeks to the feel of cold-glazed marble and the resistance of the hard surface makes my muscles strain to the point of complete exhaustion. Still, the strenuous action of flying around the ice is the most liberating sensation ever. Um...the *second* most liberating sensation. And maybe I'm not quite as pure as Snow White.

My gaze drifts back to the wicked diversion of McHottie's tight, round ass as we keep crisscrossing each other at blurring speeds. I can't help notice his high-speed, sharp cross-overs, Mohawk cuts and pivots, while using his *long, hard* hockey stick to cup his puck with acute dexterity.

Yikes.

Only I could get hot in a cold rink thinking of a hockey stick as a metaphor for...for the metaphor I'm thinking of. I need to get laid. However, since the mere thought of doing the deed has my insides twisting into a pretzel, it looks like my ever-loyal vibrator will be getting a little more action this semester.

McHottie zips past me again and my gaze drifts right back to his incredible ass. It's probably the kind of ass with those incredible indents on either side, the ones no woman could ever achieve if she did ten thousand squats a day, the ones you want to run your fingers over and...

Get out of your dirty mind, Tracey.

Damn. It. What is it with me? After Sean splintered my heart into millions of pieces, I swore I'd stay away from all men and use skating as my only adrenaline-charged escape. My body is sending me mixed messages. Some parts of me, no need to mention which ones, are not too keen on the idea of life without steamy sex. Other parts can't let anyone get close enough to be intimate. It's a big problem. But it's okay, because I'm not looking for sex, steamy or otherwise.

My mind goes back to the thought of McHottie's dreamy, ocean blue eyes. Although I'm in a frigid ice rink my lady parts are experiencing warm wet sensations. Argh. I'm a hot mess.

Focus on the ice.

The nagging inner voice tries to keep me from making the same stupid mistakes. This time I intend to listen. I shake out of the sultry thoughts and refocus.

When everything else falls apart, skating is my release. My salvation. Despite the shit storm my life has become, it's so good to be back in skates, the adrenaline rush over-taking me, the elation of flying around the ice. It's time to go for it. A double Lutz for the last move of the day. It's my most difficult jump, but everything feels so right. I'm in the zone. The music is pushing me faster, harder. I build speed toward the opposite corner of the rink and when I glance over my shoulder, ready to push off and soar, McHottie comes into my field of vision. It's too late to pull out and we crash like the Titanic into the catastrophic iceberg. Although in this case, I'm not sure which one of us is the doomed ship and which one is the damn iceberg, because we're both sprawled out on the ice in a tangled mass.

"What the fuck?" McHottie sputters. "You're supposed to look before you go into a jump!"

Sucking in a deep breath, I answer in a strained attempt to remain polite, "Excuse me? I *was* looking, but *you* cut across my path."

Okay, I *may* have mumbled 'jackass' afterward, but can't be certain because of my collision hazed brain.

"*I* cut across? *You* skated right into my path. And you broke my hockey stick. Christ!"

"*I* didn't break anything. What are you doing on the ice with a hockey stick and puck during a freestyle session anyway? You're not even supposed to be here."

"If you look around, *Bambi*, we're the only ones on the ice," the hot super douche says while pushing himself up from the ice and pulling off his helmet. "The rest of the figure skaters left a while ago. *You* were late."

Holy oh my God! He is beyond gorgeous with his caramel, sun-streaked, surfer style hair and his tanned, chiseled face.

"It...it...doesn't matter what time I got here." I manage to put my tongue back in my mouth and use it for speaking. "This is still a freestyle session and you're not supposed to be on the ice." I push myself up.

This time the dickhead doesn't offer his hand in

13

assistance, which is, once again, fine with me. Cripes! Has every college campus changed their admission requirements for men? 3.5 GPA and Must Be Total Asshole.

"You know, *Bambi*, you might want to take a few more lessons before trying those doubles and triples. You're a walking—or should I say *skating*—disaster. If you don't kill yourself first, you're going to take out another skater while you're learning."

"While *I'm* learning! Listen, jackass." Yes. This time I went right ahead and said it aloud and I'm pretty sure his beautiful Titan godlike face grimaced a little in response.

"First of all, my name is *not* Bambi," I point out, even though I get the whole snarky Bambi reference. "Second of all, I'll have you know I was the Senior Ladies National Collegiate Gold Medalist two years in a row." I put up two fingers to fully illustrate to the Neanderthal the correct amount of years.

"Huh. Yeah?" He scoffs, while putting his helmet back on. "And who was your competition, Will Farrell?"

"Ha ha, very funny, jackass!" I yell to his spectacular ass as he skates away. What a jerk. Who cares if he has dreamy ocean blue eyes, a perfect chiseled jaw and heart stopping kiss me lips? He's still an asshole. Lucky for me there's no chance of any mutual attraction between the two of us. Unlucky for me I think my skating tights melted when I took one look at his supermodel face.

DAK

Damn. My day was already in the crapper. The thought of handling the extra graduate course *and* putting in all the practice time for hockey is weighing heavy on my mind. To add to the already stressed thoughts, Bambi and her sparkling green eyes first fall at my feet like toxic manna from heaven, and then plow into me like a bulldozer and break my favorite stick. Fuck this day.

Did she call me a jackass? Pfft, jackass. Where does she come off blaming me?

I had the right of way. She totally cut me off. Yeah, she has some skills on the ice. Her edge work is a thing of beauty and she maneuvers faster than some guys on the hockey team, with her long legs, full lips and cute little ass. But her safety skills are fucked.

"No practice today, dude?" Wolfe asks as I push past him on my way into the locker room. He's one of the best goalies on any college team in the country and one of my roommates. It's absurd his last name is Wolfe. But, well, if the name fits.

"Nah. Got some research to do. I'll catch you later at the house." Official team practices haven't begun yet, but some of the guys decided to get a jumpstart on the season. As captain I should stay, but the university is allowing me to take a graduate course early and I need to get going on research to keep on top of things before the season begins and I'm super busy.

I begged the Dean to let me take the class. He said if I managed to keep my GPA at 3.5 they would consider it. I worked my ass off and squeaked by with a 3.51. I'm not sure how I'm going to keep it up with regular fulltime classes, the grad class, and hockey, but after working so hard to convince him I could do it, I can't back out now.

"Sounds good. Have a couple cold ones waiting, because I plan on melting the ice today," Wolfe says, shaking me out of my stressed thoughts. Giving me a thumbs up, he skates off.

I give him the universal-guy nod for I-know-what-you-mean-dude, even though my mind is back on how to juggle all the shit on my plate this semester. An uninvited vision of Bambi, the one-woman terminator on ice, flashes through my head. Her ass in her short little skirt pushing backward on the ice, toward me.

What the hell?

No way do I need that kind of grief. Feisty little bitch.

In the locker room, I cram the helmet and pads into my bag and toss what's left of my stick in the trash. Shit. I loved that stick. It's been a part of my life longer than most of my friends.

Peeling off the rest of my sweat-drenched clothes, I grab a towel from my locker and head for the shower. When the water hits me and I start lathering up, all thoughts go right back to Bambi and my cock jumps in response to the mental image of her vibrant green eyes, luscious plump lips, and perfect round ass as she cut across the ice.

What? No.

This isn't my MO. Since Abbey, I make sure never to let a chick under my skin or inside my head. It can lead to the kind of commitment which risks letting someone down in a catastrophic way. For three years, I've pursued enough lusty adventures to help me forget. But never with anyone looking for long term, only with chicks who aren't interested in falling in love. I can't do the relationship thing. It's obvious in the way I failed Abbey in the most epic way possible. I'm not the kind of guy a woman can depend on, not hero material. No more relationships.

I hook up with chicks whose only interest is in racking up their score with another athlete. They use me for a good time with the added benefit of boosting their popularity and I use them to help me forget. Even more, though, the way I make *them* feel makes *me* feel good. I don't mean just physically. I mean it makes me feel good about myself again, like I'm doing something good for someone. That may sound cocky, but it's the way it is, symbiotic exploits of lust filled usage.

Huh, maybe I can use that sentence in my thesis.

And again, the memory of the adorable little spitfire yelling at me across the ice flashes inside my head. What the actual fuck? Why can't I stop thinking about this surly chick whose real name I don't even know?

Guess it's because of this shitty day, must be triggering needy hormones. Yeah. Normal, horny, male hormones. I'll work it off later tonight. There's sure to be a long line of hot rockets waiting and willing to relieve my...stress. Totally not interested in feisty skater girl.

Chapter Two

TRACEY

"Hey, girl," the cute guy sitting on one of the front row seats unlacing his skates calls out to me. "Impressive moves you got there."

"The ones when I was upright or the ones when I was sprawled out on my ass?" I grimace as I rub my backside. There's definitely going to be some serious bruises tonight.

"Both. Your jumps are amazing and you fall more theatrically than anyone I've ever seen. But then I'd like to take a massive fall between the legs of Dak Andersen myself," the friendly guy says and wiggles his eyebrows up and down.

"Humph. Dak Andersen. Is that the jackass's name?"

"That's him. Dakota to be precise. A hotter than the sun jackass, I might add." He waves his hand in front of his face in a fanning motion. I can relate.

"I'm Alex Sanchez." He pushes a black curl off his

forehead and holds out his hand. After getting my second guard in place on my blade I walk over and shake his outstretched hand.

"I'm Tracey Hayward. Most people call me Trace."

"Well, Trace Hayward, you must be new around here. Are you trying out for the team? We could definitely use you." He drops my hand and slips on his lilac colored Chuck Taylors.

"Only the club team. I'm a graduate student, can't do the national collegiate competitions anymore."

"Too bad. They could use a massive jumper like you on the senior ladies' team. But the club does some local shows and state comps you can get in on. You headed to get something to eat?"

Until he mentioned it, I didn't remember the last thing I'd eaten was an apple I grabbed for lunch. Conjuring up the thought of a nice juicy burger with crispy fries has my stomach growling loud enough for Alex to be able to hear it. "Yeah. I'm starving."

"Great! How about I treat you to a welcome to Bernard U dinner at a popular pub in town. They have a stellar selection of craft beers and the biggest burgers you've ever seen."

"You read my mind. I'm already drooling." I love to eat, and one little apple is not enough to satisfy my more than healthy appetite. Luckily, the amount of exercise I do makes up for my love relationship with food and keeps the fries off my ass. "Can you give me a minute to change out of this skirt and tights?"

"Sure, girlfriend. I'll wait for you outside. I gotta get out of this cold. It does all kinds of horrific things to my glowing skin. Why didn't I go for ballroom dancing or anything not requiring frigid temperatures and ice packs on my ass at the end of the day?" He pats both sides of his face and rolls his eyes.

"Nice eye roll, dude. Even Mae West would've been impressed."

"Mae West?"

"Yeah. She was a movie star in the..."

"Girl. Stop." Alex holds up his hand like he's stopping traffic. "You do not need to explain who Mae West is to me. She was like the original diva and one of my idols, thank you very much." He rolls his eyes again and purses his lips, Mae West style, then lets out a big laugh. When he smiles, it's warm and inviting, lighting up his handsome face.

My first new friend. It's like the first day of kindergarten when you're scared to death of the new experience, then you meet your new wonderful BFF and he or she makes everything awesome.

"Okay. I'll be out in a sec." Grabbing my skate bag and backpack, I scamper off to find the locker room.

I don't know my way around the state of the art arena yet. There are all kinds of rooms: off-ice dance rooms, two fully equipped gyms, at least two weight rooms, therapy rooms, and lots more there's been no time to explore yet. I see a sign pointing the way to the locker room and follow it. Pushing the door open, I'm surprised to find it's empty and quiet except for the sound of running water in one of the shower stalls. It's close to dinnertime, and I guess except for the hockey players on the ice everyone else headed out to eat already.

The minty smell of the peppermint soap someone in the shower is using mixes with and sort of masks some of the human smells always present in locker rooms.

Dropping my backpack on a bench in front of the lockers, I sit to unlace my skates, wipe off the blades, and put them into my skate bag. I dig through my backpack to find the cutoff jeans and tank top I stuffed in there earlier. Even though it's September, the warm weather is unusual for Mt. Desert Island. I'm not sure who had the brilliant idea to name an island this far north off the coast of Maine 'desert,' because most of the year it certainly doesn't get desert temperatures. Although right now the temp is a toasty eighty-five degrees.

I slip off my sweater, skirt, and tights, and pull the elastic from around my ponytail. The prospect of a few more warm days to head to the beach or be able to do some kayaking before the water temps become frigid has me smiling. In my contented state of mind over the weather and my new friend, I don't notice when the shower turns off. But when I look up and see *him* standing there, all six foot something inches of dripping wet naked hotness, I'm aware of the heat creeping up my neck and I'm sure my face has turned the same shade of bright red as the lace bra and matching thong panties I'm rocking on full display. Our eyes lock and neither one of us can seem to find our voices. My gaze drifts down, the trail of dark hair directing my eyes right to the magnificence between his thighs.

A loud whistle snaps my gaze back up to his face. "Jesus, Bambi." The super douche blows out with his whistle. "You're just full of surprises, aren't you?" He grins wryly, and if I didn't know better I'd swear he was staring at me with a kind of hungry glare. But since I *know* there can't be any attraction on *his* part, I assume it's my imagination and it doesn't bother me.

My therapist Gail spent months trying to convince me my theory concerning my draw to gay men was scientifically impossible. I can hear her judicious voice trying to assure me, "Your exes didn't wear signs indicating their sexual preferences. Therefore, since you couldn't possibly know what their sexual proclivities were, you can't possibly say you were or are only attracted to gay men." I could never follow her logic.

Eventually she gave up on the scientific explanations and in exasperation said, "Don't think in those terms. It's only a coincidence."

Three times? In a row? I think not.

More like my malfunctioning uterine radar honing in on them like a nuclear missile. The result being cataclysmic fallout.

First there was the smoking hot music student with smoldering gray eyes which seemed to possess the ability to burn my clothes off without his hands ever touching me and a six pack I could bounce quarters on, or lick, whichever. He loved displaying those chiseled muscles on stage when playing rock gigs in local venues. The first time I saw him perform I almost became one of those silly fan girls who fall in lust so hard they throw their panties on stage. A ridiculous gesture I resisted, thank goodness. But when he smiled down at me from the stage, I was hooked. Long story short, we became fast friends. Hung out at school, studied together, went to parties and bars together, generally did what good friends do. Problem was, I wanted way more from him than a best friend. When he didn't make a move to take it beyond friendship, I decided to take matters into my own hands. Literally.

He gently removed my hand from his crotch while explaining, "Um, Trace. This can never happen between us."

"Why, because we're friends? Isn't it a good thing to be friends before becoming lovers?" I intelligently pointed out.

"It's a very good thing, but not the reason why this can't happen," he repeated in a calm voice while stopping my hands from roaming under his shirt to trace his marble statue-like abs.

"What's the problem? You're not attracted to me or something?" I tipped my head to the side and gave him the sugariest, coquettish smile in my arsenal.

"Um, yeah. Something like that."

It took all of ten seconds for my shock to morph into tear filled hurt and then mortified indignity. Before I could stomp out of the room like an incensed ass, the rock god blurted, "I'm gay, Trace. Shit. Sorry. I thought you knew."

Oh. Okay. Disappointing, sure, but I didn't let it get to me. We remained good friends.

My next trip into unrequited love land occurred with the esoteric art student. He had long flowing hair and haunting amber gold eyes which seemed to hold the secrets of life and made my limbs quiver. Things went pretty much the same with art boy as they did with rock god. Another beautiful friend who was unable to quench my robust desires. I introduced my music friend to my art friend and hearts and flowers bloomed all around—for them. I was happy for them. Really. Sort of. Okay, I was pissed. But I eventually got over it, and didn't panic.

Having seen that look before, the first time rock god gazed at me, I'm not surprised or bothered by the way I'm imagining the jackass swallowing me with his eyes right now. I know it means nothing. What *does* bother me is his panty melting body in full view, which I, on the other hand, am more than attracted to. My legs are starting to feel rubbery underneath me. Bambi might be the right name for me after all.

"Maybe you need glasses, Bambi." The jackass smirks. "You can't see the big things right in front of you."

"My eyes are fine. For instance, I don't see anything *big* in front of me at the moment." I glance down at the Thor-size hammer between his legs.

What? I'm certainly not going to tell him he's been blessed by the gods.

He finally decides to wrap his towel around his miraculous...waist. Doesn't help though. I'm still aware of the perfect V of his oblique muscles pointing the way to wonderland.

"Never had any complaints before." He grins. "And I was referring to the big black letters on the door of the locker room."

"I came in to change my clothes." I flip my hair back in a perfect 'fuck off' maneuver.

"I can see that, Bambi." He arches a brow while

taking one more long survey up and down my body. "But *this,*" he points one finger from side to side, "is the *boys'* locker room, and unless you want to start a riot, I suggest you get out of here before the hockey team gets off the ice."

"Precisely what I was trying to do before you decided to parade yourself out here." I give it my best nonchalant tone. Jesus H. Christ. Another asshole athlete.

"Parading? I'll say it again, this is the *men's* locker room. Therefore, I'd say you and your lacy red undies are the ones doing the parading." He glances up at the clock on the wall. "And in about fifteen minutes the parade is going to turn into a stampede when the guys get a look at the way you fill that red lace." He flashes me another hormone-inducing grin.

I glance down at myself and realize my see-through undergarments are leaving nothing to the imagination. Once again, the warm blush creeping up my skin is causing my face to flame to what must be panty-matching red shades. I scramble to pull on my shorts and tank top. The pompous ass doesn't even bother to turn his head. He just stands there with that stupid hot grin on his annoying gorgeous face.

"Later, Bambi," he finally says and turns and walks away with the outline of his tight ass taunting me.

"Not if I can help it, jackass," I mutter, slip on a pair of flip-flops, grab my bag, and run from the equator-level heat of the locker room.

DAK

Holy shit! This girl may kill me. I get that she may be new and it's possible she didn't realize this was the guy's locker room, although it does state Men's Locker Room in big black letters on the door. But who wears sheer red lace lingerie under their skating clothes? Nobody wears it the way she does, that's for sure. I don't even know her; only saw her a handful of minutes ago and she's got me sweating and trembling like a thirteen-year-old virgin.

I slip on my favorite worn jeans, and the thought of the imminent danger zone known to me as Bambi floods my thoughts and other areas. Fuck. Her body! Yes. Exactly what I'd like to do to that body. And she seemed to be more than interested in my...in me.

I tried to give her a nice long look, but when I got a glimpse of her perfect tits wrapped in red, it was like Christmas morning for my cock. One glimpse at the sweet little package in lace and I had to pull the towel around me and think of depressing things, like the Ducks' record last year, to dampen my dick's enthusiastic response to the sight. I know women, and that surly chick has relationship material written all over her. Sorry. Don't do those anymore.

It's taken a long time to get myself together. My life ended the day Abbey ended. Well, almost. If not for Dalt and the guys keeping me going, I might've crawled up into a ball and joined her. They helped me rejoin civilization. Even after three years, though, it still feels like my heart is being ripped out of my chest when I think of her and the day from hell. I loved Abbey, but I can numb the pain of losing her with a never-ending line of girls looking for one night of body-scorching activities, nothing more. No entangled commitments.

I've got to get home and bury myself in research. The guys will be back to the house soon and this being the first Friday night of the semester means it's the first keg blast. There's a couple hours to get some work done before the throngs descend on the house, then I can lose myself in some party time before I need to focus on the official start of hockey season and classes, not on some hot-tempered figure skater. Definitely skating clear of that thin ice.

Chapter Three

TRACEY

When we get to The Thirsty Whale, I find it is aptly named. Not only because everything in town is named after marine life, but because the place is covered in the obligatory fishing nets, long wooden fishing spears, and even a gigantic plaster model of Moby Dick hanging from the ceiling with his huge mouth gaped open. The brewery pub is packed. Excited college students are celebrating the end of the first week of the semester. Classes begin next week. This week moving in and boring orientation filled our time. Tonight was the perfect opportunity for a raucous, welcome back celebration.

Alex informs me it's happy hour, thus the happy masses. After we squeeze our way in the door, he walks right past the hostess stand. The interior of the pub is a large expanse with dark wood tables filling most of the center of the room and booths around the perimeter. A bar, constructed of the same dark wood, lines the length of one long wall. A huge board behind the bar lists the names of about fifty in-house brewed craft beers. There's a karaoke stage in one corner and a small dance floor in front of it. The LED screens strategically placed around the room are displaying the video sans audio of various sporting events. With the noise decibel in the pub no one would be able to hear the sound on the televisions anyway.

Alex does a quick scan around the room and waves excitedly to a stunning blonde girl waving back at him from one of the booths.

"Over here," he says, and takes me by the hand to lead me through the crowded room. "Hey, girl. Been waiting long?" he asks the blonde while sliding into the seat across from her and tapping the end of the bench next to him to invite me to join him.

"Got here about a half hour ago to try to beat the crowds. Hi, I'm Nikki." She extends a hand to me. She's a petite girl, but she has a cool, deep voice. It's the kind of gravelly, sultry voice I always wished I had.

"Nikki, Trace. Trace, Nikki," Alex introduces us before I get a chance to respond. When I extend my hand, Nikki takes it into her firm grip and gives it a vigorous shake. "Hey, Trace. You a new freshman?" She drops my hand and grabs the beer bottle in front of her and takes a big pull.

"A graduate student. But I *am* new. I transferred from Delaware. Are you on the figure skating team too?" Since Nikki has the slim, muscular build of an athlete and is friends with Alex, I assume she's a teammate.

"Christ no." She almost chokes on her beer. When she shakes her head the short layers of her bangs fall into her eyes. Even with the royal blue bangs, the platinum blonde hair she has pulled on top of her head in a messy bun makes her look like Tinker Bell, if Tink had slim but totally ripped arms.

"Nikki is captain of the girls' soccer team and high goal scorer. She wouldn't be caught dead in figure skates." Alex does his infamous eye roll again and motions to the waitress to order drinks.

"Hell no I wouldn't. Those girls put the 'be' in the word be-otch." Nikki scowls.

"Nice, Nikki. Tracey is a figure skater." Alex tilts his head in my direction.

The waitress shows up and interrupts the awkward moment. "What can I get you?"

"You into IPA's?" Alex asks. "Or you want something besides beer?"

"Beer's good and an IPA would be great."

Tequila used to be my poison of choice to loosen up and enjoy an evening with friends, until the way too loose evening occurred with Sean and *his* friend. After the devastating experience, I promised myself never to drink too much and swore off tequila for the next five lifetimes.

I feel the familiar lump forming in my throat as I think back to that mortifying night. Swallowing hard, I push the memory back down where it belongs. I refuse to let all past crap ruin my fun with new friends. One beer with them can't hurt.

"You've got to try Another One. It's Maine's best

IPA. And who isn't *up* for another one? Right?" Alex winks at his apparent double entendre.

"You're such a slut," Nikki jokes.

"Oh right, and you're Sister Teresa." Alex purses his lips and flicks her off with a playful wave. "Speaking of which, how about you, Ms. Tactful? You want Another One?" He smirks at Nikki.

Even though Nikki has one empty bottle on the table and hasn't finished her second, she polishes off the second bottle and nods. "Absolutely." She smacks the second empty bottle down on the table. "Always," she drawls seductively. I love these guys already.

"And of course, all you PYTs are twenty-one, right?" the waitress asks me, while listening to Alex and Nikki's banter.

"Yeah, Molly. She's good. Trace is a new graduate student," Alex explains.

"Okay, Alex. I'll take your word for it." If Molly had asked for my ID she'd know I'm pushing twenty-two, and probably older than most of the students in the pub. My Sean-related escapades put me behind a couple of semesters while I brought myself back to planet Earth. With the transfer, I ended up losing some credits. Now I'm the old lady on campus.

"Bring us three of the Zeus burgers too," Alex adds to our order.

"You got it, Alex." Molly grabs the empty bottles from the table and disappears into the crowd.

"Molly's a senior. I'll introduce you sometime when she's not so busy. Sorry about being all bossy and ordering for you, but trust me. Your taste buds will thank me."

"Not just your taste buds," Nikki adds. "The Zeus burgers will have you comin' in your pants." Nikki makes moaning sounds, mimicking Meg Ryan's restaurant orgasm scene in *When Harry Met Sally* and damn, the girl has some serious acting skills. Thankfully the pub is too noisy for anyone to notice her adept performance.

"Okay, Nikki. How about we give Trace a couple of days to get used to you before you exhibit all your ho-ish social skills?" Alex quirks a brow.

"What? Just being honest. I'm in love with those burgers. Although I am sorry about the be-otch thing," Nikki apologizes. "But really man, those girls are *e-vil*." She shakes her shoulders in a shiver, like she's envisioning Freddy Krueger.

"Yeah, I don't know what it is about most figure skaters. Sometimes I think bitchiness is a prerequisite to being good on the ice." I try to keep my tone from sounding too gloomy, but the memory of how cruel some of my teammates at UDel had been brings back the depressing thoughts of all things Sean.

"Uh oh. Looks like our girl here has had some shitty experiences with her new teammates." Nikki shakes her head.

"No. Not with the team here. I had a problem with a gu...with some of the people on the team at UDel. It's not worth talking about."

"Oh shit. Problems with some asshole. I know the symptoms," Nikki sneers.

"It's the past. No big deal." Right where I want to

keep it, buried deep in the past, never to rear its ugly memory again.

Molly shows up at our table again and takes six glasses of beer and three burgers with fries from the tray she balanced above the heads of the crowd. My eyes widen at the sight of the pint glasses of beer in front of me. I forgot during happy hour you get two drinks for the price of one.

As if she could see right into my depressing thoughts, Nikki holds up a glass of beer and shouts, "To new friends and moving on!"

"To new friends and moving on," Alex and I say in unison. We lift our glasses and clink them to Nikki's. We all laugh as the beer from the full glasses spills down our arms. The cheerfulness of the moment wipes away the bitterness of my past.

"Speaking of moving on with new friends, I'd like to move on some of *those* gorgeous things right there." Alex sighs and gazes across the room.

Nikki follows his gaze. "Yeah. They're okay I suppose. If you like *man-whores*."

"I happen to loooove manwhores," Alex sings out and sighs again. "I hope you're not suggesting the soccer players, either male *or* female, are any better than the hockey players. I happen to know you can be quite a lady-whore yourself," he teases Nikki in a playful tone.

"Fuck you." Nikki flips him a finger and laughs.

I turn my head to see who they're talking about. The crowd parts like the Red Sea and a group of super-hot guys make their way through the room. They're all wearing t-shirts and jeans. And yes indeedy I can see why

Alex is drooling. The way those shirts stretch across broad shoulders and muscled arms, these guys turn plain old t-shirts into works of art. Hockey players. What's up with this team? Is it a requirement to be hot as fuck to participate?

"Geech. How do they not melt the ice?"

"I know, right?" Alex swoons in agreement. Nikki blows out a disgusted eelk sound.

"Oh *puhlease*, Nikki. You gotta admit every one of them is a perfect male specimen."

"I'll admit no such thing," Nikki states and takes another long drag of her beer.

My mind drifts for a moment as Nikki and Alex argue over the swoon-worthiness of the hockey gods in the pub. I notice the jackass isn't in the group. Good. I can't stand the cocky asshole. Then I remember the vision of his long, wet hair and streams of water running down his hard chest and roped six-pack. Mmmm, might be an eight-pack. Just as I'm getting what must be an alcohol induced warm tingling sensation between my legs —because I don't even like the guy—a deep voice snaps me out of my inappropriate, wide-awake, wet dream.

"Hey, Nikki. Nice to see you." One of the tall, gorgeous hockey players is standing next to our table.

Nikki doesn't look too happy to see him. "Yeah. Right," she mumbles and takes a long pull on her beer. Her posture stiffens and her jaw clenches when she puts her glass down.

"How's the soccer team this year? Any good new recruits?" The guy runs his hand through his tousled brown hair giving it an even more "I just rolled out of bed and look this hot" appearance. Apparently the guys on this team got the memo. Long, disheveled hair on men is sexy as shit because they're all rocking it in swoon-worthy fashion.

"Why? You interested in tapping the fresh meat?" Nikki glares at him through narrowed eyes.

"What? No. I just..." The guy winces his dreamy bedroom eyes and rubs the back of his neck. He looks from Nikki to me and then to Alex. "Uh...hi," he chokes out after clearing his throat. "I'm Dalton." He flicks his chin toward Alex and me while introducing himself.

Alex stretches out his hand and almost climbs over me to shake Dalton's hand. "Hi, I'm Alex and this is Tracey. So nice to finally meet you. I see you on the ice all the time." Alex is grinning and babbling like a smitten fanboy, while still holding onto Dalton's hand.

"Oh, you skate? You trying out for the hockey team?" he asks while twisting his hand out of Alex's grip.

"No, *Dalt*," Nikki pronounces his name like she's spitting out poisonous venom, "Alex is a *figure skater*." It sounds more like a question, like she's trying to get a reaction from him.

"Figure skater. No shit? Cool. That takes some crazy ass skating skills. Looking forward to the Winter Fest Show you guys always put on. Oh shit, yeah. I remember you. You did a Gaga routine last year. It was lit, dude."

Nikki rolls her eyes and takes another gulp of her beer.

"You remember my routine?" Alex puts his hand over his heart and blushes.

"Oh for chrissakes, if you two are done having your

little bromance I think your friends are looking for you," Nikki practically growls at Dalton.

"Just came over to say hi, Nikki." He gives her a sheepish look. It's astonishing how such a petite girl can topple the spirit of the massive athlete like a fallen Redwood. "You coming to the party tonight?"

"There's a party already on the first Friday?" Alex nearly jumps out of his seat in excitement.

"Yeah, sure. You guys are welcome to come if you want. Everyone's invited. You should bring your friends, Nikki." He's staring at her like she's *his* Zeus burger.

"Right. Byeee." She waves him off without looking at him.

"Okay then." Dalton shrugs. "Anyway, hope to see you guys tonight. Nice meeting you." He never takes his eyes off Nikki before making his way through the crowd back to his friends.

"OMG, Nikki! Why were you such a bitch to him? He's spectacular and he's totally into you. You should be jumping all over that. I would be if he were playing for my team. What's up with you?" Once again Alex is squirming in his seat, but this time it's like he wants to jump across the table and shake some sense into Nikki.

"He's a dick. I hate him. He thinks he's all that. And for the record, he's *into* pretty much anything with a vagina." Nikki shrugs like she couldn't care less, but her eyes glaze over, giving away her true feelings.

"Well he *is* all that and more," Alex states with enthusiasm, not noticing the hint of tears in Nikki's eyes. "Unfortunately, the V-jay rule seems to go for most of the hotties on the team." Alex pouts and takes a swallow of beer. "But you *hate* him? Sounds a little harsh. I knew you hooked up with him a couple of times, but it was before we were friends. What happened? What did he do?"

"It's a long story, which we are *not* talking about. To moving on," Nikki states again, although with a little less enthusiasm, and raises her glass." Alex and I repeat her cheer.

"Uh...*most* of the hotties?" My focus is on Alex's statement regarding the bedroom antics of the hockey players. "They're not all into vagin...uh, girls?" I ask, trying to sound as disinterested as possible. Because, why should I care? As I said, totally not interested in sexcapades, steamy or otherwise. At least, I'm not into *acting upon* my interests in them.

Sex with Sean was more in the 'otherwise' category. I mean it was good, don't get me wrong. Sean was gorgeous—on the outside. However, our sex sessions were more about him and his needs than about mine. He spent a lot of our intimate time telling me what he needed or wanted and how I should do things to provide him with those needs.

It could be the reason my confused lady parts are craving the idea of a super attentive lover now, but since Sean, the fear of intimacy causes my chest to hurt and my stomach to tighten like it's full of hard rocks.

Nevertheless, the kind of fantasy lover they write about in books, the kind who puts the woman's pleasure above his own, a guy who cares more about the girl's needs and pleasing her in every way possible...mmm, yeah, that's the kind of attentive intimacy I would love to be able to experience just once. Even if, at the moment, I'm an anxiety ridden mess when anyone tries to get too close.

Alex snickers, pulling me out of my amorous thoughts. "My gaydar tells me there are a couple of those cuties who would love to play with more than just *hockey* sticks, but they would never let their macho teammates know about it."

"Uh, speaking of ho-ish," Nikki teases. "Knock it off, Alex. Your metaphorical statement is bringing imagined visions of lust filled guy on guy scenes, causing hot wet stimulations between our thighs. Am I right, Trace?"

"Oh shut up, Nikki." Alex sticks his tongue out at her and then sweeps it around his lips in a seductive manner. Nikki throws her head back and lets out a loud laugh.

Their insinuated scenario brings back visions of Sean and his running back companion, with me somewhere in the picture. Nope. Nikki's wrong. The thought of two guys together, especially *those* two guys, isn't getting my panties wet, not at all. Although, it *is* making my hands clammy and my chest hurt.

"I'm serious," Alex's resolute voice invades my thoughts again. "This is my last year and I'm free as a bird. Therefore, I intend on doing some private investigating of my own into one particular hockey stud who has fucked me with his eyes on more than one occasion when no one was looking." He nibbles hesitantly on one of his fries. Apparently there's at least one figure skater at Bernard concerned with his daily consumption of grease.

I'm dying to ask which hockey player eyed him over.

Why should you care?

I don't. It's none of my business. "I could probably help you out with that," I mumble, before realizing I'm saying it aloud and not inside my head.

"What was that?" Alex asks.

Should I tell him if he gives me five minutes with the team my *Ute*-dar could easily hone in on his 'teammates' for him? Nope. Too soon to lay all that crazy on my new friends.

"Oh nothing. Just saying how delish the Zeus burgers are."

I polish off the last sip of beer in my glass and stuff the rest of the burger in my mouth. In this case, Nikki's assertion was right, the Zeus burger, with its herb sauce, mushrooms, and feta cheese, almost moistens my panties as much as the thought of the super douche's wet, naked, rock hard body. Maybe not. I mean the burger is good, but his body was amaz...ugh. There I go again, lost in visions of the jackass known as Dak Andersen. Yup. Time to go.

"Well, great meeting you guys, but I need to get going. Got some studying to do." I climb out of my dirty mind and slide out of the booth.

In one afternoon, Nikki and Alex have made me feel welcome and comfortable and I'm enjoying their company. But the effects of the two beers I downed way too fast are washing over me. I can't break the "no drinking too much" promise to myself after only two weeks. Besides, I *had* intended on spending the weekend buried in my books and research references. It's time to get back to schoolwork.

"Studying? No way. It's the first week. What could you possibly have to study?" Alex protests.

"It's research stuff for my thesis. Been working on it for months, but it takes a lot of time and I need to use every free minute."

"You're going to be missing a few of those minutes tonight, girlfriend, because you're going with us to the party. We got a personal invite to a hockey party and we're not missing it."

"No fucking way am *I* going," Nikki snarls. Crossing her arms over her chest accentuates her trim muscles and the tattoo of a soccer ball on her right triceps. And the look on her face—man, she flat out doesn't like Dalton. What did he do to her? I'm beginning to think I'm right, all male college students, especially all Division 1 male athletes, are assholes.

"*Come on*, Nikki. I served as your winglady on more than one occasion," Alex pleads. "I need you to have my back when I make the move on hockey boy tonight. Besides, we gotta help our new girl here socialize. She's just getting to know people. What better way to meet a ton of people than at a hockey keg fest?" Alex gives her a lost puppy kind of face and despite her determination to act tough, Nikki's stiff posture and demeanor soften and she relaxes her arms.

Before she can respond, I chime in with, "I don't think I should I—"

"I'm not going if Trace isn't going." She crosses her arms back over her chest.

Alex turns to me with the same pouty puppy dog

face. "You'll be my new BFF if you go with us, Trace. Besides Nikki, of course," he adds.

I'm sure Nikki doesn't care if I go or not. After all we just met. I'm certain she's looking for any excuse to get out of going to the party. I guess a little relaxing time with my nose out of the books doesn't sound so bad, though. "Just a half hour." I don't want to get *too* relaxed. Too relaxed has proved to be disastrous.

Alex resumes jumping up and down in his seat like a kid at the circus. I tell myself it will be fun to hang out with new friends, even if it's only a half hour. In such a short time, it will be easy to steer clear of the jackass.

Chapter Four

TRACEY

The universe hates me. The house where Alex tells me to meet them for the party at nine o'clock is right next door to mine. I mean *right* next to my rented little blue house, with the white picket fence and porch. Obviously, the house belongs to the guys at the bar Nikki referred to as man-whores. Wow. I am seriously working off some bad shit Karma. In all of Mt. Desert Island I end up living right next door to a bunch of hot, horny, hockey players. The Cosmos is clearly trying to test me. Not sure I'm up to the challenge.

I knew male students occupied the building because when I pulled up to the front of my house two weeks ago to move in there was a sign stretched across the front porch. Big black letters painted across a white bed sheet read **'THANK YOU FOR YOUR DAUGHTERS.'** All caps. I didn't get a good look at the few guys sitting on lawn chairs on the porch drinking beer. I'm sure the parents who were swarming around the streets of the town while moving their freshman daughters onto campus must've been thrilled at the sight of the welcome sign and partying boys.

I close my books around eight thirty. It's time to get ready for the trip into Testosterone Central. It's cooler outside since the sun has gone down. My mind is having a battle trying to decide how I should dress for a party at a house full of demi-god hockey players. I want to look good.

But you don't want to attract unwanted attention.

Right. I slip on a pair of skinny jeans, a lightweight red V-neck sweater, and a pair of red high-top Louboutin sneakers.

They're ridiculous, especially for a college student, but Mom insisted every woman should own at least one pair of Louboutin's. When I explained they would never work for me because the only shoes I ever wear at school are sneakers or boat shoes, these little beauties showed up in a gift box on my bed right before I left for Maine. I didn't want to hurt her feelings or disappoint her. I mean, how could she have given birth to a daughter who wasn't into designer clothes? Maybe I'm adopted.

Thank goodness she has my drop dead gorgeous sister to follow in her modeling footsteps. When I told her I wasn't interested in fashion and wanted to pursue a career in Marine Ecology she almost choked on her dirty martini. But when she got over the initial shock, she was happy I found something I love.

Both my parents support me in every way they can. Even though I'm a nerdy scientist, it doesn't stop my mom from slipping a few high priced fashion designer items into my wardrobe whenever I'm not looking, or Dad from challenging me to a hockey match whenever I'm home.

A quick review in the full-length mirror hanging on the closet door gives me my exasperating answer. The outfit works, I guess. It's the right amount of non-frumpiness, with not too much come-and-get-me. Of course, if my sister, with her long black hair, legs which go on for years, and lavender eyes, was wearing this outfit it would *scream* "come and get me." In fact, Sloane could wear a trash bag and it would do the same. The remarkable thing is she's as beautiful inside as she is out. I miss her so much. I can't wait to see her over the holiday break.

Right now, it's time to venture into the eye-candy filled house next door.

My neighbors' house is a white, three-story monstrosity. The wraparound porch, which is already overflowing with students, is in serious need of a paint job and repair, and the siding on the house is even worse. It's ten after nine as I climb the weather-beaten steps of the porch.

While I don't see Alex or Nikki out here, through the open door I can see the house is packed. I'm not too thrilled about pushing into the mass of undulating, dancing bodies, but I need to get back to socializing like a normal college student instead of a messed up basket case. Forging ahead through the door, the combination smell of cologne, perfume, beer and bodies hits me. Once I'm in the middle of the crowded living room my nose adapts to the overwhelming mixture of scents, and I don't notice them as much anymore.

The inside of the house is pretty nice considering the outside appearance. Off-white walls are peeking out between hockey and video game posters. From the little bit of floor I can see between feet, there's no dirty, stained carpet, only glossy hardwood floors. Do these sex-gods actually polish their floors? A black leather sofa, ottoman, and two gaming chairs are pushed against one wall and a huge beanbag chair is pushed against another. I guess moving the furniture to the perimeter of the room leaves space in the center of the room for everyone to mingle, though with the amount of people packed into the house, even with the furniture out of the way, it's a tight squeeze.

I begin searching over the tops of heads for Alex or Nikki. It's easy to spot the hockey players from the pub since they're all over six feet tall and tower over most of the people in the room. Not to mention there are one or two stunning, scantily clad girls draped over each one of their shoulders. I thought football players were players, but these guys are no slackers. When do they get time for classes and schoolwork?

As I scan the room, I spot *him* in the corner next to the staircase, leaning one shoulder against the wall and laughing. For a douche, he's got a spectacular smile. All cleaned up, covered in clothes, he's almost as hot as he was naked and dripping wet. His black crew neck sweater is clinging to his muscled chest and arms and his worn jeans are just tight enough in the right places to display his abundant blessings. His tousled, sun streaked, golden brown hair skims his shoulders. He could be the cover model for *Surfer* magazine. I give a little sigh as I admire the jackass known as Dak Andersen.

It's apparent most of the girls here are vying for the attention of all these male wonders of the world. I'm glad I'm not interested in the competition to get the attention of any of these visions of hotness.

You're not?

No. I'm not. I want to smack my infuriating mind.

Ed Sheeran's "The Shape of You" is pulsing through the stereo speakers and it couldn't be more appropriate for the sensations I'm experiencing while watching Dak flirt with...Alex?

Holy shit! Is that Alex he's laughing with in the corner?

Standing on tiptoes I can see the person Dak is having such a good time talking to is indeed Alex.

What the ever loving hell?

Dak must be the guy Alex said he was going to make his move on tonight. First I get my rocker and artist friends in Delaware hooked up, and now my teammate and hockey player! I guess he's technically not *my* hockey player, and I suppose I didn't actually do anything to get them together. Still, I'm beginning to think I should get business cards. *Tracey Hayward. Matchmaker. Bringing men together all over the country.*

Why should it matter to you if Dak was the guy Alex said eye-fucked him?

Right. Doesn't matter. I hate Dak Andersen. Ugh. It's *so* discouraging. Even though I'm happy for Alex...if

Dak is the kind of guy he wants. Piercing blue eyes, heart stopping smile, sculpted pecs, six pack abs, Thor-size... Uh, yeah. Who would want a guy like that?

I don't see his wing lady Nikki anywhere in sight. I guess he didn't need her backup support after all. Dak must be more than willing. I continue to search the room for Nikki's platinum hair, and my eyes connect with Dak's. He arches one brow, tips his chin at me and gives me that damn ovary-exploding half grin of his.

For a second my feet are frozen in place and my eyes remain locked with his. Heated shocks of electricity shoot down to my core simply from the intensity in those blue eyes. My mind drifts back to the way I trembled the first time I gazed into art boy's perceptive eyes.

Ugh. I can't do this. I can't get involved with another guy whose only interest is in a new BFF. Or in this case, all over the place with his sexual attraction. Anyway, I'm *so* not interested in having anything to do with another cocky athlete. I turn around and push back out through the crowd as fast as I can. When I get to the bottom of the porch steps I bend over, place my hands on my quivering thighs, and take a deep, mind-clearing breath.

Breathe. In. Out. Close your eyes and imagine in your mind what you want your future to look like.

I hear Gail's voice encouraging me as she's done a thousand times in the past. Before I get a chance to practice some calming breathing exercises, a deep, already recognizable voice startles me back to an upright stance.

"What are you doing, Bambi? You okay?"

I spin around so fast, I almost fall over. "Fine. It's...it

was really hot in there. I mean ... it was hard to breathe in there."

"Surprised to see you at our party. Nice shoes." He smirks at my shoes and then gives me a wolfish up and down scan. What is it with this guy? First he's flirting with Alex and now...Not. Happening. Again.

"Whatever. I like them," I lie. "They were...wait, what? You live here?"

"Yeah, me and three other guys from the team. You sound surprised. Sure you're not stalking me?"

"Yeah right. Get over yourself. Not everyone is falling all over themselves for you."

"They're not?" He crosses his spectacular arms over his spectacular chest and grins.

"Arrogant much?" I sneer at him. "Speaking of cocky, when I was moving in, a sign on your porch read 'Thank You For Your Daughters.' I suppose it was *your* idea?"

"No. That was Wolfe and the other two idiots. They were celebrating a little too hard. Happy to be back together I guess." He shakes his head.

A girl striking enough to be the next Top Model with long brown hair and a tight, barely there skirt brushes past Dak on her way up the steps. He doesn't seem to notice the way she rubs against him on purpose as she goes by. I don't know if I'm pleased or disappointed at his lack of attention to the striking female.

"Happy to be back together or happy to welcome the new groupies?" I direct my gaze toward the girl as she makes her way onto the porch.

He turns to see who I'm referring to. Here comes

that bad boy half grin again when he spots the brunette. "A little bit of both. What can I say? Chicks want me and there *are* some perks that come with being a hockey player." He waggles his brows.

This is ridiculous. Why don't I just ask him if he's gay? Except for the way he was flirting with Alex, it doesn't seem like he is. Could be he's a big enough manwhore he doesn't discriminate.

What's the big deal? Ask him.

I already know what the big deal is. I'm a coward, afraid to hear the answer. If he says yes I'm screwed because once again I'm attracted to the wrong guy. If he says no I'm screwed because I don't want to be attracted to anyone, especially not another arrogant jerk who's making my body do this intense hormonal dance, which I can't do anything about because I can't let him anywhere near me.

"Yeah. I saw you talking to Alex about those perks." I try to sound aloof. His brows pinch and I could swear there's a pink blush of embarrassment on his face. Yet I can't imagine this guy with all his cockiness being embarrassed by anything.

"Alex? Yeah. He's a cool dude. He's got crazy skating skills." He shifts his weight from one foot to the other.

Is he embarrassed because I saw him flirting with Alex? He wasn't trying to hide their interaction.

"Yeah. He seems like a great guy," I offer. His uneasiness is making me more uncomfortable than I already am around him.

"You two must know each other, right? Being on the same team."

He rubs the back of his neck. I'm certain now he is feeling awkward discussing Alex. Perhaps the big jerk expects me to put in a good word for him with Alex. I'm sure he wouldn't want me to give *my* opinion of him. Let's see...um...cute but a smug asshole.

"Met him this afternoon, actually. We're both on the club team, but I haven't seen him skate yet." There's a beat in our conversation, only seconds, though it feels like an eternity. I take a big breath and blow it back out. "I haven't known him long enough for my opinion to count for anything."

"You're opinion about what?"

"Um, nothing. I don't know. Anyway, gotta go. Thank Dalton for the invite."

"You know Dalton?"

"I met him this afternoon too at the Thirsty Whale."

"I should've known. My man Dalt's a fast worker." I think he's joking, but a pinched, frowny expression sweeps across his face.

"No. He wasn't trying to hit on me. It was a quick meet and greet." It's not my place to mention Dalton was totally swooning over Nikki, who seemed to want to walk through hot coals rather than even look at him.

"Oh, good." His face relaxes.

Oh good?

Why should he care if Dalton hits on me? I suppose the jackass thinks his friend is too good for me.

"I'm outta here." I turn to make my getaway before I waste any more time snarling at him for his comments.

"You leaving so soon? You just got here."

"Yeah, I have some studying to do." How does he know when I got here? Was he looking for me?

*Of course not. He doesn't even like you **and** he was flirting with Alex,* my bratty little mind points out.

"Studying? Already?"

"Yes. I suppose it makes me some kind of nerd in your eyes. I guess we can't all be the sexy cheerleader type." I start to turn away. I really, really want to get away from this arrogant ass.

"Studying is cool. Already started myself."

"Yeah. I'm sure you're getting a whole lot of studying done in there," I say sarcastically and flick my chin toward the house. The pulsating sounds of "No Church in the Wild" are blasting from the open door and the rolling bodies of dancing students move like one big mass.

"It can be a challenge sometimes." He shrugs and glances toward the door. "Hey, you need a ride, Bambi?"

"Only if you plan on giving me a piggyback ride. I live right there." I don't want him to know I live at a I-can-see-into-your-bedroom-window-from-my-bedroom-window distance from him, but there's no sense in trying to hide it. Our driveways are right next to each other. He'll find out sooner or later. I point to my pretty little blue house and start walking toward it. I can't wait to get back to its quiet, uncomplicated surroundings.

"You live right next door? No shit? One serious looking Jeep you got there." Even though I'm not looking at him, I can hear the sarcasm in his words. It's the same sound they had when he commented on my shoes.

"Yes, it is pretty awesome. Isn't it?" I keep walking, not looking back. I don't tell him I detest the color and think it's just as outlandish as my shoes, because fuck him.

If he thinks your car and shoes are outrageous what would he think about your absurd furniture?

Who cares what he thinks?

"Yup it's awesome all right. If there's ever anything I can do for you, Bambi, piggyback ride or skating lessons, just give me a shout," he calls out to me.

I come to such an abrupt stop my preposterous designer shoes do a little skid on the graveled driveway. "There *is* one thing you can do for me." I turn my head and glare at him through narrowed eyes.

"Yeah?" He grins. "What's that?"

"Stop calling me Bambi," I growl. Stupid, snarky, nickname.

He rubs his chin like he's considering my request. "Can't do it," he drawls after a few seconds.

"Why not?"

"Because you never told me your *real* name." He quirks his brow and hooks his thumbs in the top of his jeans. He looks like he's getting ready for a shootout. Where does he think he is, the OK Corral? His already dangerously too low jeans are flashing just enough skin to send heated gunpowder sparks between my thighs.

"It's Tracey. Trace Hayward," I force my dry mouth to speak. He may be a dickhead, but he's an equator-hot dickhead.

"Trace. I like it."

"So glad you approve," I sneer, because I'm never

going to let him see how he affects me. I turn back toward my house.

"But," he says after a moment, "I think Bambi suits you. So see you later, Bambi." He emphasizes the name. "I'm Dak Andersen, by the way," he calls out to me, again.

This time I don't stop and I don't turn toward him as I flip him the finger over my shoulder.

"Yeah. See you later. Jackass!" I shout back.

DAK

I could take Alex up on his offer to exchange hook up encouragements with our mutual friends when I ask him about Bambi. He wants to put in a good word for me with her in exchange for me putting in a good word for him with Erik. But I don't think he's going to need my help to get together with Erik, one of our defensemen, because it's apparent he's more than interested.

He thinks he's hiding it from the team, but I can see the way he stares at Alex when he thinks no one is looking. I want to tell him it's cool. No one on the team will think less of him. At least not if I've got anything to say about it. I don't want Alex saying anything to Tracey about me anyway, making her think I'm into some kind of fix-up relationship thing.

"Nah, man," I say to him. "I think you and Erik will be cool without me interfering and I don't need you to say anything to Tracey. She's not my type. We're kind of like oil and water. Just curious about the new girl."

Alex doesn't know too much other than she had some kind of problem with a guy and teammates at UDel.

Shit. She transferred to another school to get away from some dickhole. Some fuck-up broke her heart or did something calamitous enough to cause her to transfer to another school and lose credits. I knew it. Girlfriend material.

"Ah, sucks man. Exactly why I don't do the girlfriend thing. And, uh, don't say anything to Tracey about the two of us discussing her. Wouldn't want her to get her hopes up. Make her think I'm interested or anything. You know what I mean, dude?" I add the shitty request because I'm a guy and a total asshole sometimes. I'm certain Alex isn't buying my bullshit line about not being interested in Tracey though, especially when he does this elaborate comical reenactment of my collision with Bambi on the ice to remind me of my first interaction with her. His animated storytelling skills make the colossal crash seem funny, and we both get a good laugh. Then the craziest damn feeling sweeps over me. Disappointment. I'm disappointed not to see Tracey at the party.

Even though there's a long line of ready and willing puck bunnies, and as much as I was looking forward to indulging in one or even two of those specimens of divine womanhood, there is only one chick I want to see. That's a new one; me waiting for one specific chick. It doesn't make any kind of sense. I keep scanning the room in hopes of seeing her.

When I glance up, Tracey's standing right there and I'm as awestruck as a revirginized teen. It's like a scene from a cheesy movie when a guy sees a chick and fireworks go off in the background.

Her auburn hair cascades in waves past those perfect round tits I saw gift-wrapped in lace in the locker room earlier and those crystal green eyes drill right into my heart. My cock begs me to do something about the way I want her.

I had the chance to relieve the pressure I'm feeling since my encounter with her earlier in the locker room. Not ten minutes before, Bri, who is the type of chick I normally hook up with, was rubbing herself all over me.

All I could think about was Bambi and the way she looked up at me with those big eyes in both nervousness and longing when she tripped on her skate guards at the rink. Two minutes after, she was reading me the riot act when I plowed into her, or rather, when *she* plowed into *me* and broke my favorite stick.

Damn.

And then the sweet way she blushed when I walked out naked from the shower and her eyes ran up and down my body.

I turned Bri down. Bri, the chick with both Jesse Jane looks *and* skills between the sheets. Bri, the girl who's always up for a wild night of anything goes sex, especially if her feral partner happens to be a hockey player. Bri, the girl who never has anything but sweet compliments and hot, dirty things to whisper in my ear. I turned her down.

Not something I would normally do, deny myself that kind of coital bliss.

Now all I can do is stare at the reason for the newfound state of pain and confusion I'm putting my cock through. Bambi locks eyes with me from across the room, a moment filled with more exhilaration than scoring the winning goal in a power play or catching the perfect wave and riding it to shore.

When she turns and bolts out of the house I make some lame excuse to Alex and chase after her, even though I'm sure he saw me scoping her out.

I find her outside all breathless and flustered. I know she's feeling the attraction between us as much as I am. The way she devours me with her eyes, the pink flush of her cheeks when she talks to me, and the slight tremble of her body. She wants me.

When she says something about me talking to Alex, I'm sure I blush like a little girl. There's no way she could have heard our conversation over the crowd and loud music. She couldn't know I was asking about her.

Then she mentions knowing Dalt and my chest tightens. I don't know why. I only know Dalt is a bigger manwhore than I am and I don't want him anywhere near Bambi. No, I'm not jealous. I don't do jealousy, especially jealousy involving a bro. The hands off another bro's chick, even if it's a temporary puck bunny, is part of an unspoken bro-code.

Except Bambi's not mine in any way, so I shouldn't be feeling any of that. In fact, I should be steering as far away from her as I can. If there was some kind of problem with a dude at her last school, she's complicated girlfriend material and I sure as shit don't need a girl-friend messing with my heart again. Besides, I wasn't kidding about us being like oil and water.

But holy fucking hell, she lives right next door. I think God flipped me the finger. How am I supposed to avoid her? It's like putting a bee right next to a garden of roses. Knowing she's only steps away isn't going to help when I'm lying in bed at night thinking about her. Not that I lay in bed and think about girls, at least not one specific girl. But I can't get this chick out of my mind ever since I crashed into her, or rather since *she* crashed into *me*. Wrecking ball on ice skater girl has seized my brain and body. When I see her, my dick sits up and begs.

Chapter Five

TRACEY

The first time I saw the *Wizard of Oz* when I was around five, I gasped in shock when Dorothy went over the rainbow and everything turned to Technicolor when she stepped outside her house. The plastic flowers looked so beautiful. Although, at the time I wasn't aware of the polyethylene toxicity of said beauty. Anyway, it's the same distorted impression a person gets when walking in my house. Sort of beautiful, but in this case, too much of a beautiful thing can be mentally toxic. It's the reason why unpacking all day has me exhausted, more perceptually than physically.

My mom supplied me with a house full of Mackenzie-Childs furniture. When the delivery truck showed up at my door last week I held my breath because I knew it was going to be insane. I was right.

Mom called me five minutes after the truck pulled away all excited asking me what I thought about the "extraordinary" new furniture she got for my new house. It's extraordinary all right. With all the black and white checks, stripes, velvet, and bright colored flowers, I couldn't tell her it looks like Alice came back through the looking glass and threw up all over the place.

"Don't you just adore the Rosie Sweet poster bed?" she squealed in my ear.

"Um, yeah. It's very...umm...pink and white striped." I tried to think of something positive to say to sound grateful. The only thing I could come up with was, *No guy would ever want to fuck me in the pink bed because they'd think I was twelve years old.* Which, in my case, is fine since there's no possibility of any fucking going on in the Rosie bed or anywhere else.

Of course, I didn't tell her that. I didn't want to ruin her excitement over the outrageous stuff, which I know cost thousands of dollars. I can live with it for a couple of years, then I'll donate it to Sloane and her new NYC apartment. She's ooed and ahhed over the contents of the company's catalogue a hundred times.

Since the furniture placement is more than taken care of, I focus on putting clothes away, hanging posters, placing my books in order of subject on the built-in bookshelves, anything to keep my attention off of the groups of gorgeous women leaving the house next door.

They either had another party on Saturday, or they stayed in bed from Friday night into Sunday morning. Damn. Hockey players have serious stamina. My attention strays out the kitchen window facing the hotties' house. I notice none of the ladies are showing any indications of a walk of shame. In fact, I'd say those girls appear to be proud as hell. I guess it's some of the 'perks' Dak was referring to. Apparently it's some kind of honor to sleep with hockey players. I get they're hot, but they're just jocks. Besides, these guys define the word player. I can't help notice there are far more women leaving than there are men living in the house. Sheesh. These guys really *are* sex gods.

The fact I spent the night cuddling with my vibrator while unwanted visions of the jackass danced through my head doesn't help suppress the steamy sensations I'm feeling at the moment as I glance out the window and see one of Dak's roommates. He's shirtless, barefoot, and in low hanging sweatpants, sucking face with the same brunette who rubbed up against Dak on the porch Friday night.

The boy is ripped. He has muscles in places I didn't even know there were muscles. The tats running down the length of his arm and across his chest only accentuate his massive muscles. A big sigh escapes my lips.

Oh man. It's definitely been too long. Not that I haven't tried since the infamous night. Can't do it, though. Can't let anyone get too close. Lost in my daydream, I absently stare out the window. I become aware of my creepy voyeurism at the same time the guy looks over and catches me drooling at him and his 'girl-friend'—I use the term loosely. Her back is to me, giving me a clear view as he runs his hands down to her ass and squeezes, and then winks at me over her shoulder.

I could duck and pretend he didn't see me, but I know he did. Anyway, why should I be the one feeling uncomfortable? He's the one feeling a girl up on public display.

"Nice," I mouth to him, shake my head, and get back to unpacking. One thing about athletes, you can count on them to only be in it for the meaningless fuck.

Found that out the hard way, and I'm not talking about a hot, fun, hard way. I'm talking about the painful, demoralizing way I found out about Sean. Although, after him and all his lies and false promises, a meaningless fuck with a man-whore athlete who I'm not in love with might be nice.

Yet even if I could let someone get close again, I'm not a one-night stand kind of girl. I like the emotions, the closeness of being in a relationship, the stupid warm fuzzy feelings.

My thoughts are a tangled mess of "I want it, but I can't do it; stay away from it, run for your life." I want to hold my fingers up in a cross pattern and point them at the house next door to ward off the demon sex-gods. I can't wait for classes to start tomorrow. Then there won't be time to think about mind blowing, heart pounding, in fact all kinds of pounding—sex.

After making a quick veggie stir-fry for dinner, I hit the books to do more research for my thesis on ocean acidification and its effects on marine life. Living alone is great for allowing lots of quiet time to study. Since there are no distractions in the house, there's no need to stay locked in my bedroom to study.

Unfortunately, the luxury of studying wherever I want in the house will be changing soon, because I'm going to need to find a housemate. Even though they can more than afford it and wouldn't mind paying for everything to help me out, I don't want to depend on my parents for rent money. They helped me out more than enough during my undergraduate studies. And I'm trying to overcome all the shit that went down in Delaware and be an independent, strong adult. I can't keep relying on them every time there's a bump in my road. It's time to put on my big girl panties and figure out how to make things work on my own.

Problem is, the rent on this house is draining my bank account of the money I saved giving kayak tours in Delaware last summer. If I'm going to make my funds last, it's time to find someone to share the rent. I'm also going into Bar Harbor sometime this week to see if I can get a part-time job with one of the kayaking tour companies. The touring season is almost over for the winter, but if the weather holds up there will be another month of tours.

The companies I worked for in the past were always impressed by my knowledge of the ocean and marine life. They encouraged me to add some information about the changing oceans, not only to make the tour more interesting, but also to help make the tourists more aware of the environmental perils the ocean is facing if we don't do something.

Since my family has always lived on the coast—Long Island in the winter, Newport in the summer—the ocean is a big part of my life. Marine life has been my passion ever since I was old enough to understand the significance of the ocean. I hate what's happening to the oceans on our planet and I intend on making a difference with my Marine Ecology degree.

I was doing a lot of research on the coastal wetlands and ecosystems in Delaware, but since my move to Mt. Desert Island, my focus has shifted to the outlying islands off the coast here. The move has made for a lot more work, but it couldn't be helped. There was no way I could stay at UDel. Which brings me right back to the reason why it's important to stay focused on my research, keep my nose in the books and my mind on the environment, not on the manscape of Dak Andersen.

The physical fatigue from unpacking finally seeps into every one of my muscle cells. After finishing up my stir-fry, I decide to continue studying sprawled out on my bed. The necessary books are spread around me for reference. My laptop's also next to me in case I find a significant reference for my thesis, The Implication of Climate Change and Acidification on Coastal Ecosystems, and need to make a note.

I study for a while until my reading is interrupted. Muscled arms are reaching out, the hands are tearing off my clothes, and I don't even mind the fingers touching me. My own hands move in a frenzy to unzip his jeans to free his pulsing cock. His mouth is all over my breasts, sucking and licking, while I keep stroking the massive, thick length I unleashed. I moan in pleasure as he moves down between my legs and continues to use his magical tongue, making circles over my clit before delving inside my pussy and hitting my g-spot.

"Oh sweet Jesus!" I scream out as I detonate again and again.

"Damn baby, you're so tight. Do you think you can take all of me?" He moves up my body and places his cock at my throbbing entrance. And then the face on the sex god in front of me comes into focus and it's...mmm, Dak Andersen. I mean, yuk, Dak Andersen. Whatever.

"Yes. Yes. Please put your gigantic cock inside me," I beg.

"Get ready because I'm going to fuck you so hard you're going to forget your name," he says and pushes into me with a hard thrust. His cock is so huge it's touching every point of pleasure inside me and I'm already coming again...and again. "What do you think the temperature is at this depth?" he asks as he keeps pounding into me.

"Mmm. It's so...wait, what?"

The next thing I know I'm trying to wave the bright, irritating light away from my face. I move to get out of its path. The loud noise of my books crashing to the floor shakes me out of the sultry dream. I stretch, reveling in the sunlight streaming through the window and the afterglow of all the lovely, dirty things the guy in my dream was doing and saying to me. I'm drenched from the hundreds of explosive orgasms he brought me to. And then reality hits.

I bolt straight up. Holy shit. I fell asleep! It's morning. No! I can't be late for my first class. It's at nine a.m. I grab my phone from the nightstand to see what time it is. I usually set my alarm when I get in bed, but I didn't plan on falling asleep at eight o'clock last night and having a wet dream about—*blech*—Dak freaking Andersen.

It's eight-thirty. No time to shower. I yank off my shorts and tank top and grab a clean pair of underwear and a bra. I slip into another tank, flannel shorts, and a pair of flip-flops. In the bathroom, I pull the elastic ties from my hair and run a brush through it. It's wavy from the braid I didn't mean to sleep in all night. Luckily, it works. The soft waves keep me from looking like a complete bedhead rag. I run a washcloth over my face. While the amount of time I take to brush my teeth and gargle would definitely not pass the ADA's recommendations, the ADA isn't about to make a late grand entrance into their first class at their new school, so screw correct hygiene.

I planned on riding my bike since, not only does it save on gas money and provide some aerobic exercise, it's one of the ways I try to help save the planet from global warming. It's a small gesture. Still, every little bit helps. But this morning I'm giving up the cause because my class is on the other side of campus in Carson Hall.

Grabbing my keys and backpack, I head out into the beautiful clear morning. One thing about this part of Maine, the scenery and environment are always spectacular, no matter what time of year it is. I take a deep breath to try to soak up some of the cleansing air to calm my already hectic day before throwing my backpack into the backseat of my shiny new fully loaded Hypergreen Rubicon. No shit.

It was a graduation present from my parents. They said I deserved it for all the hard work I had done both in school and in figure skating. I'm sure it was one more thing to try to pull me out of my depression over Sean. They would have bought me a fleet of cars if they thought it would help.

The outrageous color was my mom's idea, of course. She said it represented my love for the environment and ecology. Also, "it looks hot with your auburn hair and brings out the color of your eyes." Her exact words. I held back telling her if she had to coordinate the color of my car with important things in my life, an unobtrusive blue to represent my love of the ocean would be okay with me. But only a total spoiled brat would complain about the extravagant car given to her as a gift of love. And again, I didn't want to disappoint my former-model slash current fashion designer mother with my lack of fashion sense.

Sloane has never disappointed our mom by wanting to be a nerdy scientist instead of a famous model or by falling in love with an asshole and then almost giving up everything when he dumps her. Nope. Sloane is gorgeous, levelheaded, and perfect. Besides being my sister, she's my best friend in the whole world. If it weren't for her, I wouldn't be here, or anywhere, right now.

Thanks to her, here I am, climbing into the driver's seat of my lizard green Jeep and heading off to my first graduate class in Marine Biogeochemistry.

Chapter Six

TRACEY

Racing up the steps of Carson Hall, I run smack into the rock-hard wall blocking the landing at the top of the steps. I bounce back and as I'm about to take a tumble back down the steps hands reach out and grab me around the waist, saving me from an early demise. Every muscle in my body tenses in response to the firm grasp.

"Are you okay?" The wall sounds concerned for a moment. When he sees I'm fine, the concerned tone changes to the familiar voice I know and hate. "Bambi. Wow, you've got to stop falling at my feet like this."

Oh hell no. Why is he everywhere?

"Thanks for your concern, jackass. *You've* got to stop being where you're not supposed to be." I'm trying to be aloof and cool, but his firm grip around my waist is burning right through my tank top. It's astonishing I'm not experiencing the dreaded, harsh electric shock reaction every other guy's touch elicits since hell-night with Sean. "What the hell are you doing blocking the staircase?"

"Not very nice, since I just saved your life." Dak pouts and pretends to be offended. Damn. There's something beyond sexy about a big, strong guy pouting. And man oh man, when he pouts his full bottom lip, it's all I can do to hold myself back from leaning in and sucking it between my teeth.

"I wouldn't have needed saving if you weren't blocking the steps. Do you think you could let go of me and move out of the way? I'm late for class."

And standing this close to you, while feeling the after-burn of the hot-as-fuck dream I had about you, my legs are turning to liquid again.

"Sure, Bambi. No problem." He smiles and my heart misses a beat, the effect every Mr. Wrong has on me: stuttering heartbeat and butterfly intestines.

He lets go of me and I'm surprised again to find I kind of miss the feel of his hands around me. I step around him and head toward the Marine Bio class. When I reach the door of the classroom, I realize Dak is right behind me.

"Stop following me. Go away," I snarl at him.

"Hate to burst your bubble, Bambi, but I'm not following you. Well I *am* following you, but only because you're going into *my* class."

"*Your* class? You must be mistaken. This is a *graduate* Marine Bio class. I thought you were a senior."

"I'm flattered you looked me up in the yearbook to

find out I'm a senior, but I'm also taking an advanced graduate course in my final year."

"Yeah, right. That's where I looked you up, in a *yearbook*. And *perhaps* you should hop in your DeLorean and hightail it back to the '70's. You might need to get your transistor radio." Yearbook. Is he kidding?

"Ah hah! But you *did* look me up. Thought so." A satisfied grin spreads across his face and he wiggles a finger in front of my face.

"Immature much?" He's ridiculous.

"Just don't believe everything you see on social media. I'm not that bad, or good, depending on your perspective." He wiggles a brow. "Now if you'll excuse me, you seem to be in *my* way." He gives me the familiar panty-dropping half-grin.

In my frustrated, befuddled state, I step out of the way and watch his cute ass walk past me into *my* lab class. Mother freaking hell. This cannot be happening.

Holy Mother of God and all the saints, I am heartily sorry for whatever it is I did to offend you. Could you puh-lease stop punishing me?

Dak Andersen is an undergraduate student who's in my graduate Marine Bio class. Never even heard of such a thing as fulltime undergraduate students taking graduate courses. This could only happen to me.

Shaking myself out of my dazed thoughts, I make my way into the room. Everyone else is already seated because, of course, I'm late. The only empty seat is in the back of the room and, of course, it's at the same lab table as Dak. I guess the answer to my prayer is a big, loud NO. When I sit down, he's still grinning at me like the damn cat who swallowed every more than willing canary in sight.

He leans toward me and whispers, "Looks like we're classmates, Bambi."

He's so close I can feel his warm breath on my face. I shut my eyes as my skin shivers in response. "Yeah, great." I don't look at him, afraid the longing in my traitorous eyes will give me away.

"Man, you sure know how to hurt a guy's feelings. You act like you don't like me or something."

"I don't. Therefore, please leave me alone and be quiet so I can listen to the instructor who has *important* things to say." I keep my eyes fixed on Mr. Clancy, the instructor, who is saying something, which isn't registering with my brain.

"We're going to be stuck with each other all semester," he whispers. "We may as well make the best of it. Besides, I know you like me. I can always tell. I'm never wrong about these things," he says in his usual cocky, confident, irritating way.

Astounded by the balls of this guy, I give him a wide-eyed glare. He has a pleased smirk on his face, which I would love to smack off for real. "I hate to disappoint you, *jackass*, but I'm not one of your groupies. And despite being in the same class, I don't intend on being stuck with you in *any* way. So again, *cierre su boca*," I whisper through teeth I'm clenching so hard they're beginning to hurt. Four years of high school Spanish comes in handy every once in a while.

"Mmm. Nothing turns me on like a bilingual chick.

How did you know, Bambi?" He stretches his arms up and leans his head back into his hands.

Uh huh. Bi being the operative prefix here.

With his arms stretched, his impressive biceps are on full display and my gaze lingers for a moment longer. The annoying lopsided smirk is still crossing his kissable lips. Doesn't matter. I'm feeling confident I've made my feelings clear. I am *not* interested in him and he needs to back off.

I'm more than familiar with this kind of situation. This is almost exactly how it started with Sean, captain of the football team, all interested in me and up in my space. Except he was sweet when we first met, not like this cocky jackass. I was more than interested and sweet right back because...well, he was almost as gorgeous as the jackass sitting next to me. I'd noticed him long before he began pursuing me and didn't play hard to get. He had me at hello, to coin a phrase, and I fell hard.

Sweet words of love and forever flew like pollen in the spring for almost a year. Until I walked in on him in bed with someone else. One of his fellow teammates to be exact. At first I thought I had walked into the wrong room, and then in the span of a few seconds I tried to convince myself I was dreaming or hallucinating, anything to keep myself from falling apart right there on the spot. It didn't take me long to realize the crushing scene in front of me was real. Which wasn't even the worst of it.

"Awesome!" Dak's loud outburst yanks me out of my mortifying memory. "I guess you're stuck with me after all."

"If you've forgotten the name of the person you're paired up with for the semester, the list will be hanging outside my office door for reference." Mr. Clancy glances at Dak and shakes his head. "It's the best way to help you get research done when you go out to the islands or use the research skiffs to collect specimens from the coves. This way you've always got a partner and aren't alone. I picked partners based on the topic of your theses. Even if you're not in the same major, thesis topics can require some of the same research. It works, more efficient and safe. It's the way we've done it for several years. This is only the preliminary research for your thesis. You'll get more in depth in later semesters. Any questions?"

Yes. But I'm afraid to hear the answer. I get the answer anyway when Dak leans over again and whispers, "I'm all yours for the whole semester, Bambi. Lucky the topics for our theses are similar, huh?"

Lucky? Is he kidding? This may be my worst nightmare. Teaches me to pray for favors.

"What's your major?"

If he says Marine Ecology I may jump out the window. A second story window should be high enough to break a few bones in order to miss the semester.

"Oceanography," he announces with the proud tone of someone who thinks he's going to be the next Cousteau. It eases my nerves a bit because it means we'll only share a couple of classes together. "But my graduate emphasis is in Biological Oceanography," he continues, the hellish statement ringing in my ears.

Jesus H. Christ. It means we'll be in several classes together since the two majors cross over in many aspects.

"How about you, Bambi? What's your major?" He tilts his head to one side like he's interested.

Is it too late to change majors?

Fashion design might not be so bad after all. It would certainly make my mom happy and it would keep me far, far away from Dak Pain-In-The-Ass Andersen.

"Marine Ecology," I sigh out. Because who am I kidding? It's the only thing I've wanted to do since the first time I explored the beach as an adolescent.

As much as I hate to admit it, the jackass is right. We're going to be stuck together like glue for the whole semester while we do our thesis research. I'm in trouble.

DAK

I cannot explain what is it about this chick that makes me want to push her buttons. Maybe it's because she crashed into me, broke my stick, and wasn't courteous enough to apologize or take responsibility for it. I have to admit though, I kind of like the way she pushes my buttons right back. Most of the time I don't know if I want to pummel her or fuck her. With the weird chemistry between us, she's probably feeling the same way.

She's trying hard to make me think she's not attracted to me, but I see the way she looks at me. It's not hatred in those twinkling green eyes. Well, possibly a little hatred mixed with a whole lot of attraction.

Clancy pairing us together is awesome. Working with a smart chick like Tracey will be a big help for me and take some of the pressure off of my already overloaded schedule. Also, I'll be able to spend more time with her, get to know her better and figure out why the fuck I can't get her out of my head.

Christ. What am I thinking? I need to be careful not to get too close.

After Abbey, I said 'never again' to close relationships. I never want to hurt anyone again, physically *or* emotionally. It's why I'm careful about the kind of girls I hook up with. They can't be looking for anything more from me than some toe curling pleasure.

The physical stimulation has been off the charts, no complaints there, but not a lot in the way of intellectual stimulation. Not that intellectual stimulation is what I need in a hook up. I'm only interested in mind numbing, forget everything fucking.

With Trace, there's all kinds of stimulation going on. True, it's mostly contentious, but I kinda like our contentious interactions. I even find myself looking forward to them, even if it's only to spend more time with her for studying purposes.

Yeah sure. I'm looking forward to quarrelling and studying Marine Bio with her. Nothing else.

Chapter Seven

TRACEY

"Did you sign up for the Winter Fest Show? You should do it as soon as possible. There's only a few slots for solo performances. Almost everyone performs in pairs," Alex explains to me as we sit on the benches tightening our skates.

I'm looking forward to practice with the team today. Spending so much time unpacking and organizing my research notes, I hadn't even thought about my new routines and skating performances.

"No, not yet," I reply. "Where do I sign up?"

"Oh, yeah...about that." Alex scans the rink through narrowed eyes. "You need to talk to Bri. Sabrina. She should be here any minute." He lowers his voice and gives me an intense look like he's about to tell me a state secret. "She's a senior and captain of the collegiate *and* club team."

"Oookaay. And?"

"Bri is...she's...well, remember those skaters we said had to be bitchy to be good?" Alex whispers through clenched teeth. I nod, not liking where this is going. "Um... Bri is very, *very* good. *Sooo...*" Alex shrugs. "She's probably the best skater on the team and she's helped us become Collegiate National Champions several times. But you don't want to get on her bad side. If she likes you, she's all sweetness and light, if not..." He does the same shoulder thing Nikki did the other day at the bar when she was talking about mean skater girls.

Christ on a cracker. I thought I had gotten away from this shit when I left UDel.

"Don't worry about it." Alex perks up. "I'm sure she'll like you. Bri respects good skating. When she sees your skills, she's going to love you."

As we glide onto the ice, Alex introduces me to some of the other skaters already warming up. Everyone is semi-friendly. Figure skating is a sport pretending to be a team sport. Oh sure, every skater can accrue points for the team depending on where he or she places, and everyone wants their team to win gold. In reality, however, everyone is pretty much skating for themselves. A gold, silver, or bronze medal is what everyone strives for. As the new kid on the ice, the rest of the team isn't quite sure what level of new competitor they're facing. I can feel the eyes following me around as I warm up. I feel comfortable on the ice today; more like my old self, no out of control nerves taking over. My maneuvers are flaw-less and my jumps soar and land on clean edges.

When the graceful blonde with long, lean legs and hair pulled back in a perfect ponytail takes to the ice, I know immediately it must be Sabrina aka Bri. Everyone is skating around her and gushing their greetings. She takes a few warm-up rounds on the ice and I can tell already she's a strong skater. I keep doing my thing, practicing my jumps, spins, and moves in the field. In my peripheral vision, I notice when Bri stops to watch me.

I feel good when the session ends, more like my old confident self. The hockey players are beginning to make their way onto the ice when Bri skates over to me to introduce herself.

"Hi. You must be Tracey. I saw your name on the roster and was looking forward to meeting you." She extends her hand and gives me a tentative smile, one that doesn't reach her eyes. It's like she's trying to decide what she thinks of me. "I'm Sabrina Davis. My *friend*s call me Bri."

"Hey, Br...Sabrina." Not being sure what qualifies as a *friend*, I figure I better stick to her full name. "I've been looking forward to meeting you too. I've heard so much about you." Her eyes narrow and her grip tightens when I shake her hand. "I mean I've heard about your incredible skating skills," I clarify and her facial muscles and grip relax.

"You've got some pretty good skills there yourself. You transferred from the UDel team, right?" Her tone is more amused than friendly.

"Yup. I'm a graduate student. I did my undergraduate studies there."

"Uh huh. I know some people on that team. I'm familiar with your record." She flips her ponytail back over her shoulder.

Oh shit. Does she know all about my stupid past?

"Oh. Yeah. Well then you know our team had outstanding results the last few seasons. But I'm sure the Bernard team will be able to take the championship away from them this year," I'm quick to add, not wanting it to sound like I'm suggesting the UDel team is better than Bernard's.

"I'm sure," she states in a flat tone, like it goes without saying. "Too bad you won't be able to join us for the collegiate competitions." She doesn't sound like she thinks it's too bad at all. "But there's some club comps and shows you can participate in."

Wow. This girl is as cold as the ice she's standing on. I hope I get to see the sweetness and light side Alex was referring to earlier.

"About that. I understand I need to talk to you to sign up for the Winter Fest show."

"Uh huh. What were you planning on doing, a solo or pair routine?"

As I begin to explain the solo routine I think would be perfect, I'm alarmed by a hand slipping around my waist and spinning me around. It's weird, but just like on the steps of Carson Hall, when I see who the hand belongs to, my anxiety diminishes.

"Hey, Bambi. Ready to rock some of our research work tonight?" Dak gives me a dreamy grin.

Yes fine. You're a cocky jackass, but after the dream I had I would love to do some research...of the Masters and Johnson type.

"Hey, Dak," Sabrina interrupts. Oh. *There's* the sweetness and light Alex told me about. Her tone is dripping with sugary adoration. "You know our new team-mate already?" she drawls and cocks her head to one side. It's a question, but she's smirking like she already knows the answer.

"Oh. Hey, Bri." He must qualify as a *friend*. Dak drops his hand from my waist and greets Sabrina like he just noticed she was standing there. "Sure. I know Bam... Trace. We're old friends." He winks at me and I can feel my tights moisten between my legs.

Crap. What is it about this guy?

At least he didn't call me Bambi again.

"*Old* friends? Really? I thought she was a *new* grad-uate student," Sabrina sneers. "With *other* interests."

Uh oh. What the hell does that mean?

She knows.

I should have known gossip travels like wildfire in the skating community and I'm definitely sensing some over-the-top animosity. Is there history between her and Dak? My stomach clenches, but I'm not sure if it's because of the possibility of her knowing about my UDel experience or the prospect of her having history with Dak.

"What do you mean other interests? We're lab part-ners in our graduate Marine Bio class. We'll be doing all kinds of interesting research together." Even though he's talking to Sabrina, he never takes his eyes off me.

"Umm..." I clear my throat and try to put a coherent thought together, "no. I don't have time for research tonight." Dak furrows his brow and I could swear the expression sweeping over his face is disappointment. "So, about the Winter Fest." I turn back to Sabrina to finish our discussion. "I have two solo routines I think would—"

"No." In the harsh glare of the fluorescent lighting I think I see her facial muscles tighten and she may be gritting her teeth.

"Excuse me?"

"There aren't any more solo spots open. We limit them due to time restraints. There's only time for a pair routine, but since everyone who isn't doing a solo is already paired with someone else you won't be able to find a partner."

She stands there staring at me, blinking a little too fast. It's the same expression I would give my parents when I was five years old and telling a fib. "Sorry," she bites out as an afterthought a few seconds later. By the way her hands are clenching into fists at her sides, I don't think she's sorry at all.

"I'll do a pair routine with you." I almost forgot he was standing there until Dak dropped that bombshell statement.

Sabrina lets out a snort-like chuckle until she realizes Dak isn't laughing. "Are you serious?"

"As a coronary. I think it would be awesome to take part in the show. What do you think, Trace? You want to do a sweet pas de deux with me?"

"I...I..." *Pas de deux?* He doesn't strike me as the ballet type.

"You can't," Sabrina cuts in. "You're not on the skating team," she states, placing her hand on her hip in a defiant stance.

"Not on the *figure* skating team." Dak smirks. "But I

am on the *hockey* skating team. So if I want to participate in the Winter Fest I can."

"That's ridiculous," Sabrina argues. "I've never even *heard* of a hockey player wanting to be in the Winter Fest."

"Well you have now." This time when he shares his cocky half grin with Bri, I think I fall in love with the jackass a little bit. "What do you say, Trace?"

I'm not sure how this is going to work. He may be the most skilled player on the hockey team, but it doesn't mean he can figure skate, let alone *pairs* figure skate. It's a whole different dynamic and even I haven't done a pair routine since I was sixteen. But there's no way I'm letting this bit...girl treat me the way the girls on my last team did after what I refer to as The Incident, either talking about me or snickering behind my back when they knew I could hear them, mistreating me on the ice, or completely ignoring me altogether when it came to team activities. I came here for a fresh start. I want things to be the way they were pre-Sean.

Sure, it's possible the best way to achieve the new start isn't to get chummy with another smoking hot athlete. Not to mention it's obvious Sabrina is pissed because Dak is showing me some attention.

Huh. Could be my theory of only being attracted to gay men is the fantasy my therapist said it was after all, or maybe Dak swings both ways, like I assumed when I saw him flirting with Alex. He's definitely hot enough for the whole world to want to get in his pants. Whatever he is, right now he's my only alternative to being left out of the Winter Fest and I'm not about to let that happen.

"Sure. I'd love to do a routine with you, Dak. It'll be fun choreographing a pairs number. Haven't done it in a while." I quirk a brow at Sabrina, who's starting to resemble a volcano getting ready to erupt. "I guess you can put me down for a pair's routine."

"Whatever. It's going to be your guys' humiliating funeral," she hisses and skates off to exit the ice.

"Wow." I blow out a big breath. "She's a sweet thing, isn't she?"

"She can be when she wants to be." He arches a brow.

Okay. He's also into women. This guy is all kinds of sex on legs.

"But what the hell?" His comment reminds me how annoying he is. "How are you going to do a figure skating routine? You know it's nothing like hockey, right? And as charming as you are," I add sarcastically, "it's going to take more than a sexy smile to pull this off."

"First of all, Bambi, you're welcome for getting you a spot in the show. Second of all, I use to do figure skating competitions *and* play hockey before I got into college on a hockey scholarship. Third of all, you finally admit you think I'm charming and you're into my sexy smile. I knew it."

"Oh, for crying out loud. I'm not into...okay. Thanks for getting me a spot in the show if you think we can pull it off."

"On one condition, Bambi."

"Condition?"

"Yup. I have a heavy schedule this semester: fulltime undergraduate classes, hockey, and this graduate class.

I've got to keep my grades up or I'll be put on probation and won't be able to play hockey."

"Oh, poor baby and your first world problems. What's it got to do with me?"

"I know you must be pretty smart to get accepted into Bernard's graduate program without being in their undergraduate program. They don't bring in too many graduate students from other schools. And since you're my research partner, it makes you the perfect person to help me out with extra study sessions for some of my science classes, especially Marine Bio. It all works." He flutters his impossibly long lashes at me a few times.

"Oh, it does, does it?"

"Yup." He pops the P. "You get me for a skating partner and I get you for a study partner. What do you say?"

"My schedule is completely full too. There's no extra time for—"

"Uh, uh, uh, Bambi. I'm going to be taking time for this skating show too. We'll need practice sessions, which means adding the sessions to my schedule. If I can do that, the least you can do is help me out with some extra study time."

"I don't—"

"I mean, if you really want to be in the Winter Fest." He gives me a sly grin.

I exhale and shrug. "Okay, I suppose I can work out some time for..."

He doesn't even wait for me to finish.

As he skates away he calls back to me, "We'll talk later

and figure out a schedule for research, studying, and skating practice."

He's so freaking irritating and frustrating and...hot.

It's apparent to me that instead of avoiding Dak Andersen, I'm going to be spending way too much time with him, while having to fight off my misplaced lust.

Chapter Eight

TRACEY

The words on my laptop screen are starting to blur. I didn't realize how much work this degree involved. Even though it's only four classes this semester, each class has a lab section as well as a classroom section. It's like having eight classes worth of work. And right now, I need a break from the avalanche of work, especially from the paper I'm writing for my Marine Molecular Bio class *and* the confusing thoughts of Dak which keep blocking any scientific thoughts. I need food.

The dining halls on campus are unbelievable. The Sea Star Café is on the top of the "best college food" list every year. Since the primary majors at the college focus on ecology and the environment, everything at the campus dining halls is made from scratch from organically and sustainably grown food. Sounds too good to be true, I know. What can I say? It's Maine. Except, at the moment, since I'm unable to fulfill the real pleasure of comforting sex, I'm going to settle for the next best thing to fill my carnal yearnings—a Zeus burger. Sometimes a body needs grease to satisfy its other unfulfilled desires.

I slip into a pair of jeans and one of my many Save the Ocean t-shirts. This one is black and has Save The Ocean, Save The World sprawled across the front. I'm not into advertising company logos or names on my clothes, but this type of message is something I'm willing to wear every day.

The weather is beautiful and it's still early. Since there are a couple of hours before the sun goes down, I ride my bike to the restaurant instead of drive. It's only a five minute ride anyway. The unfortunate thing is, when I decided to take Alex up on meeting him and Nikki at the Thirsty Whale again for dinner, I didn't know he had ulterior motives.

The usual Thursday crowds of football fans are yelling at the screens of the various television sets. The Patriots are the lucky recipients of the loud instructions coming from around the room. I find Alex and Nikki at the same booth we sat at last time. Neither of them is showing any interest in the latest intercepted pass, which has incurred the wrath of the rest of the students in the bar.

"Hey, girl. We have cooties or something? We thought you dropped off the face of the planet. Where you been? Haven't even seen you at the Sea Star," Alex reprimands me as I slide into the empty seat opposite them.

"Sorry, my schedule is crazy. My research project needs to be submitted in two weeks, there's a paper due tomorrow, and I took a part-time job giving kayak tours out of Bar Harbor."

"Here. Have a drink. You need it." Nikki slides a full glass of beer over to me. It's not happy hour, but she always seems to keep a spare on hand. I suppose it's her efficient way to be sure there's not too long of a wait between pints. I think the girl must be part camel. She never shows the slightest indication of being drunk. Even with her petite size, I think she could outdrink most of the male athletes in here.

I don't protest her gift. The cold effervescent liquid is just what I need to calm my overworked brain for a few minutes.

"You took a part-time job?" Alex grimaces. "I thought you had a grant or scholarship or something?"

"I do. But it's only partial and the rent on my house is killing me."

"You've got a whole house?" Nikki sits up straight from her usual slouched position.

"Yeah. My mom insisted. She did some searching online and found this pretty little house and claimed it was where I had to live. I agreed because she never takes no for an answer and, in this case, she's right. It's quiet, no distractions, it's easy for me to focus on my work. But it was on the condition they would let me pay my own rent. I don't want to keep depending on them for everything. Except, now with the schoolwork load, I don't know if I can do it. The tour season will be over in a few weeks anyway, which is good for extra time. But then there goes the extra income." I shrug and take a deep breath. The thought of juggling my schedule and my finances is exhausting.

Nikki gives a wide-eyed look at Alex and turns her palms up like someone placed a present in her hands and solved a problem for her. "Are there two bedrooms?" she asks tentatively. "In your house, I mean."

"Yeah. The second one is unoccupied. My mom wanted to furnish it, but I couldn't take another pink, storybook cottage bedroom." I shake my head at the thought of the ridiculous bed. "I put the bedroom furniture I brought with me from Delaware in there."

"Storybook cottage?" Nikki's brow pinches in confusion.

I sigh. "It's a long story."

"Who cares about the furniture?" Alex jumps up and down in excitement. "Nikki wants to get out of the dorms. She has a roommate from Hell this semester. She's looking for off-campus housing and you could use someone to share the rent. It couldn't be more perfect!" He claps his hands like he's figured out the meaning of life. The truth is it *would* be the perfect solution to my financial problem.

"Chill, Alex. She didn't even say she *wants* a roommate," Nikki says, but it comes out more like a question than a statement. "I get it if you like your privacy."

"Oh, shut it, girl." Alex rolls his eyes at Nikki. "You told me yourself it was going to be impossible to find somewhere off campus since the semester has already started. This is perfect. My two BFF's in one house. Easy for me to come over and cry on both of your shoulders when my new hunky hockey player breaks my heart."

The waitress places our food and drinks on the table and asks if we need anything else right now.

"We're going to need another round of beers in about five minutes," Nikki informs her and the waitress scurries off to fill the order.

I drown my burger and fries in ketchup and stuff a few fries in my face. Damn. Nikki as a roommate *is* the perfect solution. But Alex hooking up with Dak when the super douche keeps invading my thoughts is not perfect at all. I should tell Alex his hunky boyfriend has obvious wandering desires. I wish someone had told me about Sean. Although, I don't honestly know what's going on with the two of them, so I don't say anything to Alex.

Nikki must misinterpret the confused expression on my face because she says, "Don't feel like you need to say yes. No pressure. I just started looking. I'm sure I can find someplace."

"No." I ignore the clenching in my stomach over the thought of Dak and Alex. "It would be great if you could move in with me, Nikki. Alex is right. It would be the perfect solution for both of us. Besides, I'd love you as a roommate. And at least you know I won't be the room-mate from Hell."

Wait till she gets a load of the décor.

Hmm. Yeah. Nikki isn't exactly Goth, but her tastes definitely don't run in the Disney princess area either. She may decide my house is one of the nine circles of Hell after all.

We're all lost in the delicious mesmerizing flavors of our food for a few minutes. Alex appears to be in a race to see if he can lick his plate clean the fastest. He manages to take a breath in the middle of inhaling a bite and lets out a big whistle. "Look who just came sauntering in, all by his gorgeous self. Mm, mm, mm. That boy is heaven on legs."

I glance over to see who he's referring to and almost choke on my glorious mouthful of Zeus burger. "Oh por puck sakes. Bhat's he booing here?" I hiss out between burger bits. If he's here to see Alex, I don't want to be here to witness it. I can't think about Dak with Alex.

Or is it the thought of Dak with anyone *else you can't think about.*

No. It's not. Why should I care? I hate him.

"Probably came in to grab a bite to eat. What else? Right, Nikki?" Alex shifts in his seat.

"Undoubtedly. What else?" Nikki asks in this sarcastic tone.

I glare at Alex. "What's going on? What are you up to?"

"No idea what you're talking about." Alex puts a hand to his chest and does his best imitation of shock. "We're here enjoying a nice meal with our new friend. What could we possibly be up to?"

"Not *we. You*," Nikki mumbles into her beer glass. "What could *you* possibly be up to?" She glowers at Alex over her glass.

"We've got to go. Right, Nik?" Alex swallows the rest of his beer.

"Leave? But I haven't..." Nikki appears to be as

puzzled as I am. I guess she's not in on Alex's shenanigans, whatever they are.

"Yes, Nikki. *Remember?* We've got...um...shit to study." Alex throws some money down on the table and slides out of the booth.

"Leave? What are you talking about? Even though you've become a member of the Olympic speed eating team, I haven't finished. And you haven't even gotten your beer order yet," I protest.

Isn't he supposed to be the one interested in Dak?

"The beer's all yours. We forgot we've got...you know, like, schoolwork." Alex is a bad liar and Nikki doesn't seem to be too happy to join in on his little plan. "You can take your time to finish. Enjoy yourself. Come on, Nik," he persists, one hand planted on his hip.

"Yeah. Okay. Fine. Coming, *Match.com.*" Nikki gulps the last of her beer and slides out of the booth with a reluctant sigh.

"Shit to study? You two aren't even in a class together. What are you—"

"Hey, Bambi. Just the person I want to see." Dak steps around Alex and Nikki. "Hey, Nik. What's up, Alex?" He flicks his chin at the scheming Alex and his reluctant co-conspirator.

"He calls her Bambi. Isn't it adorbs? Nothing's *up* at the moment, Dakota. Expect *that* to change soon though." Alex grins and winks at me.

How many years would I get for strangling a fellow figure skater?

"You're just in time to keep Trace company. Nikki and I are off to go study something," Alex says.

"Oh, yeah. They're off to study shit for the class they don't have together." I smirk and flutter my eyelashes at the two traitors. "Oh, by the way Alex, remind me next time I go out for a dive in the tropics to bring you back a beautiful sea urchin as a pet," I say in a sugary voice.

Dak tries to interject. "Uh, Trace, sea urchins are poisonous and you can't—"

"Mind your own business, Dak. A poisonous urchin would be the perfect pet for this guy." I glare at Alex.

"Girl, bye." Alex waves me off and gives me a I'm-so-pleased-with-myself expression. Nikki, on the other hand, shrugs and gives me a sheepish, so-sorry look as they both make their way out the door. I'm totally confused. I thought Dak and Alex were into each other. I don't understand anything anymore.

Chapter Nine

DAK

"Have fun you two," Alex calls to us before the door closes behind him and Nikki.

When he sent me a text to meet him at the Thirsty Whale, I knew something was up because he's never asked to meet me before. I thought it had something to do with his getting together with Erik, and after a weight training session at the gym with the guys, I was starving and a little curious, so I agreed to meet him. If he'd mentioned Trace was going to be here, I would have shown up an hour ago and waited for them like some lovesick fanboy. The mixed-up, inexplicable thoughts of her are completely screwing with my ability to enjoy any other girl. I need to figure out what's going on with her and me, or, since there *is* no her and me, at least with my overzealous interest in her.

Even though I told him I wasn't interested, it looks like Alex is up to some shifty, matchmaking tricks after all, although I'm not as ticked off by the idea as Trace appears to be. From the scowl on her face and her suggestion of offing him, I don't think she's too happy about Alex's antics.

Doesn't matter. Aside from the temperature-rising thoughts of her which keep filling my mind, a deal is a deal and we need to get this project done whether she wants to study with me or not. If it takes Alex to get us together in the same room, I'll take what I can get.

Professor Clancy gave us the assignment last Friday to go out in the research vessel and collect phytoplankton samples to bring back to the lab for analysis. It's research we're both going to need for our theses topics. My topic involves plankton calcification under rising carbon dioxide scenarios; in other words, changes caused by ocean acidification. It's similar to Trace's topic, which means we're going to need a lot of the same info. The problem is, it's been a week since Clancy gave us the assignment, with two weeks to get out there, collect samples, do our lab analysis, and submit our results, and even though Trace and I made a deal for her to help me study if I skate with her in the Winter Fest, she's avoiding me like the plague.

She keeps making excuses. Something about another paper she has to finish and then something about a kayak tour she has to take out on Saturday, and on and on the excuses flow.

The truth is, I'm not too excited about the venture either. The combo of a girl and me in a boat has me kind of jittery. Good thing the research boats aren't small vessels. Since they accommodate all the equipment, they need to be at least thirty feet. The research work is important for both of us, but since the accident with Abbey three years ago, taking a small boat out isn't something I'm prepared to do. I'm feeling comfortable nothing short of a major hurricane is going to flip a boat the size of the *Arctic Tern*. The good news is, major hurricanes are unusual for Maine. But if we do happen to get heavy winds, they're just enough to make for some interesting swell for surfing along the Portland coast, not enough to cause an *Into the Storm* type of catastrophe.

It's completely weird. I can enter the back door of a barrel and ride it without a blink of the eye, or smash a two-hundred thirty pound defenseman against the boards without hesitation, but the thought of rowing in a canoe has me trembling like an abandoned kitten. Canoeing, kayaking, and playing hockey used to be my favorite things to do in my free time, besides surfing and making love to Abbey, until that fateful day. I haven't climbed into a canoe or kayak since.

The thing is, whatever size the boats are for class research, I need to grow a pair and do it. Got to get my work done for this Bio class and there's only a week left to hand in our first assignment.

"What are you doing here?" Trace's seething comment brings me out of my thoughts.

"Mind if I join you?" Not waiting for an answer, I slide into the bench seat opposite her.

"Sure. Why not? Have a seat. Oh wait. You already did." She breathes out through her nose and purses her lips.

A cute waitress comes by and puts two beers on the table.

"How thoughtful of you, Bambi." I grin. "You ordered me a beer."

"I didn't. They were—"

"Anything else?" the curvy blonde waitress inquires with a smile and flutter of her lashes.

"Sure. I'll have what she's having. I hear the burgers are intense."

"They're amazing," the waitress, in a tit revealing tank top, confirms with another smile and flutter of her overworked lashes. Her hungry gaze has me wondering if she's referring to the burgers.

A couple of weeks ago I would have jumped all over her obvious invitation. Now, the unexpected object of all my desires is sitting across the table scowling at me. The waitress lingers for a long moment.

"That's it for now, thanks," Trace says flatly.

"Be right back," the waitress says without looking at Trace, but gives me another ravenous up and down scan before hurrying off to place my order.

Glaring after her, Trace tilts her head in annoyance. "Seriously?"

"What?"

"Since *you* joined *me* without my invitation, do you think you could put away your slutty charm for five minutes?"

"I'm just sitting here. I didn't do anything," I protest, but since I'm doing it with a big grin on my face while stealing one of her fries I don't think she's buying my innocent routine.

"Wait for your own food," she snaps and moves her dish away from my reach.

"I'm a growing boy, Bambi. I need sustenance from you *now*." I run my tongue over my lips to affirm my double meaning, and since she's snorting air through her nose like a bull ready to attack, I think she gets it. I can't help it. It's so easy to get her riled and I get hard watching the fury flame in her eyes every time I push her buttons.

"You're such a pig." She rolls her eyes.

"You know, you should stop calling me names. You're giving me a complex," I quip and reach for another fry. She tries to smack my hand away, but I'm too quick and manage to steal another two fries from her plate.

"What. Are. You. Doing. Here?" she asks again. "Did you come in just to steal my dinner and give me indigestion in the process?"

"No. Alex invited me." I sit back in my seat, arms crossed over my chest, and give her a smug grin.

"Oh, Alex invited you," she drawls out and crosses her arms over her chest to mimic my pose, only her chest is way more interesting than mine. I can't keep my gaze from dropping to follow her movement.

"And he was so happy to see you. I wonder why he isn't here giving you *sustenance*? And by the way, my eyes are getting jealous." She waves her hand in front of my face and then in front of her eyes to indicate where I should be looking. "They would love it if you would look up here at them."

"Huh? Oh. Sorry. I was admiring your shirt." It's not

a *total* lie. I love all her Save the Ocean inspired t-shirts, and the way she fills them out.

"Right. So why are you here?"

Before I can respond, the waitress comes back to our table with my burger and another plate piled high with fries.

"What the hell? The rest of us didn't get a separate plate with all those fries," Trace protests in sheer disgust.

"Are you sure I can't get you anything else?" the persistent waitress asks in a breathy tone without acknowledging Trace.

"No. Thanks. That's it for now." I smile, enough to be polite, not enough to be encouraging.

"Okay. Well my name is Ginger. If you need anything, anything at all, just give me a call." She bends over to take an empty beer glass from the table and almost shoves her full tits in my mouth before wiggling her ass away. Normally my cock would have insisted I follow that action. Now the only thing he wants is the spirited chick glaring at me from across the table.

"Oh for fuck sakes. She just put women's rights back a hundred years. Would it be too much to ask for you to stop eye fucking other girls while you're sitting with me?"

Wow. I know I hold a special ability to irritate her, but she's beyond pissed right now. Methinks the lady doth protesteth a little too mucheth. Do I detect a *Trace* of jealousy?

"Would you prefer I eye fuck *you*? Because I would be more than happy to."

"I would prefer you leave me alone." She throws her napkin on the table and starts to slide out of the booth.

I grab her hand to keep her from getting up, and for a second she doesn't pull her hand away. "Sorry. I'm just messing with you. I swear I wasn't flirting with that chick. I would never do that while sitting with you."

"No. I suppose there's plenty of time when you're not with me." She gives me a smug look and pulls her hand from mine.

"Um...well..." I'm not about to tell her I haven't even glanced at another girl since I crashed into her. That is, since she crashed into me, because the only one my dick wants these days is her.

"Forget it. It doesn't matter. Got to go. Schoolwork to do," she says, and I swear a shadow of sadness, which matches her curt, disappointed tone, fills her eyes. Now I feel like a complete douche. I love messing with her, but I don't want to hurt her feelings.

"I'm sorry. Don't be mad. I'm not interested in that girl. I only want to set up a time to get together to do our research project. There's one more week to get it done. What do you say we get together this weekend?"

"Yeah, the research project. Okay." She sighs. "Put your number in my phone and I'll text you a time that works for me."

This side of Trace is a far cry from the confrontational side she's been showing me. I type my contact info into her phone, entering my name as *Jackass*, then slide the phone back to her. I figure it will give her a laugh. But she doesn't look at it before getting up and shoving it into the back pocket of her jeans. She stands there without saying a word.

The expression on her face has my chest hurting. My childish behavior can't be the reason for the level of pain I see in her eyes. It's something much deeper than what passed between us.

Sure. I wouldn't call our interactions the most pleasant since we met, but I hate seeing her like this. While the strangest urge to wrap my arms around her and comfort her sweeps over me, she might kick me in the balls if I try to touch her. And since I like my balls and want to keep them intact I only say, "I'll be waiting for your text to find out what time you want to get together."

"Okay. See ya." No sarcastic remark, no name-calling, no nasty glare. Just "see ya" and she turns to leave.

"Trace," I call after her. She glances back at me. "I'm sorry," I offer again, because I don't know what else to say to make it better.

"It's fine. Don't worry about it. It's not your problem." She sighs again and heads for the door.

This unusual girl has seeped into every pore of my skin and if she has a problem, I think I want to help her fix it.

Chapter Ten

DAK

Trying to organize my notes and put a thought together while all this commotion is going on in the house is like trying to organize the Florida Keys after Irma. Another Friday night keg party is in full swing and the house is rocking. There's no way I'm getting any studying done here tonight.

And this stuff has to get done before we can get out on the water and finish our research, if we ever get out on the water, because there's been no word from Trace. I thought about going to the library, then the brilliant idea occurs to me that since she isn't at the party, I'll walk over to her house and see if she's home. It's an uninvited visit, but it doesn't look like she plans on extending a welcome anytime soon or even text me to set up our research time. Inviting myself over is the only alternative.

I push through the crowded living room, giving friendly smiles to the ladies vying for my attention, avoiding any further contact than the casual grin. There're plenty of other hockey dudes here tonight to fulfill their fantasies. Speaking of which, I also want to avoid all the guys. I'm not in the mood to face the million questions about what I'm doing going over to a chick's house to study, especially on a Friday night. They wouldn't believe me even if I told them Trace is my lab partner and nothing else is going on. They're kinda working with one-track minds when it comes to chicks. Don't judge them too harshly. They're hockey players.

I make a stealthy exit out the side door. The only thing I can think about right now is getting my Marine Bio work done, and getting it done *with* Trace. Not only because I'm lusting after her like a fool, but because we've got to get this assignment done. For real. My main concern is the assignment. Sort of.

As I step up to Trace's door, I can hear soft music coming from inside the house. It's something classical. This girl is all kinds of different. Good different. I like the soothing music. Although, I don't even know who lives here besides Trace. She could have a roommate who likes classical music. Or she might live with her boyfriend who likes classical music. My chest tightens at the thought.

I knock tentatively. No answer. I knock a little harder and hear the muffled steps of someone moving to the door. Trace opens the door and gives me a startled, wide-eyed look. One glimpse of her and all the air punches out of my lungs.

Her dark auburn hair is tied up in ponytails on either side of her head. She's wearing shorts so short I'm sure they can't be covering the cheeks of her ass, and the tight white tank top with no bra underneath, which reads *Save A Wave Ride A Surfer* leaves her lush, round tits on full display. The best part is the orange and pink striped knee socks she's rocking. Fuck. She looks like a porno kitten version of Pippy Longstocking and my cock is enjoying the vision.

"Oh. It's you," she says flatly. Not exactly a heart-warming greeting, but when she tilts her head to one side, causing both of her side ponytails to sway over her nipples, my groin area warms nevertheless. "What do you want?"

What do I want?

I want to pull that tank top off you and suck those perfect tits until you moan in pleasure, and then I want to drop those tiny little shorts and lick you until you come all over my tongue and scream my name, and then I want to show you what it feels like to ride a surfer.

Obviously, I don't say that out loud.

"What do I want?" I say instead. "What are you doing?"

"What am *I* doing? What are *you* doing?" She puts her hand on her hip to punctuate the defiant question.

"I mean, what are you doing opening the door at this time of night without asking who it is first, knucklehead? It could be dangerous."

"First of all, there's a peephole." She tilts her chin toward the small glass opening in her door. Her lips curve in a smug grin as she counts off a numbered list to mimic the way I gave her one at the rink. "Second of all, did you come over to call me names?"

"Cute," I acknowledge her imitation of me. "First of

all," I count off in a list right back, "it's good there's a peephole. Second of all, you should never open your door to strangers. And third of all, no I didn't come over to call you names."

"Well thank you, Captain Safety. I'll keep it in mind." She starts to close the door in my face.

"Wait." I reach out and stop her from closing the door with the palm of my hand. "I...I thought we could do some research prep." I tug my backpack off my shoulder and hold it out so she can see I came equipped with study materials. Jeez. She has a way of making me feel so welcome. "Lovin' the shirt, by the way," I say to show how her mock displeasure rolls right off my shoulders, because I know deep down, okay, maybe deep *deep* down—she likes me.

She holds onto the door with one hand and grips the frame on the opposite side with her other hand, only opening it enough to allow her thin body to fill the doorway. When she catches me practically drooling as I take in the sight of her from head to toe she glances down at herself and makes a quick move to cross her arms over her chest. I snap my eyes back up to her eyes before she slams the door in my lecherous face.

"You want to study *here*?" She says it like I asked her to have my baby or something.

"Well...yeah. That was our agreement. Remember? You never sent me a text. So..." Christ. This is the only chick I know who acts like I'm *bothering* her, and I don't mean in a hormonal way.

"It's kind of noisy over at my place. I'm not getting

much work done. And we need to get on this. There's only a few days left."

I don't tell her that even when there isn't a party vibrating the walls of the house, I can't get any work done because the noises inside my head caused by the graphic imaginations of her screaming out in pleasure in response to my sexual abilities are too fucking distracting. "What do you say? You up for it?" *I certainly am.*

"Well…" She squints at me and purses her lips to one side. "Okay. I guess. Come on in." She pushes the door open wider with her hip so she doesn't need to drop her arms from covering her chest. She keeps her back pressed against the door, giving me plenty of room to move past her without touching her. "Only to plan out our schedule. I'm not having sex with you," she adds matter-of-factly.

"Huh. Must be something wrong with my memory." I scratch my head.

"What do you mean? Did you forget something?"

"Yeah. I don't remember *asking* you to have sex with me?"

She glares at me and lets out a big exhale. "Very funny, jackass."

"I'm only here so we can make some kind of research and study plan. No hidden motives. Okay?" It's almost the truth.

"Okay. I'm studying in the living room." She points to the arched doorway in front of me. "Make yourself comfortable while I go change my clothes."

"No need to change on my account. It's an interesting invitation across your chest." I give her the grin most girls drop their panties for about two minutes after I unleash it. Not Bambi. She rolls her eyes so hard I think they might get stuck in the back of her head. I think I hear her mumble the word 'pig,' one of her favorite terms of endearment for me.

"Holy shit! Did your fairy godmothers have a wand fight over the colors your living room should be?" I can't believe what I'm seeing. Bambi lives in a princess cottage.

"My fairy godmothers?" She arches her brow and smirks.

"What? I'm secure enough in my manhood to admit I dig the whole Disney princess thing."

"It's Mackenzie-Childs furniture."

"What, she didn't want it anymore so she gave it to you?"

"Who?"

"This Mackenzie chick."

"No. It's the name of the company." She giggles. "They're considered works of art. My mom gave them to me. I know it's a bit much. What can I say? She loves me."

She sighs and affection fills her eyes as she gazes across the furniture filled room. The corners of her mouth turn up. Damn. I didn't think it was possible, but she's even more beautiful when she smiles. I can tell she's relaxing a little, even though she's still got her arms crossed over her chest.

"I like it. A Disney princess house suits you." I can't take my eyes off her when she smiles again, this time so wide her eyes crinkle up in a totally sweet way. And fuck, it's like an arrow straight to my heart.

"Take a seat. I'll be right back." She gestures toward the sofa. While I make myself comfortable, I watch her climb the stairs. Yup. I was right. Those shorts don't completely cover the cheeks of her perfect ass. I love her ass, which leads to the need to readjust myself before the pressure of my zipper permanently disfigures me.

Aside from her obvious gorgeousness, which got me hard at first sight, there are so many different sides to this girl. She's smart and sassy, with a touch of insecure sadness. I've got to admit I want to get to know every one of them. If she doesn't strangle me first.

Chapter Eleven

TRACEY

I can't believe I'm wearing this shirt, because—of course—mister all-American- perfect happens to also be an avid surfer. I saw the pictures on his Facebook page. Yeah. I stalked the jackass's Facebook page. Doesn't mean I like the arrogant pig. Although the horrific truth is, I might be spending a little too much time thinking about riding *that* particular surfer boy. Yeah. Yeah. I know. It's stupid.

I slip on a pair of leggings and a loose off the shoulder sweatshirt. I hate the restraint of a bra when I'm at home studying so I don't put one on. The loose sweatshirt will keep me from revealing my assets to the object of all my unwanted desires.

I go back downstairs to find Dak making himself comfortable, his arms stretched out on the back of the sofa and his legs crossed on top of the Tra La La coffee table. Not kidding, that's the actual name of the black and white checked table, which matches the black and white stripes and checks on the sofa with the Musette flowered cushions.

God save me from my mom.

Dak said it looks like a Disney princess house. I'd say more like a Mad Hatter tea party gone wrong house. Whatever it looks like, Dak appears to be right at home, even though the sight of his big frame lounging on all this country garden furniture is a bit peculiar. My mom would pass out if she saw him with his size huge feet up on the two-thousand-dollar table. Whatever. It *is* a college student's house, after all, not high tea in an English drawing room. She can't expect prim and proper.

"I was making some hot chocolate. I know it's still too warm outside for it, but it helps me relax when I'm studying. You know, the whole comfort food thing?" I shrug. "Want some? Or I have beer or wine if you want." He's my first guest, so I force myself to be civil.

"Hot chocolate sounds good. Haven't had it since my mom used to make it for me after junior hockey games. Need help?"

"No thanks. It's already made. Be right back." While I pour our drinks, my mind drifts to the thought of a cherubic little Dak racing around in his hockey uniform while his mom bribes him with hot chocolate to get him to behave. But when I come back to the living room, the sight of the broad-shouldered, scorching hot guy filling my sofa dissolves the vision of the cute adolescent.

"Damn. You've even got cups to match your furniture. It feels like a movie set or something." He lets out a big laugh.

Yup. The cocoa is served in fashionably correct Odd Fellowes mugs, which match the flowered cushions. "Not a movie set." I smile. "You've entered the parallel universe of Terace Hayward."

"Your mom?" He chuckles again and shakes his head.

"That's her." Anyone who knows my mom would know I'm not making this stuff up. There's already matching coasters on the table to place the mugs on— Mom's thorough decorating scheme.

Dak blows out a whistle of air. "What is she, like, some kind of fairyland interior decorator or something?"

"No. Thank God. It might be even worse than it is if she was. She's a former Victoria's Secret model and a fashion designer these days."

He leans forward like he needs to get closer to hear me better. "Are you fucking with me, Bambi?"

"About what? Even though you keep calling me Bambi, I would not fuck with you." Nope. Not in any way.

"Your mom was *not* a Victoria's Secret model!"

"Yes, she *was*. Her geeky scientific daughter couldn't follow in her footsteps." I shrug.

Is it creepy he's getting all excited about my mom? Creepy or not, if he met her I'm sure he'd be even more excited. She's still drop dead gorgeous. Truth. My dad and her are like Mr. and Mrs. Olympia with Sloane as their little Miss Olympia offspring. It's discouraging to be the ugly duckling in the family.

"That explains it." He nods and gives me an all-knowing grin like the heavens opened and revealed some important secret to him.

"What?"

"Why you're so stunningly beautiful."

What?

It's like he read my thoughts about being the ugly duckling of the family. Oh, I know I'm not ugly. I'm not fishing for compliments to boost my ego. But when it comes to my practically perfect, beautiful family, they're a tough act to follow.

Though I don't need some guy telling me how beautiful I am to make me feel better about myself, I confess, when the sex-god known as Dak Andersen says I'm *stunningly* beautiful—even though I hate him—it does tickle me a little bit. Okay. I'll admit it. After more than a year and everything before, it's possible a part of me needs a small compliment here and there from a guy. It doesn't mean I'm ready to give up my membership card in the Rights for Women sorority. So don't judge.

"Right. Thanks." I try not to sound too pleased. "You're not so bad yourself."

Why the hell did I say that?

I can't even stand him. I don't want him to think his ovary exploding looks have any effect on me.

"Well thank you, Bambi. I thought you'd never notice," he says all smug and sure of himself.

Crap. Now he's got this seductive glint in his dazzling blue eyes and I'm getting moist between my legs. Ugh. Why does he have to be so annoyingly sexy all the damn time?

"Is your roommate home?" he asks.

"Uh...no. No roommate. Yet," I squeak out as I manage to unlock my eyes from his baby blues. Damn. I wish Nikki had moved in this week instead of next. Her presence would be a welcome safety net from my own desire to jump all over this guy. "Uh, we better get started on our schedule," I suggest, hoping it didn't come out as tense as my clenched lady parts. "It's getting late and your cocoa is getting cold."

Sitting next to him on the sofa, I open my laptop to my calendar. He slides over a little closer and when his thigh brushes against mine it's like getting zapped by the electric shock of a jellyfish. In a good way.

I can't explain it. When he touches me, I hold my breath waiting for the panicked reaction to sweep over me: hyperventilating, fists clenching, hammering pulse. Yet it doesn't come. It's absurd that he should be the one who breaks through the barricade I've built both mentally and emotionally around myself. I've got to get a grip before all my well-laid future plans go right down the orgasm trail along with all my vows of celibacy.

I focus on my computer because no way can I look into the eyes I can almost feel burning into me from inches away with the ability to hypnotize my vagina. "Okay, let's see. How's tomorrow afternoon to go out and get the samples? It will give us all week to do the analysis and write it up."

"Why not go out in the morning? Then we'd have the rest of the day and Sunday to do the lab analysis. It's better to get out on the water early while the sun's shining."

"Can't. I'm doing a kayak tour early in the morning. It takes two to three hours."

"You mentioned the tour thing in class. Are you working for one of the companies in the harbor?"

"Yeah. I got my certification a few years ago in Delaware. It was required by the college to take out the school's kayaks and the tour guide job was a fun way to make some extra cash. Hey, why don't you come on the tour? I'll take a double kayak out. You can pair up with me so there won't be an uneven number of people. Then we can go right out after the tour. It will save time."

"Can't. I...I just remembered, I have hockey practice in the morning. How about I meet you at the dock at one? Should give us plenty of time before dark." He shifts a bit, fisting his hands on his thighs.

He isn't as smug and relaxed as he was a minute ago. What's that about?

"Sounds good. The tour is done by eleven. I can meet you at one."

"And...uh...speaking of hockey and skating schedules, have you thought about our Winter Fest routine and when you want to get together to practice?"

Thought about it? Oh no. Only when I breathe.

I can't get the idea of skating with him out of my mind. All good skating routines should show emotion, but a *pair's* routine is intimate, familiar on a very personal level. I'm not sure I can handle or even want that kind of closeness with Dak. I need to keep my distance.

"Um, yeah. I've thought about it a little. I thought you might want to help pick out the music. Any ideas what you'd like to skate to?"

If he says Romeo and Juliet, I'm changing schools again.

"Well the music you're listening to is pretty cool."

I didn't even realize my IPad was still playing. I usually keep something classical on low in the background when studying. It helps to block out the rest of the world. Unfortunately, it hasn't help block out the thoughts of Dak ever since the first day we collided on the ice.

"Um, Pachelbel? You want to skate to the *Canon in D*?" I can't hide the surprised tone in my voice. I've skated to it before in competition because it's my all-time favorite classical piece, but I hadn't pegged Dak as a classical kind of guy.

"Nah. Just kidding." He smiles and my ovaries quiver at the sight of his dimples. "I mean I like it, but I was thinking something more contemporary for the show."

"Oh, right." His words extinguish my thought of licking those dimples. "Me too."

"A Jason Mraz song could be cool. His music got me through some tough times. Like his duet with Sara Bareilles, "You Matter to Me." It would be perfect for a pair routine. And he did another duet with Christina Perri, also pretty hot, "Distance." Do you know them?" His leg is pressing against mine now, and when I look up, his eyes are darkened to an inky blue and I can't turn away from their spellbinding hold.

Okay. Now I'm completely baffled. Sara Bareilles, Christina Perri, and Jason Mraz? The man-whore-hockey-god has the musical interests of a teenage girl.

And tough times? What kind of tough times did this cocky ass ever encounter?

I know I'm being a bit harsh. Dak doesn't deserve my caustic attitude, even if he did crash into me on the ice and blame it on a so-called lack of my skating skills. He's not the one who caused my current distrust of the opposite sex. But he does have the unfortunate honor of being the current available cocky athlete for my venting hostility.

Every second I spend with him only succeeds in bewildering me more. Turns out this arrogant guy, I *thought* was the king of manwhores has a whole other sensitive, romantic side going on. Sara Bareilles? No way. What did he do with the cocky jackass who was making it a little easier to resist his gorgeousness?

"Wow. You're one big mystery wrapped in an enigma, aren't you? You've got the same taste in music as a twelve-year-old girl." I can't help myself from spitting out the snide comment. He seems to bring out the worst in me. Besides, sometimes a woman has to behave like an adolescent. It's how the universe works.

Dak smiles at my snarky words. "I can't help it if I'm a hopeless romantic, can I?"

"Hopeless, maybe. Romantic? Don't think so." I smile and shake my head.

"Once you get to know me you'll see, I can be all kinds of romantic, Bambi."

There's the stupid sly grin again, which makes my easily impressed heart go boom inside my chest.

"I'll take your word for it," I say in an I'm-absolutely-not–interested tone. "And by the way, I think they're both perfect choices."

"Yeah? Okay. Let's do it, like a mashup or something." His lips are so close we're sharing our breath. He smells like a mixture of peppermint, vanilla, and leather, like Christmas and all kinds of bad choices rolled into one hot package. I'm lost in the combination, adrift in the intimate circle of Dak and me. There are no cautionary thoughts of his activities with other girls *or* guys.

He leans in before I know what's happening and kisses me with a feathery soft touch. His lips are warm and full and I whimper at their soft caress. He uses the opportunity to slide his tongue between my parted lips. I can't resist the seductive invasion of swirling motions he's making and I return his kiss. For a moment, there's nothing else but Dak here with me at this minute, his lips on mine, our tongues tangling, my breath coming too fast, the heat building between my legs. He cups my face in his hand while his other hand slides down my neck and pushes the loose fabric of my shirt further down off my shoulder. I jump back, away from his touch. It's too much.

"What are you doing?" I push his hand away, but not before his touch causes my body to tremble and the heat to sweep down to my core.

Oh for crying out loud. Snow White would not get herself into a situation like this.

"I...I was...I don't know. I thought you were feeling the same thing I am." He reaches out to brush a strand a hair off my face. I push his hand away again.

"Sorry. Not happening."

"Wow. Okay." He holds his hands up like he's surrendering. For a second a wounded tinge of disappointment crosses his face and I almost feel bad for the way I treated him.

Then the jackass shows up again when he says, "No problem, Bambi. Just figured the night is young and I know you want me."

I can't keep myself from laughing at his cornball line. "You must be mistaking me for one of your groupies." I brush back a pigtail to emphasize my indifference and pray my attentive nipples aren't showing through my sweatshirt.

"Real nice," he says as I continue to chuckle.

"Sorry, but I mean, does that Casanova routine actually work on the girls?"

"Forget it," he grumbles. "Let's just focus on our project."

"I...I came out of a really bad relationship not too long ago and I can't...I'm not ready to...I'm just not ready."

"Yeah, I figured something like that when Alex said you transferred from another school because of personal problems. You want to talk about it?"

Talk about it? I'm surprised I even gave him the limited explanation I did. I've never spoken to anyone about Sean, except my family and Gail. With them hundreds of miles away in the Hamptons and Sloane in New York City, I don't speak to *anyone* about him. All things related to him are locked away in the past. I've wasted enough time dwelling on my mistakes.

"You talked to Alex about me?"

I like Alex, but it's not cool to be talking to his boyfriend about me. Seriously. What gives with their relationship?

"He only mentioned you transferred because of some kind of problem with your team or something. So what's up?"

"Nothing's up. It's in the past and I don't want to talk about it. Okay?"

"It's in the past, but you're not ready to get with another guy? Doesn't sound like it's in the past to me." He gives me this smug look like no woman in her right mind has ever said no to him.

"Sorry, Dr. Phil, still not talking about it, and I still don't want to get with you. I'm sure there's lots of people waiting in line for the honor and I'm not into being part of your fan club."

"You sure?" His eyes drop to my tits and he grins lazily.

Damn. Why didn't I put on a bra?

I nod. "Never been surer of anything in my life."

At that moment, the sound of female laughter, from the girls partying at Dak's house, floats through the open windows.

"I could be over there partying right now," Dak said.

"Um, I don't remember inviting you over, and no one's got you tied here." Oops. Ill-advised comment. His eyes get all hazy.

"Interesting idea. Wanna tie me up?"

"Nope."

"Can I tie *you* up?"

"Seriously? Sorry. I'm not into the casual, meaningless sex thing, with or without ropes. It's not my thing."

"No problem, Bambi. No need to be sorry. I'll be fine." He tips his chin in the direction of his house and grins.

Blech.

I hate this arrogant asshole. So why am I so attracted to him? What was I thinking letting him kiss me? I don't know what's going on with him and Alex, but I *do* know all about his reputation of fucking anything that brushes across his crotch. Guess he's not all about only hooking up with guys. I'm not interested in making more stupid mistakes.

So what the hell am I doing?

I'm unable to let anyone touch me in a year and now *him*? He needs to leave like five minutes ago.

He gets up and heads for the door. "I'll see you tomorrow."

"Right. I'll see you tomorrow at the dock."

"Oh, and I can get the manager at the rink to let us use it alone for practice during the week. Okay?"

"Sure. Whatever."

Sure. Why not? Let's spend every day skating to a freaking love song. Can't see any problem there.

"The bad news is, it'll be early mornings. Super early, like five a.m."

He's completely unaffected by our interaction. It was nothing more to him than another chance to hit on a new girl. No problem it didn't work out, because there are plenty of other opportunities waiting a few feet away.

It's just as well, because for all my swaggering about

finding an indifferent fuck buddy, I know I can't do it. It's not me. If all I wanted was to get off, I could handle that all by myself. Casual fucking is definitely not my thing. I can't deny I like all the feelings and cuddles and laughter of a real relationship. More than anything, I need to be able to trust the guy I'm with. Dak Andersen is *not* that guy. Besides, I'm not looking for any kind of relationship right now.

"Five?" I make an over-animated grimace. I haven't had to face the five o'clock skating torture since high school. I'm regretting this whole Winter Fest thing, for so many reasons. But participating in it is an important part of me being able to move on and find my place here at Bernard. There's no choice. I need to do a routine with him. Between his schedule and mine and the prospect of open practice ice time, there's no choice there either. Five a.m. it is.

"Not an early morning girl, huh, Bambi?" He opens the front door and leans one shoulder against the frame, facing me. "Funny. I pictured you as having all kinds of energy in the wee hours of the morning." He waggles his brow.

Why is it whenever I'm around him he triggers the urge to smack the arrogant, sexy grin right off his super-model face? The jackass doesn't need to concern himself with my morning habits because he's never going to get the chance to witness them.

I make my way across the room to stand in front of him. Batting my lashes at him a couple of times I place my palms on his chest—his rock-hard chest—and say in a breathy voice, "I'll see you tomorrow at the dock at one and Monday morning at the rink at five." His eyes, his gorgeous Caribbean blue eyes, get a seductive glint again. I finish off the sentence with a harsh, "*jackass*," push him out the door, and slam it in his dreamy, smug face. I'm going to get through this vagina teasing semester if it kills me.

Chapter Twelve

DAK

Things didn't go so well at Trace's house last night. I admit I could have handled it better. While I wait onboard for the *Tern* to be fueled up, I watch her down the beach pulling the last of the kayaks out of the water and helping to strap them back up on the trailer hitch behind the van. I can't get last night out of my mind. I can't get Trace out of my mind.

Somehow she's become the girl of my dreams. She's smart, strong, beautiful, challenging. I don't even know how it happened. I wasn't looking for a dream girl. I thought I already had my dream girl and lost her when I lost Abbey. The weird thing is, when I close my eyes, the only dreamy images filling my thoughts are of Trace. How did that happen? I didn't think I would ever feel this way again and what's more, I didn't think I wanted to.

Kissing her last night almost put me into cardiac

arrest. When she returned my kiss, I struggled to hold myself back. When she pulled away from me, I was so disappointed I let my hurt pride get the better of me. I behaved like an idiot, acting like I couldn't care less and rubbing in her face my suave idea of a relationship is to tie up the closest willing puck bunny down for a quick fuck.

It's no secret, I suppose. I always make it clear before I hook up with anyone. I don't need the complications of any chick getting any warm and fuzzy ideas about a relationship. So far, there have been no complaints from any of the ladies, and we're on the same page. Except for Trace. She is *not* on the same page. Truth? I'm glad she's not.

When I got back to the house last night the party was still in full swing. I went straight to my room and locked the door. All I could think about as I tossed and turned in my bed was Trace and how she makes me feel. The need for getting myself off while I pictured her beautiful eyes giving me a longing gaze and her naked body underneath me was overwhelming. And fuck, as much as I'm trying to resist it, I want the real thing, not some horny trip to the spank bank.

She said she recently came out of a bad relationship, which means I should back off. She's not a casual fuck girl and I'm not interested in another committed relationship, not because I think being with the right woman is a bad thing. It can be a good thing...for some guys. But *not me*. I'm done with that shit.

The courage to be responsible for someone's life and happiness again is something I lack in a big way. In the end, being responsible for someone else's life and happiness is what a real relationship is all about. Being with the one special person you want feels great…most of the time. However, if something goes wrong, it can be decimating for both people. Once you cross the relationship line, both people possess the power to destroy each other. I know what it's like to be bulldozed by love. I can't risk it again. Fuck. Did I already cross the line by kissing her the way I did? Because she's all I think about, all I see when I close my eyes. I don't get this.

I thought I loved Abbey with all my heart. I thought we would be together for the rest of our lives. I guess we were. I just didn't know the rest of Abbey's life would be so short. But if all those emotions for Abbey were real, how can I be feeling what I'm feeling for Trace now? She's so different than Abbey. I'm consumed by the guilty feeling that if Abbey had lived, in time I might've fallen out of love with her and destroyed her in a different way.

We were both young. I'm not exactly ancient now, but three or four years in time and experience in college can make a world of difference. I'm a different guy than I was when I was a freshman, learned a lot about life and love. That doesn't mean I know for sure what the future holds and I don't want to do anything to Trace to hurt her somewhere down the road. She deserves way better than me.

See what I mean about relationships? I'm a perfect example. A few months ago, I had figured out how to live my life on my terms: hockey, school, surfing, the casual hook up with the next consenting hot girl to come my way. Now I'm a fucked up mess trying to figure out what I'm feeling for Trace. She deserves more than this guarded, emotional wreck.

"Okay. Let's get this over with."

Trace's frustrated tone jolts me out of my thoughts. I was so lost in my inner turmoil I didn't even hear her come aboard.

"You're late, Bambi." I return her annoyed tone, because I can't let her hear the anguish in my voice.

"By five minutes." She checks the IWatch on her wrist and rolls her eyes.

"Ten," I answer without looking up from my work of rolling up the mooring lines, because when I look at her, I want her. It's that simple. "I logged in our time at the research center. We've got the *Tern* till six o'clock. The Coast Guard has weather alerts for thunderstorms out for later tonight. They want us back in by then. It should give us enough time to get the fifteen samples we need."

"Cutting it right down to the wire, though. The sky is clear and beautiful right now. It was perfect weather for the tour earlier, too bad you couldn't make it. Maybe another time before the season's over."

"Yeah. Maybe," I mumble and feign checking the marine radio. I already checked it when I first got on the boat. She's actually making an effort to be pleasant after the bullshit way I treated her last night, even inviting me on one of her tours. No fucking way am I getting in a kayak with her on the ocean, not after Abbey's accident.

"We need about five hours, so we should get this show on the road," she states.

I don't think she noticed the hesitation in my voice.

Even though I'm trying not to, I give her a sideways glance. Dammit. I can't help myself.

She's checking the winches for the CTD sensors, flow bottles, and messengers. The research vessel is loaded with all kinds of Sea Bird electronic equipment, much more than we'll need for this project. Beyond the sensations coursing through me for Trace, being on this boat surrounded by the state of the art gear gives me a sense of exhilaration.

I always loved being on the ocean for sports activities, but studying in a field which will help to save the ocean's marine life and environment is even more fulfilling. Being on the ocean to conduct environmental research with the spitfire checking the equipment, right now, is even more satisfying than usual.

Her spandex shorts are hugging her ass and all I want to do is pull her into me and press into her back so she can feel what she does to me.

Not what we're here for, dude.

Not to mention she would most likely punch me in the face. I've got to get my head on straight and focus on the lab assignment.

"Everything's ready." She gives me a thumbs up, unaware of both the mental and physical conflict raging inside of me.

"I'm going to head out toward Mount Desert Rock. You can drop the equipment after we get further out," I call out to her over my shoulder from where I'm standing at the helm.

"Okay!" she yells back over the noise of the engine.

I point the bow out to sea in the direction of the

lighthouse and wait until we're out of the harbor before pushing up the throttle. Built in the same design as a fishing trawler, the *Arctic Tern* can cruise at about ten knots.

When we're out in deep water, I glance back at Trace. She's standing on the working deck looking out to sea. She's wearing a white Save The Narwhal tank top. One more cock-enticing item to add to the ever-growing Awesome Things About Trace Hayward list, her incredible love of the ocean and marine life. She wears these statement shirts to class every day, and on her they're like living works-of-art advertisements to save the ecology of our oceans.

It's like the sun is radiating a circle of light around her. It could be the golden wisps of hair escaping her ponytail and glowing around her face, or the spray of sea mist glistening on her skin, or my mind imagining a cosmic aura encircling her, I don't know. I only know she's the most beautiful sight I've ever seen. Christ. When did I become this poetic mush head?

She turns and catches me watching her. Although I'm expecting her to give me one of her annoyed smirks, instead she smiles, lighting up her face and making her eyes pinch so much I don't know how she can see. With it, all my confusion and inner turmoil slide away and I'm filled with a sense of contentment like this is all perfect. I'm in the perfect place with the perfect person. The thought occurs to me I could spend forever doing this kind of stuff with her. Damn. I'm turning into a girl. It's definitely time for a night out with the guys. Beer and babes are our cure for almost anything.

"It's so beautiful. Isn't it?" Trace calls out to me.

I come out of my reverie. "Yes. Yes, it is," I say under my breath, soaking in the vision of the girl I want so bad it hurts.

When we get within a few miles of Mount Desert Rock I put the engine in neutral and give Trace the go ahead to drop the equipment. She's already got the bottles and messengers clipped on the winch line. She drops the CTD first so we can measure water temperature, salinity, and density, and then she flips the switch to lower the flow bottles. I can't take my eyes off her. It's crazy. I get an unusual pleasure merely watching her. Every time those sparkling green eyes come back to me I'm undone.

If I don't stop adoring her with my eyes, she's going to think I'm some kind of creepy perv. The way she moves around the deck and operates the equipment like an expert, like she's done this a million times before, it's fucking hot. Everything she does is fucking hot, even the way she handles scientific equipment.

The bottles are lined up down the length of the winch and they drop to various depths. Trace keeps one hand on the line so she can feel the tug each time a bottle closes and the messenger moves down the line to another bottle. Then she reverses the winch line and the bottles come up out of the water. We repeat this process several times, moving to different places so we can collect samples from various areas

Throughout the tedious job of collecting samples and replacing the bottles, I can't keep my mind off what happened yesterday. I've never felt anything like the way the brief kiss had me on fire. What do I do with these sensations? She made it clear she's not into casual sex. And I'm glad she's not. I don't think I could handle it if I knew she was hooking up with random guys. Big double standard, I know. Though I don't hold any claim to her at all I don't want to think of her with another guy. It's so fucked up.

I can't stop thinking about the dickhead in her past, the bad relationship dick. It makes me sick I might've added to her troubles last night. She doesn't need another douchebag, guy messing with her body and mind. I know the best thing to do is back off. Trace deserves way more than a fuck and run.

Lost in my inner chaos, I didn't watch the time or notice the dark, fast moving clouds rolling in, and the crackle of the VHS radio calling us startles me.

"Wow. Where did those come from?" Trace asks. She was so engrossed in pouring the samples into amber sample bottles she didn't notice the darkening sky either until she hears the hiss of the radio and glances up.

"Artic Tern, this is the Bernard Research Center, over." Before I can make it back to the helm the call comes over the radio again. *"Artic Tern, this is the Bernard Research Center, over."*

"Bernard Research Center, this is the *Artic Tern*, over."

"Hey, Dak. This is Erik at the center, over."

"Hey, man. What's up buddy? Over."

"Looks like we misinterpreted the weather, dude. The Coast Guard says there's a derecho blowing in and it's coming in fast. Over."

"A derecho? It's not the right time of year for one and even if it was, it's unusual for this part of Maine. What's going on? Over."

"Apparently the thunderstorm they were tracking has turned into a bunch of severe thunderstorms moving together. They're wreaking havoc further down the coast with heavy rains, flash floods, and high force winds. Over."

Fuck. I try not to let Trace see the panic in my eyes, but she can already read me like a book.

She comes into the cabin. "What's wrong?"

I close my eyes. Christ. This can't be happening again. I can't be risking another woman's life in a boat. Dak Andersen, fucking dipshit at your service.

"Artic Tern, are you there? Over."

"Yeah...yes, Erik, I'm here. Over." I put one finger up to tell Trace to wait until we hear what instructions the Coast Guard has given the Research Center regarding vessels out on the water.

"The bad news is, the storm is moving in fast. Really fast. You guys are the only ones still out on the water and they don't think you should try getting back in until the storm passes. Good news is, based on your location, you're close enough to the Rock to head there and hunker down. Over."

"The Rock? Dude, that's in the middle of open water. Will it be safe? And for how long? Over?" I'm watching Trace the whole time and she doesn't even blink at the news from Erik. She may be the bravest person I know. On the other hand, I'm not feeling quite so brave. I'm not worried for myself, but I can't let anything happen to her. Although, I'm sure if it came down to it, she could probably rescue my ass *and* hers if she needed to.

"It could be a couple of hours, it could be all night. It's cool, though. The main house was rebuilt and reinforced for this kind of weather. You'll be okay and the generator will keep you on limited power if the solar power goes out. The food, water, and firewood supplies are all stocked because the Marine Life Research Center crew is scheduled to be there on Monday. You'll be all set if you need to stay the night. It's all good, dude. You got the codes for the door locks? Over."

"I got them before we went out. Over." The electronic keypads on the doors for the facilities at the Rock are reset every week. It prevents random people out for a day of boating from wandering into the house or lab. Whenever students or researchers need to use the facilities, they're given the codes.

"Okay then, you should be all set. I'll keep channel seventy-one open for you. Let us know when you make it to the Rock. We'll be here all night if you need us. Over."

"Will do. We're heading over there now. Thanks, man. *Arctic Tern*, out."

"Bernard Research Center, out."

"Fuck. I'm sorry. I lost track of the time and wasn't paying attention to the weather. It's such a bullshit rookie mistake," I say after replacing the handset and pushing the throttle to full speed. I've got to get her out of this damn boat ASAP, even if the only place I can take her is a massive rock island in open water. Erik was right though. They planned for this scenario when rebuilding the research facilities on the island. We'll be much safer there than on a boat until the storm blows over.

"No need to apologize. I wasn't paying attention either."

"Wow. You're not even going to call me jackass or asshole or anything? I'm kind of missing your sugary names for me." I figure a little teasing will help take her mind off of the shit situation I got us into.

"Very funny. I'm sure we'll be fine on the island and we can use the lab there to do our analysis. We'll be too preoccupied to worry about the storm. No worries, *jackass*." She gives me a sweet little grin after adding the name I'm getting so used to hearing, I may start answering to it instead of Dak.

"There it is." I smack my hand on the helm and smile. "You're such a sweet little thing."

The memory of her scent when we kissed last night fills my senses, a mixture of coconut and pineapple, the intoxicating scent of a fragrant, tropical garden. I'd love a chance to lick every inch of her sweetness.

Focus, dude. Your negligent, horny thoughts already put you in this dangerous predicament.

Trace doesn't seem one bit concerned about the precarious situation we're in. There's a good possibility I'm falling for Super Woman.

"I guess nothing shakes you up, huh, Bambi?"

Except me standing stark naked in front of you.

Huh. I kind of like the idea I might be the only thing that can make her tremble. Oh for Chrissakes! Even when our lives are in imminent danger I can't keep my mind off my dick.

Her mood darkens and a worried expression crosses her face. "Plenty of things scare me," she says quietly and drops her gaze to her feet.

Great. I'm such an asshole. I succeeded in upsetting her yet again.

"I...I'm sorry. Look, the boathouse is straight ahead." I point toward the lighthouse. Its comforting beacon flashes every fifteen seconds. "We'll be there soon, and the wind hasn't even kicked up yet. We'll be safe there until it blows over."

I hope.

Chapter Thirteen

TRACEY

Mount Desert Rock is a barren rock island situated about twenty-five miles off the coast. No trees, no grass, just four buildings perched on desolate rock ledges since the nineteenth century. Now it's used as a marine research center. A few years ago, Bernard U received a grant to rebuild and restructure the facility to make it as hurricane proof as possible and to outfit the facility with cutting edge research equipment.

The boathouse, one of four buildings on the island, is big enough to accommodate the *Artic Tern*. Dak guides it into the slip and I hop out to catch the mooring lines he tosses out to me. My mind racing, I climb back onto the boat to help carry our samples and supplies into the generator shed, which was expanded into a wet/dry lab during renovations.

Dak thinks I'm not scared of anything. The truth is I'm scared as shit. Not of the weather though. I'm panicked I'm alone on an island with this guy who's two degrees hotter than the sun and makes me melt every time he looks at me.

Beyond wanting him so much it's making my lady parts ache thinking about it, he doesn't want me. At least he said he doesn't. Despite the fact the bulge in his pants was saying something to the contrary last night when he kissed me. And then there's Alex. I guess whatever was going on with them isn't going on any more. This whole situation is such a hot mess.

"We should get right to work on the analysis and get it done before the storm hits, then we can head into the house before the wind picks up," Dak suggests. "I'll go radio the center to let them know we made it here and start a fire in the fireplace so it's warm when we get in there. You want to start setting up the samples for testing?" he asks in a tentative tone.

I'm sure he's as uncomfortable about this whole situation as I am.

"Sounds good." I try to give him my everything is cool tone, which I can't quite achieve whenever he's near me. My heart is racing at the thought of being cozy in front of a fire with him in the light keeper's house.

While he's in the house I begin the filtration process of the samples. When the filters turn green or brown I'll know there's phytoplankton on them, then we need to make up the slides, check cell count, do the DNA and water analysis. It's going to be a long night. It could turn out to be a good thing we're stuck here with nothing to do but focus on our lab analysis. Uh huh. *Nothing* else to do.

When Dak comes back to the lab I'm deep into the filtration process and making up the plankton slides. He begins the water analysis. We're so preoccupied with the work we only exchange enough conversation to tell each other what we're doing. With the two of us working together it doesn't take as long as I thought it would to finish up and record our data.

"That's the last of the data. Went pretty fast after all. We make a good team, Bambi." He holds out his hand to give me a high five and it's like Mother Nature sees him and returns the gesture, because the wind picks up, a reverberating crack of thunder vibrates the lab, and the rain starts pummeling the roof.

"We better head into the house," Dak says in a loud voice to outrival the noise of the pounding rain and wind. "We can refine all this later so we can hand it in."

Although there are plans to connect the house and lab, construction isn't completed. When Dak opens the lab door we grab our backpacks and make a mad dash for the house. The wind gales are so strong I'm almost lifted off my feet. Dak grabs my arm and pulls me into the safety of the house with such force I fall against his chest.

It only takes a matter of seconds to get from the lab to the house, and even though I'm wearing a dri-fit tank top, it's not enough to withstand the torrential rain. I'm soaked through to the skin. By the way Dak's t-shirt has become see through and is clinging to every ripple of his chest and stomach, I can see he's even more drenched.

We stand motionless in place for a moment. He's still clutching my arm and I'm pressed against him. I don't experience any of the anxious trepidation jolting through me when I'm this close to a guy, ever since the night with Sean. Although, with the combination of my wet clothes and my breasts pressed against Dak's hard chest, I'm unable to control my trembling.

"Christ. You're freezing." Dak is the first to break the intense silence. "Let's go." In a swift move, he scoops me up into his arms like I'm as light as a dandelion wisp and carries me up the stairs. He *carries* me up the stairs! It's like something from the cover of a cheesy romance novel. Except in this case, the heroine is dripping all over the hardwood floors.

"I...I...c-can w-walk on my own," I stutter out through my clattering teeth. But my disloyal body is already settling into the comfort of his strong arms.

"Sure you can, Bambi. Your teeth are chattering."

I want to come back at him with some smartass remark, but he's right. I'm so cold I can't stop my teeth from rattling in my head. The astounding truth is, I don't want him to let me go. For the first time in more than a year I want to stay tucked snugly in a guy's arms.

He takes me into the bathroom, which connects two of the bedrooms, and sits me down on the closed lid of the toilet. I'm even colder without his body pressed against me than I was a minute ago.

I know it's more than the physical warmth of *any* body I'm missing. I want *Dak's* body, want him over me and in me and all kinds of ways, without soaking wet clothes separating us. I haven't felt like this for so long it's kind of scary.

He toes off his sneakers and pulls the soaked shirt over his head and tosses it on the floor. I clench every muscle in my body to keep myself from falling off the toilet seat at the sight of his muscled torso. Gah. It's the second time the vision of his smoking hot, dripping chest has scorched my vision. It's a good thing my pants are already drenched or no doubt he'd be able to see the wet spot of arousal forming on my shorts.

As it is, he's so concerned about my welfare, he isn't noticing the way I'm fucking him with my eyes. Thank God. He reaches behind the shower curtain and turns the water on.

Is someone taking a shower? Does he think two some-ones are taking a shower—like together?

"It'll take some time for it to get warm up here, and for the water to heat up," he says and then stands right between my knees. It might take a minute for the water to heat, but the area between my legs is already on fire.

"Man, you're so cold. Are you okay?" He kneels in front of me. His voice is so soft and filled with such a sweet tone of concern, I don't scream in his face that no freaking way am I getting in the shower with him.

He's such a presumptuous jackass. He didn't even ask me. Who does he think he is? And why is one little part of me hoping he scoops me up into his arms again and carries me into the shower before my sensible conscious has a chance to object?

"I-I'm o-o-k-kay," I manage to stutter out while the two sides of my frozen brain are doing battle over the prospect of getting in the shower with him.

"Here. Let me help you. Lift your arms." I'm too cold to care that this guy, who I'm supposed to be resisting, is about to undress me. All I want is to be warm. My shaking arms raise in response to his command.

His eyes lock on mine as he slips the tank top over my head and tosses it somewhere near his. As he does, the back of his hand brushes across one of my nipples. They're already hardened from the cold, but they still manage to salute in response to his touch. I can't stop myself from releasing a soft gasp when he touches me. Crap. Maybe he didn't hear it. For a second his eyes, which have never left mine, darken to the color of a tropical island sky at dusk. Yup. Definitely heard me moan. He blinks, licks his lips, and then bends over to take my ankle in his hand.

My eyes follow the path of his tongue along his lips and this time I swallow the groan easing up before it has a chance to come out. I wonder if this is how Cinderella felt when the prince knelt in front of her to place the shoe on her foot, all tingly and quivery. Especially since, in Cindy's case, he was slipping on a glass slipper, not pulling off a soaked canvas sneaker.

When Dak's fingers touch the bare skin of my ankle, it sends heated sparks up my legs. I'm beginning to warm up in the most pleasant, terrifying way. How is it possible to be this cold and heated at the same time?

Placing his other hand over the laces of my sneaker, he tugs if off. When he does, the contents of my soaked shoe pour out and pool around his knees. He doesn't even notice. He proceeds to pull my dripping sock off, then does the same thing with my other sneaker and sock.

It's crazy. The way he's fixated on taking care of me is

so freaking sensual. And again, I'm surprised to realize that instead of tensing and moving away from his touch, I lean into it.

He looks up and slips his fingers into the waistband of my shorts. Closing my eyes to block out the vision of his heavy-lidded eyes and muscled chest in front of my face, I focus on the task of keeping myself from trembling or worse—spreading my legs open to give him a welcoming invitation.

"You okay?" he asks in a soft voice. I open my eyes to find his dreamy eyes staring at me and his brow furrowed in worry.

"I...I'm fine. Thank you." Oh brother. All I can think of to say to this beautiful guy who's taking care of me like I'm a delicate butterfly needing the touch of gentle hands to be saved is a feeble thank you.

The heated sensations caused by his tenderness are spreading from my toes to the tips of my fingers and landing down between my thighs.

He slides my shorts down my legs and slips them off, tossing them to the side. My body trembles in response to the soft touch of his fingers along my skin. When his hazy gaze drifts in a slow path from my toes up to my breasts, I become aware of once again being exposed to him in nothing but my bra and panties. Even though they're more of an athletic style and not the lacy type he saw me in at the rink, they're white and soaked and are now completely see-through. Again. This thing of ending up in transparent underwear in front of him is getting to be an awkward habit.

"I'm okay to take it from here," I say and reach for

one of the folded bath towels on the shelf next to me and hold it in front of my chest.

The bathroom is beginning to fill with the steam from the warm water now streaming from the shower and my body is already filled with the steamy sensations of Dak's hands, eyes, and ripped muscles. I was right. This is going to be a very long night, stuck on an island with a sex god I can't touch. He's still kneeling between my legs and the growing ache I'm experiencing at my core to spread my legs and satisfy my need for him is relentless.

When I reach for the towel his eyes move from my now covered breasts to my eyes as he stands up in front of me. "Oh right. I'm going to take a shower in the other bathroom down the hall. I'll see if I can find us some dry clothes. I'm sure they keep some with the supplies in case anyone gets stuck here. I'll leave them on your bed. The cabinet under the sink is stocked with toiletries and there's new toothbrushes in the drawer."

Even though it's my first time staying at the house, it's clearly not Dak's. It's apparent he knows where to find everything we'll need to stay the night. I can't help wondering if he brought any of his many hookups here, even though I'm sure the university would frown on the Marine Science students using the house as a makeshift hotel.

The house has two classrooms, a recreation room, a kitchen, a dining room, a living room and is big enough to accommodate twenty researchers or students. It's kept well stocked with supplies for times when people stay here for periods of days or weeks to observe marine life.

"You sure you're good?"

"I'm good," I assure him. "You better go get out of the rest of your wet things too before you catch pneumonia."

While I should be relieved he's going to take a shower in the other bathroom, I'm feeling a little disappointed.

Stupid girl.

I know, right? He's behaving like a perfect gentleman and I'm disappointed.

Real nice, Tracey.

Okay, okay. I get it. *Shut up*, I chide my own know it all, irritating mind.

"I never get sick," he boasts and gives his right bicep a playful flex. Yup. Thoughts of big, strong Spartan warriors, cross my mind. "It will only take me a minute and then I'll head down to check out the food supply and make us some dinner. I'm starving and you must be too. We forgot to stop to eat today."

At the mention of food my stomach responds right on cue with a loud rumble.

"I guess that means yes." He laughs and walks toward the door.

"Dak?"

"Trace." He turns and gives me his infamous half smile. Between his smile, and the way he says my name in an easygoing, sensual tone, I'm sure my wet panties must be adding to the steam in the bathroom.

"Thank you for taking such good care of me." I smile and his face lights up in a bigger smile.

"No problem. Your wish is my command, milady." He gives me a charming smile and then bows.

"You're such a weirdo," I tease, even though my heart grew two sizes in response to his sweetness.

"Weirdo? Huh, a new pet name. You haven't seen anything yet." He snickers and does a little tap dance shuffle before walking out of the bathroom and closing the door behind him.

I giggle again at his dorky, adorable antics. I undo my watch and place it on the countertop. As I stand for the first time to slip off my bra and panties, my legs and body feel weak and wobbly; not from the cold but from the stirring impressions Dak left in his wake, leaving me alone with only my mixed up thoughts and feelings.

He's not a super douche, he's a good guy. There's so much more to him than he lets people see. He's smart, caring, and funny. And the hot as the sun thing he has going on isn't exactly a bad thing. But he's got a reputation for having slept with half of the girls at Bernard. I'm still not sure about the guys. I don't want to be another name on his long list. Besides, I can't get involved with anyone. I'm not ready to put myself out there. At least that's what I keep telling myself.

Dak left sweatpants and hoodie with the gold Bernard U logo embroidered across the front and down one leg folded on the bed with a thick pair of wool socks lying next to them. I also slip my watch back on, because it's my obsessive nature to always know exactly what time it is and if my fitness goals for the day are on target. The sweats are huge and I'm sure I look like I'm wearing my father's hand me downs. Not exactly flattering, but they're comfy and I'm grateful for their warmth.

I make my way downstairs feeling both refreshed and warm. The smell of something delicious—Italian restaurant delicious—drifts past my nose and my stomach makes a sound like a tire hitting a patch of gravel.

Following the aroma, I find Dak standing at the stove in the kitchen. He's wearing the exact same black hoodie and sweatpants I am, although the way the pants sit low on his hips while he's standing there barefoot looks all kinds of sexy on him.

The room is shimmering in a soft glow, lit with two candles on the table and an oil lantern on the counter. I wonder if he decided to use the candles to conserve the use of the generator or because he's trying to create a romantic ambience.

Why would he want to set a romantic scene for you?

It's possible, I argue with the insulting voice in my head. It's obvious he's not strictly into guys.

No, but he did seem to be into Alex at the party.

Then again, Alex was the one who pushed Dak and me together at the Thirsty Whale. I continue to argue with myself like a complete psycho, because it's driving me crazy I can't figure this whole thing out.

The truth is, even if Alex isn't in the picture, I shouldn't be feeling the things I'm feeling for Dak. It's way too risky. Getting myself back together was a long journey. Still is. I haven't shaken off all the mucky aftereffects of Sean yet and Dak is a complication I don't need.

"Mmm. Smells wonderful!" I try to push the thought of the whole dilemma out of my head. "A man who can cook. I must be dreaming," I tease and walk to the stove and peer over his shoulder to see what he's making. "What is it? You need help?"

"It's eggplant and spaghetti puttanesca, and you'll find I'm a man of many talents, Bambi." He gives me a wry sideways glance. "Twinsies," he laughs.

I love his laugh. It sounds full of fun and warmth. And *trouble*.

"I don't know," I manage to speak like a normal adult who isn't getting all gooey over a guy's chuckle, for God's sake. "Yours look better on you. These are so huge I could fit you in here with me." I frown and stretch out both sides of the waistband of my pants to illustrate how gigantic they are.

He tilts his head as if he he's considering my statement. "That might be the best suggestion you've had all day. You can get some dishes and forks out if you want, and hand me that big bowl." He points to a large red ceramic bowl sitting on a shelf over the counter. "The food is pretty much done." He gives the sauce another stir, ignoring his suggestion of climbing inside my clothes with me.

Or was it my suggestion? He's a man of many talents indeed, and my unwanted desire to experience all of them is getting stronger by the minute.

"I'm impressed," I say without acknowledging his obvious insinuations. "You can make a fancy dish like this in the few minutes I was upstairs."

Before he can respond, a huge streak of lightning lights up the sky outside the window and a few seconds later a crashing rumble of thunder follows. The rain is still pummeling the rooftop. Though the sound isn't as intimidating in the house as it was in the makeshift lab.

"Yikes. Thank goodness we got off the water when we did."

I'm grateful to be inside the safety of the cozy house, even though at the moment I'm questioning what would be more dangerous: weathering the storm in a boat, or spending the night alone with the smoldering volcano known as Dak Andersen.

"I'm sorry I got you into this mess. I should've kept track of the time and the weather." Dak shakes his head and puffs out a breath like he's disgusted with himself.

"I already told you it's not your fault. I wasn't paying attention either and besides, if not for my tour, we could've gone out on the water earlier and gotten back to the harbor earlier. If it's anyone's fault it's mine. You don't get to take all the credit." I give him a playful punch in his triceps.

"Ow!" He pretends my punch hurt him, even though I only tapped him. "Okay, okay. I give. You win. You're the most irresponsible one of the two of us." He smiles and winks at me.

He might be the only guy I know who can actually look irresistible when winking. A part of me wishes he'd take those warrior arms, wrap them around me, and carry me right back up those stairs. Another part of me says to run away as fast as I can. I might tell that part to shut up.

"Um...so... what's in puttaness sauce?"

"Puttaness-*ca*," he snickers and accentuates the last syllable. "It's a variation of tomato sauce. I found a jar of olives and capers in the cabinet. They're the secret ingredients to this kind of sauce. They stocked up the fresh veggies and fruit because there's supposed to be a research group staying here for a week starting Monday if the weather clears up, so I added the eggplant."

"That's one of the things I love about Bernard. They grow their own vegetables all year round in their greenhouses. What other university does that?"

"It's the main reason my mom wanted me to come here instead of playing for one of the schools in Cali that offered me a scholarship."

"Because of the food?"

"Yep," he snickers. "She's a midwife and kind of a misplaced hippie chick. Everything has to be organic and environmentally friendly. She's into the au natural scene. She'd be rockin' dreadlocks if my dad hadn't put his foot down and said he drew the line at," Dak deepens his voice and mimics his dad, "'the knotted, unwashed hair situation.' His exact words."

"He didn't!" I can't keep from laughing at the impersonation of his dad.

"I kid you not. The two of them together are a trip." He shakes his head in amusement.

"They sound amazing. And your mom is, like, the complete opposite of my mom. I mean, my mom's great, but if she never had to cook a meal and could eat out every night she'd be good."

"Yeah, my mom's pretty cool." He stops stirring for a second and tilts his head to one side like he's thinking about it and realizing for the first time how great his mom is. "She's the one who taught me how to cook. My sister never took any interest in it. I was always the one helping her out in the kitchen."

I can't resist the smell of the sauce, so I take a spoon from the drawer and dip it in the pot to get a little taste.

"You like?"

"Oh my God! It's incredible! I could drink this."

"Huh uh," he says and moves in closer to me. "I told you, one of my many talents. My sauce is almost orgasmic," he whispers in my ear. Wow! He smells as delicious as his sauce.

I breathe in his peppermint and vanilla scent mixed with a trace of burning firewood. His masculine fragrance envelops me and I can't hold back the moan escaping my lips. He catches his bottom lip in his teeth like he's trying to hold back a smile. Crap. I can't believe I moaned out loud. Again.

"Uh...what does your father do? Is he an organic farmer or something?" I move away from the stove and around to the other side of the table to put some distance and a meager barrier between us instead of throwing him down on the floor and licking my puttanes-*ca* sauce right off his rock hard abs-*a*.

"He's a plastic surgeon. We live in Malibu, but his clinic is in Beverly Hills." Dak chuckles. "Complete job security, if you know what I mean." He drains the boiling water from the cooked pasta he had put on the stove, dumps the spaghetti in the red bowl, and ladles the sauce over it.

"Now you're fucking with me." I express the same astonishment he did when I told him my mom was a former V.S. model.

"I would never fuck with you, Tracey." He places the bowl on the table. "At least not with your mind." He waggles a brow.

I'm having no problem with the cold anymore. In fact, I feel a trickle of sweat running down my spine. It's *so* hot in here!

"An au natural midwife married to a plastic surgeon? Quite a dichotomy, isn't it?" I shake my head in awe, ignoring his latest suggestive statement. Despite the fact that most of my nerve cells are busy fighting the Battle of the Resistance of the Charms of Dak Freaking Andersen, there are still a few brain cells coherent enough to register the astounding fact of an organic, almost dreadlocked midwife married to a plastic surgeon. The two professions hardly belong in the same sentence let alone in the same bed.

"Huh. I guess it is. Never thought about it because they make it work so well. My parents are a strange phenomenon these days. They still love each other. They're like a couple of teenagers. My sister and I always pretend we're disgusted by their PDA, but it's cool how in love they are. Maybe I'll be able to feel that same kind of love again someday." He sighs and my ovaries explode.

"Again?" I ask.

"I...I...mean...someday. We should eat before it gets cold. And look what I found in the hidden supply stash."

The bottle of red wine he pulls from the cabinet is a nice attempt on his part to change the subject, because there is definitely something behind his feeling 'love again' statement. Seems we're both hiding things from our past we don't want to share, so I don't press him for an explanation.

"Ooo, yummy. I'll get the glasses." I search through the cabinets until I find two glass tumblers. I place them on the table while Dak uncorks the wine and pours some into each glass.

We sit on opposite sides of the small rectangular table and Dak uses a fork and spoon to serve the pasta onto each of our plates. He raises his glass of wine in a toast. "To successful research projects and other adventures." He gives me a slight grin.

"Um. Projects and *skating* adventures," I say and clink his glass.

"Okay, Bambi. Whatever you say."

"Your parents must miss you a lot with you're being so far away." It's my turn to change the subject. I twirl a big forkful of spaghetti and close my eyes in pleasure at the first taste.

"I guess. But they get to see me a few times a year because they own a cabin here in Maine they stay in every once in a while. They spend the holidays there. So we see each other,"

"How weird. My family has a house on the ocean in Rhode Island and they spend the holidays there too. My mom says it isn't Christmas unless there's lots of snow."

"You from a warm climate too?"

"Oh, no. We live in the Hamptons. We don't always get the amount of snow and pretense of wilderness my mom likes over the holidays."

"Pretense?" he asks and I giggle at his puzzled expression.

"We own a place in Newport. My mom's idea of wilderness. If there isn't a Prada within five miles, it's the wilderness."

I don't go on to explain that if our Newport house was the size of Rosecliff Mansion and located on Bellevue Avenue she *might* be able to consider it as something other than a rustic shack. Never mind our house is on Cliff Avenue, overlooks the ocean, and is six thousand square feet. If it's not on Bellevue Avenue, it's a cabin in the woods.

"My dad loves it up there for the holidays too. He likes to skate on the pond on our property, when it freezes."

"Awesome! Your dad skates? And what else does the lucky man married to a model do?"

"He's a retired hockey player. He does some commentating now for hockey games on ESPN."

He drops his fork and it clatters on his plate. "Holy shit! Don't tell me your dad is Duke Hayward!"

"Okay, I won't." I shrug and shovel more of the pasta into my mouth. Dak's right. The sauce *is* almost orgasmic. Yup, definitely got a sick love relationship with food going on. Give me the right food and I may never need a man in my life again.

"Fuck. He was, like, one of the greatest centers in pro hockey. I can't believe he's your dad. That's why you rock so hard on the ice." He points his fork at me. "You take after him. Man, your family is so dope, Bambi."

"Yours doesn't sound too bad either." I smile. My family is very important to me and I love a man who feels the same way about his family. Well, not love. Like. I'm beginning to *like* a man whose family is important to him, and right now that man is being so cute in the way he's become all wide-eyed and excited like a star struck kid after finding out who my dad is. I'm *almost* not hating the way he calls me Bambi anymore.

"Yeah. We must be the only people I know whose parents are still married with no problems. We've got to get them together when they're all in New England for the holidays."

Wait. What? He wants to get our families together over the holidays?

I don't know a lot about Dak and his fellow hockey friends, but the rumors of their reputations don't suggest the kind of guys who would want to meet a girl's parents after one abbreviated kiss. I've never met anyone who can send so many confusing mixed messages. Not even the nefarious Sean was this bewildering. He was just a callous, dishonest, cheating dickhole.

"Uh, well, it's kind of a long drive from Newport to Mount Desert, though. There probably won't be time over the holidays."

I stare at him over the rim of my wine glass. He keeps eating. No reaction. It's like the concept of our families spending the holidays together is as normal as green Christmas trees and white snow. Before this evening is over, I'm going to pull up my big girl panties and come right out and ask him what his game is, no more guessing.

"Our cabin is in Newry, actually," he says. "About three hours west of here."

"See? A long drive."

"You make the drive down to Newport for the holidays, don't you?" He holds up the wine bottle to fill my emptied glass. I don't think twice when I push the glass toward him. I need a refill or *five*. I nod as I take a very unclassy gulp of my wine. My eyes close at the spicy sweetness sliding down my throat and my head swims in the intoxicating buzz it's creating.

"If you can make the drive, what's the big deal? They can too." He refills his glass and then finishes off the rest of his pasta.

"I'm not sure what we're even talking about right now. The holidays are a long way off. Anything could happen by then." I wave my wine glass in the air to show how much space "anything" takes up. The wine in the glass does a swirling dance before flying across the table and splattering a few drops all over Dak's face.

He lets out a little sputter in response to the unwanted wine shower. Then he smiles, wipes off his face, and runs his tongue along his pillowy bottom lip to lick off a lingering drop.

My lips part in wonder, my eyes lingering on his tongue and mouth. I manage to squeak out a feeble apology while trying to pull my gaze away from his mouth. By the heavy-lidded way he's staring at me, I'm not sure I succeeded in hiding my own longing expression.

"If you're done with your pasta, what do you say we go sit in front of the fire and have dessert?"

"Ugh. I'm so stuffed. I don't think I could eat another bite of anything."

"No problem, because you don't bite this kind of

dessert. I found another hidden treasure in the supply closet." He goes to the cabinet and pulls out a bottle of tequila. "Guaranteed to warm you from the inside out and make you forget all your troubles."

I glower at the bottle like he's holding a viper, while reminding myself Dak isn't Sean. He has a sweet, sensitive side, which I never saw in Sean. I dismiss the trepidations the sight of the deceptive liquid sends through my body.

"No troubles—*yet*." I glare at him through narrowed eyes. I'm not the naïve little girl I was a year ago.

Chapter Fourteen

DAK

The fire is already roaring, but I get a few more logs from the built-in alcoves on either side of the fireplace and throw them in to add to the welcome heat. Trace is sitting on the leather sofa with her legs tucked under her. The way her skin glows and her long wavy hair glistens with strands of gold in the firelight, she takes my breath away.

"Mmm. This feels wonderful. Is there anything better than sitting in front of a fire while the weather rages all around you outside?" She sighs in contentment.

Uh yeah, I can think of some things better than *sitting* in front of a fireplace during a storm. Kissing, licking, sucking, fucking to name a few. But she's in a fragile place right now and my head's not exactly in a great place either. This *is* nice, though, sitting with Trace in front of a toasty fire while the wind and rain howl outside.

There are no trees or anything on the island to

protect the house, so we're at the mercy of the elements. Being here like this with her, it's like we're the only two people in the world and I can't think of anyone I'd rather be stranded with. I sit next to her on the sofa and pour a shot of tequila for each of us.

"Here's to warm fires and good friends," I say, tossing back the shot. The fiery liquid slides down my throat and does the job I said it would of warming me inside and out. Trace hesitates, then drains her glass. She lets out a cough and gasp afterward.

"Whoa. Burns." She blows out a long breath. "One is good for me." She puts a hand over the top of her glass to stop me from pouring her another shot. "I thought we could start putting together the choreography for our skating routine. I downloaded the songs onto my laptop and cut them to put them together. I can make an outline of the moves as we listen to the music. What do you think?"

"Sounds good. Let's do it."

She hops up and goes to get the backpack she dropped by the door when trying to escape the rain.

Funny. I haven't wanted to figure skate since I got serious about hockey. I'm all about working together with a team of guys with one goal—to win together. The aggressive game play of hockey is more my speed. Although I don't think I've ever felt the kind of stimu-lating excitement for a game in the same way I'm antici-pating practicing and performing this routine with Trace.

The thought of holding her in my arms while we do an intimate skate routine causes my cock to jump. If I'm feeling this way while *thinking* about it, I'm guessing I better not wear tight pants while skating with her or the whole audience will know what's on my mind.

She sits back down next to me and leans over to place her laptop on the coffee table in front of us. She boots the computer up and after a few clicks the velvety notes of J. Mraz's voice singing "You Matter to Me," fill the room.

"I edited both songs together so let's listen to the whole song all the way through "Distance,"" Trace suggests.

She takes a bottle of something out of her backpack, pulls up the legs of her sweatpants, and rubs the oily liquid onto her long, slender legs. Man. I can think of all kinds of interesting things to do with that oil and her beautiful body. She puts the bottle back in her bag, sits back, and closes her eyes like she's absorbing the lyrics and sensations of the music.

As I watch her all I know is I want her. I'd like to lay her down in front of the fire and push deep inside her. I want to tell her what she does to me. I have to keep reminding myself she's not the kind of girl I hook up with.

When the notes of the song swirl around us, soothing the menacing sounds of the savage storm outside, I want to slide my arms around her and show her how much she already matters to me. An electric surge ripples through me, something I haven't felt for any girl since Abbey. It's fucking scary and exciting all at the same time.

After all the chicks I hooked up with in the past year, trying to forget, how has this girl cracked open the prison

I keep around my guarded heart? I wanted to avoid complicated, but what she's doing to me and the feelings I'm experiencing for her are about as puzzling as it gets.

Truth is, all thoughts since I first laid eyes on her have blurred with the need to touch her, to peel off her clothes and run my hands over her creamy flesh. All I can think about is what her legs would feel like draped around me and the sounds she'd make while I pleasure her in every way possible.

The braces around my heart are tough shackles to break, and based on Trace's statement about her past bad relationship, I'm sure her heart is as guarded and fragile. I'm torn between wanting to show her how fucking incredible I can make her feel and not wanting to risk shattering her heart. Although, if she wants me, I don't know if I'll be able to resist.

After the last notes of the combined songs pulse through the speakers, Trace opens her eyes. Even with the reflection of the fire flickering in them, they've darkened to sultry emotional heat.

"Those songs get to me. They're so perfect," she says in a hushed voice.

You're so perfect, the cornball line bubbles inside me. I swallow it before it comes out of my mouth.

"I think at the beginning we should do some slow circles around each other like...wait, let me show you."

She gets up and runs around the other side of the sofa where there's more floor space. I twist around to watch her impromptu demonstration. She bends at the knee and rises on each foot a few times like she's warming up for stroking on the ice and then she starts making these balletic turns with her eyes fixed on the imaginary me she's supposed to be spinning around. It's crazy. I'm not even touching her and I'm hard just from watching her graceful movements. I've never seen anything more beautiful.

"The whole thing should be slow and dreamlike, but playful too. You're doing the same circling thing while the piano's playing and then we stop and gaze into each other's eyes. Then you run the back of your hand down my cheek when he's says something about sad eyes. And then right before he says the thing about hiding, I'll duck down under your arms like...well."

She tries to twist herself up in a position to show what two people would be doing at the same time, but she can't quite make it work. I'm so mesmerized watching her it takes me a minute to jump to my feet and come around to help her.

"Show me what you want me to do." We circle around each other and I stop and gaze into her eyes and then run the back of my hand down her cheek as she suggested. I don't know if it's her or me trembling, but the current running through both of us is all heat and desire as we stand frozen in place drowning in each other's eyes.

"Um. Right. That's pretty good," she says, bringing us out of our trance. "Now I duck down and you cover me like this." She gets into her position first and then she shows me mine relative to hers.

She stands and moves back around the sofa to get the computer off the table and places it on the back of the sofa so she can start the song from the beginning. When she hits play we get into position and do the few moves she's choreographed so far and I feel every emotion, like the song was written for us.

"I'll jump up into your arms, your hands on my waist, and we can do a loop lift at this point." She hops up into my arms to demonstrate and I get even harder to greet her. I hold her, my hands around her waist, our eyes locked again, because I never want to stop drinking in her beauty. Is it wrong I'm a little thankful for the treacherous storm stranding us here?

She breaks the mutual trance when she wiggles out of my grasp and says, "We can do a step sequence to get moving around the ice and side by side spirals or mirrored spread eagles to match the lyrics. I don't know. We can work it out when we're on the ice. When he sings the title, "You Matter to Me," we should do a star lift or cartwheel lift, or a double twist lift. Something like that. Something big. Then you can spin me down and around your body to exit. Oh, wait. Can you do those? I know you haven't figure skated for a while and lifts are difficult if you've never done them before. Damn. I'm not even sure *I* can still do them." She giggles. Her eyes are sparkling in the firelight and I'm completely enthralled by the passion she has for skating and creating this routine.

"I'm sure you can do anything you put your mind to." I swear her face lights up a little at my statement, but I can't be sure because as far as I'm concerned this girl has a glowing angelic aura around her twenty-four seven. Okay. I guess angelic is the wrong word to describe my sexy hallucinations of her, but she glows nevertheless. "I've done those lifts in the past. I'm sure it will come back to me if we practice off-ice for a while first."

"How about spins and jumps? You tell me what you can do and I'll only put in those elements."

"Don't tell anybody this..." Placing my hand next to my mouth, I stage whisper, "Whenever I get some time on the ice alone, I practice jumps and spins to see if I remember how to do them. It helps to keep up my strength and agility for hockey too. The guys would never let me hear the end of it if they saw me. I love 'em, but they can be assholes sometimes." I grimace at the thought of what Wolfe would say if he saw me doing a camel spin.

"Your secret's safe with me." She snickers and runs two fingers across her lips to show they're zip sealed. Now all I can think about is unzipping those lush lips and reliving the sensations I felt last night when her tongue tangled with mine.

"Wait. Are you telling me you practice those things in hockey skates?" She's staring at me all wide-eyed like I told her I climbed to the peak of Mt. Everest.

"It's no big deal. Doing some of the toe jumps can be a little tricky though since, you know, no toe picks, but I make it work. I have figure skates too, so no worries for the routine. It'll be safer and more stable doing the elements you're putting in. I'm okay with doubles, possibly a double-double combo, but I don't think I can handle triples without a lot more time to practice."

"Since it's not the Olympics, I think doubles are more than enough." She smiles and then sucks in her bottom lip and teases it.

Is the room swaying? Damn. She's rocking my world. My mind and eyes are once again locked on her full, pink lips, and the only thing I know at this moment is *I* want to be the one suckling that lip.

"Let's see...what else?"

Her question snaps me out of my daydream of tasting her lips...and neck...and breasts...and well, every part of her luscious body. Being alone with Trace on our own secluded island and standing so close to her has my mind drifting to places it shouldn't be visiting.

"There aren't a lot of big crescendo parts to the music. It's soft and romantic throughout, so I think it needs to be really touchy feely through the whole thing. What do you think?"

Is she kidding?

"Touchy feely sounds good," I say and move closer to her to get started on the practice right this second.

"Okay. How about you try a simple cradling lift? You know, you scoop me up in your arms and rotate, like, three times and I'll..." She squeals when I cradle her in my arms before she finishes her sentence. She circles one arm around my neck and I spin her around a few times. At first she giggles and then something happens and she melts into me, closing her eyes and resting the side of her head onto my chest.

Her hair smells like the organic peppermint shampoo they keep in the showers here. It's the same soap I've used ever since I was a kid. My mom was instrumental in voicing her opinion to the Board of Directors of Bernard on what types of soap products they should use to match their organic environmental stance. My mom can be an extremely persuasive person.

The familiar peppermint scent mixes with Trace's sunshine citrus scent on her skin from the oil she rubbed on her legs and hands. I inhale so deeply I may swallow her. She smells like a fresh spring day even in the middle of a horrific storm.

When I stop spinning she looks up at me with those big round eyes. They're like shimmering emerald pools, piercing my soul with tenderness, like she's trying to ask me something without speaking. The only answer I can give is to bend my head down and place a gentle kiss on her lips. It's all I can handle in this minute without wanting to completely devour every inch of her.

When she responds to my kiss by sliding her other arm around my neck too, pulling me closer and then parting her lips to welcome me in, I'm almost ready to explode. Having her in my arms and kissing her with such tenderness has my heart pounding against my chest so hard I'm sure she must be able to feel it bouncing against her.

She slides out of my arms abruptly and pushes me away, again. "This is a really bad idea."

She walks away and flops onto the sofa. My cock is an iron rod and it's not happy. It's had just about enough of this restraint stuff and the loose sweatpants I'm wearing are leaving nothing to the imagination. The way it's straining in protest is on full display.

I try to will him to chill out as I walk around and join

Trace on the sofa. "Trace, you must be able to see what you're doing to me." There's no point in denying what I can't hide. My words come out in more of a growl than I intended. "We need to talk about this. Last night—"

"I know." She holds a hand up to stop me. "You said it was a bad idea for you too and I get it. I know there's this thing going on with Alex, and even though he pushed us together at the pub, I would never want to hurt—"

"Wait. Trace, what are you saying?" This time it's *me* holding up a hand to stop *her*. "You're dating Alex? But I thought he was gay and into—"

"Of course I'm not dating Alex, jackass." She frowns and smacks me in the chest. In an instant, the sensual, giggling girl I had enveloped in my arms a minute ago is gone and feisty, sexy Trace is back.

But what the fuck did she say?

"I mean *you*." She takes the laptop from the back of the sofa and sets it back down on the coffee table. "*You* would never want to hurt him. I would never want to hurt him either, but I know you like him and—"

"Stop." This time I stand up away from her and try to think with a clear head. Both heads, because right now my cock isn't allowing either one of us to think about anything but getting inside her. "Are you saying you think I'm gay and dating Alex?" Well that statement worked as an instant dick deflator. "Why? Where did you ever get the idea I'm gay and why would you think I'm dating Alex?"

What the fuck?

I knew we both had some past issues standing in the

way of our getting together, but I can't even wrap my head around this conversation.

"Uh...I thought you were gay because...well, because I'm attracted to you. Long story." She stretches an arm out in front her, fingers up like she's stopping traffic. "Let's just say I've done my fair share for mankind to bring hot gay men together," she says. She moves on without further explanation, before I get a chance to think about or voice confusion over the little gem of a statement.

"And then Alex told me he's into some hockey player who's also into him and he was going to get together with him at your party, and then I saw you talking and flirting with him at the party, so I thought you two were a thing. Even though Alex kind of pushed *us* together at the Thirsty Whale the other day. I admit I don't quite get *that* but..." She stops, gives a one shoulder shrug and takes a breath, the first one since beginning her whole outrageous verbal vomit.

It takes a second for the exchange of the last few minutes to sink in. When it does, the only thing I can do is throw my head back and laugh. I suppose some guys would be offended by the woman of their dreams mistaking them for a gay man, but she's so damn adorable waving her hands around in nervous animated gestures to try to explain herself, I can't be upset. Besides, she's never experienced my ability to pleasure a woman to the point where she's moaning my name in prayer-like groans. If she had, she would know I'm one hundred percent into women.

"Tracey. Baby." I kneel down on the floor between

her legs. "I am not gay." I kiss the inside of her thigh and even through the thick sweatpants I feel her quiver. "Alex *is* into one of the guys on the team, but it's not me." I kiss the inside of her other thigh and she lets out a little whimper. All I want to do is strip off those gigantic sweatpants and lick and suck her into ecstasy. But this conversation can't wait. This is a misunderstanding of epic proportions and it needs to be cleared up ASAP. "The night you saw me talking to Alex, at the party, we were talking about *you*. I was asking him about you so I could find out more about you." I push myself up and sit next to her again. "So now, how about you explain the thing about you thinking I'm gay because you're attracted to me. I sort of get the Alex mix up, even though my rep for sleeping with so many...never mind." Probably not cool to rub it in her face, yet again, the possibility of my having slept with half the girls on campus. "Anyway, I can understand the Alex thing. But what the hell does your attraction to me have to do with me being gay, or in this case, not gay?" I add, to be sure we're clear.

"I'm sorry," she sputters. "It's so stupid." She shakes her head and wipes away a lone tear which has managed to escape down her cheek.

"No need to be sorry, baby girl." I use my thumb to follow the same path her own fingers took in wiping the tear off her face. Christ. The last thing I want is to make her cry, at least not in sorrow. After I rock her world it's okay with me if she cries in uncontrolled passion. "No harm done. I mean if I *was* into guys, Alex isn't a bad pick." She wrinkles her brow in bewilderment.

"No. I told you. I'm not into guys. Alex is a cool dude, and I don't have any problem admitting it. But my lust filled yearnings lie in the soft, curvy, land of desire, not in the hairy *ball*-park, if you know what I mean."

I cringe. Eww. Another dick deflating image crosses my mind. Which is a good thing because I'm still stroking her face and fighting the overwhelming urge to climb on top of her and soothe all her worries in others ways. I drop my hand.

The asshole at UDel must've fucked with her mind more than I thought. Does she think dating her causes men to become gay or some crazy shit like that?

"I'm only trying to understand where you're coming from. Is this something to do with the past bad relationship and the reason you said you weren't ready to hook up with anyone?"

She nods slightly, like she's reluctant to tell me what's weighing heavy on her mind. But then she does.

"I have a weird kind of problem..."

Hmm, I'm not liking where this is going.

"What do you mean 'problem'?" I ask, not sure I want to know the answer.

Trace is interesting, beautiful, and smart, and I can't deny how much I want her. Whatever her problem is, I want to help. She's shown me her tough, independent exterior. For the first time I'm seeing the vulnerable side. I want to be the one there for her, the one who helps her figure things out.

The one?

I mean...I want to help her, if I can.

"I...I'm only attracted to gay men," she says in a voice so low I ask her to repeat what I think I heard.

"Every time I'm interested in a guy, it turns out he's gay. I don't do it on purpose, it just happens. So, I figured when I started feeling all these things for you, you had to be gay. And then Alex...well, you know what happened with Alex."

All I hear is her saying she has all these feelings for me. My heart does a fist pump inside my chest. She's biting her lush bottom lip again and my cock is beginning to revive itself.

"The last time it happened was with Sean." Her voice is still a whisper, almost like it pains her to say this guy's name.

"The bad relationship." I try to help her because I need to know what the fucker did to hurt a girl as much as Trace seems to be hurting. She nods.

"He was the captain of the football team. He had all the right moves, said all the right things when we first met."

"Fucking football players," I snarl.

"We started dating and were together for a year. We were in love. At least I *thought* we were. He kept throwing around the L word and saying things like forever, promising after graduation it was him and me. We even made plans for where we were going to live."

Her breath hitches in a sob. I want to take her in my arms and promise her everything will be okay. No one will ever hurt her again. But would it make me the same kind of dick this Sean douche was? It's a promise which has nothing to do with me. Somewhere in the future some other dickweed may hurt her and I won't be there to do anything about it. My chest tightens at the thought.

"One night...after a game where Sean threw the winning touchdown to one of the running backs, I showed up at his house," she says after catching her breath. "We had plans to go out for a big celebration with a bunch of people, but I couldn't wait to see him. I didn't wait for him to come and pick me up. I headed over to his house early. When I walked into his room he... he..." She's restraining her breath so much in an effort to hold back tears her body begins to compensate for the lack of oxygen with little hiccups.

"It's okay if you don't want to go on," I reassure her without touching her. She's breaking my heart, but if I touch her I know I won't be able to stop, and the last thing she needs is another guy messing with her feelings.

"No. I want to tell you. I never told anyone the whole story, not even my parents or sister. I couldn't tell them the gritty details of all the stupid things I had done. But I want to tell you. I want you to know."

Christ. She's opening her heart to me. If she only knew how I failed Abbey, would she want me to be the one she opens up to about this?

"He was in bed with Kyle Morgan, the running back who had scored the touchdown. I...I couldn't even move. I couldn't process what I was seeing." She rubs the back of her hand across her face, under her runny nose. I don't get up to get her a tissue because I don't want to leave her alone even for a second.

"After what was only a minute, but seemed like an eternity, Sean saw me standing there watching them. He says, 'What are you doing here?' in an annoyed tone of voice. I ran out of his house and jumped in my car. I don't even remember driving back to the dorm."

She stares past me into the air like she can see something out there I can't.

"He didn't follow me. Until the next day. Saturday."

She isn't sobbing anymore. Her voice is still only whisper, but it's flat now, trancelike. Her eyes, though, are liquid pools of fury. I don't say a word and she continues the story, causing the heaviness of lead to ball in my stomach and my fists to clench.

"He shows up at my dorm all apologetic, telling me he's tried to stop these *new* feelings he's having for guys." She does air quotes around the word new. "But he can't fight them anymore. He says he loves me and needs my help. If I spend the night with him and his football buddy, I could help him overcome his urges."

"What the *fuck*?"

"I know. That's not the most ludicrous part. No. The best part is, I believed him. Or I wanted to believe him. I thought we were in love. I thought I had to do whatever it took to save our relationship, and if this could save it, if he needed my help, I'd do anything. So I did."

I want to stop her. Tell her I can't hear the rest of this, but I can't be a coward again. Another girl I care about needs me, and I can't let this one down too. I listen as she purges her soul.

"I went back to his house with him. Kyle was there. No one else was home. His roommates were gone for the night, still carrying on the celebration. I already knew Kyle. I'd seen him at Sean's house a hundred times with all the other football players, although he wasn't as friendly as usual. In fact, he was cold, standoffish. Sean brings out this bottle of tequila and says we should do shots to loosen things up and get in the partying mood."

Fuck. I gave her tequila to warm things up. *Fuckfuckfuck.* But she doesn't mention it. She just keeps on venting her toxic memories.

"He got you drunk and then he forced you to..."

"No. He didn't force me to do anything. I kept drinking the shots. I knew what was coming, what we were going to do."

She hesitates for a second and I realize I'm holding my breath, afraid to hear where this is going.

"I knew it was wrong for me," she continues in shuddered breaths. "I knew I wasn't into doing what we were about to do, but I didn't want to lose Sean and he kept telling me this would fix everything. Fix us. We moved upstairs to his bedroom and drank the last couple of shots there." The shadows of the flames sway over her somber face and darken it even more.

"After that, things get blurry. Before I knew it we were all naked. I don't even remember how. The next thing I know we're on the bed, Sean's on top of me. Then he's inside me. Kyle is kneeling behind Sean. I can feel us moving together. Sean's pushing into me hard and Kyle is behind him, his thrusts into Sean just as aggressive. My head is swimming. Sean's hurting me because I wasn't ready for him. I tell him I need him to stop, but he keeps whispering, 'It'll be fine. It's so good. You feel so good. It's just you and me, babe. I love you.' When I thought about those words a million times afterward I wondered if he was talking to me or Kyle. From what I can remember, Kyle never touched me. He didn't even look at me except to throw ice daggers at me every once in a while."

The food in my stomach is churning. How could the bastard treat her like that? How could he hurt her? All she wanted to do was love him and he used her. I think I'm going to be sick. I swallow and take a few deep breaths to keep the food from coming back up. Other than when playing hockey, I consider myself a fairly mellow guy, but at this moment I want to fucking kill those motherfuckers.

Trace keeps talking in a non-stop robotic rhythm, like she's in a trance. "I must've passed out at some point, because when I woke up it was morning. I was in Sean's bed, but they were both gone. I showered and tried to scrub away the feeling of my skin crawling. I got dressed and texted Sean. He didn't answer. I called for an Uber back to the dorm. I sent him like thirty texts, and he never responded. I kept telling myself everything was going to be fine. He must've had practice or something. Then he shows up at the dorm at about five-thirty. He tells me in a matter-of-fact tone he can't see me anymore, that Kyle doesn't like sharing him. Sean informs me the thing with the star running back isn't new. It was going on even before we started dating. He only needed me as a cover to make sure no one found out he was gay. Kyle gave him an ultimatum after our night together—him or me—and he didn't want to lose *him*.

"What he's telling me doesn't fully register. I beg Sean to let me try again to see if we can make it work. I *beg* him, even though he told me he used me and cheated on me the whole time, pretending he loved me. He sniggers and says there's no way it can work and turns to leave. He stops when he gets to the door and turns to tell me like an afterthought, '*Me and Kyle aren't ready to come out, so you better not say anything to anyone or we'll tell everyone it was your idea to fuck both of us at the same time.*'

"I was stunned. Everything he did, every word he said, was like another dagger in my heart. The final statement felt like he was twisting the daggers deeper. But I couldn't turn off all the feelings for him at the flip of a switch. I still cared about him. I would never do anything to hurt him, even though I was so humiliated and devastated. I couldn't wrap my head around what he told me or understand why he'd put me through the whole thing the night before. It was like he kicked my world off its axis. I couldn't breathe. And then he walked out. After a year, he threw me away like yesterday's garbage."

"Fuck. Trace." I'm not sure what to say. I want to apologize for all the asshole men in this world who could treat a woman with such complete insensitivity and lack of respect. I also want to cut the balls off those two motherfuckers and shove them down their throats.

Chapter Fifteen

TRACEY

"I don't want to talk about this anymore."

I can't believe I told a guy I've known for a couple of weeks as much as I did. Even though I'm not ready to tell him the worst part, I'm not sorry I told him this much. It's incredible how cleansing opening up to someone on a personal level can be. For the first time in a year I can breathe a little easier. Keeping everything locked inside, never talking to anyone about it, is a heavier burden than I realized.

I'm not sure if the expression on Dak's face is concern, pity, or a little of both. I don't want his pity. I only want him to understand I'm not ready to open my heart to anyone yet, not ready to get involved. I love the way he makes me feel things I was afraid I would never feel again, but I'm also afraid of those feelings and what they can do to me. Chipping away at the stone walls I've built between my past and present has drained me. Exhaustion overtakes me.

"I'm so tired," I say, breaking the long minutes of silence between us.

"I'll carry you upstairs again and turn down the covers for you. It's been a long day," he says in a soft voice, like he's afraid I'm going to crumble right in front of him.

I sit up so I can see his beautiful ocean blue eyes. "Do you think we could sleep on the floor in front of the fireplace tonight? I don't want to leave the warmth of the fire. It's so soothing." Also, being next to him is so comforting, though I'm not sure where he wants to go from here, or if he even wants to go anywhere with me after everything I told him.

I know he's not judging me, but it doesn't mean he wants to be friends with a girl who has all this emotional baggage. I don't know what I want right now either. I *know* I'm not ready for a relationship. It's too soon for me to trust anyone with a full-on commitment. Yet what I'm feeling for Dak is much different now than it was the first day I crashed into him—or rather, when *he* crashed into *me*. The realization he's become someone I'd like to be friends with shocks me. I want to get to know him better and spend time with him. After everything, he's...well...pretty wonderful.

"You want both of us to sleep on the floor in front of the fireplace? Like *together*?" he asks in a tentative voice.

I nod. "Well, like next to each other together." I bite my bottom lip, something I'm famous for when I'm nervous or thinking too hard.

"Okay, Bambi." He runs his thumb along my lip to stop me from chewing it off. "I didn't want to leave you alone anyway. I'll stay right by your side as long as you want me to. Hey. It's like the lyrics in our skating song. It's the perfect song for us."

He stands up, taking me with him, and presses play on my ITunes app. He steps into an open area of the room and with his hands around my waist spins us both in circles as "You Matter to Me" streams through the air. I don't know how he manages it. After spewing out the events of the most soul-destroying weeks of my life, I'm giggling in his arms.

He slides me back down along his body onto my feet and I can feel the hard ridge through the soft fabric of his pants. He's devouring me with the kind of seductive bedroom eyes that could make a nun drop her panties, which is both unnerving and provocative. I want to kiss him, but I already stopped him twice. I'm certain any involvement for me right now would be too soon.

Before I get too far into my perplexing thoughts, Dak lets me go and says in an excited voice like a kid planning a camp out sleepover, "I'll go upstairs and pull the feather mattress off the bed. You get the pillows and blankets. We'll do a picnic sleepover right here in front of the fire."

"A picnic? We just ate dinner."

"I'll make us dessert after we set up the bed."

"I thought we already had dessert." I glance sideways to the tequila bottle on the coffee table. Its crystal liquid shimmers with an innocent sparkle in the firelight, not revealing the volatile effects it contains. Dak follows my gaze.

"No." He walks over and picks up the bottle from the table. "I'm not talking about this shit. No more tequila, *ever*." He leaves the room with the bottle and comes back a second later. "Let's go get the things for the bed."

He starts moving toward the steps, doing these massive double Axel jumps across the room, jumping, spinning, and landing like Baryshnikov on steroids.

"Holy shit!" I gasp. "You're good. A lunatic, but good."

"Come on. Let's go get the stuff," he grunts out while spinning in the air. And can I just say there is something so hot about a gorgeous hockey player doing massive athletic jumps and landing with the graceful precision of a ballet dancer?

"I'm coming. I'm coming." I smile and shake my head. But I walk, because my name isn't Dakota Andersen and I'm not crazy enough to do double Axels across a room full of furniture.

The mattress fortress Dak builds us in front of the fire is so cozy no one would ever guess there's a derecho raging outside and a few minutes ago the atmosphere inside was oppressive. I'm discovering it's impossible for anyone to stay mad or sad when around his slightly immature, fun antics.

I'm sitting on our fluffy, cloudlike bed when he comes back in the room carrying two bowls, a big smile across his face.

"No better comfort food than Ben and Jerry's Rocky Road," he announces and plops down crossed-leg onto the bed with two bowls overflowing with whipped cream and fudge sauce atop the ice cream. "Not exactly organic, but even Bernard has to allow for comfort food every once in a while. I did whip up real cream though. No fizzy spraying canned crap they claim is real," he grimaces in disgust. "Milady." He passes me one of the monster sundaes.

"My prince," I tease with an over-animated, rapid blinking of my lashes. "I'm not sure I can finish all this." I'm sure I *could* if his presence didn't make my stomach flutter and flip like its own version of a Cirque Du Soleil routine.

"I'll finish whatever you can't, but I bet you'll lick the bowl clean once you taste it." He shovels a big scoop of the concoction into his mouth and his eyes roll back into his head. "Mmmph almost as orgasmic as my puttanesca sauce."

I wonder if he's aware of the way he turns every comment he makes into a sexual innuendo. It's possible he doesn't know he oozes sexiness. He slowly drags his tongue over and around his freaking spoon. Yeah. He knows.

The sight of his tongue working his spoon fills my head with thoughts of him drizzling fudge sauce along my body and licking his way down my tits and stomach to the aching spot between my legs to taste what he's doing to me. I can't take my eyes off his mouth, and even before I taste the ice cream, I absently lick my lips.

"What do you think? Good, right?" He takes a big

scoop from the bowl and licks off the remnants of gooey chocolate left on his spoon, like he doesn't want to miss a speck. Watching him has heat pooling between my thighs, but he seems to be completely oblivious to what he's doing to me

"You didn't try it yet. Oh shit. You don't like ice cream. I should've asked. I'll make you something else."

I guess he wasn't trying to be seductive after all, just innocently enjoying the creamy splendor of the ingredients in his bowl and he wanted me to do the same.

"Not like ice cream! Who doesn't like ice cream?" I take a heaping spoonful and ladle it into my mouth. "Mmm. You're right. Climatic," I sigh and take another spoonful.

"I know. Right?" He polishes off his sundae and I continue to savor every spoonful of mine. No problem eating the whole thing after all.

"So, Bambi..." He's back to his teasing tone. I love the way he can change even the harshest situations to a light and playful mood. "I don't want to bring up all that garbage again, but I need to know."

"Need to know what?" I give him a sideways glance, because I don't want to talk about any of the garbage anymore either. We're having fun again and I want to keep it this way.

"You remember how you said you thought I was gay because you were attracted to me?" He asks, leaning over to take my bowl and then place both empty bowls on the coffee table. When he stretches to reach the table, his sweatshirt lifts up and his scrumptious eight pack is peeking out at me again in all its glory. Once again, I suck in my bottom lip and worry it with my teeth.

I close my eyes and take a deep breath. "Yes, Dak. Since it was only about fifteen minutes ago, I remember," I answer, opening my eyes. Thank God his abs are no longer visible. It may seem like a ridiculous thing to be thankful for, but I'm trying to exercise some restraint here. I *am*.

"You said every guy you're attracted to turns out to be...um...gay. Is that right?"

"Well, the last few, anyway." I twirl a strand of hair around a finger. Why are we talking about this again? It's obvious my bad streak is broken, since I'm sitting here with the most virile straight guy on campus.

"It was more than just Sean then?"

"There were two other guys before Sean," I say in a more exasperated tone than I intend. Dak's been nothing but sweet, since I told him about my colossal bad choices in the past. But with everything out in the open—*almost* everything, I don't want to talk about it anymore. I want us to move beyond this.

But he's not ready to move past the conversation. "Two? Really?" Dak asks, sounding more concerned than surprised.

"It was nothing like with Sean," I blurt out. "I...I only hung out with them for a while before they told me they were gay and considered me a good friend. And then they hooked up with each other," I mumble.

"Oh. Good." He blows out a relieved sigh.

"Hmm. Depends on your perspective, I suppose."

Because it didn't feel so good to me watching my

besties—the pseudo Jamie Bower and Claude Monet—sucking face. "Wait, were you worried because you thought I was a loose woman with bad judgment or because you think I possess some kind of weird power to turn straight men gay?" I'm sucking in my lip to hold back a smile, though I wasn't smiling a year ago when *I* was considering it a plausible possibility.

"What? No, of course not."

"Of course not to which one?" I can't resist teasing him.

"Of course not to both, Bambi." He smirks. "I just didn't want to think of you having to go through that kind of heartbreak more than once."

Boom. There go my ovaries again.

"Trust me, Bambi, the power you hold over me is the complete opposite of turning me gay. When I'm around you, I'm about as heterosexual as a man could ever be."

I hold a power over him?

This foreplay of words we keep exchanging has my body temperature rising. My disloyal, needy body squirms in anticipation on our fluffy bed. Thank goodness he's decided not to make another move on me, because I wouldn't be able to say no when every one of my cells is saying yes, yes, yes.

"I'm pretty beat and I know you are too. How about we get some sleep so we can get out of here early if the weather lets up in the morning?"

Right. The morning. Even though I'm relieved he's not making this any harder for me than it already is, I'm kind of sad at the thought of our mini version of *Cast Away* ending in the morning.

"Okay," I answer, trying not to sound disappointed. I don't even know what I'm disappointed about. I already decided I don't want to be another one of his fuck buddies, but these feelings I'm experiencing and the way I want to climb his body like a tree whenever I see him can't be denied. "I'm going to run upstairs and brush my teeth first."

"Yeah. Me too. I'll race you upstairs. I'll even give you a head start." He pushes himself up from the soft mattress.

"I'm too tired to race you tonight." I stand up and walk off the soft bed.

"What's the matter, Bambi, you afraid I'll..." I don't hear the end of his taunting question because I'm already halfway up the stairs before Dak even realizes what's happening.

"You're a cheater, Trace Hayward!" he calls out in laughter and runs behind me

---

There's no other light in the room other than the glow of firelight when we snuggle under the down filled comforter a few minutes later. Dak has no problem falling asleep. He's making little snoring noises almost the minute his head hits the pillow.

Lying on my back, staring at the ceiling, I'm trying to process everything that's happened in the last few hours. Glancing at my watch, I note it's only eleven. It feels like we've spent way more than a few hours together. With all the promises I made to myself when I transferred to

Bernard, how did I end up revealing things to him I never told anyone else? And how the hell did I end up sleeping next to the hottest guy on campus and wanting said hot guy with every cell in my body in a few weeks' time?

He shifts in his sleep, turns on his side facing me, and his warm breath brushes my cheek. My heart starts beating in a pulse matching the rhythmic dance of the shadows on the ceiling caused by the flickering flames. And then it occurs to me what I want and what I need to do about it.

"Dak?" I whisper, staring at his beautiful, peaceful face. I don't get any response, so I try again a bit louder, but quiet enough not to interrupt the comforting tranquility of the moment. "Dak? Are you sleeping?"

"Hmm bfflltr," he stirs and makes an attempt at the English language, at least I think it's English. I'm envious at his ability to fall into such a deep sleep so fast. It doesn't matter how tired I am, once my head touches the pillow, thoughts come whirling through my head and I lay there in an immobile dance with my brain, spinning around the thoughts of things I need to get done. And I need Dak to join in my current thought process because it concerns him in a big way.

"Dak." I touch his face softly and his drowsy eyes flutter open. His lids blink a couple of times like he's trying to focus on what he's seeing.

"Trace," he says in a gravelly voice. "Are you okay?"

"Yes. I'm fine." I shift so I'm facing him. We're so close our noses are almost touching. "I thought about what I want."

"What's that, baby girl?" He brushes a strand of hair

behind my ear and I quiver at his touch. Sparks of electricity shoot out to every part of my body. I resist the overwhelming urge to push closer to him and press my body against his.

"I want to have sex with you." I'm still whispering, but my words are resolute. Dak is the first guy whose touch hasn't sent me running, the first guy I could let get close in a long time. This feels so right. He blinks a few more times in rapid succession and bolts straight up to a seated position.

"*What*? What now? Can you repeat that, because I'm pretty sure I'm in some kind of sleep-induced coma?" He runs his hand back through his sexy bed-tousled hair. Between his suggestive disheveled appearance and the adorable look of confusion on his face, I'm already so turned on I need to rub my legs together to soothe the longing for him.

"I said I want us to have sex," I state a little louder because I want to be perfectly clear.

"What are you talking about?"

"Wow. You definitely must still be asleep if you don't know what 'have sex with me' means." Even though I'm a jumbled mess of nerves because of what I'm suggesting, I can't help giggle at the way his confused expression has morphed into one of disbelief.

"I know what *that* means." He blows out a big breath and there's no doubt, he's *definitely* wide awake now. "But why are *you* asking *me*? I thought you said you weren't into casual sex and it was too soon after what the dickhead put you through for any kind of relationship, anyway?"

"Right." I sit up cross-legged in front of him.

"Soooo?" He leans toward me and glares at me through wide eyes, like he's waiting for the big reveal on how I managed to sustain a complete mental breakdown in the past half hour.

"I'm not ready for a relationship, that's why this is perfect. Don't you see? Things in the universe are lined up perfectly."

"Tracey. Baby. You'll forgive me. I have no idea what the fuck you're talking about." He scrubs a hand down his face. "That seems to happen a lot when you're talking to me," he mumbles through his fingers. "I know there's this unbelievable attraction between us, but how exactly did you go from 'go away and leave me the fuck alone' to 'I want to have sex with you' in a few days?"

"I never said leave me the fuck alone."

"No. But you *did* say 'go away and leave me alone,' the fuck was implied. So, what's up? Why the drastic change of heart?"

"Why does it matter why I changed my mind? You never have a problem saying yes to anyone else who wiggles her ass in your direction."

"It matters because you're *not* that kind of girl."

"You know I'm not a virgin, Dak."

"I *think* I understand your sexual status, Trace. But a few days ago you didn't even want to talk to me and you were adamant about the no casual sex thing. Now you want to get naked and climb all over me? I get I'm irresistible, sweetheart, can't argue with that. And I feel the way you tremble whenever I touch you."

"You are such an egotistical jerk. And I do *not* tremble."

"Oh, you tremble, and you make little oooh sounds."

"If you could put a harness on your galloping ego for one second and listen." I move closer to him so I'm right in front of him, sure if he can see me he will be able to understand me better. "I feel like we've become good friends in the last few hours. As you said, I'm not ready for any complicated relationships and I know you're not into *any* kind of relationship. You just...well...sleep around. And since I don't want to get involved with anyone, I changed my mind."

"You don't want to get involved with anyone so you changed your mind about sleeping with me," he states like he's finally figured it out.

"Right. You said yourself we can't deny the attraction between us." He's nodding, the thought train chugging along. "I want you, and from what I...um... felt, you want me too. Since we're friends and there's no chance of us getting involved, I thought we could have sex, no strings attached. No feelings, no falling in love. You know, just for fun, and I can even throw in a little extra studying and tutoring for you." I sit up straight and flip my hair back over my shoulder, content I came up with a reasonable solution to the quagmire of sexual tension between us. I managed to explain the solution in a concise, understandable manner.

"What the fuck!" He jumps up and starts pacing the floor. Uh oh. I think the thought train has jumped the tracks. "Are you saying you want us to have, like, a meaningless fuck for *fun*? Oh. No, wait. You want it in *exchange* for tutoring?" He air quotes around the word exchange, like it's some kind of poison word. "Are you like selling yourself to me now?"

"What? No! Absolutely not. We already made an arrangement in exchange for the skating routine. I just thought—"

"No. You didn't think. Are you crazy? Why now? Why me? You know what I'm like with women. I don't get involved. I don't stay around. "

He hasn't stopped pacing, or should I say stomping back and forth like a caged tiger. If I squint, I swear I see steam coming out of his nose and ears.

"That's exactly why you. You don't want any strings and neither do I... I only want—"

"To get laid," he spits.

"No." I'm sitting on the bed, looking up at his angry face. "Well, yes. But I want it to be with you," I add in a soft voice.

His anger dissolves into what looks and sounds like disappointment. "No way." He shakes his head. "Not with you."

"So you're not attracted to me?"

"Of course I'm attracted to you. You're fucking gorgeous! There isn't any part of me that doesn't want you. But I'm not the right guy for you. You're not that kind of girl. You don't...you know. Besides, like you said, we're friends. I don't do 'casual fuck' with friends." He freaking air quotes again, this time around the words casual fuck.

"Let me get this straight." I untangle myself from the twisted blankets around me and stand in front of him.

"You can fuck anything in a crotch-length skirt that brushes past you, but you can't have sex with me," I snarl and poke a finger into his chest. His magnificent chest.

He grabs my wrist and glares at me. Then his grip softens. "They're not you. You're different." He drops my hand.

I don't miss a beat with my response. I've had a lot of experience in the arena of rejection. I was trained by the world's biggest asshole, so this latest rejection is nothing.

"Never mind. Forget it. Let's just go to sleep so we can wake up bright and early and get the freak out of here."

Throwing myself back down on the bed, I pull the blankets up so high they almost cover my head. The covers shift as he lies down next to me. I'm lying on my back, peeking out over the top of the blankets, my eyes fixed on the ceiling. In my peripheral vision I can see he's on his back staring up at the ceiling too.

"Trust me," he says, his voice so low it's barely audible, "I'm not what you need. I'm not good for you."

"I'm old enough to decide what is or isn't good for me," I answer without turning to him.

"You sure about that?" I can feel him staring at me when he asks the loaded question.

Sure, I made plenty of stupid choices in my past. But I'm older, smarter. Aren't I? When I don't answer him, he turns on his side, facing away from me.

I keep my eyes glued to the performance of the waving silhouettes taking place on the ceiling in shades of gray and black. My mind is racing as I think about Dak's words. I can't be angry with him. I know what I suggested is crazy and out of character for me, and I kind of get where he's coming from. He listened to my past horror story and was comforting and understanding. In fact, he's done nothing but take care of me all night. I don't think he's rejecting me; I think he's trying to take care of me as a concerned friend. And as crazy as it is, I want him even more now because of his reaction to my proposition.

The rhythmic swaying on the ceiling acts like a rocking lullaby and after a few minutes my lids grow heavy and exhaustion overtakes the thoughts racing through my head and the desires pulsing through my body.

This dream is even more intense than the last one. My back is pressed against his front. His arm is holding me tight against him and his leg is draped over my hip. I wiggle my ass back into him and he responds with a groan, his hard, full length against me.

I'm on fire, burning hotter than the glowing embers in the fireplace. I turn and his arm tightens even more around me. I gaze into his eyes. They sear into mine. In the dim light they appear as dark and dangerous as the stormy waters in the bay.

His hand moves to my face and he strokes my cheek with the back of his fingers. "Trace," he whispers. The sound of my name on his lips reverent.

My heart is beating so hard against my ribs it's going

to explode. I can't control it. I'm going to die of pleasure right here in my sleep.

"I *do* want you so bad," he whispers and rocks his hips into me so I can feel how much harder and *bigger* his cock is now.

Oh God. Is this real? Am I dreaming?

He leans in and kisses me with a gentleness as soft as his whispers. I return his kiss. But I can't be gentle. I'm consumed by my scorching need. I part my lips, inviting his further exploration. Our tongues tangle and I grab his full bottom lip in my teeth and bite down. I'm going to devour him if I don't get release.

"Please...Dak. Please," I beg.

This is too intense. Too real. I need to wake up.

His slips his hand into the waist of my pants and moves it between my thighs, his fingers stroking and teasing.

"I need...please," I moan.

"I know what you need, baby girl. I'm here." He licks and kisses the tender spot below my ear, and despite the molten blood pulsing through me I shiver in response. He slides one finger inside me with ease. I'm slick with the need for him.

"Fuck. You're so wet," he groans. He uses his thumb to make circles on the aching bundle of nerves at my center and then slips in another finger. I arch into his hand, pushing against it. My body is going to detonate if I don't wake up.

"Oh God...Dakota. Please," I plead. I can't breathe. I need more.

This is so real. So real.

His fingers start pumping in and out of me at a frantic pace and my hips match their rhythm. "Fuck. Tracey," he groans in a raspy voice. "Let it go, baby. I want to feel you let go."

My world explodes into a haze of blazing fireworks. I scream his name as waves of pleasure lift and rock me in what feels like an unending ride back down to Earth. The coiled tension holding me finally releases. Every muscle relaxes into him while he showers my face and neck with kisses and whispered endearments. At first I'm so filled with the blissful intoxication I luxuriate in his tenderness. But when he slides his fingers out of me, I'm jolted out of my hazy afterglow and I know.

It isn't a dream.

Chapter Sixteen

DAK

"Oh my God. What? What just happened?" Trace bursts straight up on the bed.

I smirk and sit up next to her. "Well if you don't know, then I must've done something very wrong."

"I thought...I didn't..." She's shaking even though she's swathed in the layers of blankets twisted around us from the few minutes of hotter-than-fuck passion we shared.

"Tracey, calm down. What's the problem? I thought you wanted me to."

She pulls the covers up under chin. "I thought...I thought I was dreaming." She's nibbling on her lip again.

"You thought you were dreaming about *me*?" She gives an almost imperceptible nod. Huh. Interesting. "Have you...uh, dreamed about me before?"

I know she suggested having sex with me, but dreaming about me is in a whole other realm than casual fuck. After all the excuses I gave her explaining why having sex with me is such a bad idea, it's ironic my heart is doing joyful handstands right now.

She pinches her eyes closed and groans. But they're not the sensual groans she was giving me a few minutes ago when she screamed 'Dakota.' She's never said my whole name before and no one has *ever* said it like that. This current groan is all anguish and disgust and I hate what she's feeling about what happened.

"I don't dream about...I don't usually dream so vividly." She shakes her head.

"No. I guess not." I chuckle, because her response to my hand was pretty fucking vivid.

But she's not laughing or even smiling. "I'm sorry. I didn't mean to...I shouldn't have...."

She's apologizing to me? She's too much.

"Did I...did I do that to your lip?" She runs her finger along my bottom lip and my cock gives a hopeful twitch. But ouch. Until she touched it, I didn't feel the bite mark she left on my lip.

"I guess you did." I smile and pat my lip to make sure it's all still there. Wow. If she's this much of a wild thing when she thinks she's dreaming, what would she be like wide awake? My cock is straining against the fabric of my pants, begging me to find out.

"My lip is fine, and I don't want you to be sorry about what we did...unless you didn't want to and I—"

"No. It wasn't your fault. I practically ravaged you in your sleep. God, what *else* can I do to throw myself at you?"

"Tracey, it wasn't anyone's *fault*. You didn't throw

yourself at me. It was incredible the way you rode my hand and screamed my name when you were coming...all in your sleep."

"Ugh. Could you please not be quite so graphic?" she whimpers. "Besides, I thought you said friends don't—"

"I know what I said. But as a friend, I totally didn't mind if you needed to use me to fulfill your wet dream."

Nope. I sure as shit didn't mind. In fact, I'm still so hard it hurts.

Even in the dim light I can see the deep crimson blush of her face. Maybe it's from embarrassment or it could be from the epic way I made her come all over my fingers. I'm leaning more toward the second one.

"Okay look, this doesn't need to be weird. It was beautiful. *You're* beautiful. I'm not sorry this happened and I won't pretend I am. But I stand by what I said earlier. It's obvious by your reaction you're not the type of chick who has casual hookups and I'm still dealing with...I'm dealing with some shit too. I can't be what you need." My brain is being all logical, but my dick is throbbing in disagreement.

I know I sound like a hypocrite, but I care about Trace. Even though I almost gave in to the insistent longing of my hormones to be inside her, I didn't know about her past experience. I'm not going to join the list of assholes who fuck her and move on because they can't commit. She deserves someone who has way more to offer than a hit and run.

I couldn't resist helping her find a little release, though. When she said 'Dakota please,' how could I refuse her? A guy doesn't turn down a woman in that kind of distress. Okay, so it wasn't all about *her* distress. I'm ready to ignite every time I glance at her, and when she pressed her ass against me I thought I'd let go right then. But I'm trying to think about her and what she needs and not what my raging hormones are telling me *I* need.

"What...what are you saying?" She's blinking her incredibly long lashes rapidly. And oh shit, when you see a girl do that, it can only mean one thing. She's trying to hold back tears. Her brow creases like I'm speaking another language and she can't understand what I'm saying.

I'm not sure what I'm saying. What I *want* to say is, *Tracey, let me show you how many other ways I can make you moan and scream my name in wide awake pleasure.* Then my mind goes right back to the thoughts of her deserving better...more than I can offer. She deserves time to heal, time to learn to trust another guy, not another prick who is as confused about his past as she is about hers. I can't tell her about Abbey, though. I'm not ready to lay the whole mess on her. She's had enough of an emotional rollercoaster for one night and my emotions are pretty twisted right now too.

"I'm saying, let's think of this night as two friends getting to know each other, having some fun, and continuing to be good friends. Do our project, practice and perform our skate routine and hang out whenever we get the chance...as friends." While it sounds like bullshit even to me, I can't risk the possibility of hurting her again. She's had enough assholes in her life.

Damn. I may've stepped into an alternate universe.

I'm actually saying no to my throbbing dick and the sexiest girl I know. Declining sex with her even though she offered herself to me, no strings attached. This has to be one of the signs of the apocalypse: war, famine, plague, and Dak Andersen keeps his determined dick in his pants.

"So...no sex," she says slowly. "Even after what just happened."

"Um...yeah. Even after that. I think it's the best thing," I affirm and try to smile to feign feeling good about the crap I'm dishing out. I know it's a schmuck thing to say after what took place a few minutes ago, especially since the truth is I've never wanted a woman more than I want her. Dammit. I know I'm right about this. She deserves more than a fuck and run, even if she thinks that's all she wants.

She tilts her head and those big doe eyes narrow to tiny slits. Why do I feel like the mouse about to be pounced on by the mountain lion? Fuck. I know what she wants, what *I* want. The easy thing to do would be to slip her out of those clothes and make her feel all the things I want her to feel. But she needs someone she can depend on.

"Good friends...without the spine-tingling benefits." She purses her lips and sighs.

"I don't know, I think there's lots of benefits to being friends with you."

Mental images of her naked body supply all kinds of graphic material for my own wet dreams.

"Oh yeah? Like what?" She smiles.

I'd like to take her in my arms and show her all the

benefits. "Like having a super smart study partner. Or having a friend who can do touchy feely skating routines with me. Or having a friend who enjoys good food and can eat as much as I do, even if she doesn't like to share her fries."

"You're such a jerk." She giggles and lightly punches my arm.

"So you keep telling me." She's an extraordinary woman and as hard as this is, I'm determined to do what's right for her.

"So it's okay for you to do the deed with all those other girls, but not me."

Uh oh. The lion may pounce after all.

"No...it's just. Dammit, Trace. You're not a puck bunny and you need—"

"Don't tell me what I need. I know exactly what I need. Yes, Sean messed with my head, and I was screwed in lots of terrible ways. I gave him everything I had—my love, my trust, my friendship—and he threw it all back at me and stomped on it."

"I know. And I'm not going to be the next asshole who treats you like that."

"Exactly! Having sex with you would be perfect. No chance of any of that ever happening, because you would never be like him and I could *never* fall in love with you."

"Ouch. Kind of a twisted compliment. Should I say thank you or be offended?" I scratch my head in confusion.

"You know what I mean. You could never fall in love with me either. You don't do love and feelings. Right?"

Right. I don't do love and feelings...anymore.

"Forget it. Forget I mentioned it." She rubs her eyes. "I'm too exhausted to think straight right now or argue with you. Let's go to sleep."

I don't even know what to say. I get where she's coming from. No one knows better than I do. She wants me to fuck her because she doesn't want to risk being with a guy she might end up caring for. I get it. Been doing the same thing for years. Fucking *girls* that is, not guys. But should I be insulted or gratified I'm the one she chose to be her unlovable fuck buddy? Isn't she offering me exactly what I'm in the market for right now? I should be jumping all over her *and* her offer. So why am I feeling like shit about it?

"I'm pretty exhausted too. I'm not thinking right either. Let's get some sleep." A disappointed look sweeps over her face. But I need time to think about everything going down between us. She was hurt bad and she's still hurting. I'm not the right guy to help her overcome her pain.

She forces a grin, sighs, and lies down, enveloping herself back into her cocoon of blankets.

"Oh and Dak," she says from inside her sheath, "please stay on your side of the bed. No telling how I might lose my head again if you touch me and I wouldn't want to put you through that again."

I don't get time to answer before she's making soft sleep-induced breathing noises. I lie down as far away on my side of the feather mattress as I can get and stare into the hypnotic flames. It's a long time before I fall asleep.

Chapter Seventeen

TRACEY

Only two nights ago I vowed Dak Andersen didn't need to concern himself with my morning routines, because he was never going to get the chance to witness them. Well...as they say, never say never.

The weather is clear and invigorating in the harbor today. The bright, sunny day makes the adventure last night and what happened between us seem even more weird than it already does. I'm not sure what the hell happened, other than wiggling my ass in what I *thought* was my sleep into Dak's cock, and begging him to hand fuck me. At which, I might add, he has magical skills— and then freaking out when he complied. And after, even though I offered myself to him no strings attached, he wants to be friends. The story of my life.

It's possible the surreal circumstances of being trapped in a storm and stranded alone on an island led to my uncharacteristic request. And apparently the calming effects of a mind-blowing orgasm are a fantastic sleep aid. I fell asleep as soon as my head hit the pillow for a second time. Too bad those effects can't be bottled. It would be a zillion dollar industry.

Problem is, we haven't spoken one word to each other all morning. We packed up our samples and headed back to the harbor in silence. Dak is not into my proposition, even though he had no problem letting me ride his hand. He has some weird idea he's not good enough for me.

Or perhaps he only said that because he's not into you.

My snarky mind is such a bitch!

I remind myself I'm not angry at Dak. After all, I was the one who initiated the whole thing, and he did what I'm sure any guy would do. I guess I'm more disappointed than angry. At least he was honest with me, saying everything I already know is true. But I don't know what to say to him now. He assured me it doesn't need to be weird, but in the morning light it *is* kind of awkward.

I'm not sure how to think about what happened last night and everything he said. It's obvious he's attracted to me. He couldn't hide it in those sweatpants with everything he's got going on down there. For the first time in a long time I'm attracted to someone, and not afraid to let him get close to me. He's right, though, getting involved with him sexually is not a good idea. Hell. It's the same thing I've recited to myself for over a year. Don't trust anyone, don't get involved, no more heartbreak. It's the ironic reason I thought this plan was perfect—sex with a guy I like hanging out with, a guy I trust as a friend and am not afraid to let touch me, no strings.

I suppose Dak is trying to be the good guy and give me some time and space.

Or is he so freaked out by your past, he realizes he can't handle it?

Is it wrong to tell your own conscience to shut the fuck up?

"I'll jump out and you can throw me the ropes, okay?" Dak's question as we pull into the dock jolts me out of the verbal circles my mind keeps making.

"Sure." Those are the first words we've exchanged today.

"What should we do with the samples and slides?" he asks while tying off the *Tern*.

"My car is right there." I point to the outrageous green vehicle parked in the lot right next to the dock only employees in the harbor use. "We can load them in there. I'll bring them with me to class tomorrow and I'll write up a data report tonight to submit with them." As we discuss it, I'm handing him everything we need to take off the boat.

"You don't need to do the data report all by yourself. I can help."

"It's cool. Only one person needs to type it up. No sense both of us tying up our evening. I'm sure you've got somewhere to be."

Someone to be with.

"No I don't. There's practice this afternoon, but I'll be done at four thirty. The assignment is for *both* of us, Trace. I can read off the data to you while you enter it.

It'll save some time." We're being so courteous, so civil. Polite acquaintances. Like a few hours ago he wasn't finger fucking me and I wasn't screaming his name in ecstasy. Damn. I'm getting wet again merely thinking about it.

"My roommates and I always have dinner together at the house on Sundays. I don't think you've met them all yet. Why don't you come over for dinner and we can finish the assignment at my place?"

"Oh, I don't think—"

"Come on, Bambi. It's only dinner." He shrugs.

That's the problem. It's only dinner. He doesn't want to take it any further. I offered myself to him without any strings and he said no. Now my thoughts are tied up in knots wondering if he said no with the best intentions for me, or if there's another reason he doesn't want to have sex with me.

"We all pitch in and help. All except Wolfe. His cooking abilities are shit. We don't allow him anywhere near the kitchen when we're cooking." He chuckles. And I'm gone. His smile gets me every time. "What do you say? I think it's Mexican food night. You into it?"

"I hate to admit it, but you'd be hard pressed to find any kind of food I'm not into." I exhale a big breath. "Food is my only addiction."

"Fantastic! A fellow food lover. I knew it last night by the way you polished off your pasta and sund—" He stops midsentence. "Sorry, I didn't mean to bring up last night."

"You *should* be sorry," I fake admonish him, because he's right about not making what happened last night weird. I don't want anything to be weird between us. I kind of like the jackass. "Don't you know it's extremely ungentlemanly to notice how much a lady eats, let alone comment on it?" I open the back of the Jeep and place our supplies into it.

"I'm so sorry, milady." He puts the things he's carrying in the car and turns toward me. Bending at the waist with one arm behind him and one in front, he bows like he did in the bathroom last night. The memory sends a bolt of longing between my legs.

"I'll forgive you, sir, *if* you are able to satiate me tonight." He snaps upright and gives me a wide-eyed look. "Uh, with food. If you can satisfy me…with…with *food*."

So much for not being awkward.

This time when Dak bends over it's because he's doubled over in a roar of laughter. "I was totally thinking you meant food. You know, you've got a dirty little mind, Bambi."

I shake my head at the way he's having such a good time at my expense. "Ha ha. Sure you were, jackass."

I guess we're back to our teasing antics and it's kind of okay with me. Even though he causes the hormone levels in my body to skyrocket, he also knows how to make me have fun and smile again. Being friends isn't such a bad idea I suppose.

"I guess you're coming over for dinner then, so I can *satisfy* you?"

"I guess so." I shrug and hold my arms out, palms up, on either side of me in capitulation. There's no denying it, he's a good guy and not only do I lust him, I like him.

I find Nikki in the driveway of my house. She's in the process of moving in, hauling the last of her bags out of her car, a VW Beetle. When I see the bags lined up on the front porch, I can't help wondering how she crammed all that stuff into the tiny car.

"Hey, girl," she calls to me when I pull in. Her eyes open to saucer-sized orbs when Dak pulls in next door at almost the exact same time. I'm in the same sweatpants and top from last night. I didn't want to take time to shower at the house. I wanted to get out of there as fast as possible. And yup, when I follow Nikki's gaze up and down my outfit and then over to Dak, who is in the exact same outfit, it definitely looks like I'm getting home from a long winter's nap with my next-door neighbor. Except it's not winter and I'm not ready to let anyone know what may or may not be going on between him and me.

"It's not what it looks like. We're doing research together," I say flatly as I pull my backpack from the back seat.

Right on cue, Dak looks over and waves to Nikki as he steps out of his black vintage Defender. "Hey, Nik. Long time, no see. You movin in?"

"Hey, Dak. Yeah I am. Trace needed a roommate and I needed a place, so everything is copacetic."

"Awesome. You need some help?"

"No thanks, I got it," Nikki answers and slams her trunk closed.

"Trace is having dinner with us tonight. Why don't

you come with? There's always plenty of food and the guys would love to see you."

"Um, thanks, man, but maybe another time. Got to get unpacked and uh, I've...um, got a paper due tomorrow. I'll take a raincheck." Nikki is digging the toe of her Dr. Marten's into the gravel of the driveway like she's drilling for oil, *or* the more valuable excuse to keep her from having to see Dalton.

"Okay. But you're right next-door now, Nik. Don't be a stranger. It's all cool." Dak hikes his backpack up one shoulder.

"Right. Will do." Nikki nods. "I mean, no I won't." She shakes her head and forces a smile. "It's all cool," she mumbles through her teeth.

Dak turns to me, and then gives me a wink along with his sexy grin. "See *you* at six."

Oh for chrissakes. Was that necessary?

He's cute, but he's such a pain in the ass.

"Heard it called a lot of things, but *never* research." Nikki tilts her head and arches a brow at me after he goes inside his house.

"Honest. It was only research, Nikki," I insist. I pick up one of her bags to give her a hand. I'm not sure who I'm trying to convince, her or me. "We were out on the *Tern* and we got caught in the storm, so we had to stay at the lightkeeper's house on the Rock overnight until the storm blew over."

Nikki stops so abruptly on our way up the front porch steps I almost plow into her back. She drops the bags she's carrying and spins around, blinking her eyes a few times like it will help her hear what I said. "Are you trying to tell me you spent the night, alone, on the Rock, in the middle of a storm, with Dak Andersen, resident hockey sex god and manwhore?"

"I spent the night alone on the Rock with Dak. I don't know anything about the sex god thing," I answer nonchalantly, moving around her to the door, juggling the bags so I can slip the key in the latch.

"Nothing happened," Nikki says drily. I feign struggling with the key so I can think about my answer. I don't want to start out our friendship lying to her. But I positively don't want anyone to think there's anything going on between Dak and me.

"Well..." I drawl.

"Ho-ly shit!" Nikki pushes past me into the house and pulls me in after her. "You only moved here a few weeks ago and you already hooked up with one of those hockey sluts. You're a dark horse, Trace Hayward. I had you pegged for the sweet virginal type. Nothing wrong with that, but I had you figured all wrong." She snorts and punches me in the shoulder.

Ow! For a little thing, she packs a wallop. And she should know how *not* virginal I am.

"You have to tell me every single detail. Those fuckers next door may be whores, but their abilities between the sheets are well known all over campus." She walks through the arched doorway into the living room. "Holy shit!" she repeats, in more of a shriek this time. "What the hell happened in here?"

"What do you mean? What happened?" I rush into the living room thinking I might have been robbed. Everything is neat and tidy, exactly the way I left it.

"What the fuck? Did Little Red Riding Hood have a yard sale or something?"

"Oh. No." I wave her off. "It's the new furniture my mother sent me as a moving in gift. You want something to drink?"

Nikki blows out a long whistle, taking in what is now her new, totally ridiculous, home. "No shit? Wow your mom is the bomb. My mother didn't give me a toothpick when I started school."

"You like it?" I'm shocked. There is no way the girl standing there in a black tank top, black grunge cutoffs, and black Dr. Marten boots could like the flowered, checked, striped furniture.

"Are you kidding? I freaking love it. It's lit! So unique! Who else can say they live in the seven dwarves' cottage? I'll take a beer, if you have it."

"Hmm. I thought you said it looked like Red's leftovers. Now it's the dwarves'?" I laugh.

"Whatever." Nikki shakes her head in disbelief and chuckles. "It looks like somebody's idea of a cartoon character's house."

I'm so happy she decided to move in with me. I can tell she and Alex will be the kind of friends I haven't had for a long time.

"Hey, don't think you weaseled you're way out of telling me every little thing about you and Da-ko-ta," she sings out his name.

When I open the refrigerator, the inside light doesn't come on. The electricity must be out.

"There's nothing to tell, Nikki." I come back in the room and hand her the beer. "The power seems to be off.

I hope it's cold enough."

"Pretty much the whole area lost power because of the storm last night. They're still working on getting it back up. And come on, there's no way Andersen spent the night stranded with a hot chickie like you and didn't make the moves."

Um. Yes. There's a way. Apparently, I'm not the kind of chickie Dakota is interested in.

"At least tell me if it's as big as is rumored." She spreads her hands apart in an impossible length, even for a sex god.

"Oh my freaking word, Nikki!" My face is flaming, probably matching the color of the hideous flowers spewed all over the furniture.

"What? The boy has a reputation. I've heard it's magnificent. Sometimes a girl has to live vicariously through her friends." She twists off the cap of her beer and takes a long drag.

"You're ridiculous. I have absolutely no idea how *magnificent* Dak's uh...his...uh..."

"Dick? Cock? Love hammer? Is that what you're trying to say?" She wiggles her brows.

"Oh for God's sake. I have no idea how huge Dak's *cock* is." I puff out a long exhale and stomp up the stairs.

"Ah hah. But you *do* know it's huge. Just not sure of the actual dimensions. Gotcha," she calls after me, laughing. "And you've got a dinner date with the cutie patootie. I'm impressed."

"It is not a dinner date. All his roommates will be there. Remind me why I like you?" I yell back downstairs.

"It's a dinner date," Nikki sing-songs back to me.

I hear the front door open and close and the sound of her carrying boxes inside.

"Up the stairs, second door on the left," I call out so she can find her bedroom. "And no it's no-ot," I sing right back.

She stops in my open bedroom door with a box in her hand. "You can deny it all you want, skater girl. Do you know how many girls those hotties invite over to eat with them?" She cocks her head and arches her brow like she's daring me to answer.

"No. How many?" I tilt my head to match hers.

"Zippo. Nada." She makes a circle with her thumb and forefinger and peeks through it, while balancing a box on one hip with her other hand. "That's how many. It's against their rules of whoredom. No chicks allowed to spend personal time outside the bedroom." She purses her lips and tips her head toward me while making an "mmph" noise through her nose. "And I like you too." She grins and walks down the hall to her room.

"That's ridiculous. There are girls there all the time hanging out in their living room. And I didn't say I liked you. It's still open for debate."

"For parties. That's a whole different thing. It's their foreplay. Trust me, I know. And you love me, admit it."

"You're pretty knowledgeable about these hockey boys. Is this coming from experience and does it have anything to do with a certain blazing hot hockey player whose name will remain unspoken?" I ask while walking down the hall to her bedroom.

Something for sure went down between her and

Dalt, and I would say it has definitely affected her opinion of the boys next door.

"By the way, as I recall, Dak invited you to dinner too." Standing outside her door with one hip placed defiantly on my hip I purse my lips and arch a questioning brow right back at her. Two can play at this game. "What's up with you and Dalt? The tension between you two is palpable." I walk in and flop down on her bed.

I moved the plain, normal bedroom furniture I brought with me from Delaware into this room when I received all the other outrageous stuff from my mom. I'm sure Nikki is happy she won't be sleeping in fairytale central.

"Nothing's up." She shrugs and keeps folding clothes or hanging them on hangers. "We hooked up a few times and he turned out to be a dickhead. That's it. No surprises." She walks into her closet to hang some things, but not before I catch a glimpse of the dampness filling her eyes. She's trying to pretend she's all tough and doesn't care about Dalt, but I can see it's not the case.

"So that's it? End of story?" I ask when she comes out to get more clothes.

"That's it," she answers in her attempt at a cheerful voice. "I, on the other hand, *will* admit that his love hammer is as gigantic as his reputation indicates." She hurries back into the closet with a pile of folded clothes.

"Ugh. TMI. You're so gross." I laugh and throw a pillow at her when she steps out of the closet again.

She grabs the pillow midair—girl has some serious reflexes. "It wasn't gross, it was *spectacular*," she says wistfully while clutching the pillow against her chest. She's staring across the room with a dreamlike glimmer in her eyes. "It was the super douche himself that was gross." She snaps out of her reverie and resumes her attempt at brushing off her obvious feelings for Dalt.

"Whatever you say. You sure you don't want to join me over there for dinner? I could use the support of a girlfriend around all that raging testosterone."

"No can do, skater girl. But no worries. You'll be fine. Except for the douche, those boys are pretty cool. Dak is a good guy, even if he *is* a manwhore."

She smiles and throws the pillow back at me. My reflexes aren't quite as sharp as Nikki's and it hits me square in the face. We both start laughing and I'm glad Nikki doesn't seem to be sad anymore. I'm even managing to feel a little better about what went on between Dak and me. "Okay, girl. That's a pillow fight challenge that'll have to wait because I need to shower before heading over to sin city. There's all kinds of food in the fridge if it's not ruined because of the power outage. Help yourself."

"A pillow fight challenge. Ha ha. If we do it in our underwear and leave our curtains open the boys next door will probably get their ridiculous fantasies fulfilled," she jokes. "I'll take you up on the food. I'm starving. We'll need to work out splitting the food tab."

I stand up and head for the door. "Don't worry about it. We'll figure it out."

"Trace," she says before I walk out. "Thanks for all this." She makes a sweeping gesture around the room. "I don't know what I would've done."

"No thanks necessary, Nik. I'm really glad you're here."

"Me too. And good luck with Dak. You two would be great together," she says in a sincere voice and smiles.

I open my mouth to disagree, but decide better of it, because I can't deny I think so too.

I wait until six fifteen to head over to Dak's house, figuring it would give him enough time to shower and get home from practice. Since the power is still down, I wonder if they even *had* practice, or how they're going to make dinner without electricity. I swing the backpack over my shoulder and hesitantly knock on the front door.

It's crazy I'm feeling nervous. You'd think I was about to meet my boyfriend's parents or something. Even though Dak's *not* my boyfriend and these are not his parents, I want to make a good impression on his friends. I don't know why it matters to me so much, but it does. I'm going to be spending a lot of time with Dak this semester, which means I'll be seeing a lot of these guys. If I'm going to be breaking the 'rules of whoredom' Nikki referred to on a regular basis, it would be better if they like me.

The door swings open and the Titan I saw sucking face with a girl outside my kitchen window is standing there shirtless. No shirt and low hanging sweats appear to be his favorite attire.

"Hey, I know you." He gives me a sultry grin. Christ. Are all these guys blessed with a panty-dissolving grin as their trademark tool of seduction? His long black hair is wet and disheveled like he just stepped out of the shower or off the set of a porno movie. These guys should publish their own calendar. It could fund their college educations.

"Hi. I'm Trace." I hold out a hand in greeting, because an adult woman should be able to calmly shake a man's hand instead of standing here drooling over the incredible tattoos decorating his incredible muscles.

"I know who you are, sweetheart," he drawls. I recognize his voice from my first day at the rink. It's the same voice as the hockey player who pushed past me coming off the ice.

He takes my hand and pulls me against his chest. I stiffen in response to his touch and too close proximity. "Dak has done nothing but talk about you for weeks. I'm Wolfe." He's still holding me when he introduces himself.

My eyes glance toward the door. My immediate thought is escape, then my mind drifts for a moment. Did he say Dak talked about me? What did he tell him? And wait. Did he say his name is Wolfe?

"Are you kidding? Is your name really Wolfe?" I let out a loud snort-like giggle—the result of my usual anxious reaction to a guy touching me too intimately.

I know he's Dak's roommate and he's only being friendly, but I can't keep my skin from doing its usual crawl at the intimate touch of a guy. I feel the signs of dread creeping up my spine: paranoia, fear, panic. I should have stayed home. I try to wriggle out of his grasp, but this dude is strong and he's not letting go.

"I wouldn't kid you, sweetheart. You can call me Damon." He winks.

For real?

He even has a porno actor's name. Does this shit actually work on the ladies? I guess it does, because Dak had no problem using some of these same tactics to throw open the doors to my heart...and other areas. But Dak's are the first male hands that haven't caused a panicked reaction in over a year. At the moment, an imminent scream is working its way up my throat.

"Okay, asshole. Unhand the girl and let her come in." Wolfe immediately steps back away from me.

Speak of the devil with a voice like an orgasm. Dak's deep, sexy voice sends sparks through my body.

"Hey," he whispers in my ear and gives me a brief kiss on the cheek. His scent of mint and man fills my head and all sense of anxiety melts away. Without thinking, I reach up and place a hand over the spot he kissed, like I'm trying to hold it there.

When I realize what I'm doing, I drop my hand like I just touched a hot iron. Dak didn't miss the brief gesture and he gives me a confident smile as he leads me into the living room.

He's wearing a black t-shirt, the fabric straining across his broad shoulders and pecs. His jeans are hugging him in all the right places. Can we skip dinner? Because he definitely looks scrumptious enough to eat.

There's a battery-operated camping lantern lighting the room. The light is so bright I'd almost forgotten about the power outage while I took in Dak's smoking appearance.

"What? Just being polite, trying to make Trace feel right at home." Wolfe protests as he walks behind us. With all my carnal contemplations of Dak, I forgot Wolfe was there.

"Have a seat while we finish making dinner." Dak gestures to the sofa and takes the backpack off my shoulder.

Delectable smells coming from the kitchen are causing my stomach to do its usual doglike rollovers to beg for food. "Smells delish. How are you cooking without electricity?"

"It's nothing fancy, just bean and cheese enchiladas. We have a gas stove and oven. We used a match to light the burners since the electronic ignition isn't working. You into a margarita to go with the theme?"

"Uh, no. I don' think—"

"They're virgin." Dak interrupts with a grin. He must read the puzzled look on my face because he adds, "No alcohol. No *tequila*."

"Oh. Right." I smile. "In that case, sounds good."

"I'll sit here and keep Trace company. Wouldn't want her to get lonely." Wolfe sticks out his bottom lip in a pout.

"Forget it, dickhead." Dak gives him a playful smack on the back.

"Ow. What the fuck, dude? Only tryin' to be friendly to your lady friend here."

"Well my *lady* friend doesn't need any friends like you. On second thought, Trace, why don't you sit in the kitchen? We can talk while you drink your drink and the rest of us finish making dinner." Dak hangs his arm around Wolfe's shoulder. "Why don't *you* set the table, Romeo?"

"Yeah. Yeah. I don't know why I'm the only one who's never allowed to help with the cooking. Come on, Trace. You can give me a hand with the table." Wolfe pushes Dak's arm off his shoulder and takes my hand to lead me into the kitchen. Dak chuckles and shakes his head.

"Lead the way, Damon. I'm all yours." I'm not feeling the trepidation I was a few minutes ago. Wolfe is definitely into using his skills to woo the ladies, and his playful antics are making me feel welcome.

"See? I told you, Andersen, all the ladies love me best," Wolfe teases.

"Sure they do, Romeo," Dak chuckles. I follow Wolfe into the kitchen, with Dak only one step behind us.

There's another lantern on the counter and several candles on the table. Dalt and another guy I haven't met yet are standing in front of the counter assembling the enchiladas. Dalt is wearing a t-shirt and sweatpants. The other guy has gray sweatpants on too, a black apron, and no shirt. The straps of the apron crisscross over his wall of a back and the obligatory muscles of this sin on legs houseful of hockey players are on glorious display

"Hey, Batt, this is Trace," Dak says to the only guy in the room whose name I haven't heard until now.

Bat? Huh. Another porno actor name. Or it could be my dirty mind giving their names a sexual connotation. Who could blame me with all this muscled male flesh staring me in the face?

"Hey." Bat wipes his hands on a dishtowel and holds

out his hand in greeting. The front of his apron has I Like Big Buns printed across it. "It's great to finally meet you, Trace. I'm Dante."

"Hi. Dante?" I shake his hand and ask in a bewildered tone, because how is Bat a nickname for Dante? And what does he mean it's great to *finally* meet me? Crap. Dak must have talked to him about me too. They probably got a good chortle over the crazy bitch who begged to be fucked and then ravaged him in his sleep.

"Dante Battaglia. Everyone calls me Batt. And it's a tradition around here to kiss the chef." He grins and bends down, giving me a quick kiss on the lips. Yup. I'm definitely wading through a swamp of raging testosterone.

"No shit. It's a tradition?" Dak asks. "Well then. I better kiss the chef, because I never honored the tradition." Dak grabs Batt around the neck, pretending he's going to kiss him on the lips.

"Get the fuck away from me, asshole." Batt laughs and pushes out of his hold. "A tradition only for hot chicks."

"This hot chick is off limits to all you sluts," Dak says, and he's not laughing now.

I am?

"Oh come on, dude. Bros always share a good thing. House rules," Batt says in a joking tone, and resumes making enchiladas.

"Not this time, asshole." Dak hip checks him into the counter in a not so playful gesture.

"What the fuck, asshat? I was only kidding." Batt

turns toward Dak with fire in his eyes, like he's getting ready to punch him in the face.

I cough to clear my throat. "Excuse me, but you little boys do realize I'm standing right here. Right?"

"Sorry, Tracey," they both mutter.

"We're only messin' around," Batt says, gives Dak a sideways glance and shakes his head.

"Sorry, man," Dak apologizes. "Just looking out for Trace. She's not a...she's a friend."

"It's cool, man. Only fucking with you." Batt holds out his hand and they do some kind of macho boyfriend handshake thing. "You know no bro would ever touch another bro's babe, it's—"

"I'm no one's *babe*," I interrupt. "I'm here to do a bio project and I can look out for myself, Dakota. Thank you very much." Better to announce my presence with authority first thing with these guys.

I'm not one of their starry-eyed fangirls, and it's best to set the record straight if I'm going to be coming here to do projects.

"Yeah, *Dakota*. Trace can take care of herself," Wolfe says in a high-pitched feminine voice, then adds in his own deep voice, "so back the fuck off." He snickers, while placing forks and napkins around the table.

Dak mouths the word *sorry* to me. "Have a seat, Trace." He pulls out a chair for me. "I'll get you that margarita."

"Got some enchiladas coming out of the oven right now. I'll make you a plate," Dalt, who hadn't said a word through the whole exchange, announces. "Glad you're here, Trace. It's good you're friends with Dak." He places a steaming dish of food in front of me and puts one down for himself to the left of me.

"I'm glad I am too."

Dak puts a gigantic bowl filled with a mixed green salad in the middle of the table, then takes the seat to the right of me. A girl could get used to being waited on by all these Magic Mike potentials.

"I thought you might be interested in knowing Nikki moved in with me." I toss the tidbit of info out to Dalt, because I'm certain he would want to know. Since he stops mid-bite, his mouth gaped open, I think I'm right.

"She's...Nikki...she's right next door?"

"Yup. Right there," I reiterate with a slight smile. This boy has it bad.

"I invited her to come for dinner too," Dak says. "But she said she has too much school stuff to get done." He doesn't take his eyes off his plate, but I can hear the smile in his voice.

"Maybe you guys can all come over to our place next weekend. I can return the favor and you can see Nik then," I offer nonchalantly. Dak bumps my leg with his under the table and smiles down at his plate. I guess it's his version of applauding the suggestion with a high-thigh.

"You'll need to run that by Nikki," Dalt mumbles and shoves a forkful of enchilada into his mouth.

"I'll do that. So what's up with your names?" I ask, changing the subject for Dalt's sake. All the guys are seated around the table now and they've all got dishes in front of them stacked a mile high with cheesy enchiladas and a beer in hand.

"Our names?" Dante asks.

"Mm hmm," I say through the gooey deliciousness I scrape off my fork. "All your names start with the letter D, right? Is it some kind of house rule?"

"No," Dak answers. "Just a coincidence. But it is kind of cool because when we play they call us the D-structors, because of our names and the way we work together to crush the opposing teams." Wolfe gives Dak a high five and the rest of the guys all make some kind of affirming grunt through their mouthfuls of food.

"No way. They do not call you the D-structors. You guys are totally fucking with me, right?"

"We would never fuck with you, sweetheart," Wolfe grins. As if on cue they chant in unison, all except Dak, "At least not with your mind." They glance over at Dak to see what his reaction will be to their unexpected coordinated response.

"Aww how cute," I say, not giving him the chance to jump to my aid again. I need to stand up for myself when it comes to this crew of arrogant hotties. "You're like a boy band, all synchronized and shit. Are you going to start singing in harmony now?" I tease. Everyone at the table is laughing. "Oh I know! You're like the Hanson brothers plus one, right?"

"Holy shit, Andersen! She's seen *Slap Shot!*" Wolfe's full mouth gapes open in obvious surprise.

"Are you kidding? A chick who's seen the movie *Slap Shot*?" Dalt adds in equaled astonishment.

"Seen it? It was like the national anthem in our house. At the beginning of every hockey season my mom would make popcorn and my dad would make us all sit in the home theater to watch it," I explain through fork-fuls of food. "You know, like other people watch *A Christmas Carol* every holiday season, we had to watch *Slap Shot* every hockey season. I can practically recite the whole dialogue."

"Man, a chick who can recite lines from *Slap Shot* and has a home theater. I think I'm in love," Wolfe coos, and the rest of the guys mumble their agreement through full mouths, all except Dak.

He finally enters the conversation. "Her dad is Duke Andersen."

"No shit?" Batt asks.

"No shit." I smile at how awestruck these guys are by the life I take for granted.

"Wow, Andersen. You better hold on to this one or I may say screw the bro-code and sweep her off her feet for myself," Wolfe taunts.

The muscle in Dak's jaw twitches. "Enough, asshole."

"What's with you, Andersen? You on the rag or something?" Wolfe heckles.

"Shut up, man. You're disgusting." Dak throws his napkin at Wolfe. It's obvious he's holding back a smile and not really mad at him.

"Trace, you want a beer with your food?" Dak asks, getting up to head to the fridge.

"No thanks. I'll stick with the margarita. We've got the report to do."

"Yeah, *Dakota*. You've got the report to do." Wolfe purses his lips and blinks his lashes at us.

"Shut up, Wolfe," Dak and I say at the exact same

time. For a second everyone stops eating and the room is silent. Then everyone breaks out into laughter again.

"What? What's the problem? Just happy to see my man Andersen with another fine lady. He's been a mess ever since Abbey."

"Abbey? Who's Abbey?" I ask over the top of my margarita glass. The room goes so quiet I can hear my enchiladas being digested. I look over at Dak for an explanation, and he's glaring at Wolfe like he's either swallowed his fork or decided to strangle his roommate, after all.

Chapter Eighteen

DAK

Wolfe chokes on the food in his mouth. "Oh fuck. You didn't tell her?"

"For chrissakes, Wolfe. When are you going to learn to shut the fuck up?" Dalt throws a piece of lettuce across the table, hitting Wolfe right in the face.

"How the fuck am I supposed to know he didn't tell her about his girlfriend?" Wolfe pulls the piece of lettuce off his face and tosses it back at Dalt.

"His...what?" Trace gapes at me in disbelief.

Shitshitshit.

I should have told her about Abbey last night. But after everything else at the lighthouse, I wanted to give her some time.

"You...you have a...a girlfriend?" She carefully sets her fork down on the table, like if she doesn't get it out of her hand she might stick it in my neck. She keeps swallowing like she can't get her food to go down.

"No. No. I don't have a girlfriend." I place my hand over the hand she has resting on top of her fork, but she pulls her hand away from mine so quickly she almost falls off her chair.

"Trace, let me explain."

"There's nothing to explain. It's none of my business what you do or with whom you do it." She pushes herself up from the table. "Thanks for dinner, guys. I'll return the favor one of these nights. Need to get going. Got to finish my report," she says in curt sentences sounding like someone told her Christmas was cancelled...forever. She walks out of the room.

"Nice. Dickhead." Batt shakes his head and throws his napkin at Wolfe.

"What the flying fuck? Why does everyone keep throwing things at me? Sorry, Dak. Dude, I wasn't thinking."

"You never do, asshat. That's the problem." Dalt smacks him in the back of the head.

I didn't stay to watch the rest of their interaction. I needed to stop Trace from leaving. There was no way I could let her go thinking I was another douche who was cheating on his girlfriend or even worse, doing what I did to her last night while I *had* a girlfriend.

I find her in the living room, swinging her backpack over her shoulder and brushing a finger under one eye. Christ. She's crying.

"Tracey, please. We need to talk. You can't leave like this."

"Yes. I'm pretty sure I can."

Closing the space between us in two steps, I clutch

the tops of her arms and pull her into my chest. Pressed against me, she quivers. I see the questions in those doe eyes, the pained expression of 'how could you?'

"No, you can't." I hold her tighter against me. "You don't understand. It's nothing like what you're thinking. Come upstairs with me and give me a chance to explain."

"You want me to go up to your bedroom with you so you can tell me about your girlfriend?" She sneers. "You must think I'm the same stupid girl I wa—" I crash my lips into hers to stop her from calling herself stupid again. For a second she leans into me in response and then she jerks back, pulling herself out of my arms.

"Stop it. Don't kiss me...I can't..."

"Trace." I take her hand. "Please let me explain. I promise after I tell you everything if you want to go you're free to leave. I won't stop you. Please, just hear me out." She doesn't rip her hand out of mine this time, which I guess is a good sign.

I slip her backpack off her shoulder to carry it upstairs for her and grab the lantern off the table. The power isn't back up yet so the rest of the house is pitch black. She doesn't object when I lace my fingers in hers and lead her up to my room.

I'm glad I spent time cleaning it this morning, so at least the room is tidy. Except a neat room to impress Trace is the least of my worries at the moment. How do I begin to tell her about my relationship with Abbey and what happened? Once I do, will she still want to be friends with me?

Chapter Nineteen

TRACEY

Now I get it. The shit he said he has to deal with and the 'love' he hopes he can find 'again.' The reason he keeps backing off; he has a girlfriend, or he did. Someone he *loves*. Here I thought he wasn't into commitment and he didn't want to have sex with me because he thought I deserved better than a casual hook up. Wrong again. He's already committed...to someone else.

My head is spinning. Why the hell am I following him into his bedroom?

Will you never learn?

I guess not. I'm a big fool who keeps making the same bullshit mistakes over and over. My theory was wrong too, after all. I don't always fall for gay guys, I fall for *unavailable* guys.

"Have a seat," Dak says. He sounds nervous. What a joke, *he's* nervous.

I look around the room. The décor is sparse, but clean for a guy's room. A few surfing and hockey posters hang on the walls. The furnishings consist of a desk and chair, a tall chest of drawers, and a bed. It's covered in a gray down comforter with matching sheets, and since the desk chair is piled high with clothes, unless I want to sit on the floor it's the only place to sit.

Oh, what the hell. I slept next to him in a bed all night last night and the only time he touched me was when I begged him to. I sit on the edge of the bed, my hands on my lap and wait for the illusive explanation which is going to make everything between Dak and me okay.

The bed creaks in response to his muscled weight on the edge of the bed next to me. He rubs his hands over his face and keeps tapping his legs, but he hasn't said a word.

I begin the conversation, because I want to get this over with and get as far away from him as possible. Well, as far away as the house next door, at least.

"I opened up to you about some of my deepest secrets last night and you didn't think it might be a good idea to tell me about your girlfriend, Abbey, the girl you're in love with?"

I'm going to talk to Professor Clancy tomorrow, there's no way I can be lab partners with Dak for the rest of the semester. And we for sure aren't skating together. Bri will be happy to know I can't skate in the Winter Fest after all. Speaking of Bri, does this Abbey girl know how he's cheating on her? I almost feel sorry for her. I wouldn't wish that painful heartbreak on anyone.

I glance over at him in the middle of the pissed off verbal spew in my mind. His chest is heaving in shallow breaths like he's trying to get the courage to speak. He's scared...scared to tell me what he has to tell me.

"I...I don't want to tell you this," he says in a barely audible voice.

And I don't want to be sitting here listening to your bullshit story.

"No. I'm sure you don't. That's obvious. Why—"

"I'm not in love with Abbey," he says, his voice low. He's staring down at the floor, leaning over his legs, arms resting on his thighs, his head dropped forward. "There is no Abbey. Not anymore," he whispers.

"Did she break up with you?"

Probably the reason he's whoring around with Bri and whoever else. He's trying to get over a broken heart. The irony almost makes me snicker, but he seems to be hurting and even though he's hurt me with his lies, I can't be cruel.

"No. She didn't break up with me," he murmurs, still staring at the black carpet between his feet. "She died, and it's my fault."

I sit there speechless and let his words sink in. I can't have heard him right. "What? What did you say?"

"I said, Abbey's dead because of me." He turns to me.

"I...I don't understand. Wolfe said she's your girl-friend," I say in a softer voice, because now I know for sure he's hurting and it's for something much worse than a girl breaking up with him.

"She *was* my girlfriend and I *did* love her. It was three

years ago. Freshman year." He looks back down at the floor. "Abbey was...well she was great. Pretty, sweet...she was... kind of petite and fragile. She really loved me and depended on me to be there for her and I loved being there for her. We got hot and heavy pretty fast."

My stomach is a balled knot as Dak explains his love for another girl, one who is no longer here. I hear the tenderness in his voice and the pain for her loss. This is so much more than my pain over what went down with Sean. Sean is alive and my memories of him are only as a complete asshole, not as someone sweet and worthy of my love. Dak says he's responsible for her death! Whatever that means, it has to be a heavy burden to live with.

Once he begins to open up, the story pours out of him in an unrestrained flood.

"We were together for almost a year. Things were good. We were ...I guess we were in love...a couple, always together. But Abbey...well...she wasn't...she wasn't into athletic activities. She...she didn't like the water. It was okay. We had a good time together hanging out doing other things, but I couldn't imagine someone not loving being out in nature on a river or in the ocean. I felt like she was missing something. I thought if I could get her out there she would see what she was missing. I could get her to love being on the water if I showed her how mind-blowing the scenery and experience was on the river. Maybe even take her kayaking and snorkeling at some point, even get her into the ocean and teach her how to surf."

He stares across the room. His vacant gaze isn't

focused on anything. His eyes are blank liquid pools, only reflecting the imagery inside his head to himself.

"It was early spring, I needed to get some samples from the east branch of the Penobscot River for a project." He closes his eyes like he's reliving the scene in his head.

I don't say a word. He listened to my whole sordid story last night and the result was cleansing, almost healing for me. The least I can do is allow him the same opportunity to purge his soul. Whatever he's about to tell me, I owe him that much.

"The river waters were high from all the melt off. That area of the river can be tough when the waters are high, but I'd done it many times before so I didn't think twice about taking out the canoe. I liked using a canoe because it was easier than a kayak to maneuver along the bank and collect whatever specimens I needed."

He's clutching his hands together, still leaning forward on his legs. "Abbey didn't want to go. She legit wasn't into the water. I used to tease her, because she grew up on the coast of North Carolina and never got into water activities." His eyes are clamped shut, and he gives his head a slow shake, like he's disgusted with himself for having given Abbey a hard time for her lack of enthusiasm for the ocean.

"She kept telling me she wasn't comfortable being in a canoe. But I knew she could swim. We had picnicked on some of the lakes and played around in the water. She was okay with being in the lakes. I insisted she would be fine, that she would love it and she could wear a life vest. Besides, I would be there and wouldn't let anything happen to her." His voice drops to an almost inaudible whisper.

I hate where this is going. My heart is pounding against my ribs. I want to reach out and hold him, tell him everything is fine. But it's not fine. His shoulders are beginning to shake and tears are spilling over onto his cheeks. He's falling apart in front of me and I don't know if it's my place to comfort him. He opens his eyes and runs his hand over his face to brush back the tears, though he still doesn't turn to look at me. He keeps staring straight ahead at empty air.

"I launched the canoe far enough down on the trail so we would be beyond white water. The current was crazy strong there too, though, and Abbey was still extremely nervous. I kept pointing things out to her, trying to get her to relax and take in the beautiful things all around us. I rowed closer to the shoreline to collect some plant life and Abbey stood up to try to move toward me. I don't know if she thought we were going to get out of the canoe or if she was just trying to get closer to me. I don't know what the fuck she was doing...I never got a chance to ask her. The last thing I heard her say before we went over was 'Dak, I want...'"

He rubs his hands over his face and then he leaves his face buried in the palms of his hands. His pain is palpable. I reach out and touch his arm to remind him I'm here, despite knowing it's not nearly enough. His muscle tenses under my touch, but his only response is to continue telling me about the horrific memory unfolding inside his mind.

"I yelled for her to sit down, but it was too late.

When we tipped over I went under and the current started pulling me away from the canoe. When I finally pushed myself to the surface, Abbey was screaming my name. She was being pulled away by the current too." He turns to me for the first time since telling me Abbey was dead and I see the terror and anguish in his tortured eyes.

"I tried. I tried to get to her. I kept swimming until my muscles were on fire, but I couldn't reach her. Even though she had a life vest on, the water was freezing and she kept getting pulled away with the current. I kept yelling for her to swim. Keep swimming, Abbey!" he yells, like he's back in the frigid, racing waters and she can hear him. "The last thing she said before she disappeared around a bend in the river was, 'I can't, Dak. I'm sorry.' Christ. *She* was sorry. *She* was apologizing to *me* for not being able to fight the freezing water and current."

His eyes are pleading with me now; pleading with me to say something to help him understand why or how this could have happened.

"Oh, Dak. I'm so sorry," I whisper and stroke his arm. "But you know this wasn't your fault, right?"

"There's no question it was my fault. Abbey wouldn't have been there if it wasn't for me. She didn't want to go. I insisted. I told her it would be fine and she thought I would be there for her, protect her and take care of her. But I fucking couldn't. I was too weak."

It's like he can't hold himself up and he slides off the bed onto the floor. He crosses his arms onto his knees and drops his head onto them. His shoulders are trembling and he's gasping for air between sobs. I shift off the bed and join him on the floor.

"No. You tried. You did everything you could." I try to comfort him with my hands, making small circles on his back, although at this point he's so distraught he may be numb to my touch.

"Yeah. I did everything I could to pull *myself* onto the shore," he sneers into his own arms. "My muscles felt like they were paralyzed from the cold, but I tried to run along the shoreline to see if I could find Abbey and pull her out. I couldn't find her." He shakes his head.

"Dak, it was—"

"They found her several hours later, downriver." Dak finally looks up at me, his beautiful face and eyes swollen and red. "I stayed at the river to help search, even though the rescue team kept insisting I needed medical attention and should leave in the ambulance. There was no way I was leaving there without Abbey."

His voice drifts off in a distant whisper. "I saw her when they pulled her out and laid her onshore. Her beautiful hair was tangled across her face and for a second the ridiculous thought crossed my mind that it wasn't her. Can you fucking believe it? I tried to convince myself it wasn't her." His lips flatten into a tight line as he shakes his head and blows out a forced snigger.

"When they moved her hair off her face, she was so blue I almost couldn't recognize her. And when they asked me to identify her, I...I threw up. Her big strong hero, the guy who was supposed to take care of her, threw up." Still sitting on the floor, he drops his head back onto the mattress. Staring at the ceiling, he stretches his legs straight out in front of him on the floor and blows out another huge breath.

"You weren't responsible for Abbey. She was an adult, able to make her own decisions, and she decided to go with you to the river."

"She decided to go with me because she loved me and would've done anything I asked her to," he says, not looking at me.

"I get that."

Believe me, no one gets that kind of devotion better than me.

"Even so, it was her decision. It was an accident. You did your best to save her. You aren't a superhero, you're only human. You did everything humanly possible." I push myself back up onto the bed and he turns his head to look at me.

"An accident. That's what everyone keeps telling me."

"Yes, but..."

"But what?" He pushes himself up and sits next to me on the bed. He's looking at me with such anticipation, like I'll speak some words of wisdom to make this all better. I want to. I want to say something to make it better.

"What if there are no accidents? What if things happen the way they're supposed to happen? What if it was just Abbey's time?"

"You mean Abbey was supposed to die?" he asks in wide-eyed disbelief.

"I think...it could be no matter what she did that day it was her time."

"Like everything happens for a reason. Is that what

you're saying?" He smirks. "You don't really believe that."

"I don't know. Maybe I do."

"So everything that went down between you and Sean was supposed to happen?" He sneers, like he's angry with me for suggesting Abbey's death wasn't his fault.

The suggestion takes me aback for a moment. I had never thought of it in those terms before. "I suppose so, because...if...if I hadn't gone through what I did with Sean, I wouldn't be here now and I...I would never have met you."

He stares at me for a moment and then reaches over and takes my hand, lacing his fingers in mine.

"I'm glad you're here, Trace. I'm sorry I didn't tell you about Abbey last night, but I thought you'd already been through enough, talking about all the crap from your past. I wanted to give you some time. I've been trying to get past my feelings of guilt over what happened for three years. I don't know if I ever will, but I know I want to. I'm glad we're friends." He stops talking and stares at me.

"Please don't go. Please stay with me for a while. I promise I won't touch you or bother you...just...please stay."

He won't touch *me*. I know. He made the vow of never touching me again perfectly clear last night. But can I make the same promise to him?

Chapter Twenty

DAK

One of the things that always gets me about the show *Outlander*—yeah, I watch it on the DL. The guys would never let me live it down, even though it's totally not just for chicks. There're a lot of rugged fight scenes between all those Scottish dudes. Anyway, one of the things that always catches my attention is the vivid green of the open fields of grass where they film. It's like the true green I used to color my drawings of grass when I was a kid. The same color of the vibrant green eyes staring at me right now. The eyes which were like a molten aphrodisiac the first time I gazed into them. Trace is staring at me with such intensity I think those eyes are piercing right through me and cleansing away all the black webs of guilt clinging to the recesses of my heart.

She's the best thing that's happened to me in a long time. I pray she doesn't realize what I already know. She's too good for me.

"Between the two of us we're a big enough melodramatic shit show to deserve our own reality series don't you think?" she purses her lips into a half smile and shrugs.

"I guess we are." I return the smile. It's incredible. With a few words, she's able to bring me back to the here and now, pull me out of my tortured past, help me ease the heavy guilt burdening me.

I was scared she was going to think I was the biggest loser when she found out what happened to Abbey because of me. Instead, she's telling me it's not my fault. Maybe she's right. It's possible everything happens for reasons unknown to us. But even if she believes there are obscured forces in the world mapping our paths, I don't know if she'll want anything to do with me. This whole thing might be too much drama for her. She's recovering from her own 'shit show' as she put it; she sure as hell doesn't need to deal with mine. But despite my fear of her walking out of here and never wanting anything to do with me again, it feels like a colossal weight was lifted off my chest and I can breathe for the first time in a long while.

"I can't let you weasel out of doing your share of this research report. I suppose I'll have to stay for a while." She gives me a little push against my chest and I grab her hand and hold it over my heart. She leaves her hand in mine and keeps penetrating my soul with those doe eyes.

"We better get started before it gets any later." She slips her hand from mine and picks up her backpack from the floor, pulls out her laptop and notebooks, and drops the bag next to the bed. "I can use my backup battery if we need it since the power's still out."

"I have an extra battery too. Let me get my laptop." I jump off the bed to retrieve my computer and external battery from my desk.

"You sure you're okay? We can work on this tomorrow if you want. We've got a few days. I'll bring the samples in tomorrow and tell Clancy we'll turn in the paperwork in a couple of days."

"No. I'm good." I swipe a hand across my face. Christ. I've never cried in front of a girl before. I never talked about any of this to a girl before either.

"Dak, I'm sorry about what I suggested last night. I understand now why you can't help me out. Like you said, I don't want it to be weird between us."

"It's cool. Nothing's weird." We've shared so much, and since she brought it up, I need to know what prompted her to make the outrageous request last night. "I'm a little confused why you had such a radical change of mind, though. And what do you mean 'help you out?'" I sit next to her on the edge of the bed.

"Forget it. Sorry I brought it up. I don't want to talk about it anymore."

"There's something you're not telling me. What is it?"

"Nothing. There's nothing." She's biting on her overworked bottom lip, again. I know she's thinking hard about something.

"I would say the request you made was based on the dream-provoked...or should I say finger-provoked orgasm, but you made your proposition before the incredible incident even occurred. I heard your moans when I pumped my fingers inside you last night. But again, it was *after* you asked me to fuck you. So why did you change your mind?"

"Can you stop it with the blow by blow description already!" She puts her hands over her ears. The fifty shades of red creeping up her neck and face after I mentioned finger fucking her is the only proof I need to confirm Trace is not the type of girl to want, or ask for, a one-night stand.

"There. That's exactly what I'm talking about. You can't even hear me talk about putting my fingers inside you, but all of a sudden you're into a casual fuck like nothing matters. Why?"

"Never mind. Forget it, okay? Since when does a guy need to know the hidden meaning of life and love when a girl offers to fuck him no strings attached anyway?"

"Since the girl is you. What's going on?" I reach out for her hand, but she backs away from me.

"I thought you said you wouldn't bother me if I stayed with you. I'm going. We can finish the project tomorrow," she snarls and stands up to leave, but this time I manage to grab her wrist. There's no way she's running out of here and leaving this bullshit hanging in the air between us again.

"We can finish it now. What aren't you telling me? I opened up to you about some shit I never told anyone because I trust you like I've never trusted anyone. You obviously don't trust *me* because I know there's something you're not telling me. What the fuck is going on?"

"I trust you. It's why I asked you to...to..."

"To fuck you."

"No. Why do you always put it like that?"

"How else should I put it? Isn't that what you want? You want to get laid. You want me to fuck you. That's what you're saying, right?"

"No...well, yes. But...fine. You're right. I didn't exactly tell you everything last night. After...after Sean came to my apartment the last time...um...things kind of got worse."

Oh fucking hell.

"How can they have gotten any worse?"

"Trust me. They did," she whispers.

"Christ. How much more crap do we need to rehash tonight."

"See? I told you. Never mind. I don't want to talk about it and you don't want to hear it." She tries to pull her arm out of my grasp, but I pull her back to the bed.

"No. I want to hear it. I need to hear everything the prick did to you. Tell me what else happened and what's going on with you."

Although it sickens me to hear the levels of douchery the asshole put her through, I need to know and she needs to share all of it if she is ever going to move on from the pain. She says it was even worse than what she's already shared. Once again, I'm consumed by the desire to beat the crap out of the motherfucker.

"Like I said, I was...crushed by what happened." She blows out a long breath and hesitates before speaking again to tell me the worst part of the trauma she endured. "The whole thing was so surreal. I felt like I was walking around inside a nightmare. I couldn't eat, couldn't sleep, couldn't focus on schoolwork. A few days later when I went to skate practice because I thought skating would help take my mind off of everything, I see a bunch of the girls standing in the corner of the locker room all focused on the screen of a cell phone. They're all giggling and pointing and making comments like 'holy shit' or 'what a slut' and other things. When they see me they get quiet, their cackling becomes snickers and their loud comments become whispers. When I ask them what they're looking at, they snicker again and walk out of the locker room. I didn't know what was going on. A few seconds later one of the girls I hung out with from the team comes back in the locker room and pulls out her cell phone. She says, 'Holy shit, Tracey, what were you thinking letting them take pictures?'

"I asked her what she was talking about, and let who take pictures? I had no idea what she was talking about. She holds her phone out for me to see. I looked at the screen, but there was no way I could be seeing what I was seeing. It was a picture of me naked on Sean's bed, with Sean on top of me. You couldn't see the face of the other guy, but you could see him naked from the waist down, standing next to the bed. Kyle had managed to take a picture showing enough to make it appear to be the two of them having sex with me. She asked if it was me, but she knew. My face was crystal clear on the screen. I ran into the nearest stall and threw up."

Fuck.

Bile begins churning in *my* stomach and it feels like

it's about to flame out of my eyes. If those assholes were standing in front of me right now I'd rip both their heads off and spit down their necks.

"Christ. Trace..."

"It was pretty bad." She shrugs, like it's taking everything she has to keep going. "I sent Sean a text and told him I had to see him right away, told him to meet me at the quad. He didn't answer. So I threatened to out him and Kyle to get him to answer. He answered in about five seconds, said he would meet me in ten minutes. When I saw him after not seeing him for several days I didn't know if I wanted to kick him in the balls or hug him."

"Hug him? Are you fucking kidding me? You should've cut his balls *off,* never mind kicking him. Why the fuck would you want to hug him?"

She went through a different kind of hell than me, but it was hell nevertheless. I'm so angry I can't manage to be sweet and understanding. I feel like I can spit nails at the two dickholes who took advantage of her. My thoughts are back to beating, murdering, slashing.

"I know. So dumb."

"Fuck that noise. *You* weren't dumb. You just—"

"I *was* dumb. Even after everything he did, I missed him. We were together for a year. I couldn't believe that was how it was supposed to end. I confronted him with the picture posted on the university's social media site. He claimed he knew Kyle was taking the picture. They had discussed using the night and the photo as some kind of insurance. But he swore he didn't know Kyle was going to post it, not unless he had to.

"I asked him why he would do such an awful thing, because I still didn't get it. If they were so into each other why didn't they just go their merry way and leave me out of it? He said Kyle thought guys on the team were getting suspicious and they needed some kind of proof they weren't having a relationship. The night with me and the photo was supposed to be their proof. Kyle decided to post the picture in case I said anything about the night with them. If he posted the picture, it would look like they were two macho football dudes fucking the same girl.

"Kyle figured if I said anything after the picture was out there, everyone would think I was trying to cover for sleeping with both of them and they would believe the star football players on campus rather than me. I knew he was right. No one would take my side over theirs." Her gaze drops to the floor and she shakes her head, like she still can't process what happened.

"I told Sean if I ever meant anything to him he would make Kyle take down the post. Sean stood there staring down at the ground. He couldn't even look at me. He said he tried to get him to take it down, but Kyle said none of their teammates would want anything to do with them if they found out about their relationship and they might even be thrown off the team. He convinced Sean the picture was their insurance no one would ever question their relationship. That's when I knew. It took that one final, awful jolt for me to realize Sean never felt anything for me." She looks up at me again and brushes one lone tear off her face.

"It was only a horrible game of pretend, a cover-up. In the end, the university got the photo taken down, but enough people had already seen it. My life on campus or on the skating team was never the same. I kept spiraling down into a pit of depression until my parents finally insisted I drop out of school for a semester to get myself together. I was basically like a walking zombie. My heart had been ripped out of my chest and stomped on."

She sighs and the desperate sound pierces my heart.

"It wasn't any better at home. I couldn't stop thinking about Sean and how naïve I'd been. I couldn't stop the depression or the pain. One afternoon when everyone else was out I went into my mom's bathroom, found her bottles of sleeping pills and painkillers and... and..." Her breath catches and she's blinking rapidly again and I can tell she's fighting back tears.

"Jesus Christ. Jesus Christ, Tracey," I whisper over and over.

"I know. Stupid. So stupid. You thought I wasn't afraid of anything. I was the biggest coward ever. How could I let a person as heartless and empty as Sean and the insensitive people I thought were my friends drive me to the point where I took a swan dive to rock bottom? I was supposed to be smarter, stronger. I hated the girl I'd become. It was so bad. When I look back at it now all I can see is how he was so not worth it, but it was more than what he did. It was the cruelty of so many people around me afterward. I was so...disheartened, so broken by the way the people I thought were my friends treated me. I didn't want to die. I only wanted the pain to stop.

"I'm not that person anymore. I would never do

anything so stupid again. But I wouldn't blame you if you never wanted anything to do with me." Her words keep catching in her throat on short gasps.

"Oh baby." I brush a strand of hair behind her ear. "I can't believe what you had to go through. I wish I had known you then so I could be there for you. I'm here now. You're not stupid and you're sure as shit not a coward. You're the smartest, bravest person I know. You loved the fucker. People do crazy things for love."

"Did I love him? I thought I did. But how can I be smart if I fell for all his lies and then made the stupid choices I did afterward?"

She doesn't wait for me to answer; for me to tell her some guys hold superpowers at being dishonest mother-fuckers and no one, not even the smartest person, has the ability to see through their Kryptonite of lies.

"Thank God my sister came home earlier than she was supposed to. She found me and rushed me to the hospital. They weren't sure they could save me at first. After they did, I promised myself I would never give anyone the opportunity to hurt me again, never allow myself to be used again or think anyone was worth giving up my self-esteem or my life."

When her gaze meets mine again, I sweep my thumb over her cheeks to brush away the tears trailing down her face.

"Anyway, I worked through a lot of this, becoming a stronger person every day. Even so, I'm still sacrificing a part of myself to the aftereffects of Sean and I don't want to anymore."

"I'm not sure I get what you mean."

"I told you last night I haven't been with anyone for...well...for a long time. The truth is, I haven't...since that night with Sean and Kyle."

"That was like..."

"Over a year ago."

"No one? For over a year?"

"No. I was too afraid to. I didn't want to let anyone get close again. I couldn't let myself trust anyone. I...I couldn't let anyone touch me."

"What...what do you mean you couldn't let anyone touch you?"

Please tell me she's speaking metaphorically?

"What do you think I mean? You know...fingers, hands, skin, *touching*."

"But...but you let *me* touch you last night."

"I know. Crazy right? The guy I thought was the biggest super douche a few days ago turns out to be the only one in over a year I can let touch me."

"I...wait...you thought I was a super douche? I mean ...shit. I'm so sorry."

I want to hold her in my arms, but now I'm afraid to touch her. I should be able to understand. It was a long time before I could put myself out there after Abbey. But Abbey was sweet and kind and loved me. This Sean dude is nothing but a real dickhole. Although I get it was a traumatic experience and loss for Trace too. She loved the fucker, even if he *did* turn out to be the world's biggest prick. In my case, when I lost Abbey I hadn't lost my trust in other people because of her death. If anything, I had lost trust in myself. I didn't want to be with anyone else for a while because I missed Abbey so much and blamed myself for her death. I wasn't afraid to be touched. Fear of being touched is a whole other level of trauma.

"I don't want you to feel sorry for me. I want you to understand. The whole thing with Sean had me screwed up for a long time. I don't want to give him one more minute of my happiness. I gave him enough of my past, I'm not going to give him my future too. I want to move on. So...I asked for your help."

She hasn't let anyone touch her—*couldn't* let anyone touch her—for over a year and now she wants me to be the one to help her by having sex with her. Christ. I know she didn't mind me touching her last night. But why do I deserve her trust over every other guy out there?

Sure, I know all the ways to please a woman, but am I capable of helping Trace overcome her fears? I've never been with anyone who requires that kind of sensitivity. I don't do sensitivity or feelings. My mind is racing, trying to process this latest revelation. She must read the perplexed look on my face because she says, "It's okay. I get why you said no. I'm sure one of these days I'll find someone I can trust again. I waited this long. I can wait a little longer. For now, I'm glad we're friends."

Fucking hell. She's going to go out there to find some other asshole to fuck her back to happy. She may be one of the smartest people I know, but she's naïve as shit when it comes to guys. I'm sure there'll be no problem finding some douche who will be more than happy to offer the use of his dick to fuck away her fears. But he won't care about her and what she needs. He won't notice the vulnerability and longing in her eyes and she'll end up feeling even worse than she does now.

She definitely needs a friend like me to protect her from the Dick Ways of the Douchebag Human Male. If that's not a handbook already in existence I may need to write it so every sweet, unsuspecting woman out there can use it as a guide.

She looks up at me and in the glow of the lantern light I can see the shimmering hopeful longing in those beautiful eyes. I can't stop myself from scooping her into my arms and onto my lap.

"What are you doing?"

"I'm here, baby. I don't know what I did to earn your trust, but whatever it is, I promise you, I'll never do anything to abuse that trust. I'll never do anything to hurt you. You're incredible, you know that? Beautiful and smart and sweet. You deserve to be held and touched and treated like the goddess you are. If you want me to be the one to do that for you, I'm here."

She stares at me and blinks a couple of times, like she needs my words to sink in. "I...I...wow...that was ...kind of beautiful."

Her brows pinch in confusion, like she can't believe those words came out of my mouth. She's staring at me again with those sparkling eyes. And damn, my mind is starting to shut down. My need to fuck her right this second has taken over every fiber of my body. But this isn't about me, this is about Trace. I've got to take this slow and show her the level of worship she deserves from a guy.

The tension seeps out of her as she melts against my

chest. I keep rocking her in my arms. The tsunami of tears she can no longer hold back are saturating my shirt. I'd hold her forever if it would erase her past experience. I can't find the right words to make this better. In fact more words might not be what she needs right now anyway. We've shared all our past nightmares.

Chapter Twenty-One

TRACEY

D ak keeps stroking my hair and whispering things to soothe me, telling me not to cry. The comfort washing over me from his gentle touch is making me cry even harder. No one has touched me like this for so long. No. Wait. No one has *ever* touched me like this. It's strange how comfortable I feel with him in such a short time.

I tried to date once before in the past year. The guy was nice enough, but when he wanted to take things a little further I panicked and told him I couldn't see him anymore. With Dak, I find every time he touches me, I don't want to back away. I want to lean into him and let him touch me...everywhere.

The irony hasn't escaped me. The one person I can trust to get this close to is Dak Andersen. A few days ago I thought I hated him, and now we've both trusted each other with things we've never told anyone else. Who would have thought I'd be crying in Dak Andersen's arms and he'd be comforting me? Life is weird and wonderful all at the same time.

"Let's get this project done." He gently slides me off his lap and picks up his laptop from behind us on the bed.

"You...you want to do schoolwork? Like *now*? I thought you...we..."

"You kill me, Bambi. There you go with that dirty little mind of yours again," he teases.

At first, I'm confused, then I get what he's doing. He's easing the somber mood after everything we shared and is trying to relax me, maybe both of us.

"What do you want to do? Strip naked and have your way with me?" He grins.

Uh, yes please.

"I thought you said—"

"Let's take this slow. One step at a time, okay?" He runs his fingers down my arm and gives me his heart-stopping half grin and dammit, I tremble like he claimed happens whenever he touches me.

Slow? Really?

It's already been over a year without the warm touch of human hands on me and after the way he touched me last night, I don't know if I can wait another second.

He toes off his shoes and moves away from me, sliding up on the bed and leaning against the headboard, propping his computer on his knees.

"Oookay then. I guess we're going to record data.

You sure know how to show a girl an exciting evening, Dakota Andersen." I join him at the head of the bed after pushing off my sneakers and prop my computer on my knees too.

"Be careful what you wish for, baby doll." He smirks, balances his computer on his knees, and then pulls his shirt up over his head and tosses it onto the floor. "It was kind of wet," he says without looking at me.

Oh. My. Freaking. Word. Does he expect me to focus on the density of ocean water when all I can think about is the density of his roped abs and...and *other* dense, hard things?

"I think we should enter the water sample data in first," he says like he's read my mind. "What format should we use?"

"Um...I've already got a lab spreadsheet set up. We can enter the info on it. It's more organized." I boot up my computer and try to get my mind to focus on Marine Bio instead of the Anatomy of Dakota 101.

"Wow. You've already got scientific spreadsheets set up? I never had to use them before."

"Well, I have used them before for graduate research, but you're just a wittle, bitty boy, so you haven't needed them, yet."

Two can play at this game of ignoring the 900-pound should we or shouldn't we fuck gorilla in the room.

"Real nice, Bambi. You know you're about two seconds away from being put over my knee for a good spanking, right?" he teases.

"Hmmph. Promises, promises," I mumble but don't

look at him. Game on. My fingers fly across the keyboard, though I have no idea what the hell I'm typing. I may have entered in data showing the water temperatures around Mount Desert Island match those in Aruba.

I give him a sideways glance and note he's staring at me now. He leans in and brushes his lips along my neck. Oh God. I close my eyes and will myself not to overreact.

"Where's the notebook with the water temps at different depths?" I ask, ignoring his kiss. Pushing my computer off my lap, I crawl down the bed to rummage through the notebooks I had taken out of my backpack earlier.

Only when I hear Dak groan do I realize my spandex-covered ass is up in the air right in front of his face. Something hits the floor with a crash and I turn to see him sweeping all the notebooks off the bed.

He grabs my hips and flips me over and then crawls over me like a panther about to claim his prey. I'm trembling so hard with lust, but even more with nerves, I grip the comforter under me to try to hold myself steady.

When I was with Sean, it was like I handed him all the power, all the control over me. When he broke the trust I had in him, it broke something inside of me—the ability to allow myself to be this vulnerable.

Yet here I am, leaving myself susceptible again. "What...what are you doing? I thought you said we had to get the research done." My voice comes out all squeaky, like a scared little mouse.

Okay so he's better at this game of cat and mouse then I am.

"Yeah. We need to get it done," he whispers and licks my neck. My eyelids close and I drop my head back, arching my neck in an inadvertent invitation to his tongue.

"I...I thought you said we should take it s-slow." He's barely touched me, but I'm quivering like it's my first time.

Technically it *is* my first time with Dak. I'm not counting the sleep-muddled episode which occurred last night. The way he's consuming me with those scorching eyes, there's no doubt I'm wide awake right now.

"Oh, we're going to take it slow. Nice and slow. You tell me if you want me to stop. I'll only do what you feel comfortable with." His eyes are filled with more than hungry lust. Along with desire, there's warmth and concern. I'm overcome with something other than nervousness. Excitement and anticipation.

"So, a year since you've had any release. That can't be healthy. We need to take care of that," he says against my skin, and resumes trailing kisses down my neck.

"I didn't...mm...say there...there was no release."

God. Can we hold the conversation?

"So?" Dak asks as he pulls his head back and looks into my eyes. "What'ya do?"

"Seriously?"

"I'm curious what kind of experience I'm working with here." He gives me a slight smile, but not his usual sly grin. This time his smile is sweet and matches the concern in his eyes.

"If you must know, I have a very cooperative vibrator."

"A vibrator. No shit?" The twinkle in his eyes and mischievous grin are back.

"Yes, and I recently gave him the fond name Jackass." I flutter my lashes and smirk back at him.

"Is that right? I might have to meet my rival and see what he can do."

Any residual unpleasant thoughts of Sean vanish when Dak slips his hand under my sweater, trailing his fingers up toward my already throbbing breasts. I buck under him at the intimate invasion.

"Is this okay?" His tone becomes apprehensive and his hand stops just under the swell of my breast. "Should I stop?"

"Yes...I mean...yes it's good. Please don't stop." He slides his hand out from under my sweater anyway and pushes up, resting back on his feet, his knees on either side of me.

Damn. Is he afraid to touch me now? I may explode into a million needy pieces if he doesn't do something right this second. What can I say? After a year, as much as I love my baby pink vibrator, it's nothing next to all the hot things Dak has going on.

"Lift your head up a little." I follow his instruction. His hands slide under my sweater again and he pulls the sweater over my head and tosses it on the floor. I'm wearing the same red lace bra he saw me in the first day at the rink. He licks his lips.

Electric heat pulses through me from the craving in his eyes. My senses take over and my hips push up, begging him for what I need. He uses the opportunity to hook his fingers into the waist of my leggings and slide them off me He sits back again and sets me on fire with his heavy-lidded glare.

"Fuck. I haven't been able to get the sight of you in those little pieces of red lace out of my mind since that day in the locker room. You're so beautiful. I got hard every time I thought of you standing there in them."

"You...thought about me?" My voice is so raspy I barely recognize it.

"Oh yeah I thought about you. About kissing you, touching you, tasting you. I can't get you out of my head," he whispers and crawls up over me again.

He slides his hand under my back and with what I'm sure is well-practiced dexterity unhooks my bra. "Is this okay?" I nod, because I'm sure at this point I may only babble if I try to speak.

My brain no longer has the ability to form coherent words. I'm on sensory overload. He slips my bra down my arms and pushes it to the side. When I gasp at the cool rush of air across my tightened nipples he bends his head down and presses his lips to mine, moving his tongue into my parted lips. My tongue sweeps over his and his kiss deepens. It becomes hungry, ravenous. I respond with the same greedy exploration of his mouth and tongue.

I love the way Dak kisses, like he can't get enough of tasting me. Like I'm the only one who can satisfy his need. I'm on fire. I may come before he even touches me again.

Running my hands down his chest, I trace the lines of his toned muscles. When my fingers sweep over his nipples they pucker in response and heat pools at my core. I push my hips up into him. I can feel the hard ridge pressing against my thigh through his jeans. My body is screaming for him to be inside of me, but he continues his slow, sensual exploration. He pulls his mouth from mine and moves his lips down my neck, chest, and stomach, kissing and licking, leaving a trail of goose bumps along my skin as he goes.

"Oh, God. Dakota," I moan.

"You good?" He tilts his head up, his eyes filled with a mixture of longing and concern.

"So good," I manage to breathe out in a murmur.

"I'm going to kiss and lick and taste every inch of you." He drops his head and whispers against my skin between the demonstration of those licks and kisses and I lift my head to watch.

Watching him move in a sensual, languid pace down my body may be the sexiest thing I've ever seen *or* experienced. "I'm going to worship you with my mouth. Are you okay with that?" He glances up from under his dark lashes.

Oh yeah. I'm so okay with that.

"Completely," I sigh out and he lets out a throaty chuckle.

When his tongue brushes across my nipple, I drop my head back, consumed by mixed sensations of longing and euphoria.

He sucks on my attentive nipple and I can't hold back the loud groan escaping my lips. The aching need between my legs throbs. When he moves to my other nipple, giving it equal attention with his mouth and tongue, the sounds of pleasure pushing out of me become even louder.

"Shh, baby. The guys are all home. Use your inside groans," he whispers and I can feel his smile against my skin. "Mmm, you taste so fucking good. I could swallow you up."

"Dak. I'm... Dak. I'm going to come."

"Yeah, you are, baby girl. That's the idea." And then he slides my panties off.

"Fuck." He groans. "I love how wet you get for me." He bends my legs and brings his head down between my thighs. It only takes one long lick of his tongue down my center and I go off, moaning his name and other ecstatic prayer-like words.

"That's it, baby. I want to feel you come all over my tongue." He doesn't even give me time to come down from the first orgasm before he's licking, sucking, and talking me into the next one. "Mmm, Bambi. You taste like coconut and oranges, like a tropical dream."

He uses his tongue and teeth to take turns teasing my clit. I weave my fingers through his long, silky hair and rock into him. I can't get enough of the way he tastes me, consumes me. And then he sucks on me like a starving man, like he can't get enough of me either. He slides two fingers inside of me and begins to pump in and out, first at a slow pace and then faster and harder while continuing to lick and suck. The aching pleasure I'm experiencing is almost too much to bear.

I push into him, my rhythm matching the thrust of his fingers. Tipping over the edge, I explode again, and before I come back down I'm detonating for the third time, unable to hold back my scream. I'm confident the rest of the guys in the house won't believe our Marine Bio research project was this exciting.

My bones are molten putty. The release I experience is unlike anything...there are no words.

"Oh my God, Dak. That was...did you see what happened?"

"Uh, yeah. I was right here." He chuckles, sitting back on his legs with a pleased grin.

"I mean, I didn't get all weird while you were doing it and I came *two* times. I never had multiple orgasms." I sit up and throw my arms around his neck.

"I'm pretty sure it was three times, and that's because you've never been with the right guy, baby girl." He chuckles, wrapping his arms around me.

When I gaze down to admire his magic lips, he wipes his fingers across his mouth and licks them. He. Licks. His. Fingers. Just like he did with his ice cream last night, like he's trying to get every last drop of me.

"Mmmm, Bambi. I could spend the rest of my life without any other nourishment but going down on you. You taste so delicious."

Oh. My. God. I'm getting all hot and bothered again from his words and the way he's worshiping me with his eyes. He pushes me back, crawls over me again, and brushes his lips along mine with a tender kiss. I can taste myself on his lips and it's *so* hot.

"I want you," I purr and reach toward the thick bulge still confined within his jeans.

"I love that you want me and you've got me baby, but

it's getting late and we're scheduled to be at the rink at five." Without another word, he rolls off me and moves off the bed. I'm overwhelmed by an immediate sense of loss. "Let's record this freaking data and then I'll walk you home so you can get some sleep."

"You want me to leave? But you haven't...you're still..." I reach out toward his erection, which is clearly straining inside his jeans.

"No, I don't want you to leave, but one step at a time, remember? I want you to be sure of what you're doing."

Ugh. He's so frustrating. Couldn't he tell how sure I was, how much I wanted him?

"And we've got an early start," he adds, with more exasperating words.

His cell phone pings and vibrates on his nightstand with an incoming notification. A few seconds later the muffled sound of a bird chirping comes from inside my backpack as my phone notifies me of my own incoming message. He picks up his phone, swipes his finger across the screen a couple of times, and his face lights up with a huge ear-to-ear smile.

"What's up?" I ask and roll on to my stomach to reach for my backpack on the floor next to the bed. Dak groans again behind me and when I look back at him, he's staring at my bare ass.

"You're killing me, Bambi. Did I ever tell you how much I love your ass?"

"Really?" I twist around like I need to get a good look at the ass in question. "It's a skater's ass," I offer, like it's perfectly normal to be discussing my bare ass.

"Yeah. Trace Hayward's skater ass." He teases while ogling my ass. "'And all I can say is thank you to whoever it was invented the sport of figure skating. It's the perfect little round apple bottom."

"Apple bottom." I giggle. "Between the coconut, oranges, and now apples, I guess I'm like a fruit salad, huh?"

"Yeah. And I intend on pursuing a steady diet of fruit."

He does?

I thought he was only supposed to be helping me get past my anxiety of being touched by a guy. We accomplished our mission. But I'm more than okay with the idea of pursuing further treatment sessions with him.

He bends over me and licks and then nibbles on my available rear end. I moan as he licks places on my body that have never been licked before. How is it possible? In a few weeks I went from not wanting to be touched intimately by a guy, to not wanting Dak to *ever* stop touching me. But he does stop, stands up again and moves around the bed to retrieve the laptop he had pushed onto the floor. Hopefully the rugged armor case he has on it did its job.

He blows out a big breath. "You need to put some clothes on or I may never do any kind of schoolwork again."

"I don't know. You seem to be showing some pretty phenomenal restraint at the moment."

I can't help noticing the huge bulge in his pants pushing against his zipper.

"I'm good." He adjusts his pants and smiles, even

though it has to be so uncomfortable. I don't know how guys do it with those things between their legs. I sit up and look around the room to see where my clothes ended up. He opens a drawer and tosses me one of his hockey t-shirts.

"Here you go. Slip this on."

"Shouldn't I get dressed? You said yourself it's getting late. We can finish the report tomorrow night."

"We've got all night. You should stay over and we can get it done tonight."

"All night? What are you talking about? We're scheduled at the rink at the ungodly hour of five a.m. Did you forget?" I ask while slipping his shirt on, since I can't locate my sweater.

"That message was from the university alert system. They haven't gotten all the electricity back online. Classes are cancelled tomorrow. That means public skating sessions will be cancelled too. We can go to the rink later than five."

"Will there be ice if there's no electricity?"

"They keep the backup generator running at the rink at all times. But they'll cancel all the sessions except for hockey practice. It's happened before. It's how they preserve the ice conditions. Good news, right? We can get things done tonight and sleep in a little later."

Hmmm. Get things done tonight.

"Yeah that's great, but we may not need the ice tomorrow anyway. We should start practicing some of the lifts and jumps off-ice."

"No problem. The dance rooms at the rink will be

empty any time we want to use them. So you want to stay over and get this research project out of the way?"

"Sure."

But what I actually want to *do* is him.

Chapter Twenty-Two

DAK

"I'll text Nikki to let her know I'm not coming home."

Trace gets her phone and taps out a message. The responding message comes back almost before Trace is finished sending hers. She sends another, and another lightning speed response chirps back. I'm sure Nikki is warning her to stay away from all of us asshole hockey players. Ever since her and Dalt had a falling out, she's not too keen on hanging out with any of us. Trace sends one more message and doesn't get any response so I guess she's convinced Nikki it's cool. Or it's possible Nikki is on her way over here to beat down our door and rescue her friend.

Except I'm not sure it's her friend who needs rescuing. I don't know how it happened. Trace has gotten under my skin and inside my mind to the point I can't think about anything but her. She's turned my world upside down and inside out. The way she responded to my touch was incredible.

She seemed cool with everything. In fact, she was so responsive, I almost came without even removing my pants. That's never happened to me before. I've never wanted a girl the way I want her. I'm still so rock hard I don't know how I'm going to keep my mind on Bio data.

Now that I know what she's dealing with, I want to take things slow. I want to make sure everything is right for her, make sure we don't do anything she'll regret later. But fuck, when I see her sitting there in my shirt and remember she's naked underneath it, my cock throbs. I keep reminding him we're trying to do the right thing here. He's not happy.

I resume my position leaning against the headboard.

Holy fuck!

Trace leans her back against the footboard, pointing her legs in my direction. She bends her knees and props her computer on them, like she's completely unaware of what she's doing to me. My t-shirt is long enough not to be able to see anything, but I know she's panty-free, since I'm the one who slid the tiny strip of lace down her long, silky legs. My mind is making its own enticing images inside my head. If she spreads her knees and shows me that luscious pussy, I'm done. There will be no Marine Bio work going on in this room tonight, only human bio of marathon proportions.

I'm thankful, sort of, that she keeps her knees clamped together and I manage to keep my eyes fixed on my computer screen. During the tedious process of recording data, she moves up to my end of the bed and slouches down so her head is resting on a pillow while she types in info. We succeed in getting our project done by two a.m.

"That's it." I shut down my computer and yawn loudly.

"I'm beat. Thank goodness we don't have to get up at four. Oh man, it's almost that time already." She grimaces after checking the time on her computer screen before shutting it down and placing it on the floor next to the bed.

"You staying or you want me to walk you home?" Technically, Trace lives close enough to walk her home, but we're both zonked and I can't think of anything I want more than to hold her in my arms while we sleep.

And again, when the fuck did that happen? I normally don't *want* chicks to stay the night and the girls I hook up with are fine with that. It can get too complicated in the morning. But with Trace, I want to take her in my arms and hold her for as long as she'll let me.

"If it's okay, I'll stay." She yawns and stretches like a tired little kitten. And there goes my cock again, informing me it's more than okay if she stays. I'm so fucked when it comes to this girl. Every move she makes and every sound escaping her lips sends all my blood flow between my legs. "I'm too tired to walk home. I'm almost too tired to get up and brush my teeth," she says and nestles into the bedcovers.

"The bathroom's right there if you want to use it. There's some new toothbrushes in the second drawer." I point to the door leading into my private bathroom.

Being the captain of the team had its advantages when it came to choosing bedrooms.

"Thanks. Be right back." Trace scoots off the bed and picks up her backpack to take with her into the bathroom. I hear the shower water running.

I get up and get a pair of gray sweatpants off the back of my desk chair. When I slip off my jeans and boxers, I can almost hear my frustrated cock breathe a sigh of relief.

A few minutes later the shower turns off and Trace steps out of the bathroom. The room fills with her signature scent of citrus and coconut and I'm intoxicated. She has my shirt on again and her hair is knotted on top of her head in a messy bun. "I took a shower. Hope it's okay." She pulls the elastic from her hair, flips her head over, and shakes out her hair. When she stands again, her long waves fall past her breasts. My breath catches. She's so fucking beautiful. I stand there staring at her, wondering what I did to deserve this gorgeous, mind-blowing woman standing in my bedroom.

"Don't wait for me," I say pointing to the bed. "I know you're tired. I'm going to use the bathroom." I drop my hands in front of me to try to hide the half-mast working its way back up.

"Okay," she says through another yawn and makes her way over to the bed.

I decide to take a quick shower too. I already took one after practice, but...well...Trace is in my bed. Even though I'm only in the bathroom for a few minutes, when I come back out she's making the sweet little sleeping noises she made the night before at the lighthouse. She's snuggled under the covers, curled up on her side. After pulling on a pair of sweatpants, I turn off the lantern and climb into bed, trying to be quiet enough not to wake her. She's already in such a deep sleep she doesn't stir. I lie on my back, staring at the ceiling wondering, again, how I got so lucky. Exhaustion overtakes my thoughts and it isn't long before I drift off to sleep.

I don't know how long I've been asleep before the stroking of a tongue brushes across one of my nipples. I can't hold back the sound of a growl coming from the back of my throat. Reaching down, I run my fingers through the silky waves of Trace's hair which are spilling across my chest. Somehow I managed to become the luckiest motherfucker on the planet. Trace is running her tongue down my abs. Christ. She slips her fingers into the waist of my sweatpants and tugs.

"Trace? What are you doing, baby?" I ask in a thick-tongued voice. I want to make sure she's awake and completely aware of what's going on this time.

"I want to taste you," she whispers, looking up at me with those big round eyes. Jesus Christ. Maybe it's me who's dreaming.

"You don't have to do that."

"I know I don't *have* to. I *want* to."

Yeah. I'm pretty sure this girl will *never* do anything she doesn't want to do again. And at this moment what she wants is to slide off my sweatpants. I lift up and let her pull them down my legs and over my feet. My cock springs up in front of her face and when she licks her lips, I don't think it's possible to get bigger or harder than I am right now.

I've had plenty of blowjobs in the past couple of years, but when Trace looks at me like she's about to devour me, I become Thor, Superman, Hercules, and any other superhero I'm assuming has a superpower dick.

Fuck. I want her. I want to bury myself deep inside her. But she's studying my dick like it's the most luscious treat she's ever seen and I intend on becoming her all-night candy shop.

"Wow," she says, and sucks in her bottom lip. She's doing the nervous chewing thing again.

"It's okay, babe. Like I said. You don't have to—"

"It's so big." She runs her fingers down my shaft. Oh fuck. I don't know how much longer I can hold out.

"Uh. Thank you?" I grunt.

I may not be Thor, but I can't complain. I've been somewhat blessed in that department. It's not the first time a girl has given me the acknowledgement. However, after resisting my craving for Trace for so long, I'm not sure I can handle much more admiration of my assets before I go off. And then she bends her head down and licks the drop of pre-cum off the head of my dick.

"Fuck. Tracey," I groan. She wraps her hand around my shaft and takes me in her mouth, an inch at a time, like she's testing to see how much of it will fit.

When I reach the back of her throat, she starts sucking and moving her tongue in ways I never felt before. I fist my fingers through her hair to direct her where I want her. But she needs no direction. She takes a long lick, from the sensitive spot at the base of my cock to under the tip of my head, like she knows all the most sensitive spots to get me crazy. Then she starts licking and sucking like I'm her own personal candy cane while her hand works up and down and around my moistened cock.

"Jesus. Fuck. Trace. It's so good...so good."

She starts making these sounds like I'm the most delicious thing she's ever had in her mouth. Normally I can go for a while with a chick's lips around me and her tongue working me. But this is Trace, and I've been doing some serious prohibition for a while now, holding myself back from her. Not to mention the way she's working me feels like nothing I ever felt before. I can't hold back another minute.

"Trace, I'm gonna come." The gravelly words push out from deep in my core. I try to pull out of her mouth but she holds on to me like a kid fighting for her favorite lollipop.

Her sucking intensifies, gets faster and harder, and I explode into the back of her throat, groaning *"Trace,"* *"fuck,"* and some prayers of thanks. The whole time she keeps me in her mouth, swallowing every drop and moaning like she's the one getting all the pleasure.

When she finally sits back, she licks her lips like she doesn't want to waste one drop.

"Mmmm. You taste so good."

Holy fuck. I swear, that gesture, and the sight of her sweet, flushed face is making me hard again.

"Fuck, Trace."

"Was it okay?" she asks as she crawls up over my body and then rolls on to her side to face me.

"Okay? That was...it was...there isn't a word invented yet." I turn toward her and brush my lips against hers. She tastes like a mixture of salt and peppermint. Like me, I guess.

"But it was good?" she asks me again like it was a test and she needs to know her grade.

"Incredible," I whisper and tuck a strand of hair behind her ear.

"Good." Her voice drifts off into a slur, and her eyes flutter closed.

I never saw a girl fall asleep so fast after a mind-blowing orgasm, even if it's one she gave instead of received. Then again I have never been with any girl like Trace. There are so many versions of her: the shy and insecure Trace, the feisty and strong Trace, and now I discover the sex-goddess of the universe Trace. At the moment, that one's my favorite. I'm beginning to think that when I'm done being her friend with healing benefits, Trace Hayward is going to be a tough act to follow.

Chapter Twenty-Three

TRACEY

The smell of bacon and eggs is better than any alarm clock to blast me out of my cozy slumber. When I open my eyes, I blink a few times at the unfamiliar surroundings before remembering where I am. Mmm. Right. I'm in Dak's bedroom, in Dak's bed. Except, his side of the bed is empty. I roll over and press my nose into his pillow and inhale so deeply I may suffocate myself with feathers. The scent of him is everywhere. It's so yummy, even better than the smell of bacon and eggs. I stretch and languish in the afterglow of what happened last night. It was amazing! He was incredible! *I* was incredible! I'm no longer an anxiety-ridden freakazoid!

I didn't cringe when he touched me. And I was the one who made him feel everything he felt last night. I did that to him. Sean's main interest in bed was to give *me* instructions on how to make *him* feel good. I have to admit, the dude knew all about the best way to give a blowjob.

The whole thing is so ironic. After allowing myself to be so controlled and used by Sean, I took a little something away from the horrible experience, which has allowed me to feel more confident after all. I may do a happy I still-got-it dance right here in bed, like the one Diane Lane did in *Under the Tuscan Sun* after sleeping with the hot Italian dude.

"You awake, Sleeping Beauty?" Dak says from the doorway. He has his sweatpants on but he's still shirtless. He's so beautiful standing there smiling at me. I could lie here all day admiring his muscled chest and roped abs or better yet, licking them. He walks over to the bed and bends down to brush a soft kiss across my lips.

"Hi." I give him a sleepy grin.

"Hi," he answers in a hushed tone. "How are you feeling this morning?"

"I'm feeling pretty fabulous." I stretch in pleasure.

"That's because you *are* fabulous." He brushes light kisses down my neck.

I run my fingers along the fuck-sexy morning scruff on his face and find myself wondering what it would feel like scratching against the skin between my thighs. The thought causes heat to coil in my stomach and I'm rubbing my legs together to soothe the growing ache for him.

He can already read my movements like a book. When he glances up his eyes deepen to a sultry dusk blue and then he returns to the exploration of my neck with his lips and finds the spot just under my earlobe, which sends my hormones racing.

"You drive me crazy, baby. I could eat you for breakfast." He nibbles along my neck.

"Dakota..." I purr.

He bends his head back so he's looking into my eyes again. "Tracey." My name is a prayer on his lips.

I'm about to tell him how much I want him inside me, right this second. Until *he* says, "As much as I want to climb back in this bed with you, baby girl, we need to get to the rink and start working on our routine. We're going to rock their world when they see us skate together." He leans in and gives me another soft kiss. How can he be all logical and shit at a time like this? I would rather he rock *my* world.

"We've got all day. Hold that thought."

What thought? I know he's got bionic abilities at everything he does, but can he read my mind too?

"The only thing I'm thinking is..." I run my fingers down his chest and his skin quivers at my touch, "...how much I really, *really* want..." I sweep my fingers down his abs to the waist of his pants and feel the thick bulge of his erection move inside his sweatpants. "To eat bacon and eggs, right now." Giggling, I grab the pillow next to me and push it into his face.

"You little tease. Get out of that bed right this second." He throws the pillow back at me, laughing, but I move out of the way before it hits me.

Scrambling out of the bed to get away from him, I run out the door and down the stairs to the kitchen. I'm still giggling when I run into the kitchen, stopping dead in my tracks when I see Dalt and Wolfe sitting at the table.

Wolfe smiles at me over his coffee cup. "Morning, sweetheart. You have a good night?"

"Did you get your *research* project done?" Dalt asks, obviously trying to hold back a grin.

"Yes, as a matter of fact we..." Holy crap. When I notice Wolfe eyeing me up and down, I remember I'm in Dak's t-shirt. *Only* Dak's t-shirt, nothing else.

When Dak walks in the room behind me, Wolfe adds, "You must've had a seriously *hard* time agreeing on what info to use, the way you were yelling at Dakota... screaming his name." Wolfe snickers into his coffee.

I turn toward Dak. We stare at each other for a second before we simultaneously raise our hands and high five each other. "Yup. It was pretty much the best research I've ever done in my life." Dak grins and moves to pull a chair out from the table for me. "Take a seat. I'll make you a plate."

I walk right over, chin held high, pull Dak's t-shirt down to my knees, and take a seat. "You guys should try some *real* research sometime," I offer matter-of-factly.

No walk of shame for me. Last night was one of the most wonderful nights of my life. I feel good about everything for the first time in a long time and I have no intention of feeling ashamed of any of it.

"Yeah, assholes. You could all use some *real* research instead of the shit you do almost every night." Dak sets a dish filled with scrambled eggs and bacon down in front of me. "Coffee?"

"Yes. Thanks."

"Cream and sugar?"

"Yes. Please."

"Milady," Dak says, placing a steaming mug of coffee in front of me. He bends down and kisses me on the cheek. This show of affection in front of his friends feels a bit strange, even though they obviously could hear us loud and clear in the bedroom last night.

Wolfe almost spits out his coffee. "Who are you and what the fuck did you do with Dak Andersen?"

"Shut up, Wolfe," Dak and Dalt admonish him in unison.

None of us laugh the way we did last night when the same thing happened at the table. It's like we're all aware Dak and I crossed beyond a friendship line. The question is, can we stick to our plan of no strings, no messy feelings and keep our friendship? No. The question is, can *I*?

After inhaling my breakfast, I run home to take a shower and change into dance clothes for our first off-ice practice session. I don't even get my foot on the first step before Nikki calls out from the living room.

"No way. Get your ass right over here, Tracey Hayward."

Wow. She's going to make someone a wonderful mother someday.

"I'm in a hurry, Nikki," I say, stepping into the living room. "What do you need?"

"I need you to tell me what the fuck happened last night. Come on, girl. Spill it."

"Nothing happened. We got our project done...it took all night." I suck in my bottom lip and worry it between my teeth.

"Tra-cey," she drawls and waggles a finger at me. "I haven't known you long, but I already know when you bite on your bottom lip, you're either very nervous or thinking really hard. Right now I'll bet you're nervous *and* thinking hard about what kind of story you can tell me instead of telling me the truth. You need to tell me. I'm dying to know. Was he as good as they say? No way, right? No one can be that good."

Um. Yes, they can.

"Nikki, there's nothing to tell. We didn't have sex. Gotta go. We're going to the rink to practice."

"Are you telling me you spent *another* night with *the* hottest guy on campus and nothing happened? Have you seen you? There is no way Dak would've missed climbing all over that body."

"We did *not* have sex. We...we...did other things. Okay? Got to go. I'm in a hurry. We'll talk later." I hurry out of the room before she can say another word.

As I'm running up the stairs she calls out, "After I get back from my touch football game, I want to hear every dirty, luscious detail."

Chapter Twenty-Four

DAK

"Let's try a reverse lasso lift at this point in the music. Rotate three times and I'll grab one foot as we spin. What do you think?"

Trace has an excited little girl at Disney World expression on her face again. I love how enthusiastic she gets when she's working on our skating routine. As much as I love hockey, that kind of exhilaration is a special experience. It's the reason I told the coach I wasn't thinking about going pro. I only feel that kind of intensity when I'm on the ocean. Trace seems to feel intense enthusiasm for everything she does, and seeing her face light up as she choreographs our routine is causing her exhilaration to rub off on me. I'm focusing on every word she says like we're practicing for the Olympics.

"Sounds good. Let's try it." We stand on the mat in the middle of the room, watching ourselves in the mirrors along one wall. I face her, her back toward me, and we hold each other's opposite hands. I spin her up and around my head and we drop one hand. Trace uses the hand to bend one of her legs up to her head, while I spin us around twice. It's a crazy difficult lift, but we do it like we've skated together for years. The fact she's as light as a feather and I bench press three times a week in the gym helps.

"Hey. That was almost kind of perfect," she says when I bring her back down in front of me with one hand.

"You sound surprised, Bambi. You gotta trust me, baby." I tap her nose with my finger.

"Hmmph. If I didn't trust you, *jackass*, there's no way I'd let you throw me around over your head." She flicks my nose in response.

I rub my nose. "Or let me fuck you into ecstasy with my tongue?" I say, holding back a grin.

She closes the short space between us, her sweet breath on my lips when she says in a hushed voice, "No matter how much I adore your tongue, Dakota Andersen, you will always be a jackass to me."

I push her back against the mirrored wall and press my mouth to hers. This girl makes me crazy. Her lips are soft and sweet and welcoming. She moans into my mouth and Christ, I've got a raging hard on again. I pull her leg up around my waist and grind my erection into her and she moans again. "That's not what you called me last night when you came all over my face and screamed my name," I whisper and grind my hips into her again.

"Oh God. Dak, I want you inside me."

There's no place I would rather be. I crash my mouth

onto hers again. Our kisses become deeper, more insistent.

"Well that's an interesting routine you're practicing. Although I'm not sure the administration will allow it. The Winter Fest is a family show."

At the sound of the snarky voice behind me, Trace drops her leg and stiffens in my arms. Bri and her entourage are reflected in the mirror in front of me. I bring my eyes back to Trace and don't let her go or turn around. "We're using this room, Bri. Use the dance room next door, okay?"

She sneers. "I can see you're *using* it. But that's not what the dance rooms are for. I'm sure you can find a cheap motel room to fuck her in."

Trace pushes me back and by the way she's glowering at Bri, I think she's planning on punching her lights out. Lucky for Bri, Alex intervenes.

"You would know all about the locations of the cheap motel rooms in the area wouldn't you, Sabrina honey?" Alex snaps his fingers back and forth in front of her face. The shocked look on Bri's face is priceless.

"Alex, you better—"

"Oh shut it, Bri. The room next door is bigger and it's empty. We can use that one." Surprisingly, Bri stomps out of the room without saying another word, the rest of her groupies in tow. I guess the fact Alex is the best skater on the men's senior skating team means Bri holds no swag over him.

"Hey, Trace, Dakota. What's up? Uh, never mind. I can see what's up." Alex scans my crotch area and quirks a brow.

"Hi, Alex. Thanks." Trace sighs.

"For what? I only want to make sure there's enough time to teach this he-man how to pair skate." He hooks a thumb in my direction. "I want you guys to be so freaking good you'll blow the pole right out of Bri's stuck up ass. Eww. Now that I said it, it's kind of a disgusting mental graphic. Right?"

Trace and I are cracking up too hard to answer. "Bye you two gorgeous hunks of humanity. You may resume whatever it was you were doing so hotly when we so rudely interrupted you." Alex waves, walks out of the room, and slams the door behind him. I think he'd lock us in if he had a key.

"I fucking love that guy."

"Me too." Trace smiles. "So, where were we?" She gives me a narrow-eyed glare when she notices the lust-filled ogle I send her way. "Where were we with *skating* lifts?"

"I suppose we do need to keep practicing if we want to blow the pole out of Bri's ass." I rub a hand down the back of my neck. Hell. This much restraint can't be good for a guy's health. Might cause some kind of blockage or something. "But after we're done here, we're going back to my place...or yours. I don't care as long as there's a bed...and a wall, and a sofa and possibly a table and countertop. What do you think?"

"I think it sounds like a whole lot of furniture. We better make it my place."

She giggles. Fuck, I can't wait to bury myself inside her.

After perfecting our fancy lasso lift, which requires lifting her from a spread-eagle position, rotating once in the first position with a two-handed hold, and then her changing position in the air while we switch to a one-handed hold and do two more rotations, Trace decides we should practice a star lift. The icing on the cake is the exit. She drops in front of me and slides on her back between my legs. She's a little thing and again, I work out a lot and have my fair share of muscles, but damn. When I told her she could trust me, I didn't think she'd take it to mean I'm Maxim Tankov!

By the time we're done two hours later I feel like someone's used me for their punching bag workout right after I was run over by the Bigfoot Monster truck. Holy fuck. I thought I was in good shape. Did I travel through some kind of time warp and come out a hundred and fifty years old? Because that's what I feel like. Make it two hundred and fifty. I'd love to climb into one of the team whirlpool baths, except the side of my brain that isn't bruised and battered is revving up to get back to Trace's for the afternoon delight we discussed earlier.

I let out a loud groan, and not the kind of blissful filled to the point it aches groan I gave when she had her lips around me last night.

"You okay?" She places her hand on my shoulder.

"Yeah. I'm good," I answer, even though every one of my muscles is screaming, *no you're not, asshole. What makes you think you can pair skate?* "I just need a shower and you." I bend my head to kiss her and even that slight movement elicits a groan.

"Oh, poor baby. When we get back to the house I'll give you a full body massage. How does that sound?"

Like the skies opened up and all the angelic choirs in heaven started serenading me.

"Sounds like heaven, but I've got hockey practice at four. I'll take a raincheck for the massage. We've got more important things to attend to right now. Let's get out of here."

The drive back to our houses is quiet except for Paramore's "Only Exception" streaming from the satellite radio like a psychic reading. I'm nervous. *Me*. The guy who's seen more pussy in the last year than Tumblr. But this is Tracey and she hasn't let anyone get close to her for over a year. How do I handle that?

I glance over at her and see her gaze is fixed out the window. She's nibbling on her bottom lip again and her left leg is bouncing up and down. Even though we've already given each other these mind-stupefying oral orgasms, it's apparent she's nervous as hell too. Is she thinking the same things I am?

No matter how much I fucked around, I'm aware there's a unique trust that comes with having the kind of sex which joins two people together to the point they're almost one entity. They move together, breathe together, climax together...hopefully. That climax, the moment when there's this kind of out of body experience, it leaves you open, vulnerable, unguarded. Is Trace ready for that kind of vulnerability again? Am I? Despite our agreement for no attachments, no feelings, when I look at her, my heart races and my balls tighten. This is way more than the thrill of a meaningless one-night fuck. This is *Invasion of The Body Snatchers* level of mind and body takeover, but a good kind of body snatcher. She's all I can think about, all I want. The *only* one I want. Could she be feeling the same way, even though she said she isn't interested in anything but friends with benefits?

I reach over and place my hand on her thigh to calm her. She stops bouncing her leg up and down.

"You still with me over there?" I stroke her leg.

"I'm with you." She smiles and my heart races a little faster. The effect she has on me is unbelievable.

"We got a lot done today. The routine is gonna be awesome."

"Yeah, it is. A few more off ice sessions to get it all put together and then we can try it on the ice." She's talking to me but I can tell she's distracted. Her mind is somewhere else. Then she goes back to staring out the window and chewing on her lip.

A few minutes later I pull into my driveway. "I'm going in to take a quick shower. I'll be over in a few, okay?" She stares at me for a minute. The shy, insecure Trace is back.

"Sure. I'll...I'll make *you* something to eat for a change."

"I bought every season of GOT on Blu-ray. I wanted to watch it all again before the new season starts. You into it?" I totally do not want to watch television. What I want is her, but the "take things slow" plan is the best way to keep things relaxed and give her time to change her mind if she wants.

Please. Please don't let her change her mind.

"Definitely. By the time they start the new season I can't remember who's killed who or whose mother is sleeping with whose brother." She giggles. "I was planning on streaming it to catch up."

"You have a Blu-ray player?"

"Naturally." She sighs. "If there was room and it was up to my mom, I'd have an in-home theater."

I smile at her frustration over her mom's over the top gifts. "Give me a few minutes to get cleaned up."

She's smiling again, more relaxed. It only takes one flash of her sweet smile for me to relax too. Everything's all good. Trace and I are good together. No pressure. Everything's cool.

When I knock on her door about a half hour later, she opens it before my second knock. My breath catches like it does every time I see her, even after such a short time being away from her. It's like I forget how perfect she is, because it isn't possible for anyone to be so beautiful.

She's barefoot and wearing yoga pants with a loose off the shoulder pale green sweatshirt. It says *Save the Ocean* and has bright colored pictures of various fish and marine animals in a circle. Her wavy hair is loose and hanging down past her perfect breasts and her face is radiant and freshly scrubbed. Her green eyes are sparkling like grass after a fresh rain. The way they're tipped up slightly at the corners when she smiles at me, it's like they were made to twinkle just for me.

"Hey." She pulls me in the door and circles her arms around my waist to hug me. I put my arms over hers and press my nose into her hair, breathing her in. She not only looks like an angel, she smells like heaven. My senses fill with her distinctive tropical scent and I'm transported to Hawaii, Fiji...heaven.

"Hey." I smile into her hair.

She takes my hand and leads me into her preposterous living room. "You hungry?"

"I would think you'd know by now, Bambi, I'm always hungry."

Especially for you, I want to add, but I don't want to make her nervous again.

"It's too early for dinner, so I made us a fruit smoothie and a kitchen sink salad."

"A kitchen sink salad?"

She giggles and the sweet little sound sends my pulse into overdrive. "That's what my sister and I call it. We throw in any kind of veggie available—mixed greens, carrots, peas, edamame, kale, whatever, and then we add some dried berries and some slices of pear or apple and seeds or nuts. *Voila*, kitchen sink salad."

"Everything but the kitchen sink," we say in unison and laugh.

"We can eat in the living room while we watch some GOT episodes."

"Sounds good. No roomie today?"

"No. Nikki had a touch football game on the quad, guys against girls."

"Well if it's the girls from the soccer team, the guys are going to get their asses kicked."

"You serious?"

"Absolutely! The way those chicks maneuver on the field, they never tire out and their endurance is epic. Those guys, whoever they are, are fucked."

"I guess I need to go to the next soccer game to watch those superwomen in action."

Tracey giggles again, and I swear even her laughter sounds like angels singing.

Christ. I'm turning into Emily fucking Dickinson!

"You can set up the Blu-ray while I get the food," she says and heads into the kitchen.

Trace has a fifty-five inch ultra-high definition television sitting on a black and white checked TV stand along one wall in the room. Although my parents own top of the line media equipment at home in Cali, I never got the chance to watch *Game of Thrones* in UHD because I'm always at school when the seasons start.

She comes back in carrying a tray with our salads and smoothies on it. Placing it on the coffee table, she makes herself comfortable on the sofa next to me.

"The salad looks incredible."

"I made a raspberry vinaigrette dressing for it. Hope you like it. Did you put the first disc in?"

"Yep. Just push play on the remote."

She picks up the remote and when she pushes play, the most phenomenal graphics for any opening sequence ever, roll across the screen. We sit there for a few minutes in silence enjoying the food and the show. When we're finished eating, Trace takes the dishes back to the kitchen and hurries back to the sofa so she doesn't miss anything.

I push off my sneakers and stretch my muscle weary

legs up onto the coffee table. Trace sits next to me and drops her head on my shoulder while we watch the show. With her body pressed right up next to mine, I can't focus on how many heads the White Walkers tear off and throw.

"So Jon Snow and Khal Drogo. Fuck or marry?" I remark, trying to get my thoughts out of my crotch.

She looks up at me, her brow pinched. "What?"

"Jon Snow or Khal Drogo? Which one would you fuck and which one would you marry?"

"Well that's a no brainer. I'd fuck Khal Drogo and definitely marry Jon Snow."

"Definitely? How come?"

"Because...well, *Jon Snow*." She says it like I'm some kind of idiot not to realize any woman would want to marry Jon Snow. "Those *eyes*, and he's so trustworthy and devoted...and sincere. Drogo...well, *look* at him. I mean, mmph."

"Oh, I see." I laugh. "So it's all about the muscles, huh?"

"Have you watched the sex scenes between him and Daenerys?" She sits up so she can look directly at me and arches a brow.

"Tra-cey, your dirty little mind is showing again." I wiggle a finger at her.

"Oh right. Okay. Your turn, Saint Dakota. Daenerys and Cersei. Fuck or marry?"

"That's easy. I'd fuck the hell out of both of them. And then kill Cersei. She's batshit crazy."

"Not fair. That wasn't a choice." She grins and flops back against the sofa. "What is it about Daenerys that makes her a keeper? The long blonde hair, I suppose?"

"Nah. She's got dragons. Who wouldn't want to hang out with a chick who has dragons? That's mother-fucking awesome!"

"But you wouldn't marry her, just fuck her."

"Nope. I don't do the whole marrying thing."

"Hmm," she says, like she's mulling over all this. "But if you piss her off she could sic her dragons on you and burn you to a crisp."

"Huh. I might need to rethink this whole thing."

"Yeah you might, *jackass*."

"Come on, you calling me jackass again, *Bambi*?" I slide a hand under her sweatshirt and tickle her ribs. She falls back wiggling and gasping between giggles for me to stop. I reach for her, and when I find myself on top of her, I stop tickling her and the mood between us changes. We're not laughing anymore. Everything becomes serious, more intense. We're staring into each other's eyes and I'm wrecked.

"What was it you said to me at the rink today?" I whisper.

"I...I said a lot of things to you at the rink today. Which one are you referring to?" Her voice comes out in a nervous tremble. I know *she* knows exactly which one I'm referring to, but I'll help jog her memory if she wants me to.

"The one when I had my tongue down your throat and I was grinding my hard cock into you. Remember that one?"

"Um...yes I remember." She closes her eyes and sighs.

"Say it again. I want to hear you say it again." I take her earlobe between my teeth and give it a slight nibble. She makes an aching oooh sound and pushes her hips up into my hard dick. Being in a constant state of erection since the first day I met Trace has me ready to explode, but I won't make another move until she tells me she wants it.

"I said I want you inside me." She whimpers and circles her hips into me again.

I press my lips onto hers, hard and demanding, claiming her. Then I slip one hand under her sweatshirt again and slide up to the swell of her breast. Fuck. She's not wearing a bra and the constant danger of coming in my pants whenever I touch her warm, sensitive tits is looming large. Really large.

"Bedroom. Nikki might come home," she mumbles against my lips.

I take my hand away from her pert round breast and pull myself off of her. Part of me is reluctant to be away from her even for a second, but the other part is so wound up I can't wait to get her upstairs and onto her bed. I lift her into my arms, and she wraps her legs around my waist and presses her heels into my back, like she's afraid someone might try to pry us apart.

While carrying her up the stairs I keep kissing her mouth, her eyes, her face, and she tips her head back to receive my kisses. "This is going to be perfect," I whisper in between each brush of my lips.

I lower her on the bed and pull my shirt up over my head and toss it. When I drop my jeans and boxers to the floor my straining cock bounces against my stomach, like it's waving at Trace. Her half-lidded gaze slides up and down my body, until her eyes meet mine. And then she crosses her arms and drags her sweatshirt over her head.

I can see her trembling. I'm not sure if it's nerves or need or a little of both. I'm going to make this so good for her she'll never be nervous or afraid to let anyone touch her again.

I hook my fingers in the waist of her leggings and drag them down her legs, then do the same with the white lace underwear she's wearing. Damn. Does she own these tiny strings of lace in every color? I fucking hope so.

Seeing her lying across the bed naked gets me harder and my cock throbs to let me know what he wants, right this second. But I need to savor her first, take it nice and slow, like I told her before.

She's so breathtaking. Everything about her is perfect. Her perfect tits, not too big or small, round with rosebud pink nipples waiting for my attention. Her body; not too thin, just enough curves to bring me to my knees. Which is right where I want to be—on my knees with my face buried in the patch of curly auburn hair between her legs.

"Dak," she whispers and holds her arms out like she's inviting me in. I don't think twice about accepting the invitation. I crawl over her and push myself up on the palms of my hands, one hand on either side of her. Seeing her lying here underneath me with flickering anticipation lighting up her sweet face has me as hard as iron. But now that she *is* under me my insides are tied in knots. I want her more than anything, but can I do this? Can I be the one to help her get past her fears without hurting her again?

Her flushed pink face and big round eyes are declaring her longing. But I need to be certain this is what she wants, even though it'll be one of the most difficult things I ever had to do. I'll stop. I won't make another move until she says it is.

"You're so beautiful. I wanted you since the first minute I laid eyes on you."

"You did?" she asks in a surprised tone.

"You don't know how hot you are. Every time you said it wasn't a good idea or I said it wasn't right for us, I died a little. I wanted you so much. I don't know how I waited so long. But if you're not ready, if you want to stop, say the word. I can wait longer. I'm all yours, however or whenever you want me. If you want to wait longer or just do what we did last night, I'm okay with that. So are you sure about this, baby? Because if you don't want—"

"Dakota." She places one finger over my lips, shushing me.

"Tracey," I mumble against her finger.

"I'm not afraid anymore. I trust you. If you want me, I want you too. Please fuck me."

Jesus H. Christ!

Thank you. Thank you.

It's a weird kind of prayer of thanks, I know, but Trace asked me to fuck her and it feels right this time. Like all the planets in the universe are lined up in perfect order and the heavens opened up and are raining peace, love and harmony all over us. In my present state of

Nirvana, I can't think of anything else to say but thank you.

Before I bury myself in her I'm going to lick every inch of her again and make her heat with desire, to show her how thankful I am to be the one she chose to trust. I'll never get enough of her sweet taste. I want to feel her tremble under me and dig her nails into my shoulders when the ache of pleasure becomes too much.

I lower myself and press my body against hers. My rock hard cock throbs with fire against her stomach and I roll my hips into her. She groans and arches her back, pressing further into me.

I don't usually have a problem with stamina, but when she moves under me and those sounds leave her lips, everything is raw and intense desire. I want to push into her and hear her scream my name as she lets go and I release into her. But even more, I want this to be perfect for her. I want to show her how much she deserves to be adored.

Tilting my head, I lick her plump lower lip and then take it between my teeth and nibble. When she opens her mouth and our tongues touch, I plunge deeper and harder into her mouth, tasting her, devouring her. She follows my lead, just as hungry, just as needy.

I trail my fingers over her nipples and they pebble in response to my touch. "Fuck. You're so—"

"Dak...don't stop."

"Stop? I haven't even started. Are you ready for me?"

"I'm so ready," she moans and the sound is like music to my ears. I intend to compose a symphony of those sounds today.

I move my hand down between her legs and when I slide two fingers into her I find she's not kidding. She's so wet and warm and soft. "So fucking hot," I whisper against her lips. I pump my fingers in a slow in and out rhythm and she makes an oooh sound again and pushes herself into my hand.

I kiss and nibble my way down her body, and when my mouth replaces my fingers she threads her fingers through my hair, pulls me closer, and pushes her hips up. I consider myself pretty experienced when it comes to pleasuring a woman, but with Trace and the way she moves and responds to me, I find myself shaking almost as hard as she is.

It only takes one circle of my tongue around her swollen pink clit and she's over the edge moaning, "Dakota. Oh God, yes, yes. Yes!"

"I love the way you say my name when you're coming," I say, trailing kisses along the silky skin of her inner thighs.

She reaches for me again. "Dak, please. I want you."

"You've got me, baby." I crawl back up her body and kiss her again, deep and hard. She reaches down between us and takes me in her hand, placing my cock right where she wants it.

"Hang on a second, baby." I try to move to get a condom from my pants pocket, but she reads my mind and grips me tighter. Holy fuck. I may come in her hand.

"I'm on the pill." She lets go of me and starts nibbling on her bottom lip. "I started taking it again a few months before I came here. In case I wanted to...or I could..." She keeps worrying her lip.

I run my thumb along her lip and she releases it from her teeth. "I've never been with anyone without a condom, but I'm tested and clean. You sure about this?"

"I'm sure. I want to feel you. Really feel you," she says in a soft voice.

Every word she says, every sound she makes is like scorching heat sweeping over me. I'm on fire and she's the gasoline. I push up and position my cock right at her entrance and she spreads her legs wider for me. I can feel how wet and hot she is. Keeping my eyes locked on hers, I slip inside her. She gasps and I groan such a guttural sound I almost don't recognize my own voice.

"Is this okay?" I want to make sure she's still good with what we're doing. The words come out in a growl because she's so fucking tight.

"Dakota," she breathes out in a soft voice filled with entreaty.

"You good?" I ask again to be sure, but I'm thinking *please say yes, please say yes.*

"So good," she sighs.

Thank all the deities in the universe.

"Fuck. You're so tight. You feel so good. So fucking good." I'm buried deep inside her and there's nothing between us. She's so slick and warm. Her muscles are clenching around me. Christ. I'm like a virgin, experiencing all this for the first time. Nothing has ever felt like this before. Like her.

I rock into her slowly, savoring every sensation, and the whole time we keep kissing and she moans into my mouth. She hooks her legs around my waist and pulls me even deeper into her and I can't keep it slow any longer. I start thrusting in and out of her faster, harder, and she matches my rhythm, pushing her hips up into me with every thrust.

She's digging her nails into my shoulders so deep it's sure to leave marks like I was in some kind of catfight. But the pleasure building at the base of my spine is all I can feel. Everything becomes fast and desperate, we can't hold back. Trace goes off, dropping her head back and screaming my name like she does when she comes.

The way she tightens and clenches all around me, I'm right there with her, detonating with such force as I spill into her it feels like it will never stop. She keeps milking my cock with her trembling spasms and I keep pulsing into her as waves of release push through me

I collapse onto her, spent in the most incredible way.

"Trace." I groan. "You are so fucking amazing." My face is buried in the curve of her neck and I may stay lost right here in this silky, fragrant space for the rest of my life.

Chapter Twenty-Five

TRACEY

I haven't had many past experiences with sex. There was only one other guy besides Sean I went all the way with. He was nice. It was nice. But with Dak, the terms mind-blowing, Earth shattering, and heart pounding hold true meaning for me now. I get it. Sex with him is awe-inspiring to the point where I'll admit he deserves the title Sex God. Everything is electric, intense, toe-curling heat, and at the same time anesthetizing and mind-numbing.

At this very moment, I think Dak is numb to the point where he's going to suffocate me. I run my hand down his back trying to get his attention. "Dak?"

"Yeah, baby?" He lifts his head and starts placing little kisses along my face and neck.

"I...I can't breathe." I push against his chest.

"Oh sorry," he says and rolls off of me onto his side,

facing me. "I think you used up every drop of me. I can't even move." He runs his fingers through my hair.

"I hope that's not true." I giggle. "What will we do with the rest of the day?" I tease.

"You keep talking like that and we may never leave this bed again." He pushes into my thigh and it's clear I haven't used *every* drop of him because I can feel he's already thick and hard again.

"Can we leave the bed long enough to take a shower?" I joke, but I'm not hating the idea of staying in bed with him forever.

"Only if we're taking it together." He flips onto his back, stretching his arms over him and resting his head onto the palms of his hands. "Holy shit!" he roars so urgently I sit straight up in concern.

"What? What's the matter?"

"Your bed! It's pink and white stripes!"

"Oh that." I smile and roll on top of him, straddling him. "Is this the first you're noticing, Sherlock?" I kiss along his neck and breathe in his peppermint vanilla, now mixed with sex, scent.

"Yeah. I was a little too preoccupied to notice your Barbie Dream House bedroom before." His sultry eyes are saying everything I want to hear and then he rubs both hands over my breasts and squeezes.

"Mmmph." I roll my hips into him.

"Great idea."

"What, the shower?" I moan as he continues to knead my breasts and pinch my attentive nipples.

"No. You riding me."

Oh my God.

I love the way he uses his words. If I stay around him long enough I may be in a permanent state of orgasm.

"Unfortunately, four o'clock practice. Remember? For now we have to settle for that shower."

"Nooo. Really? Can't we stay here like this all day?" I pout and rock my hips against his thick cock again.

"Oooh fuck, Trace. You're killing me," he groans and I love it. I know he has to go to practice and I wouldn't let him miss it. But the truth is, I'm loving the way he wants me. I love the power I hold over him to make his body shake in pleasure and I'm enjoying teasing him.

"Dak?"

"Trace," he says, squeezing my tits to the point I need to force my brain to focus and my ass to stop wiggling into his hard shaft.

I tilt my head and look straight into his captivating eyes. "Thank you."

"For what, baby?"

"For doing this for me. For helping me."

"For doing this for *you*? Are you kidding me right now? Tracey, I'm the one who should be thanking you. You're the most incredible woman, in every way. You're... perfect. That's it. Perfect." He places one hand around the back of my neck and pulls me down. My breasts press against his hard chest and he crushes his lips into mine. And have I mentioned? This boy can kiss.

"Tell you what, baby doll," he whispers between kisses. "You hold the thought of riding me like a cowgirl until tonight. For now, let's take that shower and I'll worship your sweet pussy until I can't feel my tongue. Okay?"

Um...okay. Yes please.

He didn't lie. After lathering each other with soap and running our hands over every inch of each other's body, Dak pushes me against the cold, wet tiles and drops to his knees in front of me.

"This is where any guy who's with you should be all the time. On his knees in front of you."

I can't speak. I'm so lost in the passion in his eyes.

"Watch me, baby. Watch me adore this sweet pussy."

I can barely breathe. I'm soaked, and not from the shower water.

He drapes one of my legs over his shoulder and licks at me with a hunger that drives me insane. I thread my fingers through his hair and hold on to keep the one leg supporting me from buckling.

He's licking me like he's a starving man and I'm his meal, thrusting his tongue in and out of me.

Oh God.

It's almost too much.

"Dak. I'm...Dak... I'm...I'm going to come." I drop my head back against the tiles and he makes these rapid flicks with his tongue against my clit. "Yes...yes...just like that... yes!" I come so hard, I may be the one suffocating him this time. I can't stop myself from screaming his name again.

He doesn't stop licking me until I stop trembling and I may scream again because the pleasurable sensation is too much for my post orgasm throbbing clit.

"So fucking sweet," he says, standing up. He licks his lips.

When I can feel my legs again I drop to my knees and take his thick cock in my hand. This is the first time I'm seeing him in the light of day and he's even bigger than he appeared last night in the dimmed lighting. "Geez." I tilt my head back and see the most beautiful blue eyes I've ever seen focused on me.

"You certainly know how to stroke a guy's ego, Bambi." He flashes me the sexy grin that had my panties soaked the first time I saw it.

Hmm, that's not all I know how to stroke.

My mind flashes back to Sean and his directives during the act. *"Not like that, Tracey. Do it like this."* I smile at the irony of having this expertise because of that selfish prick.

I'm thankful I'm able to use my skills on a man who doesn't take me for granted, who appreciates me. I run my hand up and down Dak's wet length and he groans and braces his hands on the tile wall behind me. The steam from the hot water swirls around us. Dak towers over me. He's all ripped muscle and rivulets of water are streaming down the valleys of those muscles. He's the most beautiful man I've ever seen.

I lean forward and trace my tongue over every ridge of his cock, licking down to the base and back up, circling the tip. He doesn't take his eyes off me, his gaze both vulnerable and carnal. He groans with every flick of my tongue. I take him in my mouth as far as I can, devouring him like he did me, keeping one hand on his thick base. He's wet silk over iron and he tastes soapy and musky and so good.

I keep working him with my tongue and hand, sliding up and down and around his length. His eyes are closed and I can tell by the strained look of pleasure on his face he's going to come. The power of the control in making him come this way, the vision of him being so turned on by my actions, is almost enough to make me come again with him.

He drops one hand and threads his fingers into my wet hair to hold my head in place—like I would ever let him go right now. I take him in all the way, licking and sucking hard. His moan of my name pushes out from deep within him when he explodes into my mouth. Every muscle continues to shake as he keeps himself braced against the wall with one hand. I keep swallowing and drinking him in until he comes down from the pulsing waves of pleasure.

"Jesus...Bambi. Your mouth," he moans. "I'm ruined."

Chapter Twenty-Six

DAK

I never believed it was based on actual science, but I may be forced to reluctantly agree with those people who claim it's not a good idea to engage in the act of sex, sex involving several mind-blowing, body draining orgasms, before trying to perform some kind of athletic endeavor.

Let's just say I'm not at the top of my game at practice today. Then again, it might not be the marathon of sex we had this afternoon or the fact Trace may've sucked every drop of cum out of me with those luscious lips that's the problem. It may be because I can't think of anything but her.

"Where the fuck's your head today, man?" Dalt snarls as he skids to a stop next to me. "That was the perfect set up and you're gazing off into space, out in lala land somewhere. What the hell happened to you today? Where were you?"

"Had practice with Trace this morning. What's your problem?" I push my mask up off my face.

"Practice. Is that what we're calling it now?' He smirks. "Dude, you know there's no one happier than me you've found someone you're into again, but focus man. We want to go out on a winning season."

"I'm focused. Relax. It's nothing like that." I'm not about to tell him I can't get Trace out of every single one of my thoughts. "We had practice for our skating routine. I'm kind of sore...from all the lifting."

"You're doing what now?" His brow creases in bewilderment. He gives me a sideways glance, like from that angle my words will make more sense.

"I'm doing a skating routine with Trace in the Winter Fest. We need to choreograph and practice it. That's what I was doing today."

Right before we fucked each other's brains out.

"Stop fucking with me, Andersen. No fucking way are you doing a figure skating routine."

Wolfe sprays shaved ice all over our legs when his blades screech to a stop next to us. He spits his mouth guard into his hand and growls, "What the hell are you guys doing over here?"

"Get this." Dalt jabs his stick in my direction. "Andersen claims he's skating in the Winter Fest." He shakes his head in disbelief.

"I didn't know they did hockey demonstrations in the Winter Fest," Wolfe says while using the stick in his hand to readjust his...uh...jock strap.

Batt and Erik pull up next to us in time to hear

Wolfe's comment. "They're doing a hockey demonstration in the Winter Fest this year?" Erik asks.

"No, man. He says he's doing a *figure skating* routine with Trace," Dalt spits out the words, like they taste foul in his mouth.

"Yeah, right. Good one." Batt snorts.

He pats me on the back like I just told him the best joke he's ever heard.

"It's true. I'm doing a pair routine with Trace."

"Get the fuck outta here, bro. You can't do a *figure skating* routine," Wolfe gasps. "You're fucking captain of the hockey team."

"What the hell does that matter?" I push my chest into his to demonstrate I manufacture as much testosterone as he does.

"Wait a minute, Wolfe," Erik interjects. "Just because he's captain of the hockey team doesn't mean he can't figure skate too. They're not mutually exclusive, you know. I mean, can you *figure* skate, dude?" Erik wrinkles his brow in disbelief.

"Yeah, I can. You assholes got a problem with that?"

"No...no...guess not...whatever," the guys all mutter over each other.

"Good. Because when you see how frickin' hot our routine is, you guys are all going to want to find yourselves a partner to do a routine too." I flip my mask back down. I'm done defending this shit. I love these guys, but all their macho bullshit can be a pain in my ass sometimes. This routine is more athletically challenging than most things in my experience. So screw whatever anyone thinks.

"No thanks, bro. I'll stick to doing the horizontal mambo with my partners, if you don't mind." Wolfe shoves his mouth guard back in.

"Excuse me for interrupting, but if you ladies are done having tea over there, would you mind getting the fuck back to practice?" Coach De Luca's voice booms across the ice.

He can be harsh, but he's an awesome coach. He's brought us to more championships than any other Ivy League team in the ECAC. He knows how to get the best out of us and we respect the hell out of him for it.

"Make sure you get tickets, assholes, because it's gonna be fucking lit!" I yell over my shoulder to them, as I skate away.

———

I don't think I ever showered or dressed faster in my life. The only thing on my mind is getting back to Trace's house. Back to her. I crave her like a dying man on a desert craves water.

I don't know what's happening. Technically, we fulfilled what we said we were going to do. She's no longer afraid to be touched by a guy. But the thought of another guy touching her the way I did has my stomach roiling and my muscles clenching. I'm not ready for this to be over between us. She could be, though. Maybe she's ready to go back to being 'friends only.'

The vibration of my phone in my back pocket snaps me out of my deliberation. The text message lights up my screen.

TRACE

> Nikki messaged me. She's having dinner at the TW at 5:30 with some of the people from her football game. She asked me to come. You want to go?

Yes. I definitely want to cum with you. ;D

> You're such a pig :P

So I've been told by the world's most amazing woman.

> Anyone I know? And can that ride you promised me wait 'til after dinner? I'm starving!

Okay, so she's not ready to go back to being just friends either.

When you put it like that I'm not sure it can wait! Might need to take matters into my own hands. ;)

> OMG! Now I can't get that image out of my head.

Good. Hold that thought. See you at the TW in ten minutes.

When I walk into the pub it's not hard to find the table full of grass and mud-stained students. They pushed a few tables together to accommodate the number of people and they're laughing and chattering louder than the music streaming through the bar.

My eyes lock on the only person I want to see. Trace laughs at someone's comment and flips her hair over her shoulder. As I watch her, my heart beats faster against my ribs. The word *mine* runs through my head. The thought makes my pulse beat even stronger against my temples. I don't deserve her.

She glances toward the door and sees me standing there. Her face lights up with an ear-to-ear grin matching the size of my own. She waves to me and I swear to Christ my heart flutters, something I thought only happened to chicks in romance novels. I can now attest to the fact a dude's heart can indeed fucking flutter.

She moves her backpack off the chair next to her so I can sit down. The simple act of having saved the seat next to her for me has my ridiculous heart rippling again. Christ. I'm becoming a Jane Austen character. A *female* Jane Austen character.

I take a seat and I don't even hesitate to lean into Trace and place a kiss on her cheek like it's the most natural thing in the world. Except all the chatter at the table goes quiet and everyone is staring at us, making it seem like the most *unnatural* thing in the world.

"Uh huh!" Nikki shouts. She points her finger and glares at Trace from across the table. "I knew it!"

I snicker under my breath because in that second Nikki reminds me of Hercule Poirot solving the unsolvable mystery.

Trace shifts in her chair. It's obvious she's not loving

this unwanted attention. I place my hand on her thigh to reassure her and her muscles relax.

"So how was the game? Did the girls whip your ass?" I tease the guys from the football and soccer teams seated around the table. The question succeeds in diverting the attention right back to the anecdotes they're sharing about what went down in their touch football game and who was better.

"Our first game's tomorrow. Can you come?" I ask Trace while the others are preoccupied with their stories. I can't explain my overwhelming need for her to come watch me play. Even if I can't see her, I want to know she's in the stands supporting me.

"Sure. I might be a little late though. I got a GA position with one of the Bio professors. There's a late afternoon lab class I'm helping with."

"Okay. Hope you can make it. I really want you there." I regret my last comment almost before it comes out of my mouth. There's a chance she'll think I'm pushing her too hard. Maybe it sounds too much like a boyfriendy thing to say and we promised no messy relationship.

She leans into me and whispers, "Eat fast."

Hmm, I don't think she minds.

Chapter Twenty-Seven

TRACEY

I never inhaled food so fast in my life and I don't think Dak chewed his either. Nikki is still at the pub. The house is all ours again. We fall into the open door barely giving me a chance to remove the key from the lock. Dak's pulling at my clothes and I'm doing the same to his, like we haven't touched each other in weeks. Even though it was only a couple of hours ago we brought each other to several, *orgasmic* orgasms.

I don't know what's happening. The intense level of want is a new experience for me. We're trying to make our way up the stairs while at the same time unzipping clothing and plundering each other's mouths.

When we get to my bedroom, Dak slams the door closed behind us and pushes me against it. He pulls my sweater over my head and tosses it. In a matter of seconds he has my bra off and then he drops to his knees, pulling my shoes off, with my jeans and underwear following in quick succession. Staying on his knees he tugs his own shirt over his head, drops his head back, and scans his hungry eyes over me.

"You're so fucking beautiful," he says in a hushed voice. God. I love the way he makes me feel so cherished. Then he begins to stroke me into ecstasy with his tongue again. I lace my fingers through his hair and hold him against me, greedy with need. When the tease of his tongue has me right on the edge, he stands up.

"Nooo," I groan in frustration.

"Don't worry. Just the warm-up." He steps out of his shoes, jeans, and briefs. His erection springs free and I can't take my eyes off of him as he turns and walks toward the bed.

I'm leaning back against the door trying to catch my breath and regain the use of my wobbly legs, a state I seem to be in ninety percent of the time I'm around him. I take the time to admire every cut groove of muscle in his back and wide shoulders. My gaze drifts down to his ass. The perfect ass. I was right. He has those slight indents on either side caused by the most toned, tight glutes I've ever seen. Not that I spend a lot of time studying booties, though I plan on spending some time studying *that* one.

Dak lies back on the bed, his head resting on a pillow. He hooks his index finger and motions for me. "I believe we had plans for this evening. Bring your sweet pussy over here."

Like a good girl, I do as he asks because I'm more than warmed up. I'm on fire and drenched with need for him. I climb over him and straddle his legs.

"Tracey," he whispers and the intensity in his eyes pierces my heart and makes my legs quiver. He grips my hips. "Ride me, baby. Ride me until you can't think of anything but how good this is. How good we are." The heat coursing through me intensifies. There's nothing slow or careful about the way he's taking me now.

In one afternoon Dak has gotten me past all my apprehensions. Gone are all those anxious restraints. At least with him.

He loosens his grip on my hips and gives all control over to me. Bracing my hands on the hard planes of his stomach I willingly take it, because my need for him is scorching. I lift up and with one quick move he's so deep inside me my groan and Dak's "fuuuck" vibrate the air at the same time.

He's watching me through lust-hazed eyes as I begin to move up and down in slow strokes, clenching around his shaft with every movement.

"It feels so good," I growl.

"That's it, baby. Ride it. It's all yours."

I grind down on his pelvis, feeling him so deep and hard the heat building within me is volatile. He curls toward me and sucks one nipple into his mouth, teasing it with his tongue and teeth, and then moves to my other breast. His lips move over me, kissing and sucking and whispering words I can no longer comprehend.

I move in a faster pace, pulling up and crashing down on him over and over. He matches my rhythm. We're so connected, moving in perfect synchronization. It's all sweat, flesh hitting flesh, and currents of white, hazy heat threatening to combust.

My muscles are trembling so hard I'm no longer in control of my body and Dak tightens his grip on my hips again. I lean back and with a deep thrust he drives into me and we ignite together; our groans a combined rhapsody of pleasure.

I collapse onto him, burying my face in the curve of his neck. He's still inside me; still connected. Neither of us says a word.

No tangled involvement, no feelings, our promise to each other before this all started. I think I might be breaking my promise.

Chapter Twenty-Eight

DAK

> Hey Sleeping Beauty. Get that gorgeous ass out of bed. We're supposed to be at the rink in an hour.

I don't get any response to my text, which I kind of expected. I spent the rest of last night doing the most awesome dirty things I could think of to Trace. And by awesome, I mean by the time we were done we almost couldn't breathe anymore.

I slipped out of her bed a little while ago and deciding she deserved the extra sleep, went home, showered and made us breakfast.

> Come on sweetheart. Up and at em. There's bacon and eggs waiting for you. Opening my windows so you can smell the bacon.

I figure if anything will get her out of bed it's food. Trace loves food.

TRACE

I'm up. Just let me take a quick shower. you slave driver.

No, baby. After last night, I'm your slave to command.

Yeah? I need to think about that. I don't think there's anything left for you to do to me...I mean for me. ;)

That's what you think.

Hmm. I'll be right over. Don't eat all the food!

Our first game is a thing of beauty. Textbook how to play to win. Everything is going right.

The last few seconds of the third period I'm moving from corner to corner behind the goal, setting up for the power play, looking for some open ice. Their defense is putting on the pressure. I pass down the left side to Dalt. He shoots it over to Batt, our right winger, and he passes back to me in the right corner. Dalt manages to split their defenders, leaving himself open. He's ready when I shoot him the puck. Dalt takes the perfect shot on goal and we win 4-2.

Everyone in the arena is going crazy. My only thought is, *I hope Trace is here.* On our way into the locker room I search the bleachers and my eyes find her waving and jumping up and down. The big smile and excitement on her face have me feeling happier than winning the game. I put up five fingers to let her know I'll be out in five minutes and she nods back.

I keep trying to make my way to the locker room. I can't wait to get out of here and be with Trace. People are blocking our way, high-fiving us and congratulating us. You'd think we won the championship rather than the first game.

Next thing I know Bri's in front of me, circling her arms around my neck and kissing me. "That was amazing. You guys destroyed them." She has her lips against my ear so I can hear her over the noise of the crowd.

"Yeah. Thanks. It was a good game." I smile, trying to be polite, but I wish she'd let me get by.

"I have no plans tonight. You want to get together? It's been so long and I'm missing you, Dak." She pouts and bats her lashes at me.

A few weeks ago, she wouldn't need to ask twice. Like I said, Bri knows how to have a good time. But there's only one girl I want to be with, even if we're only going to sit on the sofa and watch GOT episodes.

"No. Sorry, Bri. Got somewhere to go. Thanks for the offer." She doesn't seem to be getting the message. I put my arm around her waist and pry her off of me and keep walking into the locker room.

The level of the adrenaline rush in the locker room is at Defcon 5. "Hey man. We're going out for a few brews to celebrate. You comin'?" Dalt yells over to me.

"Nah man. Got plans!" I yell back while stripping off my gear.

"Oh yeah. I saw sweet Sabrina hanging all over you." He smirks.

"No, dude. Not with Bri." I peel the sweat-drenched pads off. When I look up Dalt is standing right next to me.

"Shit, man. You really got it bad for this chick, huh?"

"No. We're just friends. Yeah, maybe. I don't know," I ramble because I *don't* know. I don't know what's going on.

I made promises to Trace, promises I thought would be no problem for me to keep. Except, now I'm feeling things I'm not supposed to be feeling. I opened a door I thought was chained and padlocked and I'm not sure I can close it again, or if I even want to.

"Shit. You're so fucked. I hope you know what you're doing, dude," Dalt adds.

I hope I do too.

Chapter Twenty-Nine

TRACEY

I slam the door so hard behind me it rattles the walls.

"Wow. What's with you?" Nikki glances over at me before dropping her gaze right back to the screen of her phone. She's sprawled on the sofa. When I don't answer she glances back over to me. "What's going on? I thought you would be out celebrating with the hockey god."

I heave a big sigh. I thought Dak was telling me to wait for him when he saw me in the bleachers, but maybe he was only waving hello. We didn't make any plans for tonight. He asked me to come to the game. Nothing more.

I have no right to be upset. We set up the terms of what we were doing before we hooked up and we both agreed to those terms. We never said it was exclusive. Besides, Dak said he would help me and he did. He's free to see whoever he wants. So why am I feeling sick to my stomach thinking about him and Bri.

"Uh oh. What did the douchecanoe do?" Nikki sits up and puts her phone down on the coffee table.

"Nothing. He didn't do anything." I'm trying to sound indifferent, but I can't keep my voice from shaking. I walk through to the kitchen. I could use a beer...or ten, but I settle for water.

"Don't tell me nothing happened. Yesterday you were all bubbly, whispering and giggling with the superhero, and tonight you look like someone stole your puppy. What's up?" Nikki is standing in the doorway of the kitchen, her hands on her hips. Such a perceptive, persistent little thing. Good friends can be such a pain in the ass.

Before I can answer there's a knock at the door. "I'll be right back, and then you're going to tell me how badly I need to kick that boy's ass."

I smile at her threat and the thought of her trying to beat the crap out of Dak to protect me. Truth is, the way she's ripped, she might be able to hold her own against the jackass. I hear Nikki's irritated voice coming from the living room and there's no mistaking who it is she's talking to.

"Hey, Bambi. Where did you go? I thought you were going to wait for me. And what's up with Nikki? Did she run into Dalt tonight or something?" Dak crosses the room and leans in to kiss me. I turn toward the counter before his lips touch me.

"What's up, babe? I thought we could go over to the Blue Goose and grab a beer with some people to celebrate. Want to go?" He presses into me, moving my hair back and brushing kisses along my neck. Dammit. I can't keep myself from trembling at the touch of his lips on my skin.

"Um...no...I..." I move away from him because I can't think while he's this close and kissing me.

"It's cool. Want to hang out here and watch more episodes of GOT?"

"You don't have to. You can go celebrate with...with whoever you want to." I suck in my lip and bite down because dammit, I am not going to cry. It's ridiculous. I hold no claim to Dak. We're friends. Friends with bone-melting benefits.

"Oh...okay. I thought...nah it's cool. I guess we accomplished what we said we were going to. You're all good now so..." Although I'm expecting his usual cockiness, there's no mistaking the disappointed tone in his voice as he turns to leave.

"I saw you with Bri. You had your arm around her waist and you were kissing her."

If we're going to remain friends, even though being *just* friends now is going to be extremely difficult, if not impossible, at least for me, we need to be honest with each other.

"What are you talking about?" He closes his eyes and shakes his head like he's trying to make sense of my words.

"I *saw* you with Bri after the game. She was all over you. It's...it's fine, you can be with whoever you want. We were only...we never said—"

He closes the distance between us before I even

realize he's moved. Cupping both sides of my face with his hands, he crashes his lips onto mine. "Listen to me," he says, his lips touching mine. "I don't want Bri or anyone. Let's get one thing straight. While we're doing this, if you still want to do this...whatever it is we're doing, there can't be anybody else. It's just you and me, while it lasts. Agreed?"

"Uh, agreed." I try to nod, but he's holding my head between his hands.

"So, you want to keep doing this?" he asks, his eyes piercing straight into my soul.

"Yeah, sure." My words don't match the level of certainty of how much I want him. "But when it's done, if one of us wants to move on, we'll tell the other one before we hook up with anyone else. Agreed?"

"Agreed."

"And no messy feelings or falling in love. Right?" I ask.

Tell me I'm crazy. Tell me we can't go back from all the feelings we've already unleashed.

"Uh...right. Sure. That was the deal." He lets go of me and runs his hand through his hair. "You know me, Bambi."

"Yeah. Me too." I give him a forced smile because I *do* know him. And I wasn't supposed to be feeling any of this for him.

Chapter Thirty

DAK

The weeks are flying by. My schedule is gruesome, keeping up with classes, games and practice, both for hockey and the Winter Fest.

The team is killing it though. We can't do anything wrong. Every pass goes right where we want it. Wolfe is like a cement wall at goal and nothing gets past him. With only one loss, it looks like we're on our way to another championship, maybe even another seed in the Frozen Four.

Trace and I are rocking our skating routine too. We're on the ice every morning at five and in each other's arms every night. In between, we do our research together, study together, and hang out, going to lunch or dinner, or the movies or watching our favorite shows. There's a couple of shows besides *GOT* we never miss, like *Vikings*, and I turned her on to *Outlander*.

She likes those reality shows like *Crazy Ass House-*

wives or whatever it's called, and I can't stand that shit. So we compromise; I watch some of that crap with her and she watches *The Walking Dead* with me. I think Lisa is the biggest crazy bitch on her show, but she thinks it's Dorit. She says Daryl is the main alpha hero on *TWD*. No way, it's Carol. We agree to disagree. Life is good. She's even agreed to come to my parents' cabin with me for Thanksgiving because her parents can't come up for the holiday this year.

The truth is, I can't remember a time when she wasn't a part of my life or what it was like without her in my life and I don't want to. If I lost her now it would be like losing one of my limbs. But I don't know if she's feeling the same way.

We haven't discussed what this is going on with us. I'm afraid to verbalize it, afraid to say it out loud or I might ruin it. I came close to letting the l-word slip from my lips a couple of times when we were in the middle of making love. Yeah. It's gone way beyond fucking. I swallowed the tender words before they came out because I don't want to scare her away.

Even now, sprawled on the ice after taking a fall together when attempting a new side-by-side jump, we're giggling and rolling into each other's arms like two puppies in love.

"You totally tripped me, Bambi."

"I don't think so, *jackass*. You moved in the wrong direction." She sniggles and throws some loose ice at my face.

It's reminiscent of the time we collided the first day we saw each other. Instead of snarling at her like I did that day, I roll over on top of her and press my lips to hers.

"Wow. Someone's ready to quit for the day." She runs her hand along the hard ridge inside my pants. Even though we're lying on cold ice, when I'm near her I'm in a constant state of heated rock hard pressure.

"We better leave before we melt the ice," I tease and nip at her lip while grinding my hard shaft into her leg.

"Mmm, yeah. I love Saturday mornings. We can go back to my place and you can make me breakfast. I could go for French toast."

"French toast? Not what I had in mind to eat." I waggle my eyebrows.

"Tell you what, Andersen," she says and pushes me off of her and stands up. "I'll challenge you. If I win, you make me French toast." She extends her hand to help me up.

"What if *I* win?" I grip her hand, pull myself up, and stand in front of her, nose to nose.

"If you win I'll give you *whatever* you want to eat." She flutters her lashes. Christ. My dick sat up and begged.

"You're on, Hayward. What's the challenge?" I slide away from her before I act on the urge to drop her skating pants and start licking her right on the spot.

"One on one. Whoever scores the first goal wins." She gives me a devilish grin and does a scratch spin.

"Are you sure? You're totally going to lose. Or is that what you had in mind?" I arch a brow.

"We'll see, jackass. Go get hockey sticks and a puck because I can already taste that delicious French toast."

"You ready, sweetheart?"

She looks so fucking adorable, her knees bent, hockey stick in hand, focusing intently on the puck between us and then on my face.

"Oh I'm ready, *sweetheart*. Let's go."

I figure I'll be a gentleman and go easy on her, give her the first go at the puck. Big mistake. She skillfully slides it from her forehand to her backhand and then back to her forehand. I'm awestruck by her control. When I come back to my senses, I'm sure she's going to go for open ice. I move toward the puck and she swipes it across to her backhand again. Holy fuck! She totally fakes me out with the 1-2-3 deke, skates up to the goal, and flicks it into the back of the net.

"I'll warm up the car while you're putting the equipment away." She smirks and flips her ponytail back.

"What the hell, Bambi? Where'd you learn to play hockey like that?"

"Oh, didn't I mention I was on an All-State hockey team when I was in high school?" she says as she glides off the ice.

"Uh, no. No you didn't mention that," I call after her. I should have guessed it with a dad like Duke Hayward. Damn. She totally hustled me.

No problem, though, because I have a feeling when we get back to her house we're *both* going to get our rewards.

Chapter Thirty-One

TRACEY

I'm nervous about meeting Dak's parents. I don't know what he's told them about me, how he's explained our relationship. I'm not exactly sure we even *know* how to define our relationship. Beyond saying it was exclusive for as long as our sexcapades last, he's never called me his girlfriend. I never used the word boyfriend when referring to him either. He made it more than clear he doesn't do girlfriends, so I don't want to send him running if I use the word.

It's the reason why I didn't initially accept his invitation to his parents' cabin. We're just friends. Fuck buddy friends. I didn't think it was my place to impose on his family Thanksgiving. My parents weren't coming up for the holiday and I had decided to stay at school and get some work done on the long weekend. Dak kept insisting he wasn't going to leave me alone for four whole days, like it was an eternity.

I remained reluctant until he enticed me with his mom's homemade sweet potatoes, cranberry sauce, and stuffing. It was an offer I couldn't refuse.

"Just a heads up, my parents are going to be all over you," Dak says, keeping his eyes fixed on the road ahead. It's about a three-hour drive to Newry and the further west we go the higher the snow piles on the sides of the road get.

"What does that mean?"

"They're pretty psyched I'm bringing a girl home. Especially my mom." He chuckles. "And when they meet my girl, they're going to flip out even more."

His girl?

He slides his hand along my leg and a familiar jolt of pleasure stirs between my thighs.

"You've never brought a girl home before?" I'm surprised he never took Abbey home, but I don't want to mention her name and get him thinking about all that again.

"Only in high school when I had parties at my house or something. Just a bunch of people. Never anyone special."

Does that mean he thinks I'm someone special? He glances over and gives me the grin that makes me want to demand he pull over so I can straddle him right here in the car.

I'm thrilled he considers me a special enough friend to bring home to meet his family, but now I'm even more nervous I won't live up to their expectations.

"Holy shit! This is *not* a cabin!"

When we pull up to the enormous structure, the ground to roof windows which cover the entire front of the home are glowing from the interior lights. Although there are wood logs and stone pillars between the gigantic windows, this is not the cozy *log* cabin I was expecting. This thing appears to be about seven thousand square feet and the type of "cabin" you find listed in the homes of the rich and famous registry. I've seen my fair share of estate-size houses both in the Hamptons and Newport, but when you're expecting a 'cabin' this can be a little intimidating.

"Yeah it is. It's made out of logs."

"Yeah. Millions of them. It must've taken a whole forest to build this."

Dak jumps out of the car and comes around to open my door. "Come on, Bambi. You're going to love my parents. They're awesome." He opens the back door and gets our bags. "My sister's kind of a pain in the ass. It's a package deal though. Nothing I can do about her," he adds with a smile.

When we get to the massive, double-arched wood doors, they swing open before we even knock. A petite woman with braids down to her waist flies out the door and throws her arms around Dak's neck.

"My baby boy! Finally. I thought you would never get here." It's easy to see where Dak got his drop dead gorgeous looks. His mom has the same sun-streaked caramel color hair, intense blue eyes, and full lips.

"Mom," Dak laughs, trying to get a word in as she showers his face with kisses, "I sent you a text when we left. We made it in exactly three hours, which is record time." He struggles to hold on to our bags while his mom continues to squeeze him.

"Come on, Sea. How about you wait until the boy gets inside before you suffocate him? How do you do? I'm Dak's dad, Steve." He takes one of the bags from Dak and holds out his other hand to me.

Wait. I might need to revise that. Although the tall, handsome man in the doorway has raven black hair, except for the touches of gray around the temples—he has the same ocean blue eyes and gorgeous chiseled features as Dak. Now I see where Dak gets his impressive athletic body structure. His dad's head almost skims the top of the doorway and he appears to be in great shape for a man of forty-something.

"Hi. I'm Tracey." I shake his hand.

"Oh, Tracey. I'm so sorry." His mom lets go of Dak and envelops me in a big hug and I notice her intoxicating scent. "I'm so happy you decided to spend Thanksgiving with us. I'm Season, Dak's..." she stops midsentence and takes a big inhale and then holds me at arm's length. "Eden's Garden!" she exclaims.

"Yes. How did you know?"

"Aphrodisiac." She grins and points to herself. "It drives Steven crazy." She puts her arm around my shoulders while walking me into the house, leaving Dak and his dad on the porch. The delicious aromas filling the house are exactly what a holiday house should smell like: cinnamon, apples, cranberries.

"I'd say that's...um...let me see, lemon, sweet orange, and a touch of coconut. Am I right?" Season says, focusing on my scent instead of the mouthwatering aromas of the house.

"Yes. That's amazing. Sometimes I add a little pineapple. How did you guess with one sniff?"

"Oh I'm an Eden's Garden girl from way back." She winks. "It's how I hooked Steven."

"What the hell are they talking about, Dad?" Dak asks as he and his dad walk into the house behind us.

"I think they're talking about essential oils." His dad chuckles. "Your mom swears that's how she got me to fall in love with her. Even though I keep telling her I was head over heels in love before I even got close enough to smell her damn oils."

"Uh huh. Sure you were, Steven. Take the bags up to your room, Dakota. Your bed is big enough for two." She winks at me again. "Tell me sweetheart, does your scent drive my baby boy crazy with lust?" Season keeps her arm around my shoulders as she walks me into the enormous open living room expanse of their home. I giggle at her question and can't keep the pink blush from warming my face at her personal inquiry.

"Jesus Christ, Mom! Give me a break!" Dak shrieks from behind us.

"Oh stop it, Dakota. I can already see it all over you two. There's no denying sexual magnetism."

"Oh for fuck sakes, Mom!"

"Language, Dakota. Have a seat, Tracey." Season directs me to the huge cream-colored, curved sectional sofa. "I'll be right back. There's some mulled cider on the stove."

"What? You can talk about doing it but I can't say

the word out loud?" Dak shakes his head, protesting his mother's comments.

"Only if it's used in a romantic connotation, not in a vulgar one," his mom says in a flippant tone and walks into the kitchen.

"Forget it, son," his father calls out as Dak runs up the curved staircase with our bags. "You know your mom. There's no filter when it comes to sex and love." He smiles and sits in one of the matching recliner chairs in front of a floor to ceiling stone fireplace.

The firebox is so gigantic I could walk into it, and the burning logs are the size of small trees. I force my mouth from gaping open as I take in the rest of the room. The ceiling is crossed with hand-hewn trussed logs. The wide plank pine floors are buffed to a high gloss finish and the exposed logs, which make up some of the walls, match the natural cherry wood planks and logs across the ceiling. A shiny black grand piano takes up one corner of the room.

The house has an open layout. The large living room opens to a dining area, a game room, and the kitchen. The glass windows and doors which make up the whole back wall of the open layout look out over a patio with an outdoor fireplace and the nearby river.

The lights of the ski lift at Sunday River Resort are twinkling in the distance. Dak pointed it out to me on our drive in. He said their "cabin" sits at the foot of the mountain range, and if there's time, he'll take me snowboarding. I spent many winters on skis in Aspen, but never on a snowboard. Therefore, when I challenge him to a race it'll be me on skis him on a board. Ever since I deked him, we've gotten into this habit of daring each other with challenges. Too bad it's going to frustrate him again when I get to the bottom of the hill first if we get to race.

His mom comes from the kitchen with a tray full of steaming mugs of cider. "I added some spiced rum. I hope that's okay," she says, placing the tray on the round ottoman in front of the sofa. Actually, it's more like a small table at about five feet across.

Dak comes back in the room and walks over to the fireplace. He picks up an iron tool from the rack on the mantel and pokes at the fire. He almost doesn't get a chance to replace the poker before an absolutely breathtaking teenage girl comes running down the staircase and throws herself at him.

"Hey, doofus. You made it." She has the same jet black hair as Dak's dad. Wow. I'm assuming this is Dak's sister and if so, their parents should have had lots more babies because the combination of their DNA made gorgeous offspring.

"Hey, brat." Dak smiles, lifting her off the floor in a big hug.

"So this is the girlfriend. Hi, I'm Heaven, the big jerk's sister," she says, turning to me.

Girlfriend? Did Dak tell them I was his girlfriend?

"Trace, this is my pain in the ass sister I was telling you about."

"Suck it, Dakota." She grins while coming over to shake my hand.

"Steven, we have to do something about the language of these two hoodlums we've raised." Season makes a faux tsking in disapproval sound, yet smiling at the antics of her children.

"Don't look at me. You were the one who insisted on the 'lenient parenting' thing so they could become 'strong, independent' adults." Steven laughs, air quoting around the words lenient parenting and strong and independent.

"You know you should've spanked me when I made bad choices." Season sits on Steven's lap, whispers something in his ear, and I could swear Dak's dad growls.

"Jee-sus." Both Dak and Heaven groan.

"Gross. Get. A. Room." Heaven adds in disgust. I can't keep from giggling, because I think it's adorable how in love their parents are and how open they are about their feelings.

"Heaven. What a beautiful name," I comment, trying to change the subject and alleviate Dak and Heaven's obvious discomfort from their parents frisky open display.

"Heaven-ly." Dak says, plopping down on the sofa next to me.

Heaven stomps her foot. "Shut the fuck up, Dakota!"

"Heaven!" her mom gasps.

"Excuse me? What's happening right now?' I'm confused about why Heaven is so angry Dak called her heavenly.

"Her full name is Heaven Lee Andersen." Dak throws his head back and lets out a big snorting belly laugh.

"Dad, tell him to shut up." Heaven crosses her arms over her chest and pouts.

"Sorry, sweetheart. Another bad choice I should've spanked your mom for, but she was in the throes of childbirth and she chose the moment to get me to promise to let her give you the name. Afterward I couldn't—"

"Yeah, yeah, I know. You couldn't go back on a promise," Heaven drawls in revulsion and flops down on the other recliner.

"It's a beautiful name. Unique. Just like my beautiful, unique baby girl," Season offers without apology.

I'm so glad I agreed to come with Dak. I'm in love with his family almost as much as I'm falling in love with him.

Chapter Thirty-Two

DAK

Except for the way Trace beat me in a race at Sunday River, Thanksgiving was awesome. My parents loved her, like I knew they would. Trace and Heaven became best of friends in the few days we were there. I think the way she smoked me on the ski slope made Heaven adore her even more.

We decided to leave Saturday, giving us Sunday to practice our routine a few extra hours. The festival is in three weeks and our routine to the mashup of "You Matter to Me" and "Distance" is jam packed. We've put in lots of fancy choreographed steps, several lifts, side by side double Lutzes, a throw double axel, death spiral, and combinations of a variety of side by side sit spins. It's demanding, but we decided to go big or go home. I'm a little nervous about taking on such an experienced routine. We've practiced enough, though. I know we'll nail it.

The chemistry between us as we skate in front of the filled to capacity arena is enough to cause the ice to steam. We're so in tune with each other, every move is in perfect synchronization and our routine is flawless.

When we complete our last spin and I end on one knee with Trace draped back over my leg, I can't resist bending my head down and brushing my lips across hers. Lost in the adrenaline rush and my intense feelings for her, I almost forgot there are a few thousand people watching us. When the crowd stands and goes wild, clapping and cheering, and I hear the loud whistles of my teammates in the front row seats, I'm reminded of their presence.

Trace beams from ear to ear, her eyes filling with tears of joy. My chest is ready to explode with pride. I'm so thrilled I was a part of making her this happy.

The audience is yelling for us to do an encore.

"Let's do it baby," I say into Trace's ear so she can hear me over the crowd.

"But we haven't even practiced it," Trace objects, but I can tell by the adventurous gleam in her eye she's considering it.

"We've messed around with the Steffanina choreography we watched on YouTube a few times. We can pull it off. Besides it's the song that was playing the first time you came to my house for the party. Remember? I'm going to use every emotion I was feeling when I locked eyes with you across the room. Let's show 'em how it's done."

I stand, pulling her up with me. I gesture to the guy up in the window of the AV room overlooking the ice. He's a friend of mine and I talked to him before the show. I told him if the routine went as well as I thought it was going to, we were going to do another more upbeat routine and for him to be ready with the music.

When I give the guy the signal, the crowd comes to a hush until the first notes of "Shape Of You" fill the arena and the audience is on their feet again screaming their approval.

We get right into the chorography we practiced from the dance tutorial. We tweaked it to make it work on skates. Since the moves are all on lyrics the body rolls, stanky legs and controlled arm movements were fairly easy to incorporate.

The audience is so into it we almost can't hear the music. When the last notes blast through the arena, Trace and I hit our final pops, ending in each other's arms, and everyone in the Bernard Arena goes crazy.

"We just blasted figure skating at Bernard into the twenty-second century, baby girl!" I yell into Trace's ear while lifting her off her skates and spinning us around. She has her arms around my neck and her head tucked into the space under my chin. It's her favorite spot on my body. Uh, other than the one between my legs, that is. She says it's the place she feels safest.

"Let's get out of here and celebrate," she says.

"You don't want to wait for the final bows?"

She shakes her head and I'm loving the heat in her eyes. "Okay. I'll meet you back at your house."

We drove over in separate cars because Trace had last minute GA work to do.

I try to drive at a safe speed to get back to my place to take a quick shower. I know I'm breaking speed limits for campus streets. Can't help it. Tonight's the night I'm going for it.

I'm going to tell her everything, not holding anything back. I need to tell her I'm in love with her. She has to know what she means to me and that I don't want this thing between us to ever end. I think she's feeling the same things and it's time we say it.

When I pull in my driveway, Trace's car is already in her driveway.

Damn. The girl always manages to beat me at everything.

I almost can't squeeze my car between all the cars parked on our street to get into my driveway. It's Friday night and the streets are filled with people taking part in all the festivities going on during Winter Fest.

I rush into the house and head up the stairs to my room, stripping my clothes off as I go. All I can think about is getting over to Trace's with the bottle of champagne chilling in the fridge. I bought it earlier today with plans to help set the mood and start our celebration.

After I peel off all my clothes, I stretch back on my bed for a second to try to get my thoughts straight and think about everything I want to say to her.

"Hey, Dak. Your routine was impressive. It got me so hot for you. I had to come over and show you." Bri climbs on top of me and she's completely naked except for a string of cloth posing as underwear.

"Bri, what the fuck? What are you doing here?"

"I'd already skated so I left right after your routine. I've been waiting for you. I used your bathroom to freshen up and get ready." She bends over and hangs her tits in my face. When she starts rocking her hips into my cock, I grab her waist to stop her and pull her off me.

Next thing I know I hear a gasp coming from the doorway. When Bri turns because she hears it too, I'm able to see the doorway and Trace standing in it with her hand over her mouth, her eyes brimming with tears.

"Do you mind?" Bri hisses at Trace. "We're kind of busy here."

"Get the fuck off me." I push Bri to the side. "Tracey, it's not what you think."

When I stand up and Trace sees me standing there stark naked, she takes one more glance at Bri and back to me. Bri's lying across my bed, propped up on her elbows, her mouth pursed in a smug grin.

"No... how...how could you?" Her eyes are conveying all the heartbreak I know she's feeling. I can almost hear her heart shattering. Even though it's a misunderstanding, I'm destroyed knowing I put that pain into those beautiful eyes.

"Trace, please." When I walk toward her, she bolts back down the stairs and out of the house. I start after her, then remember I'm naked. Grabbing my jeans, I try to pull them up while chasing after her and trip over the legs.

Fuuuck.

Chapter Thirty-Three

TRACEY

I fly into the house, slamming the door behind me again.

"Hey! You guys were spec—"

I don't stop when Nikki greets me. I run up the stairs and collapse on to my bed.

I don't even try to hold back the flood of tears. How could he? After everything, how could he? My heart feels like it's cracking open. This can't be happening again, not with Dak.

"Oh shit. What did the asshole do now?" Nikki is standing in my doorway shaking her head.

"Nikki, how could he?" I sob. Before she can say another word, a loud knock rattles the front door.

"Don't...l-let...h-him in," I hiccup between the sputtered words. I will not let this break me again. "I don't want to see him, *ever*." My heartbreak quickly morphs to anger.

Another knock, even louder and more frenzied, shakes the door.

"I got this," Nikki says and heads down the stairs.

"What did you do, asshole?" she snarls when she opens the door.

"Nothing, Nikki. It's a misunderstanding. Let me in." Dak's demanding voice floats up the stairs and my heart clenches in pain.

"A misunderstanding. Yeah, I heard that one before. No way, hockey boy. She doesn't want to see you."

"Nikki, I swear to God if you don't move out of the way I'm going to—"

"You're going to what? Come on, douchebag. Let's go. I've been dying to kick the shit out of one of you hockey sluts for a while now."

"Come on, Nikki. Let me in. I need to see her. I need to tell her...something." I can hear the anguished plea in Dak's voice. It almost makes my traitorous body want to run down the stairs and throw itself into his arms.

After everything he said about it being just him and me, he didn't even have the decency to tell me our time together was over before going back to Bri. And why would he end it exactly the same way Sean did, on this night of all nights? How could he be so cruel? Maybe he's been seeing Bri all along. Just one big lie...again.

"Go away, Dak. She doesn't want to see you," Nikki tells him again.

"But we're supposed to go to Newport for Christmas break tomorrow," Dak insists.

Shit. I forgot about that. My parents were looking forward to meeting Dak. I don't know how I'm going to explain to them I did it again, allowed another lying, deceptive, snake into my heart. My mom will want to move in here to watch over me 24/7 after she finds out I made the same stupid mistakes.

"You should've thought about that before you did whatever the fuck you did. Goodbye, Dakota." My heart slams against my ribs when I hear the front door slam closed.

"Merry Christmas," I whisper.

DAK

I fucked up big time. I know it wasn't my fault Bri ambushed me in my room. What *was* my fault was not telling Trace how much I love her before it happened. If she knew how I feel she might've given me a chance to explain. I should have told her she's my sunrise, my sunset, my air, my water. She's become my universe. Now she won't even take my calls.

I texted her about a thousand times over Christmas break with no response. I can't even believe she was ever mine to lose, but I miss her so much my heart hurts. How do I breathe without my air or survive without my sunshine?

"Dakota, open the door, honey."

"It's open, Mom. You can come in." I'm stretched out on my bed staring at the ceiling when my mom sits on the edge of the bed next to me.

"Why don't you come down and eat something, sweetheart? You've been in this room all week. Todd called. They're going to Sunday River tomorrow. He thought you might like to go." She brushes the hair out of my eyes the way she used to when I was little. "Heaven's going. You should go and make sure she doesn't get into any trouble. You know your sister." She chuckles. I know she's trying to make me feel better, but I can't think about going to the slopes. The last time I was there I was with Trace. God, I miss her.

"I don't think so, Mom. I'm not in the mood for snowboarding."

"Dak?"

"Yeah, Mom?"

"What happened between you and Tracey?"

"Mom, I don't want to talk about it."

"Okay, but...are you in love with her?"

"*Mom.*"

"Fine. We don't have to talk about it. All I'm going to say is, if you love her...truly love her...don't lose her. Fight for her, baby. I saw the way she looked at you when she was here. The girl is head over heels, as your dad would say. And we were so thrilled to see you smiling and happy again. Don't give up on her." She stands and gives me a kiss on the cheek.

"Mom?" I call to her before she leaves.

"Yes, sweetheart?"

"Thanks."

"Follow your heart, baby boy." She smiles and closes the door behind her.

Follow my heart. Fight for her. How, if she won't talk to me or take a call from me? I know Mom's right, though. I may be able to live without Trace in my life, but I don't want to. I need to get her back.

Chapter Thirty-Four

TRACEY

This may be the first Christmas ever I'm looking forward to getting back to classes. Having nothing to do over the break, I can't stop thinking about Dak. I miss him so much. Even though he crushed my heart in almost the same way Sean did. I can't help thinking it must be me. Beyond having the faulty ability to choose the right guy, what's wrong with me that I'm not enough for the man I love?

Sitting on our front porch in Newport, taking in the view of the churning ocean, the thoughts of Dak swirl through my head like the lacy snowflakes swirling through the air.

Dak would love this. I wonder what Dak's doing now? I wonder if Dak is with Bri?

It's crazy how he became such a big part of my life in such a short time. Ugh. How did I let this happen? What happened to my Snow White plans?

"Hey, honey. Sloane and I are headed out to a spinning class. Why don't you come with us?"

My family has fawned all over me the whole break because after telling them about Dak, they're certain I'm going to slip back into self-destructive mode. I keep telling them they don't need to worry, because that's never going to happen again. I'm a different person than I was a few years ago.

I'm all grown up and realize how valuable my life is with everything going for me and a bright future. I'm my own woman. I don't need a guy to complete me. Yada, yada, yada. All the right platitudes keep swimming around in my head. I shouldn't be flippant, because they're more than platitudes. They're my truths now. Nevertheless, I'm aching for Dak. I fell in love with him, and even though he crushed me with his dishonesty, I can't just turn it off. But I know I need to. It's the reason I deleted all his texts without reading them and haven't answered any of his calls.

"No thanks, Mom. I promised Dad we could play a one on one on the pond."

And I do not have the energy to keep up with you and Sloane in your spinning competition.

"Okay, sweetie. See you in a bit. Don't forget we're going into town tonight for a nice dinner before you leave for school tomorrow. Make sure you take a shower and comb your hair." She bends and gives me a kiss on the cheek.

"I will, Mom. Don't worry."

Um, I *might* have let myself go a little since coming

home. Everything will be okay, though. I'll get it together and be fine...eventually.

You've *got* to be fucking kidding me.

When I pull into my driveway on the Saturday before classes start again, I can't miss the white sheet hanging across Dak's front porch. The huge black letters on it read, *"Sweet babe, in thy face soft desires I can **TRACE**."*

He's ridiculous. So why are there butterflies flitting around my insides?

"OMG, girl! He's quoting William Blake for you! Be still my heart!" Alex squeals when I walk through the door.

"Hmmph. How do you know it's not there for Bri?"

"Bri? Oh please. Who would woo Bri with poetry when she'd open her legs for a Chai Latte or even a plain old coffee for that matter?"

He's bad, but I can't keep from smiling.

"Hey, girl. We missed you," Nikki calls from the kitchen. "I'm making dinner. You hungry?" She comes in the living room and we say hello with a shared hug.

"Starving, as usual."

"Hey sorry about that." She flicks her chin toward Dak's house. "Dak kept bugging me, asking me if I had talked to you and when you were coming back. I finally caved and told him you would be back today and they hung the sheet thing this morning."

"They?"

"Yeah. I couple of the other he-men over there helped him,' Alex chimes in. "It's not like I was spying on them or anything. I *happened* to be in the kitchen when they were hanging it. I saw them through the window, stretching up to reach the top of the porch and flashing all those lovely, chiseled abs." Alex sighs and waves his hand in front of his face.

"Well it's ridiculous and he needs to take it down," I say in an annoyed tone.

He's quoting poetry for me?

The butterflies in my stomach swoon again. No. I'm too easy. He was fucking Bri, or about to!

"I don't know. The boy has it ba-ad for you. He's moping all over campus, ambushing Nikki and me every time he sees us to ask about you. He's a mess."

"Oh boo fucking hoo," Nikki grumbles. "He deserves it for what he did. Let's eat and change the subject."

"Yeah. Let's change the subject before I lose my appetite," I suggest.

"Come on. There's nothing that could make *you* lose your appetite," Nikki teases.

No, only the hollow in my heart from missing Dak so much.

Chapter Thirty-Five

DAK

We don't have any classes together this semester so I don't see Trace every day on campus. I catch glimpses of her every once in a while around campus or getting in and out of her car. She won't even look at me.

The team won the ECAC championship, which means we'll get the automatic bid for the Frozen Four. The guys are celebrating like crazy. I can't get into it. Nothing seems worth celebrating without Trace. I miss her laughter, her enthusiasm, her exuberance about everything, and yeah, I miss her body too. I even miss the way she beats me at everything. I just miss *her*.

It's been a month since Christmas break. The guys are sick of seeing me mope around all moony over her. Wolfe told me to, and I quote, "Stop acting like a girl. Go over there, throw her over your shoulder, carry her back here, and fuck her brains out." He's a fucking caveman.

When I explained to him forcing myself on her could be considered rape he said, "Nah. The chick is totally in love with you, dude. You just need to remind her."

Caveman, like I said.

I had a long talk with him about respecting women and their space and *not* going to jail. He shook his head and said, "Obviously, asshole. I didn't mean you should force yourself on her. That's disgusting. I'd beat the shit out of you if you did. I meant you should remind her how much she wants you and misses you. There won't be any forcing involved."

Anyway, they all agreed to help me with my Win Trace Back Project. Since she won't take my calls and I don't know if she's even reading my texts, I came up with the idea of the sheets, using some word play on her name. It's fucking brilliant. She can't miss those.

Every few days we hang another one. After Blake I followed up on Tuesday with, *Beauty is a precious* ***TRACE*** *that eternity causes to appear to us and that it takes away from us,* by Ionessco. On Friday it was, *When I* ***TRACE*** *at my pleasure the windings to and fro of the heavenly bodies I no longer touch Earth with my feet: I stand in the presence of Zeus himself,* by Ptolemy.

Thank goodness my crazy hippie chick mom made me read poetry and philosophy and shit when I was younger. She said it would help me grow into a more "sensitive" man all the ladies would love. That's all she needed to say to convince me.

This week I dipped into my music titles. First with, *Lost without a* ***TRACE,*** by North Road. Today we hung up *Without a* ***TRACE*** *of Doubt in My Mind,* by The

Monkees. You never know where inspiration is going to come from.

It's Friday and the guys are setting up for our weekly party. I'm hanging in my room, trying to study. My mind keeps drifting back to Trace. If I can't get her to soften up and talk to me using poetry what the fuck am I going to do?

The front door opening with a crash against the wall behind it blasts me out of my thoughts. And then I hear the voice I've waited to hear for over a month.

"Where is he?" she demands. Hmm, her voice isn't exactly soft, but at least she's here.

"Tracey!" the guys shout. "Thank fuck." Wolfe's version of a prayer.

"He's in his room," Dalt answers in a shaky voice. It's incredible how that adorable girl can scare the crap out of those big macho cavemen. I think about going down to her, but decide it's better if we talk alone in my room, so I wait for her to come up.

"Is he alone?" she snarls in her cute as fuck angry voice.

"Of course he's alone. Haven't been able to get him to *look* at another chick since you," Wolfe grumbles.

"Not that we *tried* to get him to look at another chick," Batt quickly adds.

I swear to Christ those guys are afraid of her. I chuckle to myself.

When I hear Trace stomping up the steps, I go back to reading my notes and pretend I didn't hear their conversation.

"You." She points a finger at me. "You need to stop this craziness right now."

The fiery little girl standing in my doorway reprimanding me is the cutest damn sight I've ever seen. I want to run to her and wrap my arms around her and never let her go, but I don't want to scare her away before we get a chance to talk.

"Hey, Trace. I missed you." I stand up, but don't take a step toward her.

"I...I missed you too." Her voice softens and she starts biting on her bottom lip.

"Can we talk?"

"First, promise me you're going to stop putting up those ridiculous sheets. People are starting to give me nicknames like sheet girl and poetry girl."

"I heard someone call you Trasheet Hayward the other day. Thought it was pretty clever."

"Dak!"

"Okay, okay. I promise."

"Okay then." She's shifting back and forth on her feet like she's nervous. "So talk."

"Why don't you close the door and have a seat?"

"I'll sit, but the door stays open." She plops herself down on the edge of my bed.

"That's cool." I hold back a smile. She's so damn cute when she's all feisty like this. I sit next to her on the edge of the bed.

"I'm so sorry, Trace. You've got to know nothing happened between me and Bri. I didn't even know she was here. She got here before me and was hiding in my bathroom or something."

"And?"

"And I was lying on my bed thinking about you and she jumped on top of me. I was trying to pull her off when you came in."

"Okay."

"Okay, you believe me?"

"I suppose I have to. No guy would hang gooey poetry all over his front porch if he was fucking around with another girl."

When I try to pull her into my arms, she pushes me away.

"No." She stands up.

"But if you believe me, please come back to me, baby. I know I was a total slut in the past, trying to use sex to numb my guilt. I don't need or want that anymore. I only want you. I love you, Trace." I'm trying not to beg, but if I need to, I'll get down on my knees and beg her to take me back.

"You...you love me?" she asks in a hushed voice and sits on the bed again.

"So much. I should've told you a long time ago. I was afraid it would scare you away. I was going to tell you the night of the show. Then the shit went down with Bri and you wouldn't see me or take my calls. I miss you, baby girl. Come back to me, *please*." I stand and reach for her, but she holds her hand out to stop me again.

"Dak, listen. I was a mess over the break. Missing you, hurting, thinking about you."

"Oh baby..." she puts a finger over my lips to shush me the way she does. I shiver from the slight touch. My body's aching for her.

"I had time to think about a lot of things. I love you too, Dak." My heart does a backflip. "But..." and then it crashes down to my stomach, "I need some time. I was a disaster for a long time before I came to Bernard. You helped me get rid of all the awful anxiety I was hanging on to. I think I helped you a little too...get over some of your guilt about Abbey. Somewhere in there, even though I tried to fight it, I fell in love with you."

God. I want to touch her, hold her, kiss her.

"I fell apart a little bit again when I thought you lied to me. I don't want to need a guy to hold me together anymore. I need some time on my own. I want to find a way to be strong all by myself without leaning on you or anyone else. I think you might need that too, find out if you can get past your guilt about Abbey without using sex to numb your feelings. I think I should take some time to find out if I can be strong by myself, before I'm strong *with* you, and I think you should too."

"How...how much time?"

I hate this. What if needing time is just another way to say she's done and never coming back? Although she did say she loves me. I'll have to hang onto that and give her the time she says she needs.

"I don't know. Maybe weeks. Maybe months. We'll see."

"I'll wait for you, Trace. I'll wait as long as it takes." She leans in and brushes my lips with hers and the fissure in my heart cracks open.

"Bye, Dakota. I love you," she says and walks toward the door.

"Bye, Tracey. I love you too." She's already gone and doesn't hear me. I'm falling in love, *am* in love and she's walking away. But I have to let her go, give her the space she says she needs. That doesn't mean I'm done trying to find a way to win her back.

Chapter Thirty-Six

TRACEY

I t's Saturday night and Nikki and Alex are insistent I go with them to the Blue Goose for the annual talent show. Anyone in the area with an act is invited to participate. Apparently it's the event of the season. It's been sold out for months and they got me a ticket.

"I'm not into it. Can you sell the ticket? Or I'll give you the money for it. You guys go. Have a good time."

It's been weeks since I talked to Dak. I miss him so much. I'm okay though, learning to be a strong, independent woman, like I planned when I came to Bernard. But I'm not into going out to party and risk seeing him out with another girl.

Alex and Nikki see him at the keg parties and he meets them for lunch some days at the Sea Star. They say he asks about me every time he sees them and hasn't looked at another girl once. I hope that's true. I can't even think about him being with Bri or any other girl. He said he would wait and I want to believe he will. I ache to see him, but I never join Nikki and Alex at the parties or their lunches. I can't be that close to him without wanting to climb into his arms and never let go.

"Come on, Trace. It's time to join the human race again. You're a co-ed for chrissakes, not a nun," Nikki persists. She's smoking hot tonight in a short black skirt and black tights. She's rocking a red lace-up bustier top, which is pushing up all her assets, under a black leather jacket, and of course her black Dr. Martin boots.

"Wow, girl. What's up? Hot date tonight?"

"Could be. We'll see how it goes." She gives me a sly grin.

"Bitch you are *so* coming," Alex says. "You can see for yourself if Nikki has a hot date."

"Okay. If it means I get to see Nikki break the heart of some poor unsuspecting boy, I guess I need to go."

"Hell yes!" Alex cheers. "You want me to do your makeup? I know just what would pop with your auburn hair."

"Sure. Why not? I could use a makeover."

"Wear your fabulous purple bandage dress with the lace panels."

"Really? It's a bit much isn't it?"

"Uh, *no* girlfriend. The color's perfect on you and it can *never* be too much. The three of us are going to be so smoking hot tonight when we walk into that bar it's gonna be all eyes on us."

Nikki and I can't stop laughing as Alex parades up and down the room like a model on a catwalk. My mom would love him.

When we walk into the Blue Goose an hour later and I take my coat off, Alex whispers against my ear so I can hear him over the crowd, "Girl, every guy in this place just got a big old hard on for you."

"Eww. Shut up, Alex."

"I'm serious. Can't you feel the way you're being fucked by hundreds of eyes? It's a good thing you can't get prego from eye fucks or in about nine months you'd be having multiple births."

"Alex!" I shriek in laughter. "You know, you seriously need to get over your shyness and say what you feel."

"Whatever. Just sayin'."

Nikki is pushing us through the crowd to a table in front of the stage. The Blue Goose has a dinner theater-sized venue where touring musicians and bands wanting to do more intimate shows or try out new music can perform.

"Where are we going? Aren't all the tables in front already taken?"

Alex quirks a brow. "Connections."

"I guess *so*."

I'm impressed with all the people here. Nikki's sitting at a table in front of the stage with a reserved sign on it. Alex and I take seats next to her.

"Looking good, sweetheart." There's no mistaking the taunting voice. I turn to see Wolfe sitting at the table next to us with several other guys from the hockey team. There's another table next to them which also has members of the team seated around it. My heart deflates a little because Dak isn't one of them.

"Hey, Wolfe," I say. "What's up?"

I'm surprised to see Dalt and Batt are missing from the group too.

"I'd show you, sweetheart, but it would ruin you for every other guy in the world."

For crying out loud! Has every guy at this school lost his word filter?

The guys at his table whistle and high five him.

"Nice, asshole," Nikki sneers.

"You're looking pretty scrumptious yourself, soccer girl."

"In your dreams, hockey boy." Nikki gives him a teasing grin.

"Aw, come on, Nik. You know you love us *big* hockey men."

She laughs. "Fuck off, Wolfe."

Thank goodness the lights dim and the host of the show comes out to announce the first act, because there's no telling how far down into the gutter this conversation is headed. We order drinks and settle in to the sweet notes of the guy on stage rocking us with an acoustic version of Peter Gabriel's "In Your Eyes."

Several Long Island Ice Teas later, having broken my not-to-drink-too-much rule, we're all enjoying the exceptional level of talent in our small college town. Every few minutes my mind drifts to how much more fun this would be if Dak were here. My stomach clenches when I think about where he might be and who he might be with. It's ridiculous to be feeling this way. I was the one who asked for the space. I can't expect him to wait forever.

Alex jumps up and says he has to go.

"*Go*? Go where? It's not over," I say in confusion.

"It's the last number," Alex says like that explains why he's leaving. "I'll be right back." He hurries off through the door on the side of the stage.

"Oo-kaay. What's up with him?" I ask Nikki. She shrugs one shoulder and chews on the straw in her drink.

The host steps back on stage. "I want to thank everyone for coming out tonight. Before we announce the winner, we've got a special treat for our last act. Please put your hands together for a new group made up of some of the members of our own champion Bernard hockey team with a supporting role from one of our figure skating champions."

"What's going on?" I whisper to Nikki. She shrugs again, sucking on her straw like it's her lifeline to oxygen.

"Ladies and gentlemen, please welcome The Players!" The stage goes dark and the crowd erupts, especially the tables filled with hockey players next to us. When the spotlights come back up there are five guys on the stage with their backs to us. When the first notes of "I'll Make Love To You" by Boyz 2 Men pulse through the speakers, the group does sliding sidesteps together from one side and then to the other with some kind of grapevine steps afterward. When they turn to face the crowd I gasp so hard I almost swallow my tongue.

In the back line are Dalt, Batt, Erik, and Alex, and front and center is...no fucking way. *Dak*? They're all dressed in matching black button-down shirts and black pants, the same outfit Alex had on when we left the house. And they're all as scorching hot as the sun. Dak has a *microphone* in his hand?

"He can *sing* too?" I ask Nikki. It's a rhetorical question because I don't expect her to know the answer.

When Dak begins singing the whole group dances in synchronized choreographed steps, and the room fills with the sounds of girls—and probably some guys—screaming.

How is this possible? Dak sings like a rock star. Of course he does. And the hockey players can dance like B2K? I look at Nikki again in wide-eyed disbelief.

"What. Is. Happening. Right. Now?" I loud whisper.

"He's making every girl in this room fall in love with him, that's what. But there's only *one* he wants." She grins and tilts her head. Dak is staring at me while dancing and singing directly to me. I can't even hear my own thoughts because of all the *awws* rippling across the room.

"But...but...how..."

"It's Jeka Jane choreography. Dak got Alex to help him teach it to the guys. They worked on it for weeks, or should I say Alex has pulled his hair out for weeks trying to get these hockey jocks to jook, wop, pop, wobble, and Cupid Shuffle." Nikki chuckles.

When the music swells, Dak jumps off the stage and drops to his knees right in front of me and when he sings the title line, "I'll Make Love To You," I almost fall off my chair. This must be what it means to swoon. Nikki giggles and grabs my arm to keep me from falling.

The music ends and the audience goes crazy. While

on his knees, Dak drops his mic. He motions for me to bend down so I can hear him. I do as he asks, holding on to the sides of my chair to keep myself from toppling over. Between the alcohol laced ice teas and how much in love I am with this boy, I'm head over heels as Dak's dad would say. I can't hold back the tears in my eyes or the heat pooling between my legs.

"You look like a goddess tonight, baby girl," he whispers in my ear. "I'm so in love with you, Trace. I know I don't deserve you and I don't have all the answers, but if you come back to me I'll spend the rest of my life trying to find the answers with you. Let's figure things out together. I'll spend every day worshipping you, proving to you you're my whole life, the only woman I want, forever. I love you, Trace. Are you with me, baby?"

I take a deep breath and try to find my voice. How did I become the luckiest girl in the world?

"I'm with you. I don't need any more time." Pressing my lips to his, I whisper against them, "I'm in love with you too." When I throw my arms around his neck, he stands up, circles his arms around my waist, and lifts me off the floor. We stand there holding each other so tight we may never let go. I nestle my head into the curve of his neck under his chin: my safe place, I missed so much.

"By the way, Andersen, you win this one. I can't sing." I smile against his skin. "Can we get out of here so you can start submitting to all my demands, or whatever it was you just sang to me?"

Dak's throat vibrates with this kind of growling noise and I think that's a yes.

After a few minutes, we become aware of the audience still clapping and cheering. The hockey players at the tables are whistling. When I look up, the other guys are still onstage. Alex and Erik are sucking face like there's no one else in the room, and Dalt is undressing Nikki with his eyes until she jumps up and says, "I'm outta here."

Epilogue

TRACE

April

"Now remember, paddle straight into the waves, find the sweet spot on your board, put your palms flat right below your chest and pop up in one quick movement!" Dak yells above the rush of the incoming waves. "Ready? Here it comes, get in position. Remember, once you're up keep your feet planted on the board, knees bent, arms loose, and keep your eyes pointed in the direction you're going. Okay...go. Paddle like you're getting ready to go into a quad jump, Bambi. Give it everything you got!" he calls out. "That's it baby girl. You're fucking phenomenal!"

"Woohoo! You go girl!" I hear Alex cheering me on from the shore as I glide all the way into shore without falling.

Dak is giving me surfing lessons while we're on

spring break in Malibu. It's as big of an adrenaline rush as a triple-triple combination jump. I'm not as good as he is...yet. I'm working on it. One of these days I'll be able to beat him in catching the perfect wave and having the longest ride to shore.

Batt is stretched out on the sand enjoying the warm weather. Wolfe spent a few minutes getting surfing lessons from Heaven, although he seems more interested in lying on a blanket with her than surfing.

"Let's take a break for a few minutes," Dak says, paddling up and sliding off his board next to me on shore. "I want to make sure Heaven's okay."

"You can see her from here. She's lying on a blanket with Wolfe." I tighten my lips to hold back the smile.

"Exactly. What the hell does he think he's doing? I told those whores before we got here Heaven was off limits. She's only a kid for chrissakes."

"She's eighteen, Dalt. She's not a kid. Have you noticed the way she more than fills out the bikini she's wearing?"

"You mean the bikini she's *almost* wearing? What was my mom thinking letting her go out in something like that?"

"Uh, I'm pretty sure she said your mom bought it for her." I smile at how cute he is about protecting his baby sister from the big bad Wolfe. By the way Heaven is giggling, I don't think she's too interested in being protected.

"Come on. Grab your board. I need to beat the shit out of Wolfe and then we can all go get lunch in the café on the beach."

We took a trip together out to California for spring break, everyone except Dalt and Nikki. Nikki said she had to help out at her family's alpaca farm and finish some school projects over the break. Dalt didn't give a reason why he couldn't come. I'm convinced it has something to do with not wanting to be so far away from Nikki. Dak's parents were thrilled to let the rest of us stay at their huge Malibu home on the beach.

I wish everyone were here, since this is going to be one of the last chances we'll get to be together before the undergrads' commencement. It's coming up soon, when we get back. It will be strange not having all the guys living next door. I know it's already weighing on Dak's mind. He gets all somber when we talk about it, even though he's happy they went out on a phenomenal season. He says between winning the Frozen Four and finding me, it's the most magical year of his life. He says those kind of swoony things a lot. He's my one totally awesome thing, which has changed my life forever.

We spend lots of time on the water. I convinced him to take one of my nighttime kayak tours in Bar Harbor. I kept pointing out constellations like Ursa Major and minor and Gemini with my laser pointer, telling stories about the history of the American Indians on the island, anything to keep his mind off of worrying about me being in the kayak. In the end, he loved it and we kayak all the time now.

We have two graduate classes together next semester. Although, he has a few more undergraduate credits to take before he gets his degree, which makes him eligible to play hockey again next season. He moved into my house, or should I say *our* house, and even though I told Nikki she didn't need to leave, she moved into a house with Alex and some girls from her team. She red-shirted for a year when she took a few semesters off. She has one more year of classes and soccer. She said the way I kept screaming "Dakota" multiple times in the middle of the night was keeping her in a constant state of horniness. I try to keep it down, but Dak...well... I'm a lucky girl.

Dalt is planning on getting his MBA. He moved into Nikki's old room. He always has his headphones on listening to music, which may be the reason our noisy sexcapades don't bother him. He also had an offer from a team in California, so he may decide to play hockey for a few more years and not stay here to get his Masters after all. He says he'll see how things go, whatever that means. Wolfe accepted an offer from an AHL team out there already.

It seems like everyone knows or at least has an idea of what they want to do after school. We've all promised to keep in touch and get together when we can and not let our lives drift apart.

As for me, I'm learning new lessons about love and life every day. Although, I was right about some of the things I learned before. Love can be destructive, and sometimes it sucks big time. Anyone who opens their heart in a relationship risks being hurt. But with the right person, love can also be completely wonderful. The thing is, I learned you'll never find that person if you close yourself off, trying to prevent the hurt. Maybe there isn't someone for everyone, but if you don't put yourself out there you'll never know.

I rarely think about Sean and what happened. He's a faded bad memory. As hurtful as people can be and as painful as life is sometimes, I truly believe we need to go through the heartbreak and pain to get to our happily ever afters.

Have I learned to be strong on my own? Pretty much. So has Dak. But I'm still searching for answers. Although, now we're searching for those answers together. When we combine our strength and love of life, we're unstoppable.

Oh and obviously, I discovered my *Ute*-Dar isn't broken after all. I mean, it found Dak, and he's pretty a-freaking-mazing.

It turns out life isn't always perfect. Truth? Sometimes it totally blows. But with Dak, the love of my life and my best friend, life is more than perfect and we intend on keeping it that way, forever.

Before You Go...

If you enjoyed my book please take a second to leave a short review. These reviews help me as an author be found by other amazing readers like you.

Thank you so much! :)

Keep reading for a ***sneak peek*** at the second book in the On the Edge Series, Cross Drop.

Sneak Peek

ON THE EDGE BOOK #2

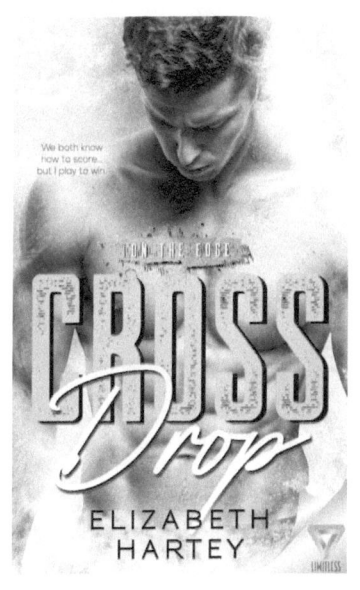

ON THE EDGE BOOK #2

CHAPTER ONE

DALT

"I might have to *nut*meg one of those fine young soccer ladies tonight," Wolfe snorts into his beer.

"Keep your eyes off Nikki and your dick off her teammates," I warn my hockey brother.

"Pfft. No worries. Any one of those fine young ladies would kick Wolfe in *his nut*megs if he tried anything," Dak taunts.

"Andersen, my man, you underestimate my talents," Wolfe says smugly and pats Dak on the back.

"Talents?" Batt sprays his mouthful of beer in laughter. "Is that what we're calling your ho-ish charms these days?"

"Who you calling a ho, dick brains?"

"You. You're a fuckin' pig." Batt laughs again.

Wolfe's brow creases in thought before his face

relaxes into a wry smile. "I proudly accept your assessment, bro." He raises his glass in a toast and Batt clinks his against it.

"'Accept your assessment.'" Dalt chuckles and shakes his head. "Wolfe, my man, you're an enigma wrapped in a slut."

"An enigmatic slut!" Wolfe shouts. "I thank you for the compliment, oh captain my captain." He bends at the waist, bowing to Dak, and in the process spills half the beer in his glass.

The degenerates—aka, my hockey teammates—and I are having our own party at a separate table from Nikki and her friends, although the party celebrating our win over Brown today is somewhat tamer. My boys are drinking beer instead of shots. They insist on filling a mug for me to toast the winning goal I scored in overtime. But I'm sticking to water and electing myself the designated driver for me and Nik tonight.

"Seriously, though. The soccer ladies are really gettin' their party on tonight." Wolfe flicks his chin toward the table where Nikki and her teammates are celebrating the big win they had over New Hampshire today.

"I know. Nik was on fire. She scored three goals in the first half of their game and one in the second." A contented smile crosses my face at the sight of my beautiful girl having such a great time. The way she works her ass off in school and leading her team as captain, she deserves a night out to let loose.

"Yay, Nik!" Batt hollers to her, raising his beer mug in a cheer.

Nikki waves, raises a shot glass, then tips it back,

emptying its contents with one swallow. The pyramid of empty shot glasses on the table in front of her and her teammates is evidence of the slightly excessive but well-earned celebration.

The adrenaline rush from the game and the enjoyment of seeing Nikki laugh and have fun is all the festivity I need. Just watching her makes me happy. Her joy for living, even when she hasn't overindulged in too many shots of Red-Headed Sluts, is contagious. If it's possible for someone to seep under your skin and infect you with happiness, Nik has me chronically afflicted.

She glances over every few minutes and waves or blows me kisses. I nod and smile back. No airborne kisses, though. I'm sure as hell not going to let the asshats at my table see me blowing kisses to a girl. Even if she *is* the most incredible girl on the planet.

Don't get me wrong, these guys are my brothers for life and if I needed anything they'd have my back faster than a slapped puck shoots across slick ice. That doesn't mean they're not always on the lookout for ammunition to bust each other's balls.

Like the time Wolfe was sitting next to me in our Public Speaking class. He caught me grinning and staring all dreamy-eyed at Nikki when she was giving a speech. He leaned over and whispered, "Yo, dude. You growin' a vagina over there?"

Imagine what would happen if they caught me catching and blowing kisses across a bar like some lovesick teenager. The never-ending rank-out which would ensue has me cringing just thinking about it. No thanks. I like my balls just the way they are. Besides, Nik knows how I feel about her. I don't need to make a public display or spout romantic sentiments. I *show* her how I feel whenever we're alone. When I'm done showing her, she gets the message loud and clear.

"Holy shit. Looks like Nik's on fire tonight too!" Wolfe yells across the table.

Here's the problem. Well, not exactly a problem, more like a dilemma: an I'm-one-lucky-sonovabitch versus sometimes-I-wish-I-wasn't-quite-so-lucky, dilemma. Nik is every guy's fantasy come to life. She can keep up with the guys at everything. At sports? A champion at everything she tries. Soccer? She moves the ball with such speed and accuracy, she makes any guy playing against her resemble a statue. Talking teams? She can rattle off players and team stats faster than Howard Cosell ever could. She can match any guy beer for beer and then some. But even with all her badassery at keeping up with the boys, she's a goddess of womanhood, with an angel face, and a body built to bring men to their knees. Full tits, round ass, lean muscle, platinum blonde hair down to her waist. Yup. Every man's fantasy, and there isn't one guy in this bar right now whose dick isn't pointing right at her. The fact her exuberance has escalated to a this-may-be-something- she'll-regret-in-the-morning level isn't helping to keep the drooling dirtbags away from her.

She's on top of one of the tables at the Thirsty Whale Pub, dancing and singing "We Could Be Heroes" at the top of her lungs. Which isn't bad—Nik's hot when she sings and dances. Except the way she's obviously feeling the shots has things a little too torrid. Her micro-mini skirt is flashing glimpses of her lacy purple thong and tight, apple bottom cheeks to everyone in the bar as she sways. The only way I'd be enjoying this level of heated happiness is if she were doing it solely for me on top of my table at home.

"Nik's got a fine ass, dude. Now I see why you're so fucked when it comes to this chick." Wolfe continues his astute commentary as he leers at Nikki.

"What the fuck are you doing eyeing my girl's ass, dickhead?"

"It's kinda hard to miss, man. I mean look at her. She's rockin' that thang. Am I right, guys?"

The other guys at the table don't say a word. Instead, they all fidget uncomfortably in their chairs, trying their best to look anywhere but at Nikki. Every guy may want her, but a fellow hockey bro knows better than to ogle another bro's girl. Batt's right about one thing. Wolfe, our goalie, is also our resident pig. No filter. No restraint.

By the sound of the loud whistling in the bar, I think it's time to break up the party before I have to break up some guy's face. I especially don't want to have to break Wolfe's face since he's one of my roommates and also one of my best friends. Besides, he's a good goalie. The team needs him.

Still, that doesn't mean I have to be happy about him ogling Nik. "Look away, asshole, or the only puck you're going to be stopping is the one I shove up your ass."

"Geez." He places his hand over his heart pretending to be wounded. "I was just trying to give you a compliment on your lady's fine—"

I shove him out of the way. Making my way to the

table where Nik is doing her burlesque routine, I reach up to take her hand to help her down.

"Let's go, sweetheart. I think it's time to get you home to bed." She bends over and gives me her pearly white ear to ear smile.

"*Can't hear you, hockey boy,*" she sings to me in the tune of the song, while continuing to sway her hips, "*music's too loud.*" When she leans toward me the whistling in the room gets louder.

I cup the hand not holding hers around one side of my mouth and yell, "I said I think it's time to get you home to bed!"

"*Ooo, yay. Bed! I'm cooomming, oh mighty sex god,*" she continues singing, but adds a prolonged moan to the word "coming." Then she winks and jumps off the table into my arms.

Jesus. Oh mighty sex god?

See what I mean? She has a joyful spontaneity, always the first to take a running jump off the rock diving cliffs of life, or tabletops in bars. Maybe the party should have ended five shots ago.

The room is too crowded to carry her to the door. I have to put her down. She's a little wobbly. I keep my arm around her waist to be on the safe side. As I steer her toward the door, I'm hailed with an outburst of loud boos and hisses from a table full of douchebag football players. When I glance over and answer their jeers with a dagger-dripping looks-might-not-be-able-to-kill-but-I-*can*-glare they get the message and shut the fuck up. Nik, oblivious to my telepathic interaction, dances and sings her way out while the rest of the students in the bar clap and cheer her exiting performance.

Tucking her into the passenger side of my car, I make sure she's all buckled in and secure before I go around and get into the driver's seat. Almost before I'm in the seat Nik is out of her seatbelt, climbing into my lap, one knee on either side of my hips, begging me, "Please, Dalt. Now please. I need you now. *Please.*"

See what I mean? Every guy's fantasy.

My life hasn't been perfect, but I have had some great days: the first day I put on a pair of hockey skates, the day I got a full ride to Bernard University to play the greatest sport on the planet. And the best day? The day I laid eyes on Nikki for the first time. Now my girl is straddled across my hips begging me to fuck her. Can life can any better than this?

Her hot girl skirt hiked up on her thighs, she's grinding down on me and kissing me, pleading with me to fuck her. It's blissful torture.

"I want you, Dalt. Right now. Right now, please. I'm so hot for you. I need you inside me."

"Wait, Nik, honey." I chuckle and moan at the same time, trying to keep her overactive fingers from roaming to places which are adamantly protesting the idea of stopping her.

"Nooo. Come on, Dalt. I can't wait."

Damn. She's like a female Bruce Lee, fast hands moving everywhere at once. She fumbles with the button of my jeans.

"Nik, sweetheart," I smile. When my button pops open, I place my hand over hers to stop her from tugging down my zipper. I need to slow her roll for her sake and my cock's. He's pushing with rigid determination against that zipper and in imminent danger of getting snagged.

"Come *on*, hockey boy. Need to nail your big, *hard* love hammer," she purrs into my ear.

"My *love hammer*?" I have to smile. She's so damn cute. But I've never seen her like this. Like I said, she has a pretty high tolerance for alcohol, at least for beer. She may have met her match with the multiple shots of Jäger-meister. I'm sure anyone with a functioning metabolism would have.

"Mmm. He wants me. I can tell," she coos, stroking her hand down my jean-covered shaft, sending my hormones into overdrive.

"Fuck, Nik"

"'Zactly what I had in mind"

Normally, there's no way I'd have sex with a girl who's feeling her alcohol like this. I'm a hockey player, not an asshole. But Nik and I have been together for months and our hot and heavy addiction to each other is nothing new. Needless to say, my *love hammer* is ready to do some nailing of his own to give my eager girl what she needs and no amount of advice from me is going to calm him down. Neither one of us can ever say no to this girl.

When I run my hand under her skirt and feel how wet her sliver of a thong is, I can't get my jeans unzipped fast enough, while taking care not to damage anything. As soon as I do, Nik reaches down between us, wraps her hand around me, and places my hard as fuck cock right where she wants it.

She has me so crazy out of my mind I might come in

her hand. Trust me when I say stamina has never been a problem for me before. Before Nikki, that is. She gets me racing in ways I didn't even know there were roads.

I rip her thong off and she lifts up and drops back down on me with a quick, hard push. Then she lets out a loud groan of pleasure, loud enough it's a good thing there's no one else in the parking lot.

She keeps moaning and pulling up and pushing back down on me. Doesn't say a word; just makes the sexiest *ahhs* and *mmms* I've ever heard. Every tight clench around me when she pushes down sends more blood rushing to my cock, making it demand a release. I focus on holding back, fighting to hold on a little longer, making sure I give her what she needs first. Doesn't take long. Her legs begin to tremble and clamp around my hips. All I can hear as her warm pussy convulses around me and I explode into her is, "Ah, ah, mmm, yes, yes, *yes!*"

Nope. Life definitely doesn't get any better than this. I hate to admit it, but sometimes the idiotic things which come out of Wolfe's mouth are right. I'm totally fucked when it comes to this girl.

To be honest, I've enjoyed more than my fair share of fangirl honeys. It's the same old story of being one of those popular hockey jocks on campus who can pretty much have any girl he wants anytime he wants and has a reputation for taking advantage of the gratuity. I'm not bragging, that's just the way it is for me and my team-mates. All good guys, just not relationship material, and none of the guys are shy about letting it be known. They make it clear what's happening before hooking up with a chick. I'll admit I've done my best to enjoy the perks of the long line of enthusiastic puck bunnies who have been on the same page of the 'no monogamy' clause in our policy.

Nik's changed it all for me. It's the craziest damn thing. I wasn't looking for it and never thought I *wanted* to feel any of this for one girl, but I'm not interested in any of the ready and willing fangirls anymore. Nik is the only one I want, every day, every night, all night, to the point of distraction. Like I said, blissful torture.

To add to the fantasy, Nikki brings her spontaneity into bed or...at the moment, car. She approaches fucking with the same gusto she approaches everything in life, with natural enjoyment. She isn't one of those chicks who wants to get down and dirty as much as any guy but thinks she has to pretend to be all timid and standoffish about it. Pretentious bullshit isn't for me. Nik knows what she wants and she's not shy about letting me know. Tonight, though? Tonight, she's even more spontaneous than usual.

We shattered together in mind blowing ecstasy, but she's still clenching around me working my cock, moaning my name. She's got me hard as iron and ready for round two.

"Mmm. Dalt. I want more," she pleads, planting kisses all over my face.

"Nik, honey." I'm smiling so wide my face hurts.

"Hmm?"

"How 'bout we wait 'til we get home? I can give you anything you want on a nice comfortable bed. Doesn't that sound good?"

"*Anything?*"

"Everything."

"'Kay. Let's go." Just like that she plucks herself off me and climbs back into her seat. I tuck my disgruntled cock away and reach over to pull her seatbelt across her, buckling her in once more.

"You good over there?"

"I'd be better over there," she says in a flippant tone. I'm sure she'll be down for the count by the time we get home. Or maybe not.

When I turn the ignition key, the radio blasts Charlie Puth's "Let's Marvin Gaye and Get It On" and Nik joins in with her own level of slightly off key singing. When she flails her arms around as she rocks to the beat, I narrowly miss getting punched in the face.

Oh boy. It's going to be a long night.

NIKKI

"Are we there yet? What's takin' so long."

Geez. Why is he driving so slow?

"Yup. We're here and it only took five minutes. Not too long, right? You okay?"

I don't know why he keeps asking me if I'm okay. I'm fine. Do I look like something's wrong with me?

"A-OK." *Except, I can't move. Why can't I move?* "Get this thing off me."

"Just a sec, Nik. Let me come around to your side to help."

When the car stops moving, Dalt hops out.

"Get this stupid strap off me."

"I got it. Here we go. Come on, sweetheart."

He bends down and swoops me up into his arms.

Wheee. I'm flying.

"Oh hi, hockey boy." I wave at his beautiful face. "Are you gonna carry me?"

Mmmm, he smells good. I'm gonna' keep my nose planted right here in this little space under his chin.

"Yeah, baby. I'm going to carry you. How you doing?"

"I'm doin' great! How you doin'?" Whoa! My voice got real low. Ha! I sound like Rocky. "Yo, Adrian." Amazing! I sound just like him.

Dalt's chest rumbles when he laughs.

"Mmm, you smell good 'nough to eat." I lean my head back to see him. "And you're *beautiful* when you laugh."

He chuckles. "Thanks, babe. You're pretty gorgeous all the time."

He's still smiling. I love when he smiles.

"Listen, Nik. Can you stand right here for just a second while I unlock the door?" He props me up against the wall.

"A'course, I can. Standin's easy. Do it all the time." I wave a hand through the air to accentuate how ridiculous the idea of my not knowing how to stand is.

Whoops.

I can stand, just can't wave my arm around while I'm doing it. I'm melting, shrinking just like the Wicked Witch.

"Whoa. Hold on. I got you. Put your feet under

you." Dalt wraps one arm around my waist while pushing the door open. "There we are. You good?"

If he asks me if I'm okay one more time.... Do I have two heads or something? Wait. It kinda' does feel like I have two heads. Why are my legs bein' so dumb? Dumb legs.

"Yup. Standin' all by myself. Told ya I could do it. If this floor would stop moving it would be way easier though."

Dalt smiles at me. He's so happy tonight.

"You're pretty when you smile, Daltie."

Wait a darn minute.

"This isn't home. Did you get lost, my honey man?"

He lets out another big laugh. We must be having a lot of fun.

"Yes, it is. It's my house. Remember?"

"Oooh. I remember. *Bed!*"

"Yes. Definitely bed." He grins and nods a bunch of times. He thinks I'm super smart for remembering where we were going.

"*See?* There it is. You have such a beautiful smile. You know that?"

"I love that you think so, baby. Can you sit here on this chair for a minute? I'll get us a couple of bottles of water to take upstairs to the bedroom. Okay?"

"Okie dokie. Oh wait. I have to take my clothes off for bed. Why do I still have all these stupid clothes on? I hate clothes. My shirt doesn't want...to...to come off. It's...it's stuck."

"How 'bout we wait 'til we get upstairs before we take your clothes off?"

Aww. There he goes, smilin' his come-n-fuck-me-smile. "Daltie." I waggle my finger at him. I know his tricks. "You wanna help me get my clothes off so we can hide the puck again?"

"Hide the puck?" He snickers. I'm very funny tonight. "First let's have some water. Be right back." He starts walking away from me.

"Wait!"

"What is it, babe? You okay?"

"I wanna show you somethin'. Let me just...uh... push...myself up. There. Watch how easy this skirt is. Boom. See? Just a few little snaps. All gone."

"Jesus, Nik. I think we might have to lay off the Jägermeister forever. It's a little too dangerous."

Mmm. I love the way his eyes crinkle when he smiles.

"Oops. Oh no! What happened to my undies? They 'dispeared. Had 'em a minute ago." I try to bend down to search between my legs. They must be somewhere. Whoa! My head does not like bending over.

"Okay. That's it, you need sleep." Dalt walks across the room and scoops me up in his arms.

"You gonna' carry me again?"

"Yup. I'm gonna' carry you again."

"Okay. I'll be right here. Right here on these muscles." I pat his chest, his beautiful, rock hard chest, to make sure he knows where he can find me. "I'm gonna' put my face right here. 'Kay?" All of a sudden, I'm on my back with my arms wrapped around Dalt's neck.

"Here we go, baby. Doesn't the bed feel comfy? You lay back. I'll get these boots off."

"Wait, Daltie!"

"What is it, baby?"

"I love when you call me baby," I whisper in a tiny little voice right against his beautiful soft lips so he can hear me.

"And I love calling you baby because you *are* my baby. But I want to take your boots off and then get some water for you. Okay?"

"'Kay. Wait!" I pull him back down.

"Ooph. What do you need, sweetheart?"

"My legs are weird."

"Your legs are weird?"

"Uh huh." I nod. I don't feel like talking anymore.

"What do you mean? Nik? Are you still awake? What do you mean your legs are weird?"

"Umm. Sticky...yuk." My eyes won't open but I can hear Dalt talking to me.

"Sticky? Did you say...Oh. Fuck! No condom!"

"Night night, Daltie. Love you."

Acknowledgments

First, I would like to say thank you to anyone who has read this book. I'm so in love with these characters and group of hockey hotties, I couldn't wait to share them with the world. Hockey has become my passion, so it's been a blast writing these books.

Second, I want to thank my Beta readers for all the wonderful suggestions that made Trace and Dak really come to life, especially fellow author and friend, Jessica Calla. Your words of inspiration kept me plugging away at this one to make it even better.

And of course, I have to thank everyone at Limitless Publishing for helping me make this book the best it can be. Everyone there works together like a fine-oiled machine, making the publishing of a book seem easy, even though it's not. To my editor, Felicia Sullivan, I can't thank you enough for your wonderful editing skills and the way you were willing to work with me and my quirky bad habits. I promise to never let my characters say 'yeah' again. Well, almost never. It's hard to break habits!

Most importantly I want to thank my family who has been nothing but supportive in this crazy new venture of fulfilling a lifelong dream to write novels. I could never do it without your help in tackling the mountain of dirty laundry, dishes, rooms or even helping provide some hot meals when my creative juices are flowing and I don't want to step away from my keyboard. Whoever said being married to a doctor was tough never tried being married to a writer. Some days I'm on another planet and walk around talking to myself to get a scene right. So. thanks again for understanding and taking my crazy in stride.

If you loved Dak and Tracey I hope you will take the time to leave a review or contact me to let me know. Links to all my social media sites are available on my website, ElizabethHartey.com And stay tuned for the upcoming novels in the On The Edge series to read Dalt's, Batt's and Wolfe's stories. Happy reading!

About the Author

As a lover of the northeast United States, Elizabeth moved with her husband to the Poconos several years ago to open a Chiropractic Clinic. Four children and a menagerie of animals later, she has finally found time to fulfill her lifelong dream of writing novels. A dreamer at heart, romance is the genre she spends most of her time writing and reading into the wee hours of the morning. When not juggling work responsibilities and writing, she enjoys hiking the beautiful hills and woods around her home, swimming, knitting, travelling, and spending time with her family. She is an avid hockey fan, which means she has to compromise with her husband, one night of hockey for her, in exchange for one night of football for him.

Website:
https://www.elizabethhartey.com
Newsletter:
http://eepurl.com/cZCEuL